LEGACY

Katelyn Costello

Legacy

This novel is entirely a work of fiction. The names, characters, and incidents portrayed in it are the work of the author's imagination. Any resemblance to actual persons, living or dead, events or localities is entirely coincidental.

First Edition

ISBN: 978-1-7369598-2-4

Cover Design: Jane Farrell

Also by Katelyn Costello

The Frituals Saga

The Frituals

Rebellion

Until all the Stars are Found

Legacy

DEDICATION

To all those that have found a home in books.

Contents

Legacy

Chapter 1 Jamie

"You know the more you itch it, the worse it is going to be," Moraine said, not looking up from the thread she was slowly pulling from her dress.

Jamie gave his beard one last vicious scratch before dropping his hand to the filthy hay. "I am going to rip this thing off my face if I have it for much longer." He groaned, tilting his head back. There was nothing he could do about the months old beard growth. He didn't dare complain when the guards were near. He was sure they would have had too much fun threatening to give him a close shave.

"No, you won't. That is what you said two days ago. And the week before that."

Jamie glared at the Queen. She held his gaze for a second before she rolled her eyes. "What—what were you going to say?"

She shook her head. "It isn't helpful. We just have been in this cell too long." She leaned against the wall, staring at the stone ceiling high above them. "The both of us are getting crabby. It is better if I just say nothing." She rolled a matted lock of her red hair between her fingers before picking the knots apart.

"I am sorry to complain about my personal hygiene in a cell after a month."

The queen scoffed. "You and I both know it's not that. Not entirely. A good part of it is the flea bites. They are flaring up again. Mine are too," she said, pulling up her sleeve to reveal the red, swollen bumps on her arm. "If you keep itching, you are going to make them bleed again, and then you are going to get more bites."

Jamie looked down and saw a small bright red smear on his hand. "Too late." He quickly rubbed the blood off on his pants and pressed the pad of his thumb against the still itchy spot on his chin. "Goddess, we need to get out of here."

"Something will come up. We will figure a way out," Moraine said, and not for the first time Jamie wondered who she said it for. Did she say it in the hopes that she could convince herself of the fact or because she truly believed it and wanted Jamie to believe it too?

Jamie got up and moved to the door. His knees creaked and popped as he stood. The only thing he could do was sit or lie in the same positions in the damp hay. It didn't matter how old he was. Anyone would creak and pop if left in these conditions.

"You know this room used to be a nice little hideaway from the court." The Queen sighed.

Jamie nodded. "So you've said." He leaned against the wall next to the door and peered sidelong through the small window, hoping to make out which guard was on duty.

"I got a chair specially ordered from Gradatia with the softest weave and plushest goose down." She pointed up to the empty torch brackets. "I had the option to light a few torches, but I rarely did. I liked the dark, the quiet. I didn't have questions coming from every side..." she trailed off. "It's far too quiet now," she said almost wistfully.

Jamie leaned against the door, careful not to knock it in the frame. The guard on duty was a little way down the hall; it looked like he was adjusting a torch on the wall. The guard turned and made their way back toward the cell.

"It looks like Kane is on today," Jamie said, quickly stepping away from the door. He paused before shifting their food tray to the small door in the wall. The cracked china rattled on the bent tray. Moraine shook her head again and sat back. "What? It can't hurt to try. Maybe he will find it somewhere in his black heart to be generous for once." Jamie highly doubted that based on the last few interactions, but they needed food.

Moraine scoffed at the idea, but didn't discourage it. As Moraine had explained in one of her many stories, before she had turned this room into an office, a place for her to escape the complexities of court, it had been a cell. Chima used it to keep powerful enemies close. The former Queen had installed a small cabinet in the wall with a door both within the cell and outside in the corridor, allowing for the passing food or other such items without having to access the cell. The door creaked as Jamie closed it, leaving the empty tray within.

"Are my little tower prisoners hungry? Isn't that just so sad?" Kane chittered.

Jamie quickly moved away from the door and took his seat at the wall, as far from it as he could.

Kane stepped up to the door and smacked the top. The sound it created was loud, the door bouncing in the frame in booming thuds that echoed in the small, empty room.

Jamie startled at the noise. Kane had woken them this way more than once, sending Jamie's heart racing in this chest. He watched the door warily. *One of these times, the door is going to come off the hinges.*

"Isn't that just too damn bad?" Kane whipped the tray out of the cabinet and launched it down the hall where it ricocheted off the wall to the sound of shattering of dishes and metal bouncing.

Moraine sighed, no doubt wondering how there could be any dishes left in the castle with the way they had been treating her things for the last month.

Kane turned back to the door and scowled down at them. Jamie became very aware of his hands laying in the hay at his sides and did his best not to move. *Do I look like I am hiding something? I am just sitting here. He doesn't think I am up to something, right?* Jamie's gaze drifted from the door. *Don't move too fast. He will think you're scared and jumpy. Don't move too slowly. He will be suspicious.* Kane made a sort of huffing sound, as if annoyed that the two cellmates had done nothing wrong. He smacked the door once more before stepping away and continued to patrol the hall.

Jamie dug around in the pile until he found one of the remaining bits of stiff hay and dug at the dirt between the grout lines on the walls. The scratching sound on the stone made his skin crawl, but he would rather deal with that than boredom, or the questioning thoughts of his daughters. It was something he did to pass the time when he grew tired of counting the stones in the walls, but there weren't many bits of hay he could use anymore. Most of it had gone soggy, mildewed with age. He coughed, his chest aching with the force of it. Moraine looked sad. *Damn her Elven blood.* He swallowed the bit of phlegm and went back to picking at the wall. The Dark Ones hadn't given them any more hay. Why should they? They were prisoners. *They don't care about me. They just want the girls.* He looked to the corner where they had piled the hay that was clearly molding. Soon they wouldn't have anything to sleep on that hadn't been touched by mildew. Once again, looking at the hay made Jamie think of the prisoners down below. *How are they fairing? How many people had gotten sick? Are they getting food? Has anyone died? Did they hurt them after the others escaped?* "Do you think they are going to move us back down there?" Jamie asked, tossing the bit of hay away.

Moraine stood with a groan and moved to the door, probably to check for Kane.

Or she is stalling.

She paced the room before speaking. "If I were them, I wouldn't allow a move until we were at the very end of our rope. I would let those below continually question and hope we were okay and then bring us down there when we are absolutely broken."

Jamie sat back and watched the queen pace back and forth for a few moments. "You can be awfully cruel, you know that, right?"

She shrugged. "Yes, I can be. I avoid being like that. But it is smart to know what your enemy is like. You must think like your enemy to defeat them. That is how we got into this mess. Lack of knowledge, if only we had known the scope of their power." She paused. "My sister was like that. She did the same thing when she took control from my father." Moraine lifted her sleeve and scratched at a bite marring her pristine skin. They both stared at the small streak of red before she hid it behind her sleeve. The light blue fabric was dotted with red. "They want to use us as leverage, which is why we have gotten through this relatively unscathed. We must not have been as much of a threat as the other kingdoms before they fell." She scoffed.

"To what purpose? Why keep us locked up?"

She stopped. "Well, you are obviously leverage for your daughters. They are going to keep you, use you as a tool. It has already happened once," she said, pointing at the nearly healed line down the side of Jamie's face.

He nodded, the memory flooding back to him in an instant: of the pain of the blade slicing through his skin, and the look of panic on Shauna's face through the black Magick portal, trying to answer the questions posed to her. The queen rubbed at a dirt spot on the back of her hand. "I don't know why I am still alive. If the information Alexis has been bringing us is true, then I am the last Elven monarch 'standing'," she said, wrapping air quotes around the word. "Why not just take me out? It would make it that much harder to unite the kingdoms and the races." She paced the room again, lost in thought.

Jamie thought about that for a moment. With all five kingdoms collapsed but not entirely under the Dark Ones' control, all were vulnerable. They would need someone or something to unite all to succeed. "Do you think they are trying to keep you from doing that? Like, keep people from rallying behind you?"

The Elvin queen laughed, but there was no mirth in it. "Oh, my friend, you give me too much credit. I am not a good queen. I have barely held Cabineral together. I am not the one to rally behind."

She went to the wall and peered up at the arrow slit high on the wall. The only access to the outside world.

"Do you think my girls could do it? Maybe the Frituals together or Taytra and her Rebellion?"

Moraine looked down at Jamie, her face unreadable. "I don't know," she breathed.

Chapter 2 Taytra

Taytra didn't know where to look to find peace. She had come to the wall to walk under the bright light of the moon, to feel the way the brisk night air was warmed in her lungs. To forget who she was for a moment. But she was so tired. She sat against the wall, the rough stone at her back both steadied her and sent shivers of fear down her spine in the same breath. Here on the wall, under the blackness of the night sky, she could relax, take a deep breath, and ignore the weight that hung on her shoulders. Before her lay the inner circles of the city of Hollens and the many gates that stood between her people and the enemies that lay at her back. But if Taytra turned and peered over her shoulder and looked over the battlements, she could see them. A shiver ran down her back and goosebumps prickled on her skin. Whether it was just from the cool fall night, or the sight of the hundreds of Dark Ones all gathered in one place, she couldn't say. Under the sweet, clear, star-filled sky, a seething body of torches moved through the night, illuminating rippling black cloaks, glinting orange off blades, and of angry faces. The faces that had destroyed everything her people had, leaving them with just the clothes on their backs, and the breath in their lungs.

Taytra Flynn turned away from the enemy and leaned forward, dropping her head to her knees. Her neck was a series of tight knots. The ache she felt down her neck and the center of her back as she stretched the tender muscles was welcome. *You need to slow down, Flynn.*

She looked to the stars and took a deep breath in, then slowly let it out, watching as the cool autumn air transformed it to mist and carried it off into the sky. This watch on the wall was meant to be relaxing, a step away from the many questions, and valid complaints from the people of Cabineral Lake. A moment alone. But when she was alone, the memories washed over her like a tidal wave. The cold was like the nights she slept on the floor of the dungeon. She missed her father, how he had rubbed her back until she fell asleep. Trying to make her feel safe in a place where they could have been hurt at any time. Now she flinched when anyone touched her back.

Can you see these stars too, Shana? She wondered. It was almost a prayer. A message she hoped Shauna would hear wherever she was. *I miss looking at the stars with you. I will bring you home safely. I promise. I will do whatever it takes.*

She jumped and reached for the knife at her belt, hearing the blast of trumpets around her. Her heart rate spiked for a moment as the echoing blasts were taken up by each point around the city. But she slumped back when she heard the rhythm. Two short blasts, one long, announcing that the curfew had fallen over the city. "Shit." Taytra sighs, leaning her head back against the wall. She had been on the wall too long if the curfew had been called. "Shit, shit, shit." Taytra was supposed to meet with Ward, Andrew, and possibly Paulo at the eighth bell. The trumpet blast meant she had missed the eighth bell by a long shot, and it was closer to the tenth.

Even though she wasn't in a cage anymore, Taytra had never felt less free. She felt constrained by responsibility. Something she didn't want but couldn't escape. She stood and leaned out over the parapet, feeling the wind rush up the wall, running through her hair.

Since arriving at Hollens, her life was reduced to prepping or waiting to attend meetings. Meetings where she wasn't allowed to speak. The council of Hollens believed they had all the expertise needed. That they didn't need additional information from outsiders. Especially from those who they saw as barely having reached adulthood.

"I don't understand what experience they want us to have. I watched people die. I have killed people who wanted to kill me," she had shouted at Serena. The half-elf had merely nodded. She was trying her best.

Taytra understood there were lives at risk. She knew the risks. She had lived with them, and all she wanted was to do what she could to help her people. She wanted to learn from those on the council, to take their knowledge and use it. But these men acted like the passage of information was a family heirloom that must never see the light of day.

Ward and Andrew won't be mad. They will give you a recap. She thought, turning to the watchtower. Her footsteps echoed against the stone, amplified by the quiet pressure of the night air. She reached for the door handle as it was pulled inward away from her. She jumped back, an apology on her lips as the male strode forward. His eyes were downcast, caught on the bit of parchment in his hand as he ran into Taytra. The paper fell as the two collided.

"I'm sorry." The man grunted, stepping back. "I should have paid more attention." He looked up. "Oh, hey."

Taytra quickly looked away, immediately feeling guilty. "I'm sorry I missed the meeting. I was just coming to find you and Andrew."

Ward smiled. "It's okay. I thought I would find you up here. You missed dinner again," he said and slipped the small pack from his shoulder and passed it to her. "Paulo could only stay for a short time. He had to meet with Serena and Lyra. We didn't get through much."

"Would we have gotten much done if I were there?"

He paused. "No—not to say it would be worse. I think it would have gone the same. There wasn't much to cover today."

Taytra nodded and slid back down to her spot on the floor. "It's nice up here," she said simply.

"I know," Ward said, smiling softly, plopping down beside her and turned his face to the stars.

She pulled open the bag and picked out the contents one by one: a hunk of bread, a bit of dried pork and cheese wrapped in a cloth, and a skin of cider, the soft leather warm to the touch. She uncorked the skin and took a deep sip of the warm drink. The liquid warmed her stomach, and she shivered again against the cold.

"If you are going to hide up here, you should at least wear a cloak," Ward said, unbuttoning his own and slinging it over her shoulders.

"I'm not hiding!" Taytra insisted, but when Ward raised an eyebrow, she went on, "Okay, maybe a bit, but I am working. Someone has to be on guard duty."

"See, the thing is with that argument," he said, tearing off a small portion of the bread, "is that you are not a member of the guard at Hollens. And they only let us volunteer in the morning. And I know you did a sunrise shift this morning. You will spread yourself too thin if you keep this up," he said. His tone was firm but not patronizing. He had learned what she needed.

"I know."

"I can show you where I got this one." He pulled the edge of the cloak tighter around her shoulder, pushing her hair out of the way. "It was a little shop. They didn't have many left."

"Yeah, we will need to go see." She pulled her knees up to her chest and looked up at the sky.

"What's up?" Ward asked.

"I don't know," she muttered, watching her breath float away. She glanced over at Ward. "I mean, I—" The look he gave her was comforting but said *come on. It's me.* But he waited while she searched for the words to turn the feeling into something a bit more tangible. "I don't know. I just, I have a lot of questions, but feel like I don't even want the answers." She set the food to the side and got up and moved back to the wall, leaning out over the plain. Taytra watched the Dark Ones move like ants before turning away from them. She looked up at the sky full of stars and then dropped her head, staring at her hands. The memories fought for a place in her mind again, the questions about her family and her home threatening to bubble to the surface. She had been pressing a wall between her fears and her responsibilities. She didn't have time to let them consume her. But she knew the dam would break soon. Taytra didn't know when she balled her hands up into fists, or when she got the thin scratch on the back of her hand. She wanted to punch something, she wanted to run, she wanted to fight someone. She wanted to cry. "Do you think Shauna is okay?" It came out quieter than she wanted. Taytra swallowed hard, trying to dislodge the lump in her throat.

Ward didn't answer at first. He moved to her side and looked out over the plain. Out of the corner of her eye, she watched him clench and flex his hands like he was grasping for answers. "I don't know," he said, leaning down on the wall. "I don't know." Their hands drifted closer together on the wall.

Taytra closed her eyes. "I know you don't know. I don't know. You are being logical again." Her throat felt thick. She could feel tears pricking behind her lids and turned to walk away, not wanting him to see her cry, not again. It was happening too much as of late.

"Tay." He grabbed her hand and held it lightly, his calluses rubbing against her knuckles. She stopped walking, and he turned her hand over, lightly running his thumb over the creases in her palm. "I know you are stressed and hurting." He paused, tugging her gently, so she turned to face him. "I want to tell you everything is going to be okay. That Shauna will be here tomorrow or, or something like that. But I can't. I can't lie to you. I wish I could. But I won't, especially with this. She means too much to you."

She watched his fingers work over her skin. It tickled slightly, but she didn't pull away. "I know. I just wish I could get these answers easily. Or that people would listen to me."

"I listen to you." Taytra rolled her eyes, and Ward smiled. "Well, most of the time." He bent down and handed her the bread. "You need to eat." Taytra rolled her eyes again. "You do. What else did you eat today?"

"I don't really remember. I was in the market most of the day trying to see if I could make any deals with the vendors to bring to the next meeting."

"Exactly. You can't work as hard as you are and not eat. You will break. And that would be a win for them," he said, gesturing to the army on the plain. "I know you want everything fixed as soon as possible, but right now we need to play by their rules. That means we need to go slower, be more calculating with the council. As much as it feels like it sometimes, they are not the enemy." Ward's eyebrows scrunched down. "Wait a second. I thought we were getting some supplies from the city? Isn't that what they told us? I mean, it isn't a good amount at all. But wasn't Serena going to negotiate something for us?"

Taytra shrugged. "They did, and I spent a few hours going over all the supplies we got trying to figure out how to divide it. It doesn't work for one meal, let alone three meals a day. And you saw how that meeting was? They didn't let me get a word in edge wise. They looked at me with disgust whenever I tried. For some reason, I am not good enough for them."

Ward sighed. "I know. It was a really rough meeting. I don't know what I expected, but that wasn't it. Andrew was pissed. He thought your reaction was justified."

Taytra nodded. "I just don't understand any of it. We have nothing. I feel awful, like how can they think that three hundred people can fit into thirty tents? If they were like bigger tents, that could fit several people, that would make sense, but not those ones. Those tents are tiny!" She turned and pointed to the tents near the gate that can fit three, maybe four, small people. "I can't tell people to cram into those tents." She readjusted the cloak again. "I am really grateful for the room they got us at the inn, and I know you and Andrew think we should stay there because, as leaders, we need to rest, but I don't feel comfortable staying in a proper bed while others are staying on cots or on the ground."

Ward nodded. "I can understand that. Where would you rather stay?"

"I don't know. I don't—just—I don't want people to assume I think I am better than them."

"I have heard no one say anything like that. They are mad, yes, but not at us. They are frustrated and want to be treated fairly, but they see we are working at it and doing our best."

Taytra rolled her eyes at the overly optimistic words. She knew he meant them, but they were also a sort of mantra that, if repeated enough, would come true. "Yeah, even Mr. Kendle?" she asked, referencing the man who had spent ten minutes cursing at Andrew yesterday because his food delivery was late.

Ward scratched at his beard. "I don't think there

is anything we can do to please him. He was just as grumpy at home before this whole mess started." He sighed. "I don't blame him, though." Ward put an arm around her, and she leaned into him. "Everyone is tired, and they are still scared. We are safe here, but they haven't had time to process that yet. I don't expect tensions to drop for a few more weeks. Hopefully, by then, things will be more settled."

Chapter 3 Philippe

"Philippe Mattick, get up," a gruff voice said, pushing roughly against Philippe's shoulder.

"Where?" He squinted, trying to bring the room into focus. His right eye opened a crack, tight, hot, and raw. His face felt like a thousand fire ants had bitten it. He could barely make out the shape of the Dark One in front of him in the darkness. A groan escaped Philippe's lips as he sat up. The world spun as the blood rushed away from his skull, leaving behind a dull thumping wave of pain.

"Up. Let's go," the guard barked again.

"I'm going," Philippe mumbled, rolling over to his side, and slowly pressing himself to his knees. His world spun, and his head felt like he was on a runaway horse. He sat hard, taking a few deep breaths to steady his world. Gingerly, he reached up and slid his hair, matted with dirt and blood, out of the way. With stiff fingers, he reached up to touch the lump on the back of his head. *What happened?* His left eye was swollen shut and the sensitive skin on his cheek felt like it had a deep gash in it. He tried to remember what had happened since the cave. Broken bits of memory flashed in his mind's eye. Stumbling behind a horse, his hands tied in front of him, tripping into sand, a spear butt in his side. Vaguely, he remembered being thrown from a horse and dragged along the ground. *They thought I was casting.* Philippe looked down at his torn shirt and pants and saw the cuts from being dragged through the dirt. *How am I still alive?* He wondered, looking at the deep cut going down his thigh. He almost wished he could go back to sleep or get knocked out so he wouldn't feel the pain coming into sharp focus as he woke.

"You are required for a meeting. She won't be kept waiting." Through his blurry vision, Philippe watched the dark shape bend and cut through a cord. Philippe tensed as the male came closer and sawed through the tie at his ankle. "Let's go," the guard ordered again.

The elf forced him through the tent flaps into the darkness of night. Torches lit the way every ten feet, but the world was a blur to Philippe. *Where are we going?* he wanted to ask. He jumped at sudden motion and tripped over a tent line he couldn't see at his feet. Each stuttered jolting step sent a sharp pain through the many scrapes and bruises that covered his body. *Where is Shauna?* He thought, but the only thing around him was the shadows of torchlight and the guard.

Finally, the guard turned and pointed to a tent. "Here."

Philippe strained his eyes, trying to open them a bit more, blinking rapidly, trying to bring the shape into focus.

I don't want to be blind to whatever happens. His breath caught in his lungs. *I want to see my captor. Face them. Goddess, please let me see.*

The guard shoved him into a chair before

shackling Philippe's hands and feet together and looping the chain through a spike in the ground. The guard eyed him up and down for a moment before turning to the tent flap. "She will be here shortly."

Who? Shauna? Manon? Who else would it be? They were the only women he had seen of late. Who was in charge here? He squinted at his legs. There was enough slack in the chain. *If I pick up the chain, I could make a run for it.* But the logical bit of his brain fought back. *I wouldn't get more than four feet if I tried to run right now.* He shifted his weight, looking at the end of the chain looped in the stake. "What's that?" he murmured, squinting at the bit of metal. The chain was a brownish gray, tarnished from use, while the stake was dark, an inky black that rippled as he watched. Pulsing like it had its own heartbeat. "Magick," he growled in disgust, turning away from the sight of it. The chain rattled as he turned, and he whipped back around when he saw movement. He squinted at what looked like a small orb. *Is this bad? What—* It zipped away in an instant, melting right through the tent wall like it wasn't there.

"Shit," he muttered thickly, leaning forward and pressing his hands over his eyes. He willed the pain to go away for a few minutes so he could focus on whatever was about to happen. Blinking open his eye, he tried to take stock of himself and his surroundings. The red markings of his Magick had faded, replaced by streaks of dirt, cuts, and pink, sunburned skin. He paused, running a finger over a thick black band of Magick on each wrist. Like the stake on the ground, it pulsed like it had a heartbeat. His stomach roiled. *Get off me!* he wanted to snarl. Philippe snapped his fingers, but no Magick popped to light. He did it again, picturing the flames that used to dance across his skin. Philippe reached within himself to where he thought his Magick used to lie. It felt like he was stumbling through the dark, searching for the edge of a table or door frame to ground himself in the darkness. He cried out in surprise as pain lanced up his arm, and he watched the black bands tighten, pressing deeper into his skin. His markings flashed black before they faded to nothing. Another black orb went zipping away, this time in a different direction.

Philippe spun to the door, hearing people approach. "Did I say I required your assistance?"

"No, ma'am. I just assumed that—"

"Exactly. You assumed. Now I am going to *assume* you left your post unattended to come offer me help. And that could be considered an abandonment of your duty, could it not?"

Philippe could hear the panic in the male's voice as he floundered for an answer. "Uh—right, ma'am. If I have your leave, I think I should go check my sector."

"Go."

Philippe sat up straighter, his side barking in protest. The word was short, clipped, but carried enough weight and authority to send the elf sprinting away.

Philippe bowed his head when he heard the tent flap being pushed open. Keeping his eyes downcast until she was right in front of him. She cleared her throat, the sound jarring in the tent's quiet. He slowly raised his head. This was the Dark One who ran this group. The dark cloak on her shoulders made her pale, nearly translucent skin look sickly. She pressed thin lips together, her eyes boring into his. Her eyes raked over his body, like she was judging his worth and determining if he was a threat. He wanted to say something, to snap at her, to stop staring. To ask what she wanted. But the pain radiating in his body told him to stop, to wait. She was likely the one who ordered it. Or at the very least, hadn't made the others stop. "Philippe Mattick," the elf said.

Should I acknowledge my name? Deny it? But that wouldn't work. They knew exactly who he was, who he had been traveling with. *Where is Shauna?* He wondered again. Philippe looked up at her but said nothing, waiting to see if she would say more. The glare on the elf's face deepened. *Okay, not the right idea.*

"Yes?" He left off any form of honorific. *Better to be punished for no title than for giving her the wrong one.*

"You will address me as Hunter. You previously were a member of the Dark One's fold. Is that correct?"

Philippe wouldn't say he had much choice in the matter. The elders from Cabineral had wanted to get him out of the city as fast as possible. He had tried to convince them he couldn't ride like they wanted; they pushed the pace even when he had nearly fallen a few times. The only thing he had done was stop and fix his stirrups, hoping the minor adjustments would help him keep his seat. He constantly wondered what would have happened if he had been a better rider. Would he have escaped the Dark Ones? Would they have found the other Frituals? Even though he had been taken and the dark Magick they had used to control him had been strong, he had to fight for her. He hated how feeble that fight had been. And he would do whatever it took to fight for her now. *Where is she?* He tried to reach out to her and felt the band tighten on his wrist again.

He looked again at the elf in front of him. He had

listened to Damian's orders for a short period. But none of it had been his choice. The Magick Damian had used *made* him follow those orders. Would this elf want to know that he had followed the orders Damian had laid out for him, or to admit that none of it had been his choice? He knew the Dark Ones hated humans, more specifically that he and Shauna could control Magick. If he admitted he had followed the orders, even reluctantly, by a member of the Dark Ones, would it help or hinder him?

She cocked an eyebrow at him, coming down to crouch eye to eye with him. "I asked you a question, Mattick. I didn't say you could touch your Magick."

He tried to keep his face as even as possible. *How does she know* It had to be the black bands. She had to be connected. His good eye darted over her, trying to see if she had a matching band on her arm or something else that signified how she would know about his Magick. "Ma'am, you already know the answer to that question," he replied. He kept his tone even, firm but respectful.

She held up a blade for him to see. "I believe you know what this is?"

Philippe nodded, his chest tightening at the sight. The blade in her hand was long and thin, sharp and, like every other damn thing with these elves, was coated in an inky black layer of Magick. Unlike the blade that Damian had fashioned, this blade looked primed, like it was used regularly. It was a truth blade. "Yes, ma'am."

"Do I need to use it today?" she asked, trailing the tip over his skin. "Were you a part of the Dark Ones previously?"

Philippe looked at the elf. "Ma'am, I did at one point follow the orders given to me by leadership in the Dark Ones." The blade slowly spun in her hand, the point pressing into her fingertip. He swallowed hard. "But I didn't do it of my own volition. They made me follow orders. I was controlled."

"Did you feel you were accountable for your actions?"

The question took Philippe aback for a moment. "I— Accountable for my actions, Hunter?"

She nodded.

His thoughts spun, trying to find an answer he wouldn't be punished for while also being one that would appease her. "No, I was under Damian's control. For a time…" He had listened until Shauna was there. He didn't want to capture her. He remembered telling her it would be okay, that she would be safe. She had writhed in his arms, doing everything she could to fight him. Then they made him stay away. Damian knew he had lost control of Philippe. He had done what he could for Shauna, trying to stop them from hurting her, to advocate for her safety.

"For a time?" she pressed.

"I did what I could to protect Shauna. They punished me for it," he said through gritted teeth.

The elf rotated the point of the blade on her fingers, and torchlight danced over the blade, flashing orange. "Is it true that on the plain below Fuegaste peak you killed Dark Ones using Magick? Magick that should not be yours to control?"

Philippe bit his tongue. These were the sort of questions he had expected. Questions that would get him in trouble. Things that twisted his words, that had a grain of truth to them. "I can control Magick," he said simply.

"Did you kill Dark Ones using Magick you should not control, Magick that doesn't belong to you?"

"I defended myself when attacked. I used Magick." He left out the information about charred ribs of the Dark Ones, the smell of their burning flesh, and the singed grass at his feet.

She gripped the handle. "That is what I thought."

"Thought? You already knew this. There were bodies on the plains. You saw them when you took us," he spat.

She bent low, her face inches from his. "Yes, I did. But I needed you to admit it." She leered over him. "But just wait. You will want to practice your confession for when we see Nurzan." She turned and strode out the tent flap, barking an order to someone to return him to the other tent.

Philippe's mouth went dry. "Nurzan?" The tent doors blew open in the wind and sent a chill down Philippe's spine in the silence. *Who the hell was Nurzan?*

Chapter 4 Shauna

The guard at the door shot Shauna a look as her stomach growled for the fifth time in as many minutes. It felt like her stomach was trying to eat itself. She tried not to focus on her stomach, or that because of the shackles on her wrists, Shauna hadn't been able to feel her hands for several hours. She shifted again, trying to find a more comfortable seat on the cold ground. The guard walked out of the tent, and she looked around again. She strained against the chains, trying to see into the far edges of the tent before slumping back into the chair. There wasn't any sign that Philippe had been in this tent. *Please let him be okay,* she implored the Goddess. Her injuries ached, and she shifted again, trying to relieve the pain throbbing in her side.

"Stay still." The guard stuck his head back into the tent, barely controlled annoyance edging his voice.

Shauna froze, holding his gaze for a moment,

before ducking her head and letting her shaggy hair cover her face. The guard watched for a few more seconds before turning back out of the tent flaps. The wind blew the door open, and Shauna watched through the floating fabric as the guard snapped to attention and saluted to someone out of view. The guard bowed, his hand in a fist over his chest. "Hunter."

Shauna turned her head so she could see through the ragged cut of her hair while keeping her head down. "How is our little Fritual?" a voice asked from outside the tent.

The guard glanced at Shauna and back at the officer outside. "There is nothing of note to report, but she is fidgety. The noise is annoying."

"Well, you are annoying, so the feeling is mutual. Go."

"As you wish, Hunter Fayanna." The guard bowed and scurried away.

Who is Fayanna? What is a Hunter?

She moved into the tent with an effortless grace. It wasn't unlike the way Queen Moraine moved through the castle. An easy confidence that came from knowing you are in charge. "Come sit with me," the elf said, and with a wave of her hand, the manacles that had held Shauna's wrists behind her back and her ankles together dissolved into a black mist that floated upward through the hole in the tent.

Shauna watched, a mixture of fascination and fear roiling in the pit of her stomach. She moved to rub her wrists, pleased to be free of the metal chafing her skin, and paused when she saw that there was a thin black ring of Magick set into each wrist. *You didn't think she would fully release you, did you?*

Shauna moved slowly, partly to let her stiff body have a moment of peace, but also to observe this female. She watched the young girl, but not with the same unmasked vitriol most of the other Dark Ones threw her way. All the Dark Ones Shauna had faced up to this point had been male. To be female, and in a position of power within their ranks, she must have been extremely powerful. Her eyes were gray like Shauna's, but they were harsh, raking her body in a way that made her squirm. It wasn't like the males, whose gazes were probing and unclean, hers was controlled, calculating.

She sat back. "So." Shauna flinched at the firm set of her voice. It demanded respect and only accepted the answers she wanted to hear. "I hear you hurt your foot on your journey to the peak. It may need our help."

"I— Yes, ma'am," Shauna whispered. *Maybe Philippe's plan in the cave worked? Do they trust him?* When the officer said nothing else, she continued, "I had an altercation with a boar. Phi— My companion killed it. But not before it cut my foot," Shauna said, not wanting to reveal too much.

The officer rolled her eyes. "Be honest, girl. Do you think you need to be checked out? Nurzan wants you in one piece. The last thing I need is you getting a fever because the injury is infected."

"Yes, it should probably be checked. It was bleeding again when we tried to escape."

"I'll be back." She turned to the door.

Nurzan? The name wasn't familiar to Shauna. It sounded mean, like the kind of name Father would give the bad guys in the stories he would make up when she and Tay were kids. But if he—Nurzan—wanted her in one piece, maybe they would be safe from harm? *But what will he do when he has you?* Shauna looked down at the bits of black Magick circling her wrists. Not for the first time, she noticed how empty she felt. She never really noticed the warmth she felt when she had her Magick. Shauna felt full, whole. Now she felt empty, hollow, like there was a space next to her heart where her Magick should reside. It felt cold. Shauna pushed away the feeling, searching for the Magick within her. She thought she could just feel a tiny spark, but then she felt a burning pain in her wrists and stopped. Shauna looked down at the black bands. The surrounding skin was angry and red, the bands looking tighter, sinking into her skin.

The image of the cave, flashed in her mind: of stepping out from behind the boulder to be taken by the black snakes of Magick, she could almost feel it wrapping itself around she and Philippe. That was the first time she had felt the emptiness. Shauna had thought it was because she was passing out. *This must be what is blocking the Magick. If I can't cast, can I talk to Philippe? Philippe?* Shauna called into the void. She closed her eyes, searching for the connection that they used to have. The Fritual Magick that they had, trying to find a small spark of his Magick. Her mind felt dark, empty. A cavernous space she hadn't spent time in.

"You cannot use Magick when you are here."

Shauna's eyes snapped open, and she jerked my head up. The Dark One was back with a healer in tow. Her arms were crossed, and she glared down at Shana. She hadn't thought about how quickly she would come back. Shauna didn't even hear her boots or the tent flap when she came in. How long was she standing there?

"There is a reason you are bound. It isn't just for

fun," she snapped. "You will not attempt to use any Magick. This will be your only warning. If and when you try to use Magick, an alarm goes off. We know you are casting." She looked to the healer and waved him forward.

"May I?" he asked, bending to Shauna's feet.

A bead of sweat slipped down her forehead and her stomach rolled over in knots. The idea of this dark elf touching her made her sick. "I—I, uh, yes?" Shauna said, as if she had a choice in the matter. The elf dropped to his knees, laying out a wide assortment of products. A pair of scissors, a needle and thread, a bowl of water, a cloth, a vial of a green liquid, and a roll of bandages. She watched as he unlaced her boot and pulled down the sock.

Shauna gritted her teeth as he pulled the sock away from her skin. During their attempt to escape from Fuegaste Peak, the dried blood caught in the fibers. The cut was only a few inches long, but it was angry. The surrounding skin was flushed and red, coated in dark scabs. "I will have to clean this up. You can't be infected."

"Thank you?" she said, not fully understanding what was happening, but thankful that her foot could breathe without the constrictions of the sock and boot. "What are you doing?" Shauna croaked when he lifted the scissors.

He glanced from her to his commander. "I am a healer. You are in the beginning stages of an infection. These stitches need to come out and your foot needs to be cleaned. If I can, I will redo the stitches. But we need to clean out any debris that will lead to further infection."

Hunter Fayanna nodded. "I will send food to you soon. Remember. Don't cast. I will know if you do. Healer, come to my tent when you have finished." She glared down at him until he ducked his head.

"Yes, Hunter," he whispered.

She nodded, held Shauna's gaze a moment more, then turned and left.

The healer watched her exit, waiting several heartbeats before he turned back to Shauna and picked up the scissors. She looked away as he carefully slid the blade against her inflamed skin. There was a quiet snip as the stitches were cut. The water he used to clean was lukewarm. It stung a bit as it sank into the cut. She looked down, and the cloth was stained pink with her blood. It was hard to look at the long angry red cut, but the dull ache she had gotten used to had faded. He pressed the skin around the cut before pouring a thick green liquid over her foot and wrapping it back up in a clean bandage. "I don't think it would be smart to redo the stitches right now," he said. "You need to keep it clean. I will come check it daily." He looked up at her, his mouth half open like he wanted to say something.

She leaned forward. "What did you say?"

"Nothing. I didn't say anything." He collected his things, nearly dropping the roll of bandages, and scurried from the room.

Chapter 5 Taytra

All Taytra wanted to do was to bust the door down and give those *men* a piece of her mind. Her people had nothing. The Dark Ones had taken their homes and burned what little they had created in their short weeks on the plain, forcing them to beg in the street for food. They hadn't been allowed a meeting with the council for days. Serena had fed them bits of information, what she was pushing forward and what was getting pushed back to a different meeting, but it wasn't enough. She wanted to thank them. But to scream at them. She wanted to grovel at their feet. What did it matter? She had already seen people begging in the street. They could work together. If only they would let her in the room so she could tell them that.

"Tay," Ward said, glancing up from the list of potential arguments he, Andrew, and Taytra had created. "You're doing it again."

Andrew slid to the floor to sit beside them. "Isn't it better if she gets it all out here than in there?"

"I don't know. Maybe if they see how adamant she is, they will listen to one of us?" Barin suggested from his spot down the hall.

Taytra shot the three of them a glare but continued to pace, stopping for the briefest moment to glance out the window. "Do you think they are finally going to help us, or are they going to keep putting it off?" A small delegation of the people from Cabineral Lake waited below to hear today's progress. Several held children in their arms, dirty from head to toe. The sound of a baby crying floated up to the window, and Taytra turned away from the sound. "This isn't right. Sure, we are safe, but they can still die," Taytra grumbled under her breath, shooting a glance at the door. "Several people have come up asking if they can work. This isn't what they signed up for."

"We know. We were there when they asked," Andrew said.

"I don't get why that request would be denied? Would they rather us act like beggars for the rest of our time here? How long are they going to let us stay here?"

Ward sighed and rolled the bit of parchment up. "I don't know, Tay. Hopefully, we will figure that out shortly." He tapped the space between him and Andrew. "For now, can you come sit? Just try to relax for a moment. You don't want them to think you are crazy."

"She is crazy," Andrew said with a grin, earning himself a light punch as Taytra slid down beside him.

"Can I see the notes again?" Barin asked from the corner. "I want to double-check something."

Ward nodded and passed the elf the scroll.

Taytra stared at the door, listening to the muffled voices behind the thick oak planks. "What time did they say we could come in for the meeting?" she asked for the third time.

"When they get to their community forum section, baring they get there before lunch. Otherwise, we will have to wait until they finish their break," Ward said.

"And how long is it until the lunch bell rings?" she asked, leaning across Andrew to gauge where the sun hung in the sky.

Andrew gently shoved her back to her spot. "We have about thirty minutes," he said, his voice bordering on exasperated.

"Right." Taytra wondered how much of that feeling was directed at her, or the men behind the door. She grabbed her hair and started braiding and unbraiding the long strands. "I have more to say than time before they go to lunch," she said, staring at the flagstones, mentally preparing to sit for a few more hours.

"You guys are still waiting to go in? I thought they would have been done by now." Taytra jumped at the voice as Paulo came around the corner.
She looked up at him, green markings flickering on his wrists. "Did they send you out scouting again? Did you see anything? Did you run into Dark Ones? Why did you use Magick?" Taytra asked, jumping to her feet, the questions pouring from her.

Paulo held his hands up. "Whoa, okay. Yes, you have been waiting." He laughed. He looked around Taytra at the boys on the floor. "Is she always like this? Shauna never was."

Taytra jumped at her sister's name. It always took her off guard. Mention of her sister sent equal parts hope and fear singing through her veins.

"Occasionally. It's a Flynn thing." Ward laughed. "The more stressed, the more questions."

Paulo nodded. "They sent me out scouting again, but I didn't see anything useful," he said to Taytra. "I used Magick to help a few farmers on the way back. With the Dark Ones nearby, they needed to get crops in fast before they razed the fields."

Taytra sank back down to the floor. "Oh, okay."

Paulo gave her a little smile, then went to the door. "Well, I am going to be nosey." Taytra couldn't help but perk up as she watched the elf knock on the door.

The door cracked open, and a small man stuck his head out. "Right." He pulled his head back in and looked at the men inside.

Lyra moved down the hall to the group. "Are we still waiting to get in?"

Taytra opened her mouth to reply when the man came back out. "Thank you for the reminder. We were about to break for lunch. You all may come in. Unfortunately, we do not have enough chairs for all of you, so some of you will need to stand against the wall."

The reminder? Did they really forget we were out here, or were they avoiding meeting with us again?

"That won't be a problem," Paulo said, holding the door and waving the rest in. A table dominated the room so large Taytra had to assume they built it in the room. The dozen men who ran Hollens sat around the far edge of the table, leaving five chairs open near the entrance. Serena sat on the rebellion's side of the table, her raven hair in an intricate braid down her back. Paulo, Barin, Ward, Andrew, and Alois sat, while she and Lyra stood. Taytra planted herself between her friends from Cabineral, a hand resting on the back of each chair. While she would have preferred to sit and have a place at the table, she knew the boys had been right. They hadn't taken the women seriously at the first meeting. They would play by these men's rules. Taytra wouldn't lie, though. She felt powerful standing in front of these men looking down on them with her friends at her side.

"Welcome to the Frituals, their entourage, and the leaders of the Cabineral rebellion."

Alois hmphed at the idea of being called an entourage. "The last time I was in an entourage, I was seventy-five."

The Councilmen ignored Alois and continued, "We are sure you have many questions, but we have a limited amount of time. Please allow us to go over certain rules, then we shall touch on your questions or requests."

Taytra scowled. These men were very particular about their wording. She didn't like the way they said they would 'touch' on the things they wanted to discuss. It sounded to her like they didn't want to 'touch' on them at all. Taytra peered over Ward's shoulder at the list of notes they had scribbled down. Again, they all nodded their agreement. "That is fine," Lyra said.

The men in the room snapped their eyes to her, and they held her gaze. Something about the way they stared at her told Taytra even Lyra was not welcome to speak. *Just wait, I haven't even gotten started*, she thought, narrowing her eyes at them.

"As we were saying," a different man said, "we have decided that—"

"I am sorry, my old Elven ears may have deceived me again, but did any of you introduce yourselves?" Alois interrupted. "I prefer to know how to address who I am speaking with, especially with conversations as important as this."

Barin glanced over at Alois with a small smile.

"We did not," Serena said. "We apologize. It would be good to establish a working relationship." She shoots the men a pointed look. "I am Serena Nightcastle, also known as the Guardian. I am a guest of this panel currently. But I have helped the city of Hollens for over eighty years."

One man huffed, his face flushing red for a moment, mumbling something Taytra couldn't quite make out, but the three elves by her side stiffened.

"I am Paulo, I am the earth Fritual from Gradatia," Paulo filled in, trying to keep the meeting moving.

"My name is Lyra, Apeito Fritual. I am from the northern regions. Before all this, I was a seamstress."

Barin stood and gave a small bow. "I am Barin. I feel I should give you the knowledge that my surname is Nurzan. My father is General Nurzan." Taytra jolted at the name. For a moment, she saw the elf in front of her, the belt raised over his head. Ward's hand slipped off the table to touch the side of her leg, bringing her back. Barin was not Nurzan. She watched as Barin turned to each of the men on the far side of the table. His voice was firm, but she could see in the way his jaw ticked that this was a vulnerable moment. Something he carried that he wished to put down. "I want nothing to do with my father. But they trained me to be a Dark One. My father nearly made me one of his Hunters. I can help you understand his tactics."

"Right. Should we have any questions, we will reach out to you, Barin," the man said almost dismissively.

The elf sat back down, his jaw working.

I see you! I understand, Taytra thought, *I know how hard that was for you!*

"My name is Alois. I was a monk in Bulandon. While I could never control spirit Magick, I studied it."

The group continued introducing themselves to each of the men of the Hollens. The men shifted, as if knowing basic things about each member of their party made them uncomfortable. When it got back around to them, they shifted for a moment before the first man straightened the paper on his desk. "Right, well, thank you for that. Let's continue. We realize that some of you are elves and some of you can control Magick. However, here in the city of Hollens, you may not cast."

Taytra looked around in shock. *Are they really going to just ignore what we just did and still not going to introduce themselves?* She caught Paulo's eye and raised an eyebrow at the markings still glowing a soft green on his forearms.

"Is there a particular reason for this?" he asked, turning to the unnamed speaker. "Prior to this meeting, nothing had been said to me. For example..." He lifted his arm so all can see. "I just returned from a scouting mission *you* asked me to go on. On the way back, I helped to collect the harvest. In doing so, I used my Magick. No one said anything about me using my Magick then."

"You were not in the city walls. Magick is not allowed in the city of Hollens. We are the city of men. Men do not do Magick."

"I am sorry. That is wrong. Even if you don't believe us, you have to have heard?" Taytra interrupted. The men turned to her for a beat, then away. "No, no. You will not ignore me. My sister is human. My sister is a

Fritual. My sister can control Magick. Would you stop her from doing Magick in the city?"

"Yes, because Magick is banned in the city," the man said quickly, but he looked at Paulo, not her, when he addressed the question.

"You have three powerful, extremely intelligent people that can control Magick sitting in front of you and an army of your enemy at your door. That enemy will not care about your rules and will use their tainted Magick to tear down your walls. Are you not going to use them if and when it comes to it because you don't believe in the use of Magick?" Taytra asked, the question directed at Serena. The older woman was rigid, fire dancing in her eyes. *She didn't know.*

"We don't expect you to understand. Just need you to follow our rules," one man said.

"It is always easier to follow rules when you understand them," Taytra said. "Could you go more into the reasoning for choosing this?"

"No," the men said. "You are in our city. You must follow our rules. Now, if you don't mind, stop interrupting so we can finish this meeting."

Taytra's face flushed red in anger, but she bit her tongue. *So, you want to be petty.*

"Good, now to reiterate you will not cast Magick."

"What are you going to do to stop this?" Serena asked. "How do you plan to enforce this rule that I am just learning about at this moment?" She leaned forward, her voice dangerously calm and collected.

Taytra grinned. *I need to take notes from her.*

"Now that we have that cleared up," the councilman continued again, ignoring the direct question. "We understand that you, Barin, have not completed your

Frituals ceremony. If, because of safety reasons, you cannot do your ceremony outside the castle walls on Samhain, you may do it within the walls. Those are the only circumstances in which you may do Magick within our walls."

Barin nodded and glanced at Alois, who gave a loud sigh, and shrugged. "We can work with that."

"Next thing, we understand the people that have come into our city with very few belongings—"

"Nothing. We came to you with nothing," Andrew cut in.

"As such." The man glared. "We will give you some things to survive." He passed a paper to Andrew. "We calculated this number based on the number of people you have," he said as if it would explain away any questions.

With one glance, the anger in Taytra's chest expanded, and she looked to Serena. The woman stared hard at the men.

"This won't be enough," Andrew said slowly, his eyes flitting from the paper to the men around the table. "How did you calculate this? Did you receive the wrong numbers? Are these any bigger than the tents we have now?"

"No, that is correct. You will have forty tents and one hundred loaves of bread along with at least one large cauldron of stew per day. We considered your second request as well for your people to work, but that is being denied, with prejudice. Please do not submit it to us again."

The three young leaders looked at each other. "I am sorry, but you can't be serious," Taytra said, and Ward give her a warning tap on her leg, but she ignored it, stepping closer to the table.

The first man scoffed. "We are entirely serious. If you want to interrupt again, you can leave."

Ward put up a hand. "With all due respect, sir, I don't think Tay is interrupting. You finished a sentence, your mouth was closed, thus not interrupting. She is a leader of this cause, and we are just trying to understand. We have over three hundred people that came with us from Cabineral. We had a thriving community before we needed to leave. However, we cannot feed three hundred people with one hundred loaves of bread a day. Those are starvation rations—"

"And from what I can tell, your city isn't starving," Taytra cut in. "The generous luncheon you have scheduled this afternoon tells me you aren't starving. Or do you take food from your people too?"

"You should be grateful for what you are given, children." The man stood, red in the face, spittle flying across the table.

"That's it." Taytra smacked the table. "I am sick of this. We are young, yes. However, we are not children. Every person in this room is an adult—"

A council man stood and smacked the table too. "Girl, stop talking—"

"Do not interrupt me," she roared in response, and the man sat down, taken aback by the ferocity of her response. "You want to know what we are grateful for? To be away from the Dark Ones. To have a wall between us. For that, I thank you." Ward touched her shoulder, and she shook him off. "However, there are three hundred people downstairs waiting to hear what we can give them. We have over sixty children and a few dozen elders. They have been sick and held in cells. They trust us. Our people want to work. They don't want to beg or stand in a breadline all day to be told we ran out of the food we were given again. We have blacksmiths, seamstresses, and healers. They want to take their lives back. If you won't provide enough to give them at least one square meal a day, let them work for themselves. Surely there are places where they could assist and make their own wages to support their families. We have done all you asked, but our people need something. This is a misuse of power," Taytra shouts, her chest heaving with anger.

The men all yell at her, standing and shaking their fists.

"This is an outrage."

"We have been more than generous!"

"What do you know of starvation?"

"Councilmen of Hollens, is this how you act?" Serena stood, her voice booming through the room, cutting down all the others. Serena raised a hand, and the men turned to her, slowly sitting and looking at her like a mother who had scolded them. "I have to say I agree with *Lady* Taytra," she said, putting emphasis on the honorific. Taytra never wanted it, but if it worked now, she would hug the woman. "I know Lady Taytra can seem... brusque," the half-elf said, gesturing at Taytra. "However, she is a strong woman. And she fights for her people. She is a powerful ally. Who I agree with as I told you before. This gift, while gracious, is lacking." She scanned the men. The word 'gift' twisted with disgust. "Their people have nothing but the clothes on their backs. They were told this was a city of peace, a haven. They waited while you deliberated whether or not to let them in. As a result, they watched as everything they had burned. I ask again that you at least give them a bit more food daily and reopen the idea of letting at least some of their people work. It could be very beneficial to your economy."

The men turned to each other, whispering.

"We don't like outsiders," one said.

"I understand that," Serena said, voice tight with motherly annoyance. "However, the people of Cabineral can't go home for who knows how long. They may never go home. This could be some of your new citizens' first introduction to you. You wouldn't want to make it a poor interaction. I would also encourage you to consider what your residents will think, knowing their leadership gave so little to those that ask for the bare minimum."

"But what do these children know of strife?"

"These children, as you call us, have seen how quickly cities and entire kingdoms have fallen. We want to help prevent that," Lyra said. "Might I remind you that five of us here were born before your grandfathers?" She cocked an eyebrow, waiting for them to respond.

"Why didn't you just stay in your city? If not for you, we wouldn't have a mess like this to clean up?" another man whines.

"Mess to clean up?" Ward snapped, his composure broken. "We escaped our kingdom. Half of us spent weeks in a dungeon. Would you rather we rot in a cell?"

The men look at each other and all nod. "We are done with this conversation. You are dismissed. We are going to lunch," the man who let us in said, leading the men in standing, and guiding them all from the room.

"We waited hours for you. What happened to letting us go through our notes?" Barin snapped.

"You know?" Taytra leaned across the table,

getting as close to the men as she could. "My mother always said if you had to resort to name calling or making fun of someone, it was because you didn't have a foot to stand on in an argument. You know what you are doing is wrong. You are just too proud to admit it."

One man bent and lifted a bell. "You have less than a minute to clear out of this room. After that, I will call our security, and we will forgo any future meetings."

"Is this really necessary?" Serena asked.

"I am going to murder someone," Taytra said to Ward. "I swear to the Goddess I will."

"I think I will do it with you," Ward said, pulling her out of the room with him.

Serena followed them out, cursing under her breath. "When I have a chance, I would like to meet with all of you again, to learn what you need. We will get through to them. Men are stubborn. Please know I am doing my best to break through," she said, before giving the collected group a small bow and heading to the Goddess forsaken lunch.

Chapter 6 Jamie

Like many nights in the last month, Jamie found it difficult to sleep. The shadows that lay in the corners played tricks on his eyes, making him startle awake when he drifted toward sleep. The quiet, crackling torches in the hall sent flickers of light dancing on the walls of their room, giving just enough light for Jamie to see the shape of Queen Moraine. Her words echoed in the night, ricocheting off of everything she hadn't said, spinning into a tight spiral of dread.

Were his children okay?

His life was reduced to a series of unanswerable questions. It was no wonder he couldn't sleep.

He got up and paced the room for a few minutes. Eight steps one way, and eight steps back. He moved to the door, trying to see who was on patrol tonight. The male stood with his back against the wall, chin tilted down to his chest. In the amber torchlight, Jamie saw the deep bags that hung under his eyes and the thick line of stubble shadowing his jaw. Jamie turned, checking to make sure that there were no other guards in the hall. "Alexis," he called quietly. The boy didn't move. "Alexis," Jamie called again, louder this time. The boy shifted slightly, then jolted awake, twisting left to right when he realized he had been caught. But none of his vile superiors were around. "Alexis, it's just me. It's Jamie."

The boy turned, and Jamie watched as the panic melted from the boy's shoulders. Alexis held a finger to his lips and moved up the hall to the junction, peering down the side hallways before coming back. "Jamie, I am so sorry. I should have been more focused. If they had caught me sleeping, I am sure they would have blamed it on you." He ran a hand over his close-cropped hair, the skin beneath flushed with embarrassment and the adrenaline spike that came with fear. "How are you two doing? They haven't pulled you back in for questioning again, right?"

Jamie stood on his toes. "Not since Kieran pulled me out a week ago." Jamie tested the edge of his lip with his tongue. "I think most of the swelling has gone down by now, but there is still the bruising."

The undercover guard nodded slowly. "Okay, so maybe it hasn't happened yet," he said so quietly Jamie wasn't sure he heard him correctly.

"What? What hasn't happened?"

Alexis shook his head. "I don't know anymore. It's honestly getting difficult for me to tell whose plan is whose anymore. Or which plan being leaked is real or fake." He ran a hand over his face. "Sorry, so there have been whispers that you needed to be moved back down to the dungeons for security reasons. And that Moraine would be questioned again prior to confirm she couldn't break the locks or trip the alarms."

"I won't be able to," the queen said from behind Jamie. She had sat up from the floor, dusting off what dirt she could before coming to stand beside him at the door. "I am aware of how they use dark Magick, but I don't know how to control it."

Alexis bowed his head slightly to the queen as she approached the door. "Of course, your majesty. I apologize for not greeting you. I wasn't aware you were awake. I am just relaying what I have heard."

"Of course," she replied primly.

"Once they confirm you cannot break out on your own, they will move you to the dungeon. But I must warn you, your majesty, they will probably rough you up a bit before bringing you down."

"I would expect that," she said, "but thank you for the warning, nonetheless."

Alexis glanced down the hall and lowered his voice further. "We are working on a plan to get you out if they move you to the dungeon. We will make sure you have a rough idea of the plan before that happens." A door thudded down the hall, and Alexis spun away from the door to the far wall. "Stay safe."

Jamie and Moraine sank back into the thin pile of hay. "Do you think he knows anything else?"

"I don't know." Jamie paused. "What if it isn't the right rumor? Sounds like both sides are feeding each other information. It probably is best that we don't know. Especially if you get pulled in for questioning."

The queen nodded, and they turned to the door, listening as Alexis exchanged terse pleasantries with the newcomer. They heard the thud of Alexis's fist hitting his chest and the salute of "for the Dark Ones" followed by the heavy footfalls of someone walking away.

Unsure of whether it was Alexis outside their door or a different guard, the two stayed silent for a few minutes. *What sort of escape plan could they be making?* There were hardly any guards left on their side. That was the main reason Taytra had gotten out. They took the guards who were on their side and fought their way out, taking a small militia with them. Jamie knew for a fact they didn't have that available to them. Jamie turned to the door. He wanted to ask Alexis if there was any news about his daughters.

"I still think we should let them starve." The voice, the guard outside, was not Alexis but that of an elf. A moment later, the small food flap in the wall is unlocked and a tray of food shoved in with enough force to slam open the inner door and fly into the opposite wall, splattering food everywhere.

"Well, that answers that question," Moraine murmured, reaching over for a bowl. While most of the thick gray porridge had flown across the wall, a bit stuck to the side of the bowl. She delicately crooked a finger to scoop up the tasteless gruel.

Jamie grabbed the other bowl and wiped away a bite for himself. The lumpy food was gray and flavorless but edible. It wasn't good by any sense of the word, but it quelled the gnawing feeling in his stomach, at least for a moment. He shoveled the food in and swallowed as quickly as he could so he didn't feel it sliding down his throat. As disgusting as it was, they didn't know the next time a meal would be flung through their door.

"Are you two done yet? It isn't like you had a lot to eat," the guard said, peering down at them through the bars of the small window.

"Just hold your horses. We are nearly finished. We might even give you a tip today," Jamie grumbled.

The guard's eyes burned with hate. "What was that, human?"

"Nothing," Moraine said quickly. She glanced at Jamie, shooting him a look fit for a queen holding court. "What do you think you are doing?" she hissed.

Jamie ignored her. The words fell from him, soothing some of the anger in his chest for the moment. "Just answering your question like a good little prisoner. Isn't that what you wanted?" he asked sarcastically.

The guard hit the door, the sound echoing in the small room. "Be careful, little human. You won't be needed for much longer. Then Kieran will let us do whatever we want to do to you. This door may hold you, but it also protects you," he growled, kicking the door for good measure.

Jamie froze, his anger gone in an instant. To Jamie's relief, it held. His heart pounded, and he clenched his hands into fists to hide his shaking. He glanced at Moraine, and she too was frozen, eyes locked on the door. *Shauna? Taytra? Something must have changed. If they weren't useful anymore, that would mean something had happened to one or both of the girls.* Jamie stood and moved to the edge of the door, trying to see where the guard had gone.

We are a tool, Moraine had said. *They have kept me alive for leverage. If they don't need me, something happened.*

"We can't jump to conclusions," Moraine whispered, but the drawn-out way she said it was as if she was trying to convince herself of the words.

Jamie peered down the hall. There was nothing

more he wanted than to pound on this door until his fists were bloody and it shattered from its hinges. He clenched and unclenched his hands. He wanted to burst from this hold and run across the kingdoms to find his children. He needed freedom. He needed time, and that was a luxury the Dark Ones would not give him. "I know. I am sure we will hear more soon. These bastards just love to rub it in."

Chapter 7 Taytra

Taytra moved through their little tent city, torch in hand. Her night was quiet, no meetings to be had, no jobs to be done, but she wanted to avoid the quiet of her mind. She observed families settling in for the night. Bodies spilled out of the tents, grateful to finally have a bit of cover against the chill of the fall air. One father sat outside, leaning against the tent pole, guarding his family. His head bowed forward onto his knees in sleep, his hand resting on the arm of a small child reaching out of the tent to him. *He is going to be stiff all day tomorrow,* Taytra thought sympathetically. It was a pose she saw many take, always close to their families but on edge, leaving space for those inside to rest.

She made her way over to the guard tower right by their group and pulled a hay bale target down. She had made it *very clear* it hadn't gotten past her that the council insisted they had to stay here, right by the gate and the barracks. Where, if something went wrong, they would be the first to know, or the guards of Hollens could quickly be dispatched to take care of any rabble rousers.

She moved the target to the wall and quickly strung

her bow, a quiver of arrows hanging ready at her hip. She had discovered one of the best ways to put her mind at ease was to work. If she couldn't help someone else, she would exert herself, hone her skills so she could help from the future. She pulled an arrow from the quiver. The wood was smooth and well-crafted. Unlike the knobby, uneven arrows she had practiced with in the forest, made quickly out of necessity, these were created with care. The shafts sanded smooth and points rounded with tiny bits of metal. She knocked the arrow to her string, careful to not bend the delicate feathers on the fletching. She drew the arrow back, her arms shaking from the weight of the draw. The moment she released it, she knew it was a bad shot. The bow shifted in her grip and the arrow dipped, clattering to the cobblestones at her feet, the sound bouncing off the surrounding buildings. Someone from the guardhouse poked their head out.

"Don't mind me," she called. "Just practicing."

He nodded and pulled back inside.

She sighed and drew another arrow, focusing this time on the way her fingers curled around the bit of wood and willing her hand to stay steady. *Better* The arrow sunk into the bale of hay two inches from the ground, but at least this time she hit her target. "Just goes to show you better arrows doesn't mean better aim," Taytra grumbled. She turned to grab another arrow and noticed Serena leaning against the wall, watching her. "Hi," Taytra said, feeling a bit of something fall into her stomach. She couldn't quite tell if it was dread, anger, annoyance, or maybe a bit of all three. "How long were you watching?"

"You are doing a good job, you know," the half-elf said.

"Right," Taytra said, pulling another arrow. "You tell that to the council." She drew the arrow back quickly and released. The arrow impaled the center of the bale. She paused, staring at it. She didn't do that very often, so when she did, she let herself take it in. *I am getting better. I can protect people. The practice is working.*

"I have spoken to the council about it. Like someone else I know, they are very stubborn." Taytra glanced at the woman. She was smiling, her eyes dancing with amusement at her little joke.

Taytra allowed herself to smile back. *She didn't cause what happened at the ceremony. She wanted to protect Shauna, too*, she reminded herself. Taytra turned back to the target, reaching to draw another arrow, but her hand grazed the air. She glanced down. The quiver was empty. *I should have brought more. No reason to carry so few.* She took a deep breath. It wouldn't hurt to speak with her. She had been encouraging all the others to, so she could as well. "I don't think I ever really thanked you. For Sam and Clive. Thank you for taking care of them. I—I don't like to think about what could have happened to them if you hadn't found them." Taytra quickly turned away, embarrassed at the way her eyes burned at the thought. She hurried to the target, collecting the arrows.

Serena nodded. "May I?" she asked. Taytra nodded, handing her the bow and an arrow. The woman took the bow, testing the draw. She lifted an arrow to the string and prepared to fire. "You have surprised me. A lot."

"In what way?" Taytra asked, crossing her arms.

The elf released the arrow, and it thudded deep into the hay bale a few inches from center. "You were stronger than I thought you would be." She lowered the bow and turned to Taytra. "Over the years, I have met many people like you. They have an anger that boils under their skin. They get into trouble. There is a lot of fighting. But it isn't very often that those people can temper that anger." Taytra passed her another arrow, nodding slowly. "You have become a good leader. You have made mistakes but you have also owned up to them. Or you have admitted when you don't know exactly what to do." She released the arrow, and it thudded next to the other. "That is a big step in being a leader. Humility."

Taytra handed her the last arrow and grabbed a hay bale, then pulled her whetstone from her pocket. Once settled, she drew the knife from her hip. Watching as Serena fired and moved to collect the three arrows. "Well, I didn't exactly have a choice."

"No, you did. And you chose the harder path." Serena grabbed a few of the hay bales and pulled them over for the two of them to sit. "Here is an example. You spoke today at the council. You admitted you were young but had experience you wanted to share to show why you were acting certain ways, yes?" Taytra nodded. "Well, may I remind you of your good friend Neander and how he took over leadership when you fled? From what I have gathered, there was no collaboration. It was his way or nothing."

Taytra scoffed. "He's a prick."

Serena laughed. "As someone sitting on the council who has to work with him, I can neither agree nor disagree with that statement." But she nodded vigorously. "You have learned well and you are open to keep learning. I definitely wish that the men of Hollens were as adaptive as you. Men are stubborn as hell."

Taytra laughed. "You aren't kidding. I have never met so many men that I want to smack upside the head in one setting."

Serena grinned. "Me too, but I wanted to make sure you know you are doing a good job. It's going to get worse, but you, Ward, and Andrew are doing well, given the circumstances." The half-elf looked around and saw a few practice blades on a rack on the wall. "Any idea whose blades these are?"

Taytra shook her head. "They were there when I got here."

Serena got up and tested the weight of the wooden blade. She spun it in her hands, moving through a series of moves.

"Andrew tried training me for a little. I haven't picked up a blade since we got here. They injured me when we were leaving the forest," Taytra said. "I took them out, but not cleanly."

"Well, is it healing, okay?" Serena asked. When Taytra nodded, the older woman smiled. "Good." Serena handed her a blade. "Let's see what skills you have. Keep moving. Make sure those skills are flexible."

Taytra hefted the blade, shifting her footing. She scoffed. "You know, Ward always wanted me to train in a skirt in case we ever were caught unawares. I think I did it twice. I much prefer pants." The cheap skirt she had gotten for a few stones in the market was made of a thin itchy fabric, but the skirt had enough space for her to take a stance similar to what Andrew had drilled into her head.

"I can't argue with that sort of thinking. My father had similar instructions for me when I was younger. Though I never tried to wear pants. I didn't have anyone to swipe them off of either. So I just did what I could with my skirts." Serena circled Taytra. Her steps were long and even. The woman stood in a crouched position, blade held out in front of her with steady hands. Taytra tried to mimic the woman's sure stance, but her arms shook from the weight of the blade. She took a few quick steps forward and back, and Serena jumped back in response, the action just as smooth as Taytra would have guessed. The elf raised an eyebrow, nodding at the movement. "Good, that was good. Okay, I see how you fight."

Taytra laughed. "Really? You can tell how I fight from one movement?" She jumped into action when the elf lunged and blocked the move, the movement more reactive than strategic.

"When you have been training as long as I have, you learn to read people pretty quickly," Serena said.

Taytra nodded. A thought hit her as Serena moved again. Taytra blocked the first strike but missed the second by a few inches, receiving a solid tap on her arm. "Ow." She laughed. "You know, my father would tell my sister and I your story around the time of the testing. This year, he mentioned how your father was a swordsman. Is that true?"

"Yes, it was. My father was human. He died a long time ago." The elf paused, sticking her sword in the dirt while she tied her hair up. Not wanting to be surprised again, Taytra kept her blade up and ready. "He started teaching me when I was ten. He had been a part of the rebellions and had seen what vile things men could do. Being a halfling, he didn't want me to be hurt. It started small, with knife work. But I was fascinated with the swords he had. He would spend hours and hours sharpening them." She smiled fondly. "I met Matron getting a blade. I told him it was for my father. But it was really for me. I wanted my own." She pulled the dull training sword out of the dirt. "Father didn't want me to accidentally stab anyone with his sword. He may have wanted me to be safe, but he still thought I was going to be too jumpy with a blade."

Taking advantage of her just grabbing the blade, Taytra swung her blade in a quick zig zag formation that Serena parried. The two went back and forth for a few more minutes. Taytra could feel the muscles in her shoulders ache with the familiar work and knew she would be sore tomorrow. It felt great. And then she finally landed a blow. It was light, a quick stab that made it through the parry, sliding along until their scabbards clanged together, just nicking the elf's side.

"Next blow is the winner," Serena said, spreading her stance more evenly.

Taytra grinned. Over Serena's shoulder, Taytra could see a guard moving along the wall to the bell tower. She just had to keep the women focused on her for a few moments and she was sure she would get her opening. She danced around the woman, making a few moves the other could easily block. Serena wiped her forehead with the back of her hand, quickly shifting to the offensive. Taytra saw the man through the window and spun away. The evening bell was loud. It echoed off the flagstones. The sound made Serena look up toward the guard tower where the massive bell was housed. Taytra struck, hitting the woman in the thigh. Serena jumped back, yelping in pain and surprise. She glanced at Taytra, then at the bell tower, laughing. "Good job. I should have seen that coming. That was good." The elf put out a hand and Taytra shook it. "Well done."

"Taytra!" Andrew called. He was leaning against the wall on the far side of the courtyard. "I am glad to see you remembered something from our training sessions." He pointed back to the tents. "Sam was looking for you whenever you get a chance."

"Okay, thanks." She turned back to the elf. "Thanks. I needed that." She wiped sweat on the back of her arm.

The elf smiled. "I could tell. Go on. And please, if you ever need anything—even if it is just something to hit—let me know."

Chapter 8 Shauna

The wind howled outside, snapping the untethered doors and sending sand skittering all around Shauna. She looked up, waiting to see if a guard would come in, but she still couldn't see anyone outside. Shuana hadn't seen a Dark One in hours, and it left her mind doing somersaults. In Damian's camp, even if she couldn't see a guard, she could hear them. But here, the silence served as her captor. She was thankful for the tent over her head that blocked out most of the cold, and to be away from those who leered over her, watching her every move, but it was making her paranoid. Shauna jumped at every sound. She was afraid of every thought that drifted to Philippe, wondering if the band on her wrist would rat her out.

She shivered again as she closed her eyes, trying to turn away as tiny specks of sand pelted her. Shauna couldn't help but wonder if Philippe was okay. Did they give him shelter? Had they had sent the healer to see him? Could he feel his powers, or were they also muted in the same way as hers? Did he feel unclean with the dark

Magick on him? Did he shy away from thoughts of her for fear it would set off the Magick that bound him? She looked down at the black bands on her wrists poking out from beneath the ropes that bound her. They shimmered in the gloom, radiating from her veins like a pulse.

Shauna's thoughts also kept going back to that woman. She had never seen a woman in power among the Dark Ones. The camps were almost entirely devoid of women. *Most women wouldn't be dumb enough to join the Dark Ones, or to fall for their tricks,* She thought, but this Elven lady, Fayanna, had. And apparently people had thought she was smart enough to give her this top-ranking position. They had called her a Hunter. —*Who are the Hunters?* There hadn't been anyone she could recall with that title with Damian. Her power unnerved Shauna. The way she stood. The way she had looked at the healer. *I need to learn more about this woman somehow. Maybe that healer will tell me something?* It would have to be a time when we were alone. If she knew more about her, she would have something. Without Magick, Shauna felt nearly useless. The next best thing would be information.

There was a rustling sound at the tent flap, and a Dark One entered. He looked down at her with a sneer of disgust plain on his face. He spat in her direction, "Hunter Fayanna wants to speak to you."

Shauna put her hands out, waiting for him to cut the ropes. He scoffed in response and batted her hands away. "Oh." She struggled to stand, trying to shift her weight underneath her. When she didn't move quick enough, the guard yanked her to her feet, shoving her toward the door.

The guard grabbed at her elbow, and without

thinking, she recoiled from the elf's touch. *Please, for the love of the Goddess, don't do anything stupid.* Shauna folded into herself, not wanting him to think the movement was her actively trying to fight him, but to mask it as one of fear. "I—I can walk." her voice cracked from disuse.

"You better keep up." He glared but didn't reach for her again. "Don't try anything."

She nodded vigorously, and he stared her down. She forced herself to meet his gaze. *Don't flinch. Don't flinch,* Shauna told herself. It felt like he was trying to read her mind and see if she was lying. After an agonizingly long moment, he nodded and opened the tent flap for her to pass through.

The tent city was smaller than she had originally thought. It probably only had about thirty tents in it. *Thirty tents, with three to four beds,* she did the math. *That could mean around one hundred of them.* Not that the information helped her yet. It's a smaller group than what had been used to take over Cabineral, but that didn't mean they were any less powerful. *I need to figure out how I can access my Magick.* Her hand stung as the band tightened on her wrist, and she shied away from the thought, focusing on where the guard was taking her. Shauna looked up at him, fearing for a moment he would know what had happened, but either he didn't notice or he didn't care.

Like Damian's camp, everything centered on one area of the tent city. This one had a large bonfire. *Where do they get the fuel for it? Do they carry all that wood with them or—* her thoughts stopped. Through the dancing flames, she saw him. Philippe. Their eyes locked, and she didn't care that the guard took a hold of her elbow and pulled her around the circle, yanking roughly on her already sore arm. She paid the Dark One no mind. Shauna just needed to get close enough to Philippe to know he really was okay.

Like her, Philippe had the Goddess damned black bands around his wrists. His face was an open book. Happy to see her, but concern, and anger flushed his cheeks. He took a half-step toward her before he froze. He glanced down, and she saw the Magick there was some sort of tether, holding him to a stake in the ground a few feet away. His face darkened in anger, his lips drawing in a tight line. Shauna wanted to move to him. She wanted to cut the Magick from his arms. His own Magick, so new and foreign to him, pulsed in deep burgundy lines on his skin. With each heartbeat, he touched the idea of his Magick, and the black band squeezed. *At least he can touch it. I still can't feel anything.*

Shauna tried to read his face, to understand what was going on, what she should say. What did they know? They obviously knew they were Frituals, but what did they know about *them?* What did the Dark Ones have that they could use against them? *Knowledge is power,* she reminded herself. *Give nothing but take all you can.*

Fayanna strode between the tents, coming to stand between she and Philippe, looking them up and down like they were prized animals in a competition.

The Dark One at Shauna's side shoved her, and she stumbled, crying out in pain when she put too much force on her injured foot. "Kneel in the presence of the Hunters," he barked, standing over her.

"You idiot!" the elf snapped. She quickly closed the gap between them and reached out a hand to help her to her feet. Shauna hesitated before taking it, fearing what would happen if she denied the action. "Nurzan wants her in one piece. Prisoner or not, we need her alive," The Hunter snapped. "What happens after Nurzan has her is up to him."

Shauna recoiled at those words. *Nurzan must be the leader.* She wracked her brain again, trying to think of when she could have met him. Or what she could have done to be on his list. *Done? All I had to do was exist.*

"You are dismissed, but stay in the area. I will call you when we are done."

"Yes, Hunter." He saluted, his fist crossed over his heart.

She wanted to turn to Philippe, to see if the name meant anything to him, but she didn't want to bring any more attention to him.

"Shauna Flynn."

She turned to the elf, trying to keep the fear from my eyes. She was a Fritual, obviously people would know who she was. But something about the elf knowing her full name unnerved her.

"Have you heard of General Nurzan before?"

Shauna racked her brain trying to think if she had ever heard the name before. *Do what you did with Damian,* she tells herself. *Tell the truth when it works for you, and half-truths when it doesn't.* She flashed through her time in the camp and stopped, running through the memories. There was one moment. *Was it him?* The black reflective disk Damian had created and the brief conversation she had with Damian, as he used her father and the blade against his face as a tool to get her to talk. He had shown the person on the other side great respect. But wouldn't he have said their name? She tried to remember if she had seen a face, but her mind kept stopping on her father, the knife at his temple. "I don't know. I don't think anyone told me who he was," She lies, trying to sound unsure, scared. It wasn't hard. The voice she had heard through that Magick was deep and powerful. If this Nurzan was who she thought he might be—well, she didn't want to think about that yet.

Fayanna smiled, but there was no warmth in it. "Oh, my dear, if you knew about the general you would remember him." She stepped closer. "Your sister will definitely remember him."

Her stomach dropped. "My sister?" Her mouth went dry. *Taytra. What did he do to my sister?* she swallowed hard, trying to force the bile down.

The elf laughed at the shock on Shauna's face. Her world felt like it was closing in around her. The sound of the fire turned into a dull roar. She stared hard at the floor, trying to stop the world from spinning. Fayanna's words cut through. "Oh yes, I know all about your big sister Taytra. She has made a pretty good name for herself, leading a rebellion. Starting a coup right under Nurzan's nose. Not before he gave her a good beating." She smacked her hands together for emphasis.

Shauna jumped at the movements. *So she is alive. He hurt her. He hurt her, but she is alive. She is a leader.*

"I know for a fact that she has a bounty on her head. Not as big as the one for you, of course." She put a hand on Shauna's shoulder and guided her to a bench near the fire. Now she was facing Philippe, but she did everything in her power not to look at him. She couldn't have the Hunter hurt him too. "Like I said, Nurzan wants both of you in one piece. He wants to make sure he talks to you," she said, and her voice shifted to a sweeter, more comforting tone. "But there are a few things I have to ask you before we see him." The elf simpered. She sat on the bench beside Shauna and draped her cloak over the bench behind her. In the firelight, the skirts she wore looked more like a dark blue than black. "Your friend Philippe over there admitted he killed a few Dark Ones when he was escaping Fuegaste Peak. What do you say to that?"

Shauna glanced at Philippe, then back to the woman. He leaned toward her, his hands clenched into fists. His expression was locked in one of anger, and he openly glared at the Hunter. She didn't even acknowledge the anger. Her lips were pursed, and she had her hands clasped in front of her like she was attempting to look patient, but the way she kept glancing between the two of us, waiting for Shauna to answer, was anything but patient. "We were trying to escape. They attacked us. We tried to get away, but they stopped our cart." Shauna said, finally.

"So you admit to the fact that you attacked them? And some may have been killed in the process?"

"Well, I mean, they attacked us first. It was self-defense. Any time I have hurt a Dark One, it has been in self-defense," she said. This was such a weird conversation to be having. Who would have thought she would have to defend herself to a Dark One?

The elf narrowed her eyes. "You killed Dark Ones before Fuegaste Peak." It wasn't a question.

"I–Well, I have been named Fritual for about a month now, and it definitely has not been the easiest time for me," she hedged. "You know, of course, that I was captured by Damian, not long after I was named." She twisted, trying to deflect from her and her supposed actions.

Fayanna crossed her arms. "Oh yes, I know of Damian. I hear your sister stabbed him at your ceremony?" She leaned back. It was like she was trying to make nice, even though she was holding Philippe and Shauna hostage.

This plan of half-truths wasn't working well for her. "She was trying to protect me. She is good at that." She glanced at Philippe. He looked just as guarded as she felt.

The elf leaned forward. "So how many elves would you say you've killed?"

From the corner of her eye, she saw Philippe shaking his head. She kept her eyes on Fayanna. "I don't know."

The Hunter narrowed her eyes. "You don't know. Have you killed so many people with a Magick that isn't yours that you can't even count them?" Her voice was low, threatening. There was something cat-like in her demeanor. If she had a tail, it would have lashed at her side.

"No! No!" Shauna jumped in. "I just—I am not the type of person to tally the people that have attacked me," she fumbled.

Fayanna nodded slowly. "Perhaps I underestimated you," she says quietly, waving over one of the guards standing at the perimeter. "Take her back to her tent. Make sure your knots are very secure with this one."

Shit, Shit Shit, Shauna thought as the guard roughly grabbed her elbow and shoved her back the way they came. She saw Philippe wince at the movement and knew he was thinking the same thing as her. *Shauna, what kind of trouble have you gotten yourself into?*

Chapter 9 Paulo

"Yes, sir, we should get another round of food from the city in a few hours. I have people on their way to get that order now," Paulo said.

The man before him was more than a little upset. The answer was not enough for him. "That is ridiculous. That is the third time this week I have had to wait until the second food drop to get a meal for my family. I am here every day at dawn. I have done everything you and the other 'leaders' have told me to do. But it is never good enough for you! I need food for my children."

Paulo sighed inwardly and made a note to see if there was anything Serena could do to make the process simpler for people. "I deeply apologize, sir. As someone who doesn't have children of my own, I am sure I cannot understand the level of stress you are under."

"Damn right you can't. You don't make it any easier, that is for sure."

Paulo's stomach growled, making the two men pause. "I'm sorry." Paulo put a hand to his protesting organ. "I wait until the last food drop to eat. I am sure you understand why." The father looked down a bit sheepishly, some of his anger softening. "As you are aware, since you have been in line and will receive food from the second drop today, if you would kindly head over to the left, the individual over there will give you a ticket to get food sooner as you could not in the first round for the day."

The man glowers up at the sky. "Goddess, there needs to be a better way to do this. Families need to be fed first. I can't get a job to stop taking handouts because I have to wait in this blasted line all day." He runs a hand over his face. "I know this is better than being locked up in the cells, but at least then we knew what we were in for."

Paulo nodded. He pulled a report from the table and showed it to the man. "I am not sure if this will give you peace of mind, but I prefer honesty over withholding. Two thirds of those who came with Lady Taytra, Ward, and Andrew, either have children or have elders in their families. Those who do, go first. As such, the food runs out faster due to those larger groups in the first round. We are still looking for the best way to divide the food equally, so if you have any viable suggestions, we would love to hear it."

A woman behind the man grumbled, peering over his shoulder at the bit of parchment. "I think the most obvious thing would be to get more food from the city or let us work for it. Let me pay for food, not just bread and unflavored stew."

The man passed the paper back to Paulo. "I agree. I would much rather work for something than wait in these handout lines and do nothing. I used to have a shop, I have skills. Someone must want to take in more workers."

Paulo nodded. "I agree. From what Lady Taytra has told me, there are many among you that could be invaluable to the city. We are working towards that. Unfortunately, the city has not found an agreement they wish to move forward with at this time."

The man opened and closed his fists. "Well—well, work harder. It isn't getting any easier." And with that, the man stomped off to get his ticket for the food drop.

Those behind him followed without comment, until an elder, whose bent frame barely came up to Paulo's elbow, toddled up. "You are doing a good job, sweetie," she said, patting his hand. "Anyone with a brain can see the cards aren't in your favor. The Goddess works in mysterious ways. She will find a way to help you soon. Don't worry. Just be sure that you are looking for it so you don't miss it."

"Thank you, madam. Your words are appreciated. I am sorry I cannot get you something to eat sooner."

She gave his arm one last pat, before wandering over to the next line to get her meal ticket.

It was bad here. It wasn't as bad as it had been on the plateau when the Dark One's had burned the fields of crops to ash and destroyed wagons of food and trade goods, but he couldn't help but feel the same pang of guilt as he watched people with large families line up for meal tickets. They hadn't known what would come. They had no way to prepare their children for the way their stomachs would growl and the hollow empty feeling one felt at bedtime. Paulo felt guilty for every crust of bread he got that wasn't passed on. But the other Frituals and the leaders made it clear they had to take care of themselves too. No matter how much guilt gnawed at them, they couldn't help their people if they were sick and hungry.

"Lord Paulo, do you have a moment?" a guard asked, coming up to Paulo's shoulder.

He looked at the man, his face is tight, like he had something he didn't wish to say but had to.

Just another form of guilt, Paulo thought glumly. "Yes, just a moment." He gathered his notes and headed over to the man leading the other line. "Do you have any grievances or other comments you would like to be noted today?" The men shook their heads. "Right. I will be back soon. Please inform anyone looking for me. I will be back in time for the next drop."

"Sir, is there somewhere we could speak privately?" the messenger asked.

"Of course. Let's head to the tent," Paulo said, leading the messenger inside a large tent that had been set up against the outside wall of the city. They had established it as their main headquarters. A place where the refugees from Cabineral could easily find them without getting lost in the twisting streets of the city. It wasn't nearly as big as the one Taytra and the boys had used on the plain, but it did the job. "What can I do for you?"

The man looked, if possible, even more nervous than he had before. He shifted his weight from side to side and tugged at a loose strand at the hem of his shirt.

This can't be good, Paulo noted, shifting the piles of reports away. Turning the focus away from the man for a moment. "Please sit," Paulo said, indicating the seat across from him. "What was it you wanted to discuss?"

"Well, sir, I was chosen to speak to you by the scouts. I have the reports you asked about. There is one in particular I think you should read right away," he said, passing a few scrolls to the elf.

The scrolls in question are bent and folded, clearly clutched and hidden away from others' eyes. "And which is that?" Paulo asked quickly, breaking the wax seals and scanning the documents.

The boy pulled one last bit of parchment out of his coat. "This one, sir. It's the update you have been looking for on Lady Shauna and Lord Philippe's locations." He hesitated for a moment before passing the small square of parchment across the table.

"Yes! Finding them is the most pressing issue!" Paulo said, dropping the other reports. He looked down at the small black seal, then up at the boy. He wouldn't look at Paulo, his face downcast into his hands. His hesitation gave Paulo pause. "You know the news you bear doesn't harm you? Whatever these documents say is no fault of your own." The boy nodded but kept his face down. Slowly Paulo broke the seal and unfolded the documents. His eyes flitted across the page, reading it twice over. "Oh Goddess," Paulo breathed. "They were immediately captured? How did this happen?"

The man nodded solemnly, finally meeting Paulo's gaze. "It appears there was a traitor who infiltrated the peak. Someone who fed the Dark Ones information. They used their previous relationship with the Teachers of the mountain and took advantage of the unsuspecting Frituals. And when the mountain was attacked, feigned support and lead them directly into a trap." He paused. "We have only been able to speak with two of the Teachers. It is unknown if the others are still alive or not."

"Goddess help us," Paulo breathed, reading over the report again.

Last known location of the Frituals, Shauna Flynn,

and Philippe Mattick, are on the plains of Fuegaste peak. It is believed that they are being taken to Bulandon to meet with Lord Nurzan. Intelligence tells us this is the current leader of the Dark Ones.

"Do you know for sure if they are still with the Dark Ones? What if they were able to escape?"

The man pointed at the notes. "Read further down." Paulo turned back to the bit of parchment. "We believe they were so easily taken over because of the recent testing of Lord Philippe. He would have been tired from the exertion of the test and more susceptible to attack. And it is believed that Lady Shauna may have been in a weakened state because of the mountain and the lack of water in the area. That was from one of the Teachers. There is a caravan of Dark Ones currently headed south. We cannot get close enough to confirm if the Frituals in their midst."

"How far south are they? How many are in this caravan? They could already be in Bulandon, depending on how quickly they are moving," Paulo said, getting up and searching for a map amongst the many scrolls Serena had acquired for them.

"Yes, sir. They have at least one company of men—we would say at the very least one hundred. They are moving slowly. The desert isn't being kind to them. Thus, making it difficult for the Frituals to escape if they have a chance."

Paulo smiled wryly. "Well, I know we have escaped from groups that big before. But it all depends on the circumstances." Paulo moved to the table of reports. "Do we know who is leading that group?"

The man shook his head. "No, sir. We have been

trying to get more information on that, but no luck so far. We believe it is a Hunter. One of Lord Nurzan's elite soldiers, but we haven't figured out which one yet."

Paulo nodded. "Is there anything else you can tell me? Do you think there were any injuries in the escape? Are they hurt? Were they able to take anyone down?"

"No, sir. I am waiting for more concrete information to come in before I confirm any of that. We know they fought until they were taken, so we can infer there were some injuries, but are unaware how severe they may be. They took out at least five Dark Ones from what we could tell from the bodies around the peak and what we learned from the Teachers." He crossed arms. "I should have that information for you in a few days."

Paulo nodded. "Alright." He folded up the report and put it in the breast pocket of his shirt. "For now, I want this conversation to stay between the two of us. Until you have more detailed information, I will not be discussing this with the others. Is that clear?"

"Yes, sir. Quite clear."

"Good." Paulo moved toward the door. "Then, master." He pauses. "I am sorry. I don't think I ever asked for your name."

"Chadwick, sir," the man supplied, exiting the tent with Paulo.

The elf proffered the other man a hand. "Well, Mr. Chadwick, I anxiously await that report in a few days' time. Hopefully, it will have better news."

"I hope so too, sir."

Chapter 10 Shauna

They were on the move. If asked, Shauna honestly wouldn't be able to tell if the pit in her stomach was purely hunger or fear. Her skin felt raw and tight from the burning sun, and to her relief, her legs had cramped so much she couldn't feel the pain of them anymore. Thankfully, she would make this journey without a blindfold. Shauna caught glimpses of Philippe as they moved far ahead of her. He, too, had a phalanx of guards surrounding him. She saw he was okay, but there was never a chance for them to communicate through words, their minds, or even a basic facial expression.

Her stomach protested again, and she slumped over gently on her horse's neck, hoping to minimize the sound. She felt shaky and weak. Her head far too heavy. And in a way, she was thankful for the ropes that bound her. They were the only thing keeping her on this horse's back. And he didn't even want her here. They stood in a group, waiting for the next order, and the horse kept dancing underneath her, trying to unseat her. The horse stepped sideways into the riderless horses on either side of him, rubbing his sides against their gear.

She clung to the horse's mane, gritting her teeth as her foot caught on the horse beside her, getting stuck in his gear. It wasn't this horse's fault he was uncomfortable. *If this is how they treat their horses, they must not last long.* Most of the horses around her were lean. But they didn't look skinny, they looked strong and well-fed. *So this has to be a special sort of hell for me and my horse,* she thought, stroking his neck with the little slack she had for movement. If the horse she had been saddled with was tired, underfed, and overworked from carrying her for days, she couldn't use him to make an escape.

Shauna squinted into the distance, trying to see if she could find Philippe again. A gust of wind caught the sand, and the Dark Ones in the distance pulled up their hoods and ducked away. She did her best to hide, leaning forward again into her horse's neck, but she still got blasted by the gritty bits. She tried rubbing her face on the side of her arm, but the tiny bits of debris still got in her eyes. She looked up, blinking rapidly at each movement like tiny blades.

"Miss Flynn, are you alright?" someone said, putting a hand on her leg.

She jumped at the touch, and her horse swayed, sidestepping in alarm.

"Easy, easy," the voice said, grabbing the halter and holding the horse still.

Shauna squinted, trying to see who the voice belonged to, but her eyes were streaming with tears. "I am okay," She lied.

"Lean down for me," the voice said. Shauna hesitated, then did as she was told. A gentle hand pressed a damp cloth to her face and wiped the sand from around her eyes. "Hmm, hang on just a moment." The person left, and she heard them in the distance. "I need her down from that horse."

"But she is a prisoner. I have orders."

"And I have orders to make sure she gets to the fortress in one piece. Do you want to be the reason she goes sand blind? I am sure that would be a great conversation."

"Flynn, you are coming down. Don't do anything stupid," the guard said, untying her hands.

Shauna leaned forward, getting ready to swing her leg over when the muscle spasmed. She gritted her teeth and tried to breathe through it, hoping it would release soon. "I think I am going to fall. I don't know if I will be able to stand right," she said.

"That is okay," the softer voice from before said. "Do your best. I will be here to catch you if you fall."

What did he do to end up here? She wondered again.

Shauna leaned forward and slowly lifted her leg backward over the horse's rump. She hit the ground and immediately crumpled, her knees collapsing like they could never hold an ounce of her weight.

"Easy there," the healer said, scooping her up and lifting her under her arms. "We are going to go sit over here to the left." He slid a hand across her back and guided her as she worked to get her feet under her. After five agonizingly slow steps, he slowly lowered Shauna to the ground. Pins and needles spiked as the blood slowly moved through her legs. "Okay, let's get that sand out of your face. I apologize that this is the first time I have been able to see you today." She heard him puttering around for a moment. "Ready?"

"Yes?" she said, not sure what he meant.

A damp cloth slid across her face, gently wiping away the gritty debris. He worked his way around her face before gently dabbing away the thick crust around my eyes. "This will sting a bit. Once we get the majority off, I am going to try pouring some water over your face slowly," he said.

Her eyes already felt better.. "Okay," she said, blinking several times. Her eyes were still streaming with tears. She ducked her head when she saw several of the Dark Ones looking in her direction. She tensed and waited for them to look away.

"Are you okay?" the healer asked, noticing my reaction.

"I—Yes, I'm alright." Her eyes darted between him and the guards.

He lifted a bowl of water above her head and tilted her face to how he needed it to be. As he slowly poured the stream of water over her forehead and down across her eyes, he said, "You do not need to fear them watching you. Hunter Fayanna has put me in charge of making sure you and Master Mattick make it to the fortress with no issues. They have no say in what I do, as long as it is pertinent to your health."

"That doesn't mean I am allowed to talk to *you*." A guard walked by, and she ducked her head, avoiding his gaze.

Gently, the healer brought her face back up and shifted to the other side. "Please, you can relax, miss. If anyone questions it, I will simply say that I was conducting my duty as assigned by Hunter Fayanna and that they should bugger off unless they want to take it up with her." He took the cloth and quickly wiped away the rest of the sand. "There. Now let's look at that foot." He put the bowl and dirty cloth to the side, and shifted to her foot, propping her leg up on a small stone.

A part of her, the scared paranoid part, wanted to pull away. She still didn't understand who this elf was or what side he was on. She wanted to question his every move, and everything he said. How could he possibly have that authority here when it seemed like he was a prisoner himself? *Maybe that was him just covering his own back.* Healer or not, she didn't know if she could trust him or anything he may say to her. Maybe she was just overly paranoid after what happened with Manon and the cave. *He wanted to say something in the tent,* she reminded herself. He seemed smaller then, like being in the presence of Fayanna diminished him in some way. While here, even with the enemy all around, he was confident in his words and actions.

"My name is Galen," he said, dropping the used bandages to the ground. He grabbed a clean cloth and dabbed away the old poultice that lay over her skin. "This looks like it will be fully healed soon." He scooped out a fresh layer of a dark green poultice and laid it over the cut, careful to do a bit more where the skin was slightly inflamed. "I am from the northern kingdom. A few hours' ride from the capital city of Apeito. It snowed a lot where I lived but it wasn't often that it stuck. Made it more difficult to find strong patches of herbs in the woods."

"Why are you talking to me?" she whispered.

"What do you mean? I am your healer. I was put in charge of you," Galen said, putting the bowl of herbs down and grabbing a thick, clean bandage.

She hunkered down unintentionally and paused. *Strong. You are strong.* She forced herself to sit back up tall, trying to keep her foot as still as she could for him. "It's just, we are in a Dark One camp. If they knew you were telling me stories about your home, I can't imagine they would be happy."

"No?" he asked, cocking an eyebrow, but he didn't look up from his work. Shauna sat back quietly, letting him finish. He wrapped the bandage tight enough she could feel the pressure of it, but it didn't feel constricting. "Like I said, this should be healed soon. The inflammation is still pretty consistent, but the swelling has gone down since you got here. As long as they don't force you to go on any marches in the next week, you should be fine." He tied it off. "I will ask Fayanna to not do so. I know she was ordered to get you to the fortress in one piece. Or so I have been told many times. To do so, she will need to care for you a bit." He gathered his things back into a small backpack.

"You said you were from Apeito?" She asked as he examined the black band on her wrist. She flinched slightly when he touched the pinched skin.

"Yes. Traveling here in the desert makes me miss my snowy home. The nights aren't so bad, though."

He wiped away the dirt from her hands, turning them over and carefully examining each line and crack on her skin. *He's stalling,* she realized. "Did—did you know?" A Dark One walked by a bit too close, and she dropped her voice. "Did you know Lyra?" she breathed.

He didn't say anything at first but he squeezed her hand. He folded the cloth slowly, putting it into his bag of supplies. He didn't answer right away, and she panicked, trying to figure out how to backtrack her question. "We grew up in the same area. I knew of her but never met her. I saw her brother more often. But that was before…" He trailed off.

Before the fall, she finished. She looked out at the line of riders making their way across the sands. "Do you know how long it will be until we get there? To Nurzan?"

"We are a few days out, but you should know we are making a stop at one of the recruitment bases. From what I have heard, Fayanna was asked to stop in and make sure things were operating at standards. We should be there by nightfall." He shifted his bag, sliding his arm through the straps. He met her eyes, and she wanted to look away. His blue eyes were striking, and the pitying way he looked at her... It seemed like there was more he wanted to tell her but couldn't right now. "I have to go," he said somberly.

She nodded and watched as he walked to a guard to let them know he was finished with her for the day.

A recruitment camp. As if the main camp wasn't enough.

Shauna tried not to let her brain wander down the path of what it could be like in a camp of impressionable Dark Ones who were currently being trained to be their soldiers.

The guard came and stood over her, his dark skin was flecked with sweat and he reeked of urine and stale alcohol. "So you are the little Fritual I was sent to gather up? Hands, time to get you back on your horse." He grabbed her hands and tightly bound them again with a cord. She flinched at his rough hands and bit the inside of her cheek, tasting blood. She wouldn't say anything. *I won't let him hear my pain,* she thought as he roughly handled the raw skin of her wrists. He hauled her to her feet, pushing her forward. She stumbled slightly, blinking rapidly as she felt a blood rush from getting up too quickly. "Come on," the male said, grabbing her elbow and dragging her back to the horses.

She limped along as quickly as she could, wincing each time her foot struck the ground. She couldn't help but wonder if this was a punishment for Galen working on her foot or asking Fayanna to let her heal.

She looked up and saw in the distance the carts growing smaller. They were on the move again, on their way to being one step closer to Bulandon. He pushed her toward the line of horses. The poor horse she had been riding danced away at the sight of her. "Come on. Grab it and hold it still. I don't have all day," the Dark One snapped at one of his fellows who lost control of the horse.

She moved to try to get on the horse when they grabbed her waist and quickly lifted her up to the horse with the grace of a toddler. She scrabbled for a grip, grabbing at the horse and tried to swing her leg over as the horse danced away from her. She clung to the horse's mane, trying to catch her breath as she tried to regain her balance. *I think I will name you Dancer,* she thought, patting their neck, using the movement to calm her shaking hands.

The guard grabbed her ankles, lashing them into the stirrups. "You will be told when to move in a few minutes. Don't be stupid." The guard smacked her leg, and she met his gaze. It wasn't kind, but it didn't have as much malice as others.

Did some of them care? Maybe not about me, but did they know they were in line with cruel people? They couldn't all be terrible through and through.

She sat in the line for a few minutes. She wished she had a set of reins to move the horse around, just to move and feel in control. But she was not. Dark Ones surrounded her, shooting her looks. Letting her know clearly that they were watching her every movement.

She looked up and saw Fayanna as she strode down the line of Dark Ones, surveying her men. She found Shauna and held her gaze for a moment before scanning the line. She swiveled in her seat, following the Dark One's gaze, and saw Philippe a few horses behind her. He was hunched over the neck of his horse. He looked absolutely defeated. It made her sit up taller. *I will be strong enough for both of us.* Fayanna looked between the two of us before mounting her horse and trotting to the front of the caravan.

Slowly, Philippe raised his head and saw her looking. He tried to smile, but it was more of a pained scowl, his fat lip looking extra swollen in the sunset glow of the evening.

Are you okay? she mouthed, wishing she had her Magick.

He shrugged but mouthed back, *Never been better. Don't worry about me.*

She scowled, and the corner of his mouth perked up. He, of all people, should know that would have the opposite effect on her. *Don't be stupid.*

He shook his head and smiled. Because why would he, of all people, ever be stupid, or do anything dangerous?

"Hey!" One of her many guards smacked her leg, sending her horse skittering. "Keep your eyes forward."

She scrabbled to find a hold on the saddle as her

horse danced beneath her. "It's okay, Dancer, it's okay," she whispered, hoping to relax the creature. His eyes rolled and he tossed his head. "We will be okay." she patted his neck. His ears flicked back toward her. "Yeah, you are okay," she whispered again, hoping that no one noticed. A horn blasted through the air then, and she jumped, sending her horse skittering once more. This time, someone grabbed his halter and held him still.

"If you can't control your horse, you will need to walk," the guard barked.

She nodded, but they both knew he didn't have that authority.

Chapter 11 Taytra

Taytra glanced down at the scrap of parchment Serena had given her. "3467 Flower Road," she repeated, comparing it to the sign on the corner and the number on the building. "This is it." She reached up and gave a few quick taps on the door. She looked over her shoulder while she waited. A few people glanced in her direction, but most of the afternoon crowd couldn't care less about what she did. They were too focused on getting home after their day in the city.

"Hello?" A petite woman opened the door, peeking out. "Who is there?" Her voice had the quaver of many years to it. Her long gray hair was unbound, falling about her shoulders in heavy ringlets, held back from her face by a flowery handkerchief.

"Hello," Taytra said pleasantly. "My name is Taytra Flynn. I was told you are the head of the Library of Hollens? I tried to stop by there yesterday, but they told me I needed your permission to go because I am an outsider. I am sorry to be bothering you in your home. I was told I may find you here."

The woman pulled the door open more. "Oh, of course, dear. Please, come in. I will make you a cup of tea. It is not a problem. Come in, come in." The woman grinned and waddled back into the house. Taytra followed slowly, making sure the door was latched behind her. "Do you like cream in your tea?" the woman called from around the corner. Taytra grinned as she followed the woman back. The hallway was lined with stacks of books up to her waist, with scrolls balanced precariously on top of the tomes, the cracked wax seals slightly reflecting the afternoon glow through the windows.

"Yes, ma'am, that sounds great," Taytra said, standing awkwardly in the doorway.

"Please, please come sit. Over here on this stool. My name is Moira Senesac, but I am sure you already knew that as you came looking for me," the woman said, bustling around the kitchen. She piled a plate full of cookies and ignored Taytra's protests, insisting that she eat the sweets. "Tell me about yourself. I don't get too many visitors."

Taytra told the woman a brief rundown of her story while they waited for the kettle to boil. It felt good to get her story off her chest, and Moira was a very attentive listener. Her eyes were wide, and she nodded or shook her head the whole way through. "My! You certainly have had a crazy time. All this in a month?" The teapot whistled, and Moira jumped to her feet to fetch the pot.

"Yes, ma'am, about that," Taytra said, quickly doing the math in her head.

Has it really only been a month?

"So, you see, I want to get into the library to do some reading and learn what I can before I have to decide what to do next. I want to make sure I am always making

84

the best choices I can for my people."

Moira nodded. Pouring the hot water over a scoop of dried leaves, she brought the small teapot and two cups to the table. "Well, my dear, I think that is a great idea. Is there anyone else that would need permission? I can make sure they are added to the list."

"Could we add my partners? Ward Hendricks and Andrew Warner. I am sure they would like to do some review, and even if they can't, if we should ever need to get a hold of one another, we wouldn't want them to be locked out and unable to reach us within the library walls," Taytra said.

"Consider it done."

Taytra grinned over her hot cup of tea. "Thank you, Moira. You are too kind." She breathed deeply, inhaling the rich earthy smell of the tea. "This is wonderful."

"Everyone needs a little tea in their life. Makes everywhere feel a little bit more like home."

The two women chatted for a bit longer while they finished the tea, before Moira popped to her feet. "I have something that you may like. I took it from the library a few years ago and I have been meaning to re-shelve it, anyway." The woman scurried into the hall to be followed a few moments later by the clattering thud of many books falling.

Taytra lunged for the door, hand at her waist, ready to draw her knife, and put a hand to her mouth to stifle a laugh.

Moira stood balanced with one foot against a stack, a book lifted high above her head. The remains of the top of the pile scattered around her. "I did not mean to do that." The little woman huffed.

Taytra laughed and helped to push the pile back against the wall and to gather the books from the floor.

"Right," Moira said, holding the book out to Taytra.

"The Frituals and their Magick?" Taytra read aloud, flipping to the first page. She scanned the first paragraph and grinned. "You are right, Moira. This is something I will need to help Shauna and the others. Thank you."

The woman beamed. "I am glad. Did you finish your tea?" Taytra nodded. "Good, let's head down to the library then, shall we? I will make sure you all are in our record books personally."

* * *

The library was a massive circular building in the middle of the city of Hollens. "The stairs go all around the outside wall," Moira explained as they approached, giggling at the awe on Taytra's face. "At each half turn around the building, is a landing, taking you to different shelving locations or study rooms." She put a hand up conspiratorially. "We put any books on the elven wars and dark Magick all the way at the top. The stairs alone are a discouragement." The main circulation desk was through the massive front doors, and Taytra saw a sign following the spiral downward wings of records and to the right, up to the many stacks of books and study rooms. After making sure Taytra, Ward, and Andrew were registered as patrons who could come while they were in Hollens, Moira took Taytra to her favorite study room on the fourth floor. It had a deep fireplace and lush chairs around the room. At the center was a small cedar table with a few chairs, and a blanket thrown across the back of each. "Do you need anything else?" Moira asked.

"I don't think so. I should be set for now. But if I do, I am sure your staff will help me." Taytra put her hand out to shake the old woman's hand. "Thank you. You have been more than generous."

The woman ignored the proffered hand and pulled Taytra into a deep hug. "It was my pleasure, dear. Please come see me again if you should require anything at all. Or nothing at all. I am always up to have a cup of tea with a friend." She toddled off back down the stairs, leaving Taytra to the silence of books and scrolls.

A friend. Taytra smiled wryly. She had been making more enemies than friends lately. With a pang, she realized she hadn't thought of Jacinta or Safiya in weeks. *I hope they made it out of the city.* She prayed to the Goddess that somewhere in the kingdoms, Jacinta had escaped and was making beautiful gowns—or at least making something. *When this is all over, I will need to introduce her to Lyra. The two of them could make something beautiful.*

Studying was never something she had been good at. That was more up Shauna's alley. She scanned the stacks of books on the walls, searching for anything that would jump out at her. But it seemed like this room had a lot of reports and research on grain and pottery of all things. Taytra got to the end of the bookshelf and looked out the large window to the courtyard far below. The market was just closing for the day as the sun set. Here on the fourth floor, she was just about level with the high walls of the city. Out in the distance, ruining the view of the sunset, she could see the Dark One squadron that breathed down their neck.

From the little bits they had gleaned from Serena, the high council didn't seem to care that the enemy was at their door. They continued to insist that they were not a part of this war and thus they had no enemy. Taytra turned away from the window in disgust. She couldn't understand how anyone could be so dangerously arrogant. All she could do was pray to the Goddess that their arrogance didn't come to bite them in the ass.

Taytra moved up the spiral staircase, following the signs pointing out the different topics. Agriculture, history, biographies, mythology. She dipped into rooms, scanning the shelves in the dimming light, before making her way back down the stairs to the study room, three thick tomes in her arms. Each book fell to the table with a soft thud and puff as she blew the dust from their covers. The sun was just about to wink out of sight as she lit a candle and wrapped a warm wool blanket around her shoulders.

The wool was scratchy, but the scent that lingered on it, of parchment, ink, and wax, reminded her of home. It felt safe. Taytra opened the first book and focused on the words in front of her for as long as she could, scratching notes onto a bit of parchment.

Chapter 12 Jamie

Jamie cracked his eyes open, sleep trying desperately to pull them shut again. He sat up, running a hand over his face. Moraine lay still. *It must have been nothing*, he thought, settling back down, trying to reclaim whatever position had been somewhat comfortable. Then he heard it, the slamming of boots on stone, becoming louder with each thump.

He sat up once more, moving across the room. "Moraine. Moraine, wake up," he whispered gently, shaking the queen. A guard hit the door with a loud bang, followed by the sound of keys jingling in the lock.

"Get up, both of you!" the guard said, flinging the door open. Two Dark Ones hurried inside, pulling the captives from the room.

Jamie stumbled, stars dancing with dark spots across his eyes. He caught himself on the door frame just before he ran into it.

"Come on, Flynn," the guard said, holding up a pair of manacles.

At least we are out of that hellhole, Jamie thought

as he lifted his hands to the guard. The first time he tried to close it, he went too quickly, pinching the delicate skin on the inside of Jamie's wrist. Jamie bit the inside of his cheek, tasting blood. *There is no need to rush. I am not fighting you,* he thought savagely. The guard repositioned Jamie's hands, closing the binding with a sharp snap.

Moraine was led out a moment later, yelping as the guard dragged her by her fiery red hair. "Now look, no one was fighting you. Let me go. I can walk on my own, thank you very much," she snapped, scrabbling at the elf's fingers.

The guard didn't hesitate before striking her, his gauntleted hand thudding against her chin. "Shut it. Royal or not, I will kill you."

Moraine glared at the elf, testing the edge of her split lip with her tongue as they threw cuffs on her as well.

"Come on. We are going on a nice little walk."

Jamie did his best to keep moving, watching the guards to judge the pace. *Was this what Alexis hinted at? Or something different?* Their limited knowledge protected them from interrogations but left them in the dark, unaware of the movements that may save their lives.

While the castle was large, it didn't take them long to get to the main hall. Down the corridor, Jamie saw the large front doors that led out to the rest of the kingdom. The doors he had heard slam shut behind Taytra when she escaped. The doors he had willingly walked through a month ago, without knowing what the ramifications would be.

"Come on," the guards who held the queen said, pulling Moraine down the hall toward Kieran's lair—the council room turned into his interrogation room.

"Ya best move it, or Kieran is going to be right

mad. Take my advice, he already isn't in a good mood. Don't do anything that will aggravate him more."

Jamie watched as Moraine was led down the hall, shoved every few steps by the guards around her.

There have been whispers that you needed to be moved back down to the dungeons for security reasons. And that Moraine would be questioned again prior to confirming that she couldn't break the locks or trip the alarms. Alexis hadn't been sure whose plan it was. Jamie could only pray that it was a plan created by their side. *Either way, she was going to come back bloodied.* Jamie thought of his own interrogation and the lies he had spun to meet the narrative that Kieran had wanted.

"Come on," the guard ordered, shoving Jamie into the corridor to the left. Toward the stairs. Having walked this path once before, Jamie knew when they were getting close, but even someone who had never walked the halls of the castle could tell when they were getting close to the dungeon. The smell of sweat, human filth, and sickness smacked him in the face, coating the back of his throat like tar.

As they descended into the darkness of the dungeon, Jamie felt the desperation and fear that hung in the air. It was like a fog that clung to your skin. The families that didn't escape with Taytra a few weeks ago were thin, their hair hanging in greasy chunks that framed their sunken cheeks. He knew he probably looked little better. But they needed to see someone being strong. Even if it was fake. Jamie held his head high as he walked past them, feigning control despite the manacles on his wrists. The fathers stood their ground, catching his eye as he passed. Jamie nodded at them, trying to use the slight movement to tell them it would be okay. The mothers hid their children behind dirty skirts with hushed words. Somewhere down the block, a child cried. The sound reverberating in the silence, the piercing sound making Jamie's stomach flip. One of the guards around him broke off to find the source, and it was quickly hushed by a mother's quiet but insistent whisper.

At the end of the block, the guards opened and shoved Jamie into the same cell he, Moraine, and Taytra had been held in when they were first taken, but the black Magick seal over the lock was removed.

"Don't try anything funny," the Guard said, twisting the lock into place.

The dungeon was deathly quiet as they waited for the guards' footsteps to retreat to whatever hellhole they stayed in to pass the time. Jamie sank to the floor, leaning against the bars of the cell. *I knew it was bad. But I didn't think it would be this bad. Stupid of me.* He pressed the heel of his hands into his eyes, listening as the dungeon grew louder as children asked questions.

He listened, wishing he had answers for them, or a way to appease the adults and the questioning looks they sent him.

A few minutes later, the door at the far end slammed open and the guard pushed Moraine through. The queen stumbled, catching herself on the bars of a cell before pulling herself up. A child inside ran to the bars, reaching for her. Gently, a sibling inside pulled the little girl away. Jamie couldn't hear exactly what was said, but was glad someone was looking out for the little one. Moraine smiled gently at the child. Jamie could see the blood on her mouth and chin, but the queen made no move to wipe it away. She stood as tall as she could, scanning the room. She kept her face controlled. A purple bruise bloomed on her eye, snaking up her cheekbone to her hairline, and a small trickle of blood seeped from her fat lip.

The guard that followed her down the stairs pushed her again, shoving her toward Jamie's cell.

"Step back," he snapped at Jamie, grabbing Moraine's elbow and holding her still as a second guard stepped up to the cell door, key in hand. Jamie stepped to the far wall and waited as they pushed Moraine in and slammed the lock back into place.

She fell to the floor and this time stayed there for a moment, waiting for the guards to retreat.

"Moraine?" Jamie asked, offering a hand to help her up.

She stared at it for a moment before shaking her head, a quiet exhale of pain escaping from her lips as she moved to the cell wall, hands gripping the bars, her knuckles turning white. "We won't be here much longer. And when we do leave—" she said so quietly, Jamie wasn't sure he heard her, "—I will make sure they suffer for what they have done." She glared at the doorway where the guards had receded. "My people deserve so much more than this." She turned to Jamie. Her face was like steel, her eyes dancing with tears. "I haven't seen pain like this since Chima was in power. I swore when I took power from her, I would *never* let anyone hurt my people like that again. And I broke my promise. I have failed them. I haven't fought hard enough for them." The words ripped from her throat, growing louder in her anger. Her body shook, and she pressed a fist to her mouth to suppress the sound of her cries.

"No, no," Jamie said quietly, moving to her side. "Moraine, you have done all that you could have short of getting yourself killed." He turned her away from the door and the people around them who surely heard part of her fear.

"I have not. I need to get these people out of here. If we don't—"

Jamie grabbed her hand. "You have done exactly what you needed to do." He paused. Wrapped around Moraine's wrist was a thin black band. "What is that?"

"Queen Moraine?" a child's voice called to them.

She pulled her hand away quickly and pulled the sleeve of her dress down to cover the mark. "Yes? Who is it?"

A little down the hall on the opposite side, a hand waved through the bars. "My name is Evan, your grace."

"Evan, hush," a woman in the cell with him said, pulling him away from the bars.

"No, it is alright. What is it, little Evan?" Moraine said.

Jamie stood behind her and watched as the little boy pulled away from the woman and pressed himself into the bars. "I—I wanted to make sure you were okay. We haven't seen you in a long time. I was worried that you had gotten sick, or that they had hurt you and that was why we haven't seen you."

Moraine laughed quietly to herself, and Jamie watched as she transformed into the queen he met the day of the ceremony. She rolled her shoulders back and held her bruised head high. "Thank you for asking, it is very kind of you. I am doing well, better now that I am down here with you. This is where I would much rather be."

"Really, your majesty? You would rather be down

here with us?" another voice asked.

Jamie smiled as he watched the spark of hope come back to the dungeon. People moved to the front of the cells, faces pressing against the bars, trying to glimpse the queen. "Yes." Her voice carried down the hall, reaching each person. "I would rather be down here with you. My people. Going through the same hardships as you, rather than spend my days away, praying to the Goddess that you are okay."

"How much longer do you think we will be here, your majesty?"

Moraine folded her hands in front of her. Jamie couldn't help but marvel at how she took the many questions and complaints in stride. Holding court as calmly and as dignified in the dungeons as she would the grand hall above. She did what she could to ease some of the fear they held in their hearts, when just moments before she was rolling in the fear herself. She was firm and honest, she didn't sugarcoat anything. It was what it was.

"We are going through some of, if not the most, difficult times of our lives. I don't know how much longer we will be here." She glanced over at Jamie, no doubt thinking like he was of what Alexis had mentioned. "But I need you to have faith. We will get through this together. Support each other in the best way we can."

Jamie sat back and closed his eyes, listening to the ebb and flow of the conversation. He fell asleep at times, catching snippets of the conversations. He knew he should stay awake. Maybe someone down here knew something they didn't. He glanced over at one point, and Moraine has settled down by the door, her stained skirt delicately splayed out around her. "As far as we know, the Flynn girls, Andrew, and Ward, are okay. We have heard very little about their whereabouts," Moraine said, and Jamie perked up at the topic.

Who is asking about the girls?

"Last we heard, they were out of the Dark Ones control and were stirring up some trouble."

Jamie recognized the barking laugh almost instantly. "Good," Omar Hendricks said. "If I know my Ward and Jamie's Tay, they will be stirring up more than *some* trouble. I thought I heard the guard say a few days ago that they had put a bounty on their heads?" He laughed loud and long, just like he had in the inn with Jamie over drinks before the ceremony. "I have never been more proud as a father as when I heard my son was worth something like one hundred gold stones. Good to know someone else besides his old man knows he is worth something."

Jamie crawled up to the front of the cell by the queen. "Omar? It's Jamie. How are you doing, friend? How's your leg?"

The queen nodded to Jamie and slipped to the back of the cell, gathering herself for a few brief moments of quiet. Jamie watched as she sat back against the wall, allowing the exhaustion to show on her face.

"Jamie! Is that really you? I saw them bring in the queen but didn't see you! Goddess, I've missed you. I'm—I'm alright. My leg's been giving me some real issues, but I've been trying to, ya know, stretch it and stuff like that doctor you told me about said to do. It's just so damp down here, ya know? Gets mighty stiff."

Jamie nodded, a smile forming on his lips. Even though things weren't going well, it was nice to hear Omar's voice and to know he was okay. "I'm glad, friend.

Just wait, our kids will think of something to bust us out of here. It will be mighty spectacular. And then you can get out and move around however you want to."

"That sounds lovely, mate. I just can't wait to get out of here and eat a decent meal. Maybe grab a pint," Omar said wistfully.

Jamie grabbed the bars of the cells, craning his neck, trying to see his friend. "Well, you remember what we said the last time?"

"Nah, I can't remember. What did we say? That we'd go to James'?"

Jamie laughed. "No, we agreed the next pint was on you."

"Mate, get me out of here and I'll buy the next round for the whole pub."

The two laughed and fell into a quiet silence. Jamie listened to the surrounding cells, absorbing the many sounds of the dungeon.

"Can I ask you something?" Omar asked.

"Yes, what is it?" Jamie replied.

A pregnant pause stretched. "I've been wanting to ask you, when I saw you again, I mean," Omar corrects.

Jamie waited, listening to a child sniffle nearby. "What is it, friend?"

"When you were moved or when you were in the hall, when Tay and Ward escaped, did you—did you see Pat? I have asked around here whenever there has been a change, but nobody has seen her."

Jamie's heart sank. Pat, of course. He hadn't seen her. The sharp-tongued woman would have stood out so clearly in the crowd. If she saw what they forced Ward to do to Taytra… "What happened the night you were taken?

I was here in the castle." He was deflecting and knew that was in itself an answer.

"It was awful," the woman in the cell across from Jamie said. She cradled a tiny child to her chest. "They came after night fell. Burned down my house. Smoked me and my husband out. The moment we stepped through the door, they captured us."

Omar cleared his throat. "I was in town. Pat sent me to get a few things for the stew she wanted to make the next day. Wanted to keep going like nothing was wrong." He cleared his throat harshly. "I wasn't home when they came. And Ward refused to speak to me when they made him a guard down here. He didn't want them to tie him back to me."

Jamie shifted, looking at the ceiling. His words were more of a prayer than fact. "I am sure wherever she is, she is alright."

"So you haven't seen her?"

Jamie ran a hand over his scraggly beard. He couldn't help but ache at the bit of hope in his friend's voice. "No, I don't think I have. Not that I can remember."

"Maybe she wasn't taken?" Omar said, but the words were a bit hollower this time.

"She may have gotten away." Jamie felt a heat in his chest, an anger and a grief he hadn't thought about in a while. Losing his wife was hard, but he held her when she had passed. He knew what had happened to her. "Is there anyone she might have gone to?"

His voice was thick. "At one point, she had a cousin in Apeito, but we hadn't heard from her in a long time." There was a long pause. "We weren't sure if she was still alive. She was older. We had thought she may have gotten sick. Now I don't know." Jamie leaned his head against the bars, wishing he could see his friend's face. "I don't know if she would have made it on her own. Maybe she found Ward. For all we know, she could be with him. Maybe she found him on the road?"

An older woman in the cell next to Jamie came to the front. Her sallow skin didn't look like it could take being down here much longer. "If the Goddess wishes it, you will see your love again. But you must accept her wishes wholeheartedly. Whether you see her in this life or the next."

Omar cleared his throat again, and when he spoke, his voice was thick with emotion. "Uh, yes. Whatever the Goddess wishes. I just—I need a sign. I just need to know if she is safe."

Jamie smiled. It was sad and a little bittersweet. The last time they shared a pint of beer, Omar had spoken about how he felt alone at home with his wife, that they had grown apart and it didn't feel the same anymore. And yet, here he was, dreaming of a second chance, waiting for a sign they could try again. "We will find out soon, friend. The moment we get out of here, we will find out what happened to Pat."

Chapter 13 Taytra

Taytra's eyes snapped open. It was dark. Shadows danced around the walls as she jolted to her feet, heart hammering in shock. *Someone was here.* She panicked and flung her chair backward and the blanket that hung around her shoulders away from her. Her arm hit someone as she spun away, her fingers scrabbling at her waist to find her knife.

"Whoa! Whoa! Tay!" Ward said, hands up as he jumped away from her. "Goddess, I think I need to tell Andrew to lay off on those lessons for a bit." He laughed breathily.

"Damn it! Ward, you can't do that," she snapped, bending to pick up the chair. Air rushed through her lips in a hiss as pain lanced up her side. The cut she had from her fight with the few Dark Ones wasn't deep, but the spot was awkward and slow to heal.

"Is that still hurting you a lot?" Ward moved to her side, but Taytra waved him off. "Let me get that." He bent and grabbed the blanket from the floor and folded it, putting it back over the chair. "Are you okay?"

"I'm okay. It's just sometimes, if I move a certain

way." She turned to the window, and the sky was pitch black, but the bright moon cast icy rays of light over the city. It wasn't much, but it illuminated the gloom coated room. Taytra turned back to the table and could just make out the candle she had lit. It had fizzled down to a little nub with bits of wax spreading out on the table around the base. She squinted, swiping her hands across the table for the pack of matches and another candle. "What time is it?"

"Sometime after the eleventh bell. I came looking for you after you didn't come to dinner," Ward said. "Here." He held out a candle waiting for her to strike the match.

She rubbed her eyes. *Eleventh bell. Come on, Flynn.* She struck the match. The light flared before narrowing into a tiny flame. The wick caught a second later, the little flames casting shadows all across the room. "Shit, I'm sorry. Serena gave me the address and then I…" She gestured at the space as if that was an answer for her disappearance.

He smiled. "I found Serena too. She said I might find you here." Taytra picked up the book she had been reading, flipping to find where she had left off. "When I got here, all the workers had left. I don't think they realized you were still here. They probably did their checks after your candle went out."

Taytra looked up sharply. "If the library is closed, how did you get in here?" she asked, shivering slightly as a breeze came through the open window.

Ward unfolded the blanket and draped it around her shoulders. "Oh, don't you worry, Flynn. I have my ways," he said slyly.

She scoffed. "Yeah, okay."

He leaned over her. "So, military strats, huh?" he asked.

"Yeah," she said sheepishly, holding it to her chest. "A bit of that and some leadership of our old generals." She passed him another book. "I thought this might be a good place to learn."

"Nightcastle?" he asked, reading the name on the cover. "Isn't that Serena's surname?"

"Yeah, it's either her father or grandfather. I'm not sure. It feels weird to ask. It's at least three hundred years old."

"I mean, that's interesting. Find anything helpful?" he asked, turning the aged pages slowly.

"The Dark Ones have been around for a long time. I don't know why I never put it together, but they started just after or before Matron and the fall of Queen Chima."

Ward nodded. "The First Fritual."

"Exactly. I don't think people had the title of Frituals without there being Dark Ones around." She picked up another book and flipped through the pages. "The one thing I could not find is any record of Nurzan."

"What, hoping it would be like a fairy tale and his weakness would be in a book somewhere?" he teased.

She shrugged. "Couldn't hurt to look."

Ward reached over and plucked the book from her fingers, closing it with a quiet snap. "We can do that later. Right now, we need to put a pause on your homework for the night, Lady Flynn," he said, grinning as she danced on tiptoe, trying to grab the book from overhead. "You can come back tomorrow. For now, we need to get back to the inn and get you something to eat and get that side checked out."

Taytra yawned, stretching her hands up to the ceiling. "I forgot to go see Kathleen before I came here."

"You have been forgetting a lot of things lately." When Taytra shot him a look, he laughed. "But Andrew and I make sure it is all covered. Even this." He pointed to her side where the bandages lay under her clothes. Ward pulled a pouch out from under his cloak and turned the contents out on the table.

"What are you? A sneak and a doctor?" she teased, plucking up a small container of the salve Kathleen had been putting on Taytra's side to prevent infection, and some linen gauze.

"Maybe Kathleen let me know the steps in case we had to leave sooner than she liked. I can do it for you here, or you can see her back at the inn." The words were teasing but soft, giving her space to make the choice.

"I think you should be able to manage it without killing me. Let's give you practice."

He picked up another candle, using the first lit candle to bring the other to life. "Alright, Lady Flynn, if you would please sit yourself on this table, let us see that side of yours."

"Why thank you for the help, Doctor Ward," Taytra said.

Ward grinned and stacked the books at the far end of the table, gathering more candles to light the space around them.

"If I didn't know any better, I'd think you were trying to set some sort of romantic scene with all these candles."

Ward's ears turned bright pink, and he spluttered something that sounded like a combination of 'I'm sorry' and 'you're welcome.'

Taytra laughed, covering her mouth to hide the grin. But Ward's embarrassment only seemed to last a moment. He stepped up to her and grabbed her hips, gently lifting and moving her back until she was seated firmly on the table, feet swinging. Surprised by the sudden movement, she grabbed his shoulders and leaned in. It was her turn to splutter out an apology as the scraggly beard he had grown tickled her cheek. She dropped her hands to her lap as her cheeks grew hot.

Ward grinned. "May I?" he asked softly, gesturing to her side.

Taytra nodded and let the blanket drop from her shoulders, then lifted the hem of her shirt. The cool air sent goose bumps down her arms as it hit her skin, and she jumped when Ward's warm fingers brushed against her skin as he slowly unwrapped the bandage from her torso. She lifted one arm above her head so he could get to her side better, while the other held her shirt against her chest. She watched as he worked. He was so focused on what he was doing, she nearly laughed. But the seriousness with which he took her care made her pause. A smile crossed her lips, but she couldn't quite place the feeling that bounced in her chest. He grabbed a cloth from his pile of supplies and carefully wiped away the old poultice. When she jumped at the dull ache created by the light pressure, he paused. "Do you still want me to do this?"

"Yes, it's okay," she said, her voice hitching a bit. She cleared her throat, the noise cracking through the silence. "You can keep going."

"Okay, just tell me if you ever need me to stop, okay?" he said, his voice low and serious. He held her gaze for a moment before turning back to his work. He gently examined the cut, pressing lightly for any sign of inflammation or infection. He brought one candle closer, using its soft golden light to be sure. Taytra closed her eyes and listened to his even, steady breath and the quiet thuds as he picked up different supplies and put them down.

She jumped again, giggling as he worked the poultice onto her skin around the cut. "Sorry, it's cold." He stepped back, admiring his handiwork. "Well, am I going to survive, Doctor Ward?"

"Hmm?" He jumped. "Oh, yes. I think so. You are lucky this time."

She laughed. "Just this time?"

He picked up the roll of gauze and rested the end on the cut. "Hold this, please," he said, and she brought her hand down to hold it in place. He stepped closer, then took the roll of gauze and began wrapping it around her torso, his arms moving all around her body. He tied off the gauze and then stepped back. Taytra took a deep breath, wishing he would come back. "How's that?" he asked as he pulled at the skin at the back of his neck, suddenly self-conscious.

She let the shirt fall back to her side and took a deep breath, bending and twisting. "It feels good. Not too loose and not too tight." She looked up, and his soft brown eyes locked on hers. "Thank you." She ducked her head again as her cheeks flushed a deeper pink. *Oh, stop it. It's Ward. You don't need to act like a child at Beltane.* She looked back up, watching as he covered his mouth to hide the smirk on his lips. "How is your arm?" she asked, reaching for his sleeve.

He shrugged. "It's fine, I guess." She crossed her arms, giving him a knowing scowl. "Okay, I mean, I could also do with a redressing. I haven't been great about going to see Kathleen either."

Taytra scooted forward and hopped off the table, closing the gap between the two of them. She could smell the leather and hay from the training he must have done that evening and the sweet tinge of ale from dinner on his breath. "Master Ward, if you would please take a seat," she said in the same formal tone he used.

Once he was seated, she rolled up his sleeve, but he grabbed her hand gently and moved it away before pulling his shirt over his head. "It's, uh—it's easier to get to this way," he said, looking off to the side.

Taytra hesitated for a moment but smiled when she saw the tips of his ears were just as pink as her cheeks. "May I?" she mimicked.

He matched her grin. "Yes, you can." It didn't take as long to clean and apply the poultice around his cut. It wasn't as deep and had healed nicely into a thin pink puckered scar. She scooped a bit of the poultice and rubbed the deep green salve into the skin. "I think Kathleen would say that this has healed nicely," she said, cutting the bandage shorter with her knife before wrapping his arm and tucking away the ends. "There," she said, stepping back. "Ready for battle." She grabbed the bottle of salve and twisted the lid on before turning back to him. "I just want to—" she said, fiddling with the end of the bandage, double-checking that it was secure.

She paused as his hand came over hers, holding it steady against his warm skin. "Thanks," he said, then gave a quiet laugh, ducking his head. "Oh, Goddess, you are something."

"What? What happened?"

Still chuckling quietly to himself, he pulled her

closer to the edge of the table. "You get so focused you miss this?" he asked, using the pad of his thumb to wipe away a bit of the healing herbs that stuck to her cheek. He stood, still holding her hand, the back of his legs bumping against the table.

She should step back, give him some more space, but she didn't want to. "I guess I was distracted," she admitted, scrubbing the spot with her free hand.

Ward's eyes shifted from a deep chocolate to a soft chestnut in the firelight. She suddenly felt locked in his gaze, like he could see straight into her. "I can't get over you," he murmured.

"What do you mean?"

Is that a good thing? Do I want that? Yeah, I do.

"I—" He laughed to himself and slid his hands around her waist, pulling her closer. "I tried to tell myself not to fall for you. It started down in those cells. Sounds awful, but it did. I couldn't get over your spirit. How they couldn't break you. But I am also afraid of it. Of you and me becoming an us." He ran a hand through his hair, hair that had grown long in the last month, curling around his ears and at the nape of his neck. Little things Taytra had noticed. "I am afraid of getting too close to you and them finding out. The last thing I need—*you* need— is the fear of losing someone else." He brushed her hair over her shoulder and took a deep breath. "I've done a pretty poor job of that, haven't I? Going from the soldier who didn't want to talk to you, as ordered, to the one who breaks into libraries to find you?"

Taytra grinned. "Well, we can't all be the perfect soldier, can we?" The smile sputtered out as she thought of their escape from the Dark Ones on the plain. When she had thrown those words at him in fear and anger. How the thought of being separated because she didn't know how to fight had scared her to her core. But he was here now, in front of her. And she knew in her heart that she would go through those feelings again. For him, she would. "I— I know what you mean, though. I am scared too. But I'd rather know I had someone who wholeheartedly had my back than no one by my side at all. I want you. I want to fight with you."

He sighed and pressed his forehead to hers just like he did when he ran through the gates of Hollens. Just like in the safety of the caves. "If I am the one who you want by your side, know I will give you everything I have."

Her heart swelled at the words, and she pressed up to her tiptoes. "And I, for you," she breathed, her lips brushing his.

He pulled her close, fingers lacing through her hair, rekindling the warm fluttering feeling in her stomach. He spun her around and lifted her back onto the table, and she wrapped her legs around his waist, pulling him as close as she could. His skin was fire beneath her fingers as she drew circles down his back and sides, smiling against his lips when he jumped at a ticklish spot beneath his shoulder blade.

"We should get back to the inn," she murmured into his neck, leaving a trail of kisses down his jaw. "Oh, so now you want to sleep there? You seem to have a knack for falling asleep anywhere but there," Ward joked, his voice a low growl. "Ow! Okay! Okay!" He laughed when she pinched him in response. He grinned and kissed her again, sliding his hands around her back.

"Oh, come on, you," she says breathily, gently pushing him back and sliding off the table. "Now you can show me your oh so sneaky way of getting in," she said, tossing him his shirt.

Chapter 14 Paulo

Paulo had discovered pretty early on that the inn where they had been given rooms was only busy a few days a week. This evening turned out to be one of those days. Paulo stood in the doorway, scanning the room for a place to sit.

"We can try the one down the road?" Lyra said, looking over his shoulder.

"There we go." He grins. "This way." She grabbed the back of his coat, sticking close as they wove their way through to the back of the room. "This is *my* booth," Paulo said, sliding onto the bench.

Lyra took a seat opposite him. "Your booth, huh?" She waved down one of the staff a few tables away. A few moments later, a waiter came and took their order. Paulo couldn't help but watch some locals and how their eyes drifted in their direction.

"You!" A man at a nearby table stood, pointing at Paulo. "You are the one with the glowing green arms."

Paulo looked up, judging whether or not he should engage with this man. But the stumbling steps toward the two elves didn't give him much of a choice. "Uh, yes, that's me." He glanced at Lyra, who gave a small shake of her head.

The man stumbled closer, and Lyra yelped as the man caught his foot on the edge of her skirts as he leaned toward Paulo. "Your people shouldn't be here," he said, slurring his words and poking a finger in Paulo's face. The drunk rocked for a second, trying to find his balance.

Paulo slowly moved the man's hand away from his face. "You are entitled to your opinion, sir. If you don't mind, I am just enjoying a pint before retiring to my rooms."

Lyra shot him a look and kicked him under the table. *Don't tell them where we are staying.* Paulo saw the curling edge of her yellow markings under her sleeve as she touched her Magick.

"Teske, come on. Leave them alone." the man's friend said, coming to collect his friend. "Leave them alone. They are just minding their own business." He pulled Teske away, glanced over his shoulder and mouthed, "I'm sorry."

The two elves sat quietly for a moment, waiting for the people who watched the incident to turn away. "How did passing out food go?" Lyra asked, tugging the edge of her sleeve down and her skirts closer around her.

He shook his head, trying to focus his attention back on Lyra. "Oh, you know, had the occasional grumpy person, but it was no problem. I just wish we had more to give people."

Lyra nodded. "I spoke with Serena today. She said she keeps going in circles with these talks. For every two steps forward, she takes one back. We just need to find the right motivator." She sighed. The waiter came back with their drinks, and Lyra eagerly grabbed her cup. "So, what did you want to talk to me about?" Lyra asked, pulling the mug of tea close to her. "Thanks for this, by the way. After being on the wall all day, I needed this."

He smiled, but it didn't feel genuine. "No problem. We all need these brief moments of pause right now." He leaned back and rubbed his palms along his pants. He watched another person go by, trying to find how to explain his conversation with the guard. *Should I even tell her? We don't know how accurate the information is. Maybe I should just wait for the next report.*

"Are you okay?" Lyra asked, taking a sip of tea.

Paulo ran a hand along his jaw. "Yeah. I mean, I'm okay. Just overwhelmed." He glanced around before dropping his voice to a whisper. "I—got a report about Shauna and Philippe earlier." His eyes dropped to the wooden table in front of him, and he forced himself to look up at Lyra.

She was beaming. "Really? That is great! I thought they were going to be here yesterday or the day before, right?" She paused. "It is good, isn't it?"

"Not quite." Paulo slid the report out of his pocket. He passed it across the table. "Just read it."

"Okay…" Lyra unfolded the parchment and scanned the document. Her smile quickly disintegrated. She read the document twice before she put it down. He would have done anything to make the sadness and confusion on her face go away. She picked up her mug and took a sip, her hand trembling slightly. "You can't be serious?" she whispered. Paulo opened his mouth to respond, but she put up a hand, and he snapped it shut. She read over the paper for a fourth time. "Are you serious?" Her face went through a series of stages, from sadness to anger. She slammed the paper down. "When were you going to tell me?"

Again, Paulo started to answer, but the waiter came with their food. Another bowl of mystery stew from the innkeeper, courtesy of the council of Hollens. "Anything else I can get for you two today?" he asked.

"Not at this time, thank you," Paulo said.

"Alright. Just wave me down if you need me." The two of them nodded their thanks and waited for him to leave before continuing.

"Look, I had heard rumors when we were on our way up for that first meeting, but I needed to confirm it. Even now, I am waiting for more information." He pushed the stew away , no longer hungry.

Lyra leaned back, crossing her arms. "Who are your sources? How do you know they are credible?"

He sighed. "I don't. That is the whole point. I don't want to make a big deal out of this if we don't have any credible information." Lyra nodded, though clearly not pleased. "Okay, look, I don't know if this is real or not," he said, stabbing the paper with the tip of his finger. "All I know is it scares me. If something like this happens, we need to act. Now."

"We knew this would be a risk." Lyra sighed. She took a sip of the tea in front of her and grimaced. "So, what do we do?"

They heard a familiar laugh from the door to the inn and turned. Taytra and Ward strode in, hand in hand. When they saw the two elves, they jumped apart. As if everyone couldn't already tell the two were head over heels for each other.

"Hi," Taytra said, coming up to the table. "How

are you two? I didn't see you all day."

Lyra slipped the bit of parchment under the table, passing it back to Paulo. "Good. We were guarding on the wall and training. I have done little of it since we got here. How about you?"

"That is great. We need to stay on the top of our game," Ward said. "Tay found some books in the city library on the Dark Ones history, so we can do a bit of studying the next few days between training sessions. What's the phrase?" Ward said, not really looking at the two elves, just locked on Taytra's girlish grin.

"Know thy enemy?" Paulo offered.

Ward snapped and pointed at the elf. "That's the one! Know thy enemy." He grinned. "Well, we won't keep you. Enjoy your dinner."

The two walked away. Lyra kept looking in their direction long after they had left. "You clearly have said nothing to her."

Paulo shook his head. "No. And I won't until I know for sure. The last thing we need is a heartbroken sister."

"Don't until you know for sure. And please keep me in the loop. I want to see every report you get."

"I will. There are four people that know about this report right now. You, me, the captain who reported to me, and the scout that came back."

Lyra takes another sip of her tea, with a much steadier hand. "Good. Keep it that way. The last thing we need is for some rumors to get back to her." Lyra nodded in the direction Taytra had exited.

"I will speak to Ward before we tell her. He may know how to explain it to her. For now, all we can do is pray to the Goddess that Shauna and Philippe are okay."

Chapter 15 Philippe

The moon hung high in the sky, her soft rays taunting Philippe with the idea of sleep. His thighs ached from the countless hours of riding, and he was sure the inside of his ankles would be raw from the friction. He was grateful for two things: that they had decided to tie him to the horse, lest they punish him for falling, and that in the nearly full moon gave off enough light he could see Shauna from time to time in the distance. Her now shaggy blond hair glowed a soft copper as the torches of the Dark One passed her.

He watched as, over time, she collapsed in on herself, sure she was feeling some of the same things he was: tired, afraid, and worried. But then she'd pop up, looking around to see if anyone noticed the movement, and pressed herself up in her seat, trying to look strong and put together, unfazed by the enemy around her. He wished he could have an ounce of her strength right now, a bit of fight in him to stand up to them. But even as uncomfortable as it was for him to sit slouched over like he was, sitting up made what he had to assume was a cracked rib in his side bark in protest. He shifted his seat, trying to find a new position, wincing as the sharp pain ebbed to a dull throb. Galen had checked his side out, but there wasn't anything you could do for a cracked rib aside from resting and avoiding movement.

Beyond where Shauna sat, disguised on two sides by the mountain, was the encampment. Stone walls lined with flickering braziers, helping Philippe judge the size of it. Philippe's skin rose with goose bumps that had nothing to do with the chill air of night. Something about it felt eerily peaceful, like this had once been hallowed ground. It was a feeling Philippe would never attach to the Dark Ones. *What was this place before they took it?* he wondered, watching as the front line of their caravan broke off and sped toward the gate. No doubt warning those inside who came and who they have in their possession. They looked like a line of ants making their way across the sand. If this was simply an outpost, a training facility, he shuddered to think how big the fortress would be in Bulandon. *How the hell are we meant to escape this?* he thought, half asking himself and the Goddess. He had never been a religious person, but if she could help them get out of this, he would be more than willing to place a few offerings at her altar from time to time.

"You there, follow me," a guard said, taking Philippe's horse's halter.

Philippe stopped himself, refraining from mentioning the fact that he had little to no control over where his horse went and could not 'follow' this Dark One. He fell forward a bit, catching himself as his horse lurched a few steps before stopping.

He watched as Shauna was pulled from the line as well, but unlike him, she was taken directly inside. He watched, leaning forward on his horse to get the last glimpse of her disappearance. She was hunched over again, holding onto her horse's neck, trying to pet it and relax it. *Of course, she made friends with the horse*, he thought, slumping when she disappeared from view. He could save them both right now. He would kick his horse into a gallop and charge through the gates. They would steal a sword or spear from someone nearby and strike down anyone who got in their way and run into the desert.

"Fire boy, let's go!" the guard said and smacked his horse.

Philippe clenched his teeth in pain as his horse jumped forward, bucking slightly as he bumped into another horse. *Even if we could get away, it wouldn't last long,* Philippe thought, keeping his eyes down and pushing the dream away. If they got Shauna out of the fortress and outran the Dark Ones, they would need to find food immediately for themselves and the horses. It just would not happen. There was no point even pretending to consider it. Not right now. They would get their chance. As he was led to the gate, he focused back on the present. *They are going to break us down*. They would want the two of them as weak as possible. That was why their meals had been few and far between. The only real support they had was to make sure they were deposited in one piece. Falling apart at the seams? That was fine as long as they weren't *too* broken down. The Dark Ones needed to break them to the point where he and Shauna would do whatever they wanted. He knew this, he knew what he needed to do. Hold firm, take each blow in stride, and stay strong. But he couldn't deny he was chilled to his core by the lines of Dark Ones waiting for orders. A company of soldiers, ready to move on a single command. *If we don't comply, will they eventually just kill us?*

The Dark One leading his horse turned and quickly sawed through the restraints at Philippe's wrists and ankles. "Let's go," he ordered, pulling Philippe haphazardly from the horse.

Philippe tumbled, his knees buckling before it felt like he had even touched the ground, his side screaming in pain as he rolled away from the horse's dancing hooves. "I'm sorry," he panted, putting his hands in the air. "I— My legs."

A spear butt slammed next to his head. "Get up. Slowly, Fritual. Don't try anything."

Philippe bit the inside of his cheek until he tasted blood, fighting the groan of pain. He rolled to his hands and knees before rising to his feet.

"Next to the other one. Go." The guard pointed to the right, indicating where he should go.

The other one? Philippe started, he had expected the Dark Ones to take him and Shauna directly to cells. Instead, she stood on a small dais, flanked by Dark Ones. Philippe moved quickly to follow the order, climbing the stairs to stand beside Shauna. She stood, hands clasped in front of her, blue-gray eyes locked on the opposite wall like nothing around her mattered. Her jaw was locked in a tight grimace.

"Eyes front!" someone barked, jabbing a spear butt into his side.

Philippe hissed in pain, the sound whistling through his teeth as the wood caught one of his bruised ribs. After a few deep breaths, he willed himself to stand taller, wincing as the muscles in his stomach stretched and cried out in pain at the movements.

I don't know if you are there or not, but maybe plant the inclination to hit me somewhere else next time? he prayed. Out of the corner of his eye, he saw Shauna shift, a short bang flicking in his direction, then away. A quick check that he was okay before anyone saw it. But what he wanted was for her to look at him. He wanted to make sure *she* was okay. Facades could only last so long, but he knew Shauna was too stubborn to let them see it fall. *She is playing smart,* he reminded himself. *She is trying to distance herself from you, to keep you both safe.*

Fayanna stood at the gate, overseeing everything. Philippe shifted again, turning ever so slightly so he could see her better out of his peripheral. Her voice rang out above the clamor of bodies coming into the fortress. Her tone was clear, she wouldn't take no for an answer, and it seemed the man before her didn't like that. "Captain Avery," she snapped, "we will stay here tonight." The words were clearly for Avery, but the weight of them silenced the crowd. Philippe watched as several officers turned, whispering something to each other. She turned, a cruel smile dancing across her lips at the sight of their unease. "Do you know where I am headed with my charges?" she asked, and Philippe quickly dropped his eyes to his worn-out boots when she turned to them.

"Yes, of course I bloody well know. And that exact reason is why I don't want you here." the male said, turning to one of his own men. "Lock it down. No one else comes in. Hunter or no, we need to keep this base secure."

Fayanna rolled her shoulders back. "You think we are being followed? You don't think I have been taking adequate measures to prevent that? Captain."

The Dark One, who Philippe noticed while given

the honorific, didn't wear the rippling black cape of an officer, grew stiff. "Madam, I never—It is just—"

"Hunter," Fayanna hissed quietly, overpowering him with a word. "I am a *Hunter*. Do you know what that means, sir?"

What does *that mean?* Philippe glanced at Shauna, but her gaze was locked to the front.

"That means that my position is higher than yours. I believe that means that my orders overrule yours?"

Kinda gathered that. Can we get a bit more than that?

Fayanna put a hand to Captain Avery's shoulder, like a mother would when comforting a child. But her position was a clear threat to this elf's life, her long fingers a few inches from his throat. "So, open the gate. Let my people in. And I want those two—" She pointed at Shauna and Philippe. "—in your highest security rooms. Not cells. *Rooms*. My men are in charge of them. I want dinner in my rooms in twenty minutes, and by the Goddess, if I don't have a thing of ale in my hand in five minutes, I will murder someone." She spun her cloak, nearly snapping the male in the face. She climbed the nearest set of stairs without a backward glance and disappeared into the mountain.

Captain Avery stood there for a moment, his face flushed a deep scarlet in embarrassment and anger. No one spoke. It seemed odd to Philippe that there was such hostility between the upper reaches of their army. *Who are these Hunters? What does it mean? How do they have such authority? What do you have to do to become a Hunter? And how did a woman reach that point?* Philippe watched the Captain. He looked like he was trying to figure out how to shift the dynamic. To show he was still the one in control, that he hadn't in fact been made to look like a fool in front of so many soldiers.

One of his guards coughed, and it broke the spell. "Well, you heard her," he snapped. "Get these doors open." The crank of the gate drowned out the rest of his orders, but four men appeared at Philippe's and Shauna's sides, each firmly taking hold of an elbow and guiding them through the sea of bodies. The Dark Ones parted for them as they walked through the ranks, but they made no move to hide their disgust, leering and spitting toward them.

Philippe watched the walls around them change from stacked stones to the rough edge of stone carved tunnels. Philippe thought they would be led downward toward rooms that would be "more secure" well within the base of the mountain, but they were led up, winding up through a spiral passage.

He glanced over to see how Shauna was doing, but he couldn't get a full glimpse of her face through her hacked off hair. She didn't seem to limp too badly, so either her foot was doing okay, or she was hiding how badly it hurt.

"In here," a guard said, pulling out a thick skeleton key to unlock a door to his left. Philippe caught a glimpse of the room with a bed and a trunk of some sort before Shauna was shoved through and the door slammed shut. She was at the window an instant later, peering through at him, her eyes wide with fear, the façade broken.

Philippe expected them to open the room across from her, but they led him on another two hundred feet. "What, don't want the two Frituals to be close to each other?" he asked as they unlocked the door. The hit to his ribcage was expected. The pain lanced across his chest, and he gasped for air, a few dark spots spinning in front of his eyes. The guard slammed the cell door without a word, the echoing bang so loud he felt it in his chest.

Chapter 16 Jamie

Jamie had forgotten how bad it was in the cells under the castle. The tower cell, while rank, was manageable. It had been quiet. Quiet to the point where you could go mad listening to your thoughts on repeat. In the dungeon, there was constant noise. Children crying, moans of pain, the footsteps of people pacing the small cells, and prayers to the Goddess.

Jamie hadn't seen Alexis in days; he added the boy to the quiet list of prayers he did. One for each of the girls, one thanking the Goddess that Marion wasn't here for this and one for Alexis's safety. Jamie had to fight the images of the tired boy beaten and bloodied. Whatever plan he had briefly mentioned had failed, and they wouldn't be getting out anytime soon.

You don't know that. They may just be working him to the bone. He just hasn't come to speak to you.

The guards, who were all elves now, didn't seem to be on any consistent schedule like when Jamie and Moraine were in the tower. Jamie couldn't name a guard he saw more than once. They would come through what felt like randomly and bang on the cell bars, startling the children. They'd yell and scream orders, then laugh and walk away. If they were terribly cruel, they would sometimes take a torch with them, leaving the captives in darker shadows, until the next guard came through and put it back.

Jamie couldn't help but flinch when they came. Scooting away from the bars, lest they notice him and be reminded he was the father of not one but two of their enemies.

Moraine stood at the door, watching as they passed and cursed and spit in her direction. She stood sentinel to their attacks. Moraine waited until they were gone to move and wiped the spittle from her face.

"Why do you let them treat you like that?" Jamie asked one such time.

Moraine carefully wiped the spit and dirt from her face and turned her answer to everyone in the dungeon. "It will be very difficult, but you must not let them scare you. They are doing this on purpose to make you fear them at all costs. Those guards are no more powerful than you or I," she called down the cell block. "You can take that power they think they have away simply by hiding your fear. If they think they cannot harm you, then you have taken the power back."

A man scoffed. "That is easy to say, but what about these bars?"

Moraine grinned. "These bars?" She gripped them, slamming her hands against them. "Harmless bits of metal. They do nothing and everything. If these bars weren't here, would you be afraid of those guards? No. Because in our numbers, we could easily overpower them. Without these bars or the shadows in the dark and their little scary tricks, they are nothing." She sat beside the door. "I will stand up to their torment every chance I have. I would ask you to do the same. Show them they cannot break you so easily."

"Queen Moraine?" someone called.

"Yes?"

"If the bars were gone, would you fight them with Magick?"

Moraine looked at her hands, and not for the first time, Jamie noticed the black band on her wrist. *Why won't she say what that is?*

Moraine turned to the voice. "It has been a long time since I have used Magick. If the chance came, and I had the energy and felt it would make us safe to do so, I would use Magick."

"Would you kill guards?"

She looked up slowly, her eyes going out of focus for a moment. "I've had to kill people in the past who imprisoned me and my people. I would do it again if necessary. Let us pray it does not come to that." She looked at her hands again. "Fear not friends. Now I must rest. Your questions shall need to wait." She moved back to where Jamie sat. "I don't think things are as bad as they were with Chima, but maybe they are."

Jamie shrugged. "Nothing we can do about it or change until we get out."

"Have you thought of anything yet? Any ways?"

"Absolutely not." Jamie tilted his head back, counting the stones overhead for the eighth time today.

Chapter 17 Shauna

Shauna used to enjoy being alone. Being able to relax, sit with herself, and reminisce about the day and life and whatever went through her brain. She hadn't had a sliver of that peace since they had left Amicus's farm in the woods, but there really wasn't much to do in solitary confinement. Just her and her thoughts turning over every action and reaction from the last month, wondering what she could have changed. It certainly wasn't relaxing anymore.

She thought they would have moved on by now. She thought by how Hunter Fayanna had spoken to Captain Avery, they would only stay the night. Shauna had spent three nights in this bed now. But something must have changed. She hadn't decided if she enjoyed being away from the action or not yet. She didn't like not knowing what was going on, that was for sure.

Shauna limped to the window again. The glass was cracked and whistled when the wind blew through. When she first was thrown in here, she had considered punching out the glass and jumping to escape. The rooms they had placed them in were placed high into the mountain. The window was set into the cliff side, revealing the long fall to the desert floor. She could just make out a rough path lined by dried plants, many fallen out of the dried earth, their spiked roots reaching for the sky. Even if she could get this window open, she didn't see how she could get down without jumping. Then if she somehow survived the jump, there was no way she would make it away, without at least breaking her legs. *Be patient*, she reminded herself. The orange glow of the rising sun reflected across miles of sand, turning it to liquid gold.

She rubbed the skin around the black band on her wrist. It felt like this Magick had become a part of her, woven deep into her skin so she could never remove it. A tainted paranoid part of her that she wanted to be rid of, that she hated to admit she was afraid of. A piece of her was afraid to even touch it. The raw skin on her wrists were another story. There were quite a few scabs and blood had dried in dark crescents under her nails. She didn't mean to, but she ended up picking at the skin around the bands until the skin was raw. Galen thought she was doing it in her sleep. There was a red streak on her bed from her right wrist and a matching smear down her arm.

She turned away from the window and paced up and down the length of the room. She'd been able to work the stiffness from her body while also getting the proper rest she needed to heal. But now that they had been here for three days, she wanted out of this room. She would rather face what was going on than be stuck fighting invisible demons who weren't even her enemy.

A knock on the door sent her spinning to the bed. A moment later, she heard the lock slide, and the door opened. "Miss Flynn, I wanted to check on your foot one more time."

"Right." She bent to unlace her boot as Galen turned to close the door.

She looked up to see him setting his things on the floor and glancing through the little window at the door. When he turned back, he pulled the items out and placed them down firmly. "I am not actually here to check on your foot," he whispered.

Shauna slowly lowered her foot back to the floor. "Oh?"

"Well, I can check it if you want me too?" he said, moving across the floor.

"I—I don't know?" she bent to remove the boot. "Why are you here if not to check on me? Don't you need to follow Fayanna's orders? Keep us in one piece until we get to Bulandon?"

The elf nodded. "That was my charge, but I wanted to warn you. We will leave soon." He glanced at the door. "Best check on it in case they come."

"Who comes? Are we that close to leaving? Are we going right there? Is Phil—" She stopped the question. *You don't know who this elf is. You don't know if you can really trust him!* She pulled the boot the rest of the way off. "Why do you want to warn me?" She said, collecting herself.

"Do you know who Nurzan is?" he asked, fiddling with his supplies.

"He is the one in charge of everything, isn't he?" The elf nodded. "Is he cruel?" Her voice was small. *Of course he is cruel, Shauna. He is the head of the Dark Ones. He has been hunting you for the last month.*

Galen shook his head. "I don't believe he always

was. He is broken. The idea of the Dark Ones took over his life and took something very important from him." He wrapped a clean bandage around her foot. "I don't know what I would do if I had been in his shoes, but I would like to think I would be a better person."

There was a prickle at the back of her neck. "How do you know such things about him?"

The elf glanced up. "It would be best if you don't know who I am," he said shortly. "Just know the tricky way you have been trying to talk with Fayanna won't work with him. He can see right through it with—with most people." He stood. "You and your lover will make it through this." He dropped his voice to a whisper. "I believe in what you are doing. I don't know what will happen in that fortress, but know if I can, I will help you escape." He looked her in the eyes, his amber gaze fierce. "I fought them once and I will fight them again."

"You what?" Before she could ask another question, he was gone, supplies and all, with a thud.

"Oh, and by the way," he said, coming back to the window, "your foot is healing nicely. I think one or two more visits, and you will be fully healed."

But you didn't do anything. She rushed to the door, trying to glimpse him to ask what he meant, but the elf was gone.

She pressed her face against the little window, craning her neck. Both Galen and any guards were gone. She couldn't tell if they were just around the corner or if they really believed that between the lock on the door— and the band of Magick on their wrists—they couldn't fend for themselves. She intended to prove them wrong.

This might be my only shot. If we were moving

soon, we might not get another chance. Shauna hurried over to her bed and pulled out the bit of metal from under the mattress. It started out as the latch for the windows. A useless thing as the window had been painted closed. The first night she was held in this room, she spent a few hours pulling and wiggling the bit of metal away from the wall, then scraping the paint off the end. She was no blacksmith, but she had been trying her hand at a crude version of it. This bit of metal might be her only tool. Whenever she hadn't seen a guard, she was holding the bit of metal to a torch, trying to get the metal hot enough to flatten the rounded end. Shauna didn't know how to pick a lock, but now seemed like as good a time as any to learn. It was a very slow process. The torch was hot, but not nearly hot enough to heat the iron through. From sheer stubbornness, she'd managed to flatten the edge, using the weight of the bed frame to crush the hot metal and straighten the hook. The bedpost on the side furthest from the door was singed black from the heat. She moved to the door and looked out the window again before she crouched next to the door handle. If they were leaving, she didn't have time to let the metal heat up. She couldn't sit around and hope the iron would glow a dull orange. *Just have to go for it.* She tried to slide a bit of metal into the lock, smudging her fingers with black soot. Unlike the last time she tried, it slid in but stopped at about an inch. She pulled it out and tried again to peer inside. Shauna wished she had a hairpin or something small and more delicate she could use to finesse the lock.

She froze when the stomp of boots sounded in the distance. She pressed her ear to the door, trying to hear if they were coming her way. She took a half step back, looking up at the door. She was still crouched in front of the door when the little she could see in the lock went dark and she heard a click.

"Shit," Shauna hissed, pinwheeling backward as the door opened. She slid the bit of metal under the washstand and purposely bumped into the bed, praying to the Goddess the sound of her body thudding into the frame would distract from the metal sliding across the stones.

Fayanna stood in the doorway, peering down at her. "Just what were you doing?" she asked, as though Shauna was a naughty child.

She kept silent, shifting so she sat up on the bed, tucking her fingers beneath her thighs.

Fayanna scowled at her, eyeing the black smudges on the bedding. "Well, come on. You are needed below."

Shauna bit her tongue, afraid to ask why. She stood slowly, twisting her fingers in the blankets, trying to get some of the soot from her fingertips.

She waited, but neither Fayanna nor the guards that flanked her moved to bind her hands. "Come on, no stalling," Fayanna said, pushing Shauna down the hall. They stopped outside Philippe's room as well. He was lying on his bed, staring at the ceiling. "Mattick, up."

He slowly rolled to put his feet on the floor. He opened his mouth to say something but when he saw Shauna standing beside Fayanna and snapped his jaw shut. The two Frituals met each other's eyes as he moved across the room. She nodded, hoping he knew she was okay. He stepped beside her, and she tried hard to keep her eyes forward but they drifted to him. She took a slight comfort knowing he looked okay. The swelling around his face seemed to have gone down, and he didn't look as tired. It would be so easy to tap into the bit of Magick that connected them, to speak his name. But there was a chasm between them and no safe bridge to cross.

They turned down the opposite hall and headed down a narrow staircase. *This must have been a servants' staircase at one point.* The cramped space looked like what she had read about in old books about the high elves of old and their bustling households. Because of how narrow the space was, the two Frituals were forced to stand shoulder to shoulder. It was a risk. She reached over and grabbed Philippe's hand, threading her fingers through his for a moment. He squeezed her hand gently, a slight comforting pressure. She jumped as warmth radiated from their hands, passing through her. And she felt it, her Magick! The connection only lasted a moment before they separated, but that moment was enough. It felt like a spark had passed between them, and for a moment, she almost felt like her Magick was back. She glanced down, but her markings were hidden. It wasn't enough to set them off. Shauna glanced up at Philippe, and he looked as confused as she did. *Did that just happen?* She glanced between their hands. Everything in her was screaming to touch him again, to confirm that she wasn't crazy. She *felt* her Magick. She felt whole for that tiny moment.

Philippe looked at her and nodded. *He felt it too!*

They stepped to the bottom of the stairs, and she stepped further away from Philippe. *Did she notice?* Shauna watched the elf. Fayanna turned, motioning to one guard who moved ahead of their group. He opened a door down the hall, and she heard the jumbled noise of people speaking and moving in the courtyard. The Hunter turned and looked over the two of them. Her small mouth frowned as she turned away from them. Shauna glanced at Philippe. *She doesn't know it happened?* she racked her brain, trying to figure out how the band on our wrists wasn't set off.

Fayanna pulled open a door and motioned them through. As they stepped through the door, many of the Dark Ones turned to face them, sneering in their direction. "Stand there," Fayanna said, pointing to a spot near the wall. The two stepped to the side, and the four guards form a half circle around them. *Are they protecting us from them, or them from us?* She watched as the guard in front of her played with the edge of his sword. She took a small step back and pressed against the wall, trying to melt into nothing.

Shuana could kick him for taking the risk with so many Dark Ones around. It was stupid, really, but it didn't surprise her at all when Philippe shifted. He moved half a step in front of her and put a hand behind him, resting it on the small of his back. Slowly she lifted her hand to his, praying to the Goddess that no one looked. She brushed her fingers against the center of his palm, the rough, and callused skin comforting her. Again she felt that spark, a bit of static branching between them as she slid her fingers between his. Philippe jumped, then he gave her hand two small squeezes. she looked up to where there was a rip in his shirt, but again, his markings didn't appear.

How is this happening?

Shauna?

She jumped and pulled her hand away in surprise when she heard his voice in her head.

A Dark One turned. "What is wrong with you?" he barked.

She turned to lean against the wall. "Sorry, I just— I got dizzy."

"Humph." The guard turned away without any offering of help.

Shauna watched Fayanna as she wound her way through the crowd, but whatever was happening between her and Philippe, either she couldn't sense or wasn't trying to stop. Shauna slid her hand back up and weaved her fingers through his again. The spark was smaller this time, and he glanced over his shoulder at her, a small smirk on his lips. *Little rebel now, aren't you? Always breaking the rules.*

I don't believe I was ever told not to touch you, she replied, watching as Fayanna took the stage. *Are you okay? What happened in the desert?*

I will be okay. Nothing I couldn't handle. He shifted slightly, and she caught sight of a bandage around his torso through the torn linen of his shirt.

Did the healer come to see you too?

He shifted again. *Yes, I am not sure how I feel about him. Whose side is he on?*

Shauna nearly shook her head, catching herself. she froze, watching those around us for a moment to see if they noticed. *I think he is on our side. I can't get a good read on him, but it seems like he wants to help. He warned me we would be leaving. My foot is healed, but he keeps coming to look at it.*

She watched over his shoulder as Fayanna spoke animatedly with someone at the base of a wooden scaffold. The person took a few steps back from Fayanna as the Hunter waved her hands around. She abruptly made a chopping movement with her hand, cutting off the other elf and moved past him to the stairs. Shauna pulled away from Philippe, and he nodded. They couldn't test their luck right now.

"My esteemed followers, as you know, we were only meant to be here a short time before moving on to the Fortress at Bulandon. Lord Nurzan is expecting us." Her voice carried over the heads of the soldiers easily, her voice as soothing as a snake. "But I have discovered there is quite a bit of deceit at this base. As such, our departure has been delayed. If you were a soldier based here, working with Captain Avery, you are no longer. He no longer has a role to play within the Dark Ones. You will move on with me." She paused, allowing for the shouts of surprise and anger. She lifted a hand, and the crowd fell silent. "As of this evening, this base is shut down. Find your commanding officer to get your marching orders."

Shauna and Philippe shared a look, and as much as she wanted to know what he was thinking at this moment, she didn't dare reach out to him. Shauna scanned the crowd, but as she suspected, Captain Avery was nowhere in sight. She was sure, 'He no longer has a role to play within the Dark Ones' meant the elf was dead. The cruelty didn't surprise her. She glanced up at the blue-orange sky; there were a few hours until the sun fully rose.

Fayanna spun on her heels and came to the end of the scaffold, looking down on them. "We will not be stopping our march until we arrive at Bulandon." She leaned down over the railing, her long hair falling over her shoulder in a wave that swung in front of her face and the gleeful smile there. "You two get to leave early with me." Shauna shifted uncomfortably. Fayanna looked like someone had told her there would be extra desserts. "Get them on horses now," she snapped. "I want to be out of here in a quarter hour."

Chapter 18 Jamie

"Psst, Jamie."

Jamie rolled away from the sound and put a hand over his head, attempting to sleep.

"Jamie, wake up. Jamie! I don't have a lot of time!"

"What?" the man mumbled.

"Come here."

Jamie scrubbed his eyes with the back of his hand. "What is it?" He mumbled, blinking at the form crouched in front of his cell.

"Jamie, come on, wake up. I need you to focus," the figure said urgently, glancing up the hall.

"Alexis?" Jamie asked with a yawn, trying to get his eyes to focus. His whole body ached from the cold and lack of sleep. "What is going on?"

The young man slipped a pouch into the cell, tossing it on a pile of hay. Whatever was inside clinked together. "We move today. After breakfast, start passing these around."

Jamie quickly crawled to the front of the cell, suddenly awake. Adrenaline pounded through his veins as he picked up the bag. "Are these the keys to the cells?" he hissed, burying them under a pile of loose hay.

"Yes. We have a plan, but you have to wait until after lunch. I can't tell you any more right now, but we will need to move fast later," the boy said, standing.

"Alexis!" Jamie hissed, grabbing the bars. "Where are we going to go? How are we going to get there?"

Someone in a nearby cell started to cry, and Alexis disappeared for a moment. Jamie watched as the boy bent and reached into the cell. He spoke with the people in quiet, comforting tones. A few minutes later, Alexis came back and grabbed the older man's hand. "For your safety, I can't say any more. Giving you those was a big enough risk. Just know, we will be out of here before sundown. Pass the word, people will need to be ready to move. Either I or someone else loyal will come down to give you the signal. If not…" He pulled a large tapered candle out of his bag and lit it on a torch. "Once this burns out, start unlocking doors. Do not leave until we come down."

"We will be ready," Jamie said, watching the wax pool around the flame.

* * *

Jamie slept no more that morning. He sat with his back to the bars of his cell, watching the sliver of an arrow slit he could see on the wall slowly grow lighter with the dawn and the candle in the corner creating a pool of wax around its base. There was a quiet buzz through the dungeon as word spread. To get ready, to be prepared. But for what exactly, Jamie didn't know. He looked at the families with older members and small children and couldn't help but wonder if they would hurt their chances of escaping. *Goddess, I hope they thought of that.* He couldn't bear to leave any of them here.

"Master Flynn, Queen Moraine, where are we going?" a child with flea bites all over his face asked.

Jamie glanced over his shoulder at the queen who lay asleep on the hay. The split above her lip was becoming infected, the skin around it an angry, swollen mess. "I am not sure. My friend could not tell me. It is better for now if we don't know anything."

"You can't be serious," a man, presumably the boy's father, barked. "How can you think that?"

Jamie shrugged. "You may have your own opinion, of course. I just find that if things go wrong, it is better that the information has an end. Less people get hurt that way."

"But if we know the plan, we can finish what others started."

"I can't argue with you there. I am simply speaking from my experience so far. Many that left with Taytra didn't know what would happen that night. They just knew to be ready. Just like us." Jamie sighed, running a hand over his face. "Taytra wanted to get as many people out as she could. I know leaving us hurts her."

A hand reached out to Jamie but didn't make it anywhere near enough to reach him. "I saw both your daughters. You should be very proud of them."

Jamie nodded. "When we get out of here, I will introduce you."

The man scoffed. "I don't know if they are that great. They are still children."

Jamie bristled but took a deep breath and reined in his emotions. "My daughters are young, yes, but if the information that has trickled down is correct, they have done some pretty good things for people their age."

"I heard your daughter fought a few Dark Ones and was stabbed in the process," someone down the hall said.

Jamie flinched at the thought but nodded. "I have also heard she has gotten into a few scuffles. I am sure if she has had any injuries, she is taking care of them. I wouldn't expect any less. If she believes she is to lead those she helped escape to safety, she would lead by example."

Omar cut in from down the hall, "It is so like her to get into the fray. I wouldn't expect anything different. Besides, if there is a bounty on her head then she must be doing something right." Omar laughed. "What was it? One hundred gold stones for her? One hundred and fifty for Shauna? Who can say their daughters are worth that much? We all want to say as much when we negotiate dowries, but come on." There was a grumble of agreement, and Jamie grinned. Even though he couldn't see his friend, he knew he was enjoying this brief moment in the spotlight.

Jamie looked at the candle in the corner again. There was about an inch of wax left, the wick sputtering as it reached the base. "We will begin the process soon," he said just loud enough for those around him to hear.

Jamie began to pull out the bag of keys when pounding feet came down the stairs. Those in the cells around him retreated, tucking themselves into the walls and the dark corners of their cells. Jamie shoved the bag back under the hay and sat atop it, the lumpy bag digging into the back of his thigh.

Alexis dashed down the hall. He had a cut on his arm that dripped blood on the floor and a knife in his hand, but his eyes were bright. "Jamie, start passing the keys.

We will be out of here in an hour. Unlock your doors, but keep them pulled shut. I will be back soon to get you out," he promised before bounding back up the stairs.

Jamie grinned and dug under the hay, pulling the keys out of the bag. This set was clearly a spare as its metal was worn and smoothed from age. Jamie tried one key, reaching around at an awkward angle to fit the key in the hole. Families around him passed quiet messages around but were shushed by others. They needed to keep quiet. They couldn't let those above know what was happening. With a quiet click and a creak, the door to his cell swung open. Jamie considered just passing the keys down the line but turned and locked the door behind him on a still sleeping Moraine. Then he hurried down the line, unlocking the doors as quickly as his shaking hands could. One little boy burst out and gave him a hug before his mother could draw him back in. "It's alright," he whispered to the mother. "We will be out soon and then you can have a hug from just about anyone."

The mother smiled and nodded, tears of relief in her eyes.

At one point, Jamie heard a wooden door slam. He pulled the cell door open he was unlocking and shoved the keys in his shirt, holding the door closed. He met the eye of the father in the cell. He stood in front of three girls under the age of ten. The man nodded, rubbing his hands together, ready to help take out the guard if needed.

Jamie glanced over his shoulder, afraid to turn in case the guard recognized him. The guard stopped in front of a few cells, peering in, but there was no malice in his voice when he crossed a hand over his heart and said, "For the Frituals." The man kept walking. "Where are the keys? Where is Jamie Flynn?" He stopped in front of each cell, peering inside.

Jamie stood slowly, turning. If he had to go down now, caught not in his cage, he would. As quietly as he could, he passed the keys to the father before stepping out into the hall. He felt the eyes of every person in the dungeon on him. "I am here." His hands shook slightly, ready to fight the guard if he wasn't actually on their side. *If my girls can fight, I can too.*

The person turned and grinned, running up to Jamie. "Good! You got started already. I was confused when you weren't in the cell with the queen." He clasped Jamie's arm. "Well, how many more do you need to unlock?"

Jamie searched the man's face for any sign of betrayal, but he appeared genuine.

"Fear not, sir, I am with you. My mother escaped with Lady Taytra. It will be an honor to help the rest of us escape."

Jamie sighed a breath he didn't realize he had been holding. *This man is with us.* He turned and took the keys back from the father. "There are a few more on that side and the cell I shared with the queen."

"Great. Anyone that is free can follow me. We are going to meet at the top of the stairs." The young man ran over to the candle in the corner, snuffing it out. "Let's get our people out of here."

Chapter 19 Jamie

Jamie bent, placing his hands on his knees, willing his heart to slow. His legs already felt like lead and they hadn't gotten out of the castle yet. Jamie had insisted on guiding each group up the stairs while they waited. He had climbed the stairs four times, each time pausing before ascending to give Queen Moraine a small shake. Jamie stood, feeling a stitch form in his side. *We have to go.* Jamie turned to the last cell, the one the queen lay still asleep in. "Moraine?" Jamie called, struggling with this last lock. The queen didn't move. "Queen Moraine! We need to go." He opened the door and fell to the floor beside her. "Moraine?" He shook her shoulder, but she didn't respond, her wrist falling limp beside her. "Moraine, what is going on?" he grumbled. This wasn't like the queen.

She has been resting a lot more the last few days. She hasn't been speaking with people.

He pressed a hand to the side of her neck, feeling for a pulse. "Moraine? Queen Moraine? I need you to wake up!" At first, he couldn't find a pulse. "Moraine!" He shook her again, and this time, she let out a quiet groan. Her pulse was weak but it held. "Moraine, Moraine! I need you to wake up. We are moving. We are getting out of here," he insisted, shaking her shoulder. "I am sorry. I am sure I am not meant to do this, but I don't have a choice." Jamie pulled the queen into a sitting position, and slowly, his knees barking in protest, lifted her to his chest. He took the first few steps slowly, afraid he might miss a step and send them both tumbling. The tiny queen didn't weigh much, but he hadn't been lifting the heavy bags of flour or farm tools lately.

He looked to the stairs, dreading them. "Moraine, Moraine," he called, trying to wake her as he walked. He paused, looking to the top of the staircase. *Keep going. This will be the last time you are ever down here. Someone else can help you, just get to the top.* He stumbled, nearly missing a step. Moraine's head lolled against his shoulder, and she made a noise like a breathy groan of pain, so quiet he wasn't sure he actually heard it. "I'm sorry. I'm sorry." He winced, trying to shift his grip. He made it to the top of the stairs and pushed his way through the crowd, looking for Alexis. "Moraine, you need to wake up," he repeated, trying to keep the desperation from his voice.

Alexis saw him and brightened. "Is that everyone? We can get out of here right now!" He grabbed Jamie's arm and turned him and the queen away from prying eyes. "What is going on?"

"Alexis, I don't know what to do," Jamie whispered. "She won't wake up."

Alexis pulled the queen's hair back and looked for a pulse. He nodded assuredly when he found it. "We need to get out of here now. We can figure out what is wrong after. We don't have that much time." He signaled for one of his men. The man came over, and Jamie carefully transferred the queen to the stronger man.

"Is there any way that you can hide her face?" Jamie asked. "If the people see she is hurt or sick, it's going to scare them more."

"What would you have me do?" the man asked. "It's not as if I can put her in a sack." His voice was clipped, but not in anger or malice. Jamie saw the strain and fear dancing just out of reach on the man's face.

"No, no, you're right." Jamie turned to those around them who were already looking at the stricken queen. "What do we need to do?" The boy shifted his weight again, and that's when Jamie saw it, under the sleeve of the queen robes. That thick band of black Magick he kept trying to ask her about. His stomach dropped. It had grown, encasing her wrist and spreading to her elbow. "Hang on. Just turn slightly so I can see her," Jamie said, indicating for the man to step into a corner with him. Once they had turned away from the crowd, Jamie lifted her sleeve to get a better look. The band of Magick sat on top of her skin, the edges digging in and cutting off the circulation in her arm, the skin discolored by bruising. "We don't have time for this right now, but there's some sort of Magick that's been attached to the queen. We will need to get it off. Is there anyone that knows about their Magick that can look at it?" Jamie asked, his mind rolling though the ramifications. "Someone that can confirm whether or not they will be able to find her? Like is it some sort of tracing spell." His mind spun as he tried to imagine what benefit the Dark Ones would gain by placing the Magick on her. There were several possibilities. She had it after the interrogation but refused to speak on it. *Did she even know what it was?* She had grown more tired, she slept more, and when she spoke to the people, her posture had slipped, curling in on herself like she had been too tired to hold herself up. *I didn't even think of it. I thought it was just the lack of food.*

The boy shook his head "I don't know anybody. I don't know if Alexis does either. We might just have to risk it."

Jamie spun. "That's not okay."

"We don't really have another option," the guard snapped. "We need to get everyone out of here now."

Jamie tried to think of what to say to explain the danger that could be in it for all of them if they didn't take care of this, but Alexis hurried back over. "Is everything okay? We are getting everyone outside."

Jamie glanced at the queen, pulling her sleeve back into place, fully covering the Magick. "Not quite but we will be okay. What do you need me to do?"

The young soldier watched as the large group moved through the doors, a few people whooping with joy, while others wiped tears from their face. "We need to split everyone into three different groups. We made a plan but it was risky. One will go through the town, one will follow Shauna's path and go across the plain, and one will go through the forest. Divided we will be harder for the Dark Ones to track, but it makes us more susceptible to attack, so everyone will have to be strong and quick. We need to get out of the city gates before they wake up."

Jamie stopped. "Wake up? What do you mean to wake up?" he asked.

Alexis grinned. "We won over the cook. He mixed

a strong sleeping draught into a sauce. We made sure not to eat that portion of the lunch. It should be strong enough for most of them but not all of them." Alexis gestured to the rough bandage on his arm. "I took care of those that didn't eat it." The last few people moved out of the building. "We know some others are going to wake up faster than we expect, we just need to be out before that." Alexis closed the door behind them.

Jamie looked out and saw people starting to break out in the middle of the courtyard grouping into little pockets of people. "Do you have a plan for how we are going to do this?" Jamie asked, hurrying down the stairs.

"Everyone, please come this way. We need to stay together for now," Alexis called shepherding to the gates of the palace and to the city.

"But I thought you said we were splitting up?" someone said, shouting above the crowd.

"Splitting up? What do you mean splitting up? We can't! I need to stay with my family."

"Now hang on!" another soldier said. "We have not fully explained the plan. We need to get out of the city first. If you want to break up from there, that is on you, but those that want to stay together, we need to get across the lake. Once you get to the lake, we will divide you into groups for the trip. For now, just get to the lake!" they ordered.

Jamie stayed back with the man who was carrying the queen, careful to keep an eye behind them to make sure that no Dark Ones followed. "What happens when we split up? Where are we going to go?"

"We're headed to Hollens. That is where we heard the rest of our people have gone." The soldier shifted the queen so she could get closer to his shoulder. "That is where we last heard where Taytra, Ward, Andrew, and those of the rebellion are. Hollens is the last city that is considered a sanctuary city for the people of man. Elves are not really accepted there, but I'm sure in this case they will make an exception," the man said, indicating the queen.

"I hope you're right," Jamie said.

The doors of the gate opened and the several of them froze. Jamie knew exactly how they felt. He couldn't believe they were out, free from that hellhole. The fear of how they may be hurt at any moment remained, and yet, he was left with a new fear too. The fear of what would happen outside those gates. Of what could still happen if they were captured again. Jamie knew if he was captured, they wouldn't imprison him again.

"Come on, everyone, we need to keep moving," one guard said, waving them on. "We need to get to the boats.

Jamie took a deep breath. The autumn air was sharp but clean and pure, the smell of rain on the air was soft and so unlike the sour air that sank into their bones in the dungeons.

"Come on, Joanie, come on," a man said, pulling his wife and small child away from the group.

"Gregory, we need to stay with the group," his wife questioned, pulling back toward the group.

"Sir, wait until we get to the lake, then split. It will be safer," Alexis said.

"No, we need to go," he insisted, grabbing her arm and pulling her toward him. "We need to find a place to stay. We will be better off separated."

"Papa, what is going on? Where are we going?"

The little girl asks, clinging to his neck.

"It's okay, Annalise, it's okay," he said, smoothing her hair back from her face. "Joanie, come on," he said pleadingly to his wife. "We need to. We—we can get out of here, we can take Analisa and run."

She shook her head. "Gregory, we need to keep with the group. I don't know if I can run for long. I—" She turned to Alexis. "I—I don't know what to do."

The crowd flowed around the two, turning to watch. "Sir, please," Alexis repeated. "Make this decision when we get to the lake." He placed a hand on each of their shoulders. "We can't make any rash decisions. Especially any that could affect the rest of the group."

The man nodded. "Right, okay." Joanie grabbed his arm and pulled him close. The two hurried off, as the woman furiously whispered in his ear.

"What is the plan, Alexis?" Jamie asked, feeling in the way without having all the information. "How are we breaking up the groups?" They dashed through the city, passing by pubs they frequented often and shops whose owners had held the location for generations. Places that now looked haunted by memories.

Alexis looked over the group. "I can't make that choice for people. They will choose their own fate. Each path will have risks. They need to pick for themselves."

Jamie nodded, and the two spoke no more until they reached the lake, coming up to the many boats previously used for the testing.

Jamie turned and helped the soldier put Queen Moraine beside the lake. "We need to find a healer," Jamie insisted.

"Clearly this Magick is hurting her, and we need her." The guard looked over Jamie's shoulder at the fallen city skeptically. "Okay, sure we maybe don't need her as ruling queen, but think of it like this. When we got down there, the first thing people did was ask if she was okay. The people look to her for hope. They need to know that she is alright."

The guard looked down at the queen and nodded. "Yeah, okay. I will pass the word around and see if we can't find someone to help."

"Thank you," Jamie said. He bent and picked up the queen, carrying her to one of the first boats. Her arm swung loosely by her side. "Can I put her in this boat?" he asked one soldier lining the boats up on the shore preparing for boarding.

He looked from Jamie to the woman in his arms. "Is that?" Jamie nodded. "Yes. Yes, of course." He stepped back and held the side of the boat still so Jamie could put the queen in. She couldn't sit up on her own, so he propped her between the benches, resting her head between the bench and the wall of the boat.

Jamie stepped back onto the shore. "Someone is looking for a healer to ride with her, if we have any in our group. There was some sort of Magick that was put upon her, I think when she was taken for questioning. We are trying to figure out how to remove it. I ask you to please keep this under wraps."

The soldier nodded, took off his cloak, and draped it over the queen, covering her body up to her nose. Her bright red hair still gave her away to the keen observer but the cloak did give her a bit of privacy.

Alexis waved to Jamie from a few boats over where he was helping load people. He helped the last person in before jogging over. "I know I have asked a lot of you so far without explaining much, but can I ask for more of your support?"

"Always. What do you need, friend?" Jamie asked, climbing onto the shore.

Alexis looked around at those around them waiting to board. "I don't have enough men to cover all these boats. Could you join one of the younger soldiers to act as a support?"

Jamie nodded, watching as the first boats board. "Of course. Just point the way."

"Thank you, friend," Alexis said, squeezing Jamie's shoulder. "Birsha over there could use support. He is on the sixth boat."

"I can do that, no problem."

"Thank you, friend. I will see you on the other side."

Chapter 20 Jamie

The boats were cramped with riders, the water sitting high on the hulls, but luckily there was enough for everyone who wished to cross this way. A few men and boys decided not to take the boats. Jamie and the others tried to convince them, but the conviction in their eyes was something that couldn't be matched. He watched from his position on a boat as they ran around the edge of the lake, slipping a bit in the mud that lined the water.

"How far do you think they will make it?" a young boy asked his mother.

She pulled him into her dirty skirts, shielding him. "I am sure they will be okay." The boy sniffled, and she bent, wiping his face with her skirt. "When all this is over, we will find them again, okay? You can play together and run through the woods like you talked about." Jamie couldn't help but notice that she didn't mention how long it might be until then.

"Once we get to the other side of the lake, you will have three options. You can go back through the town and follow the roads, follow the root Shauna took across the plains, or split off and make your way through the forest and trails," Birsha, the rebel leading the boat Jamie was tasked with helping, said.

"Do you have any supplies for us? Something to make any of this easier? Food? Medicine? Weapons?" the mother of the little boy asked.

"I'm sorry, but we don't. We couldn't risk stealing supplies leading up to our escape. They were doing inventories daily in the castle." He paused. "You might find something in town, but there isn't much left. We aren't staying in Cabineral, because there isn't a place we could try to make a stand. Not in the shape we are in."

"They burned everything?" Jamie asked, looking out to the bit of trees through which their town had sat.

"Just about, though some homes on the outskirts made out okay."

Jamie felt a slight thrill of hope at those words. "I—don't know if it will be worth our time, but maybe my home wasn't burned. We didn't live in the town. Maybe there are some supplies there we can use. At the very least blankets. Maybe some salt pork." He looked around at the people in the boat. "It definitely won't be enough to feed everyone, but maybe it can be a start until we get going? A change of clothes for a few people, a blanket for the night. I think it still has a good supply of medicinal herbs that could be good to have if people get hurt or sick along the way."

"Are you sure?" Birsha asked.

Jamie nodded. "We aren't going home any time soon. I am sure my girls would want their stuff to be used. I know their mother would."

The man at the head of the boat paused his paddling to turn to Jamie. "Don't you think your home would have been targeted?" The man's voice was sharp, his eyes racking over Jamie.

Jamie considered his next words carefully. Here on a boat in the middle of the lake there was no time to start an argument. "I am sure it was if someone told them where our home was. However, if the Dark Ones focused their effort on the town they may not have gone to our home, seeing as all of my family was already captured or somewhere in the castle when they attacked the town. There would be no point in attacking it." Jamie shrugged. "But these people don't seem to follow the same logic you or I would, so who am I to say?" The man nodded, pleased for the moment with this answer.

Birsha cleared his throat. "Okay, when we land, you and a few others can head to your home. Whether or not there are supplies, we will meet behind the school house in about an hour. We need to make sure we get a good lead on the Dark Ones before they wake up."

The mother nodded. "Noah, you hear that? We are going to have to move quickly, okay? Are you ready to do some running?"

They boy popped up. "Really?" He deflated a bit. "What if I'm not as fast as I used to be. What if they come again?"

The mother took a deep breath, careful to keep her face neutral. "I am sure you will do great. Besides, you don't want to leave me behind, do you?" She gave him a small smile and a squeeze. "It won't be a race unless I tell you to. Just remember what I said in the cells." The boy nodded and buried his face in her skirts, hugging them close. "Oh, darling, we are okay right now, I just want to remind you." She rubbed his back gently but didn't try to hush his cries or tell him he was overreacting.

Jamie smiled to himself, proud of the young mother. *She is doing the best she can with the circumstances. And handling it better than some of her elders. I don't think I could be as calm as she is.* He turned to the young man leading their group. "Do you need anything from me?"

Birsha nodded, pointing behind them. "If you could watch the shore to keep any eye out for any patrols, that would be best. The members of that patrol should still be down, but we may have gotten the dosages wrong."

"I can do that." Jamie spun in his seat to look back in the direction they had come. He watched the waves that rippled out in their wake. How long had it been since he had been in his home? A month? He honestly couldn't say for sure. The sun broke through the low hanging clouds, reflecting off the water. The little home in the woods had been his parents' cottage before his. Just a simple five room home. He and Marion had moved into it and added on a few more rooms in the hopes of growing their family. He always knew he wanted to pass it on to one of the girls. He had thought Shauna may be the one to take it. Even from a young age, it seemed like Taytra would leave Cabineral to explore and strike her own path. If you had told him five months ago where he would be in the fall, he wouldn't have believed a word of it. He prayed that the Dark Ones had left the space untouched, but knew there had been truth in the other man's question. He thought of the veggies they had bought in the market that week and the animals in the barn. *Goddess, I hope the blasted fence broke again. Let them have escaped. Please don't make me find them there.*

Jamie turned back around as they pulled up to one

of the five piers on the shore, the same piers that had been used to take the families and tested youth out onto the lake at Mabon. They pulled in slowly, rocking as waves caught on their boat and the pier. Once they bumped up against it, Jamie threw a rope over a pylon to hold them secure before climbing half out. He kept one foot in the boat, using that leg to keep the boat pinned to the side of the pier, while reaching down to help others out. "Ready?"

The little boy reached up to take his hand and clambered onto the wood. He turned and puts a hand back for his mother. "Come on, Mama!" he said, the fears he had crossing nowhere in sight. He and Jamie helped her out of the boat, the child grunting with the effort as he tried to haul the women up by himself.

"Alright, I am up!" she says, brushing her skirts. The little boy clung to his mother's hand and pulled her along the boardwalk as Jamie turned to help the other three people off the boat.

Jamie hurried down to the shore where their little group waited to head into town. "Did anyone want to come with me to see if there is anything salvageable?" he asked. "You do not need to, but I would appreciate the hands if I find anything."

"I do, Mister Flynn!" the little boy said, waving his arms. "We wanted to check right, Mama?"

"Yes, we will go." She laughed and wiped at his face again with her skirt, trying to smudge away the dirt lined with tear tracks, but the little one wiggled free, bouncing on his toes.

"Oh, to feel so carefree," Jamie said, watching as the little boy ran and jumped over a puddle. "What is his name?"

"Noah," she said quietly. "He is named after his father."

"And yours?"

She laughed. "Noah's mother?" She smiled for a moment, watching the little one. "My name is Lynessa."

He pointed to a road to the left. "Little Noah, I have a job for you."

The boy sprinted up. "I can do a job for sure, sir!" He spun to his mother. "Mama, I can go just as fast as before!"

She laughed. "That is great, honey!"

Jamie crouched in front of the boy. "Now, Noah, your mama and I are going to walk back here. Do you think you could be extra sneaky and walk along the path ahead of us a bit? We need someone brave and quiet, who is also super fast to let us know if someone is there. But you can't go too far or we won't be able to see you if there is someone."

Noah turned to his mother. "Can I do this job, Mama? I will only do it if you say it is okay."

She smiled and pressed a kiss to the top of his head. "Yes, you can. I can't imagine anyone else who would be brave enough to do this job."

Noah turned back to Jamie. "Okay, I can do it now. What road?"

Jamie pointed. "This one here. You can use the trees as a guide. You shouldn't be more than ten trees from your mother. Sound good?"

Noah stood up nice and tall. "Yes, sir!" He turned and marched up the road, his hand above his eyes, shielding them from the overcast sky. He froze for a moment, then scurried off under a tree, grabbing a long, knobby stick. He held it high above his shoulder like a spear. "What happened to his father, if I can ask?"

"Noah's father was a trader." She took a deep breath as if readying herself for the emotions. "His caravan was hit a few years ago. I didn't know what had happened at first. It was meant to be a longer trading period. But then the window was long gone, and I hadn't heard from him. I ended up sending a message to his partner in Apeito and found out that they had never received his goods." She scrubbed her eyes and fell silent, watching her son as he marched a few feet and stopped, waiting for them to pass by a few trees before continuing his march. "Noah was too young to really remember him at the time his father went away for work. I told him his father wouldn't be coming back, but I don't think he fully understands it. He asked me a few times when we were under the city if his father was just in a different cell."

"That must have been really difficult. I am sorry."

She nodded. "It is okay. There was another family in the cell with us, so he got to have some socialization. It was really hard for him, though. I hope it won't impact him in the long run. I don't know how it wouldn't be though, being trapped like that." She sniffled a bit.

"You are doing the best you can. It has been really hard. I can't imagine how difficult it is to have a child trapped with you."

"But, sir, you did?" she said, confused.

Jamie nodded. "No, you are right, I did. But my daughter has grown up. She is old enough to make her own decisions and has been for a while. And boy did she like to remind me of that." He laughed. "But you are right, my child will have a very different experience than yours. Taytra understood the concept and the purpose, though cruel. Noah is young, concepts like that should be left for stories at bedtime."

Noah came running back up the road to them. "Mr. Flynn, Mr. Flynn!"

"Yes, Noah. What is it?"

"Sir, what does your house look like?"

Jamie picked up the pace a bit. "It is a sort of brown color with a big fence around it."

"I think I found it!" The boy bit his lip. "But there is some black, and the fence is knocked over."

Jamie's mouth went dry. He swallowed and nodded. "Thank you, Noah. You stay back with your mama now. I am going to be the leader, okay?"

"Yes, sir!" Noah salutes. "Do you want my spear?"

"I will be okay, thank you, Noah." Jamie hurried down the path and heard Noah's mother shush him when Jamie passed the ten tree mark. The path in front of the house was a sea of muddy hoofprints, deep crevices dried into little craters, and as the boy said, part of the fence was knocked over. Jamie paused at what used to be the gate, thinking of the sunny day when Jamie had last told Shauna the history of Cabineral Lake.

A corner of the house had collapsed the area around what used to be a window. The entire side of the house was scorched and the door had been knocked from its hinges, either by the Dark Ones or looters. He stepped into his home, taking in the ruined space. He moved into their kitchen and slowly picked up the four chairs that had been knocked to the floor, sliding them next to the table.

Noah peeked a head in. "Mister Flynn, can I come in and help you clean up? Mama said you might want to be alone."

Jamie looked around the room. "You can come in, Noah. Just be careful where you step, okay? There is glass on the floor."

Jamie walked to the wall and opened one of the cabinets. A few plates were on the shelf and a potato had grown again, its eyes spreading out over the shelf. "Looks like they took the food we had. Probably good, I don't know how much of it would still be usable now." He paused. "I think I needed to go to market after the ceremony to get food and with everything that happened, I was never able to."

"You said you might have some blankets we could use?" Noah asked. "Those would be helpful when it gets cold at night. I was always cold in the castle."

"Yes, yes, those would be in here. I was always cold too," Jamie said, leading Noah into another room. There was a small fireplace in the corner, a desk, and a trunk. The lid of the trunk had been thrown open, but it looked like all the blankets were left. "Whoever came through was probably looking for valuables," Jamie said, thinking of the bag of stones he kept under the floorboard in his room.

"This one looks extra cozy!" Noah said, holding up a thick quilt.

Jamie bit the inside of his cheek. It was Marion's quilt. The one she made before she had gotten sick. He watched as the little one wrapped it around his shoulders like a cape. "That is cozy. A very special one, too."

Noah looked from Jamie to the blanket. "Do you want us to leave it here so it doesn't get dirty?" The little one took it off his shoulders and folded it up.

"No, let's take it with us. I would rather take it and

know it is safe. Can you protect it for me for a few minutes? I have to go into a different room. If you want, you can go get your mama and pick out any other blankets you think would be good to take with us."

"Okay! I can do that. Mama is really good at folding blankets. She is a good picker, too," he said, placing the quilt carefully back in the trunk and hurrying back to the door.

Jamie followed the boy back into the kitchen and turned to the second door. This was the girls' bedroom. He opened the door slowly. Dresses were scattered about, some thrown over chair backs, some on the bed, but a few were on the floor with large boot prints in the middle of the skirts. The room was a mess, but it looked more like the sort of mess that Shauna or Taytra would leave, expecting to come back and put it away neatly when they had more time. Someone else had come through and knocked a few garments to the floor, but it looked relatively untouched. He went to Taytra's trunk, digging around for a large bag to put a few pieces of clothing in. There were a few mothers in their groups who he was sure would appreciate a change of clothes or a cloak. He did the same with Shauna's things, digging through to see if there is anything usable before turning to the door. Out of the corner of his eye, he saw Shauna's hair brush, cast aside in the rush to get out the door. He picked it up and put it back on her vanity where it belonged.

He went back into the living room. There was one more room he had to face. His bedroom with the trunk of Marion's things he had left untouched for months. The door creaked as he opened it. The bed was torn apart, blankets everywhere. He sat on the edge of the bed and put his head in his hands. This house, the little creaks he heard as Noah and his mother gathered supplies—those are sounds he knew. But someone had been here, someone he didn't know that may have meant harm to him and his family. That knowledge sat like a weight in his stomach. He took a few deep breaths and blinked away a few tears before getting back to work. He couldn't stay long; they needed to get out of Cabineral. He crouched, peering under the bed, but didn't find the loose floorboard moved. Inside the stash of money sat safe in a leather pouch. He put it on the bed beside him and turned to his trunk. He pulled out a few cloaks and a bag. He slung one cloak around his own shoulders before folding some of the clothes into the bag.

He turned to Marion's trunk and froze, then shook his head. "Lynessa, could you come here?"

"Of course, what is it?" she asked, coming from the living room with an arm full of blankets.

Jamie rubbed the back of his head. "I—I have a trunk I cannot go through myself. I think it would be better if you do. As a woman, you might be able to say what would be of more use as we continue this journey."

She looked behind him to the room and the large bed. "Your wife's?" Jamie nodded, trying to swallow past the lump in his throat. "Yes, I can do that for you." She turned back to the room. "Noah?" The boy sprinted out, a tiny cloak from when Shauna or Taytra had been small around his shoulders. "Do you think you could take Mister Flynn outside? He needs a strong body guard like you," she said before squeezing Jamie's arm and moving to open the trunk. "I will be out in just a moment."

Chapter 21 Jamie

When the three arrived back at the town, laden with clothes and blankets, the groups had already been divided for their journey. A group of thirty had chosen to go through the woods with the larger group. Choosing the journey on the road, the smallest group would follow Shauna's path across the plain. Alexis was at the center of the courtyard, his voice raised above the clatter of voices. "No matter which way you choose to go, I want to reiterate it will have its own set of challenges. You will need to be aware at all times. Especially those who are choosing to go via the road. You will be easily traceable. You will need to move as quickly on foot as you can. The Dark Ones have horses, we know they will be after us in the night. We released the horses into the city, but it will not take them long to round a few of them up." He looked over the group somberly. "Your group leaders have a plan in place, but you need to trust them. We ask that you follow any orders given. Delays could cost you or your family," Alexis said gravely. He turned when he saw Jamie and the others walking up, nodded, and turned back to the group. "For your safety, your group leaders have chosen not to share the next steps with you. If you are seen to have valuable information, the Dark Ones will be cruel to you to get it. The less you know the safer you will be."

Birsha came up to Jamie. "Your home was untouched?" he whispered, pulling the three to the side.

"Mostly," Jamie said, pulling out the clothes. "Someone clearly tried to set it on fire and went through it. I hope we have some bits that can be useful."

"If there is anything you should keep to yourself, pull it out and put it to the side. Anything else, lay out in size order as best as you can. I know you don't have a lot, but we will try to divide it as best as we can," Birsha said before walking up to Alexis and whispering the information into his ear.

Jamie turned to Noah, draping Marion's quilt around the little boy's shoulders. "Can I put you in charge of this?" The boy nodded vigorously and clutched the quilt to his chest. He stepped back behind his mother, trying to stay out of sight.

Jamie laid the last item on the ground. Looking at each garment on the ground made him think of a different time or memory of his family. "It has come to my attention that Jamie Flynn, father of Shauna and Taytra Flynn was able to return to his home for a brief time. He found that many of their belongings were untouched. As many of us have not been able to bathe or change or have warm enough clothes, Jamie brought some items to try to mitigate some of that issue." People started to rush forward, and Alexis put up his hands. "Wait! Wait! Like I said, it is a very limited stock. So, we need to do this carefully. Jamie, please come here."

Jamie stepped up, giving a small wave, then

quickly put his hand down. "Hello, everyone. First, we have three children's cloaks."

"Only three? There are at least ten children here!" someone from the back of the crowd shouted.

Jamie sighed. He knew this was the sort of reaction he was going to get. "My wife was no hoarder. My daughters are seventeen and eighteen. We are lucky we had any children's clothes left," Jamie pointed out. "I wish I had more to give, especially the little ones, but there is only so much one man can do." The crowd shifted and whoever it was that had spoken up stayed quiet. Jamie cleared his throat before continuing. "We have a few dresses for young and older women, but again not much. My girls tended to clear out things that didn't fit anymore, and we tried to take things that would be warm in the next few months."

As he spoke, a line was formed. The families walked quickly down the line, grabbing items that would fit one or more members. The clothes disappeared into the arms of people too quickly, leaving many at the back of the line with nothing. But it was good to see those that were able to get clothes smiling as they carried them away. They hurried off into the woods nearby or behind the fallen structures of the town to change out of the clothes they had been wearing for over a month.

Alexis came over. "Thank you, Jamie. This will be really helpful for some of those families. We will have to thank your daughters too when we find them. Maybe this will keep some people from getting sick."

Noah ran up and tugged on Jamie's sleeve. "Mister Flynn, which way are you going?"

"I am not sure yet. Do you know?" Jamie asked, looking up at the boy's mother.

"Not yet. I want to go where you do. I think you can keep us safe!" Noah insisted.

Jamie glanced up at Alexis and knelt so he was at eye level with Noah. He saw Lynessa over his shoulder, and she nodded, encouraging him to speak. "I want to be honest with you, little sir. I can't promise to keep you safe. I wish I could but I don't know what is going to happen over the next few weeks. But if you want to go with me, I will do my best."

The boy nodded soberly and turned back to his mother. "I think that is still a good answer, because he didn't lie."

Jamie shared a small smile with Lynessa. He hadn't wanted to overstep his bounds by speaking with the boy. And he didn't want to scare him, but sometimes the truth was a better protection than a lie. "Alexis, is there anywhere you would prefer me to go?" he asked, turning back to the rebel.

"I think you would be of most use with the group on the plain. We can't take the queen through the woods, and the other option for the town has just about disbanded already. You will have four of the soldiers we have with you, but the main group of our army will go to the woods. We will act as a lure, try to get the Dark Ones to follow us in that direction and take as many of them out along the way as we can."

"Alexis." Jamie looked down at Noah and grabbed Alexis's arm, pulling the young man away from the group. "Alexis, if you do that you might as well as commit suicide. If they catch you and you take a stand, they won't put you back in the cells. They will kill you."

He met Jamie's eyes. There was no fear, just cool

determination. "I know, and every man that comes with me knows the risks. I do not ask this lightly of them. They come with me for the good of the group. The elders and children won't be able to go fast for long. You will have to stop. The only way that we will be able to ensure that they will be safe is to take that harm away from them. Stop it before it gets to them."

Jamie searched for something to say. A way to persuade him not to take this risk, that they could find another plan. But he was right. Jamie looked over the group, the queen on a stretcher, the frail elders who he feared wouldn't make it. They needed more time. Jamie reached up and squeezed the boy on the shoulder. "May the Goddess bless your journey. Find me in Hollens and tell me about the adventure. I will do all I can to support those that stay with me and go to the plain."

Alexis nodded, tears dancing in his eyes. "I will. You are a good man, Jamie." The boy straightened and crossed a fist over his chest. "For the Frituals." Alexis moved to the group that he would be leading, and they jogged back the way they came just as the sky opened and rain started pouring down.

"For the Frituals," Jamie echoed, praying the Goddess would hold everyone close.

* * *

Jamie looked to the sky again, cursing at how quickly the gloomy skies of day were turning to damning dark clouds of night. He glanced over his shoulder to the line of his people that followed him and the trail through the woods out to the plain. While they were the smallest group to escape the castle, they are the most vulnerable. They didn't have horses or a wagon. They only had their own two feet. The tired feet that had been locked up for a month.

Jamie walked with little Noah on his back, the boy's little arms slung around his neck. He snored gently, his head resting on Jamie's shoulder, Marion's quilt tied around him fluttering like a cape. After the excitement of escaping had worn off, he had quickly tired, and he was too big for Lynessa to manage on her own.

"Are you okay, Mr. Flynn?" Lynessa asked, coming over to check on Noah, and brushing the hair out of the little one's face.

"I'm just tired," Jamie said. He didn't mention how his back ached from the weight of the boy or that his calves had been cramping on and off from the hills they had climbed.

"How long did you say it was Hollens?" she asked.

Jamie looked ahead to the plain and the tall grass that was flattened by the fall wind. "It'll be about a week. I think it's a two-day ride by horse." He glanced to the right where the queen was being carried by some men in a makeshift stretcher of blankets tied to sticks with the queen slung in between. *Do we even have that long?* He saw the Magick on her arm had shrunk. Rather than a thick black band on her skin, it looked like it had absorbed into her, following the veins in her skin. Jamie couldn't decide if that was better or worse. But the fact that she moved and now responded slightly to her name had to be a good sign. Carrying her across had to be seen as something good. Their kingdom had fallen, but they had the pieces to rebuild soon. If Moraine was really the last royal to fall, she was the one that would help bring everyone back together. *Oh, my friend, you give me too much credit. I am not a good queen. I have barely held Cabineral together. I am not the one to rally behind.* It was such an optimistic idea. One laced with a hope Jamie didn't know if he really believed in. *No, that's a lie,* he told himself. *I do have hope. I believe that Shauna and Tay are just as strong as their mother. I know they are smart enough and strong enough to take out anything that comes in their way.*

"Jamie, are you alright?" Lynessa put a hand on his arm.

He shook his head, clearing away his train of thought. "Yeah, I'm alright. I was just thinking about my girls. There's so much on their shoulders that they never expected— that I never expected. I just hope I gave them the right tools to be the kind of people we need right now."

She smiled, following his gaze to the queen. "I think you have. Those guards would spit out your daughter's names like they were a curse! If they're for us, then they are the greatest tool we have. I think they are doing well and you will see them soon. If Taytra really is in Hollens, you'll see her in just a few days. It's a good thing to have motivation to get through these hard nights." She reached over and took Noah from him. "You take a break. You have been carrying him far too long." The little boy stirred slightly, wrapping himself against his mother's side.

Jamie paused and pressed his hands into the small of his back, rolling his shoulders back. He felt a low pop in his spine and breathed through the sharp pain as the muscles relaxed.

"Front of the path, slow down," a voice called, the message echoing down through the group. The pack in front of Jamie slowed, allowing those behind them to catch up. Jamie heard someone murmur something about letting the slowest go first to allow them to set the pace. Jamie wanted to agree, to say that was a good idea, but it felt like a lose-lose situation. The elders and children would set the pace, letting everyone else conserve their energy, while they rushed their tired and frail bodies to set a pace they couldn't maintain. The pace would be slower, letting the Dark Ones have the chance to catch up. Their current tactic was to walk for about an hour then rest for a few minutes. They had to keep a steady pace for as long as they could. Jamie knew they would soon come upon the rolling hills of the plain. They would need to check ahead and keep close to the treeline. They would be exposed. There was no other way to look at it. They just had to pray the Dark Ones stayed asleep long enough for them to get away, and that Alexis's plan to draw them away worked. He knew several parties in his group were alone, their fathers or brothers, burning with anger and ready to fight, had gone with Alexis.

Jamie had chosen this group because he felt he had to protect them, though he had no real skills. He was a baker and the only thing he could beat was eggs. "I'm going to walk a lap and check on the others," Jamie said to Lynessa. He paused to speak with each family as he made his way to the rear guard. He tried talking to mothers and their children who they struggled to carry on their hips and their backs, asking if he could help. They all turned him away, wanting the control of holding their babies close, of having the choice to carry them or put them down. "Just let me know if you need any help."

The last family in their group was a mother of four, who struggled to keep her babies focused and moving forward. "Their papa and my eldest son went through the forest," she explained as she tried to carry two babies who cried and struggled in her arms to be free. "There was no way I could've gone with them. I know we wanted them to be the loudest but we didn't want them to be the weakest. My Nolan didn't want to go, but my son did. He wanted to show the Dark Ones who they were messing with."

"Would you like help?" Jamie asked. The mother nodded, and Jamie took one of the little ones. The child looked at him for a moment before crying louder. As if to say *Who the heck are you and why are you holding me*? Jamie put the child to his shoulder like he did long ago with his daughters and bounced slightly to soothe the child.

"I know it was really hard for my husband to leave us, but it would've been worse if we were there in the Dark Ones. Now he can protect us, and I can get these babies away from the city," she said slowly and deliberately, like she was saying it to convince herself as well.

Jamie agreed, "You are doing the best you can. He would be proud of you. You will have many stories to tell him when you see him again."

She nodded, blinking furiously, but didn't say anything until they paused, the group taking their short break to rest. "Thank you, sir. I can take him back now."

A young boy came up to Jamie, a friend just behind him. "Sir, we had an idea. We wanted to check and make sure it was okay with you or the others before we did it."

Jamie crouched to the boy's level. "And what was that?"

The boy glanced over at his friend, then turned back to Jamie. "My papa used to have a walking stick. I think Mister Omar did too. Could we go into the woods and get walking sticks for all the elders? To help them walk?"

Jamie looked for one of the rebel soldiers as he spoke. "I think that would be a marvelous idea. Do you want to go count how many we would need?" He waved over one of them and quickly explained the plan.

"We may need to pause a bit longer for that, but I think it will be helpful in the long run. Once we get that number, we will help the boys get that together. Tell them to come find me," the soldier said, moving to pass the message along.

"Don't you worry about it, honey. I won't be here much longer so I won't want you to worry about it," one grandmother said.

"Well, I expect you will make it to Hollens." Jamie heard one of the boys say.

"Do you see? This will help you so you don't have to work extra hard. Please let us find you something. We just want to help," the other piped up.

Some continued to insist they didn't need it but were kind and respectful and paid the boys many compliments for thinking of them. Jamie saw they wanted to be of help. They couldn't fight like their older brothers or fathers, but they could still help bring people to safety.

A pair of young women came up to Jamie, and he beamed. "Jacinta? Safiya? Oh, girls, how are you?" He pulled the two girls into a tight hug. "Girls, I am sorry I didn't see you were here. I didn't know you were in the dungeon."

He took a step back, looking over the two women. They were frail, their pale skin clinging to their faces. Safiya's once glossy black hair hang limp in a knotted braid. "We were trying to keep as low a profile as we could. I made Andrew leave without me. I didn't know what would happen if they found out." She fiddled with her finger, the place where a thin band had sat for the last few months.

Jamie sighed. "Of course. That was extremely brave of you. It was a good choice. An incredibly hard one, I am sure." Safiya nodded vigorously and bit her lip, staring hard at the ground. "Oh, come here, Hun," Jamie said, pulling her into a tight hug.

The girl buried her head into his shoulder. "My family is gone," the girl said, her voice muffled by Jamie's shirt. "All of them. Andrew is all I have left."

"You are not alone, Saf. You have me. And soon we will find Andrew, Tay, and Ward. Okay? When we get to Hollens, we will do something to honor your family." Safiya whimpered, and Jamie felt the girl take deep breaths, trying to calm herself. "You are safe with me. It is okay," Jamie said and looked at Jacinta. "How are you doing?"

Taytra's longtime friend looked numb, all emotions wiped from her pretty face. "I don't have anything left to give."

Jamie nodded. "That is okay too. We will get to safety soon. Then you can rest."

Safyia looked up at Jamie. "Can we stay with you?"

Jamie nodded. "Yes, Saf. I have to move around, but you can, of course."

Chapter 22 Barin

"How exactly is this supposed to work again?" Barin asked, pulling the cloak tighter around his shoulders. A fierce northerly wind blew across the plain, pulling the fabric away from him. Barin glanced up at the clear night sky. It looked like diamonds scattered against a thick velvet cloth.

"Hmm? Oh, right, yes," Alois muttered, looking up from one of the many notebooks he had brought out with him. Lyra and Paulo shared a small grin as the little monk flipped a few more pages. "Well, I don't know exactly how your ceremony is meant to go, Barin. I am sort of improvising," the elf said absently. "Yes, this is what I was looking for!" He gestured for Paulo to bring a torch closer so he could better examine the pages.

Enre, who had been scanning the night for any Dark Ones on the move, turned back to their circle. "Hang on. I thought one of the first things you said when the two of us got here was that you knew how to do it?" the elf asked. He was jumpy. He had his knife out, ready to throw it in the face of anyone who approached unannounced. "I don't see why we couldn't do this on the parapet. They said we could if we needed to," he grumbled, not for the first time.

Paulo glanced up from the notebook. "You know we can't push our luck with the council. We have to pick our battles."

Alois continued as if he hadn't heard Paulo at all. "Well, I know how the ceremony went for some of our kings and queens over the half millennium, so I am just taking that information and tinkering with it." The old monk beamed. "Come, come. We don't want to be out here too long," he said, beckoning Lyra, Paulo, and Barin closer. He lifted a candle with shaking fingers and tried to light it, but another gust of wind blew the candle out in an instant.

"Let me help," Lyra said. "I know we don't want to be using too much Magick, but we won't be able to get Barin's Magick fully unlocked unless we use some, right?" They all nodded. Enre twisted the handle of the knife in his hand, ready. With a wave of her hand, Lyra split the wind around them, forming a sort of tunnel. Barin watched the long grass at their feet slowly stand back up without the wind to push it over. As he looked around, he saw a circle of space forming around them where the wind wasn't flowing. When he looked back at Lyra, her looping, tattoo-like markings glowed under her linen sleeves and down to her fingertips a pale yellow color. With the wind no longer bothering them, it was easy for her to strike a match and light the deep red candle Alois held.

"Now, normally we would have someone here who represented each Magick type. We are lucky that we have another earth Magick user in our midst. But unfortunately, Enre can't really help us with the ceremony. I used to be able to use Magick like your mother, Barin, but over the last few decades, my Magick has left me. I can still sense it but I cannot access it. Tonight, I will act as a conduit for you, Barin. We will ask the Goddess to accept what I can do, to substitute for us not having Shauna or Philippe here to represent you."

"Should we have waited for them?" Barin asked. "If you think they are on their way here, I am fine if we wait. I am sure Serena can think of some way to convince the men in their high tower to let us try when the two of them are here." Paulo looked at Alois, who nodded solemnly. "What—what don't I know?" the younger elf asked.

"We didn't want to say anything at our meeting tonight at dinner because we hadn't had confirmation at that point. But now we have. A second scout returned with the news after the last bell," Paulo explained. "We didn't want to create any panic until we were sure."

"Oh, come on. Out with it. What did you find? Is my father marching for Hollens as we speak?" Barin asked, throwing his arms in the air. "I don't like when you guys do this. Why can't I know things right away too?" the elf asked.

"It wasn't so much for you, as for Tay," Paulo said. "We have gotten word that Shauna and Philippe are no longer on their way here," he said slowly, waiting for Barin to respond.

Barin just stared at him, confused for a moment. *Where else were they going to go?* Barin thought. Paulo and Lyra had been very clear when they said that everyone in their group had decided to come here to Hollens when they had finished doing their part of the mission. Paulo and

Lyra's trip was cut short when they had found him in Hollens. But Shauna and Philippe had to go to Fuegaste Peak. *Father never could hold the peak.*

Paulo seemed to read his mind and said, "Shauna and Philippe were captured leaving Fuegaste Peak. The mountain fell to the Dark Ones hours after they arrived. Philippe was able to complete his test but he didn't have any time to rest. They took a few Dark Ones down but they were pinned. They are being taken to your father's fortress as we speak. We don't know how they are doing or how many Dark Ones are still there."

Barin took a minute, processing the information. Fuegaste was one of the places his father had always wanted to take him. He felt the mountain of fire was the pinnacle of power. "So, you wanted to confirm before you tell Taytra and burn down the city to make the men here give her an army?"

"Something like that." Lyra laughed dryly. "We need to make sure there aren't any weapons nearby. Maybe also give Andrew and Ward a heads up. I know Tay has been having a hard time sitting here in the city to begin with. This is going to make it much, much harder for her. She is going to want to leave and get her sister back as fast as she can. I don't blame her."

"Neither do I. But we needed to wait until we knew for sure they had been captured and what state they were in."

"And we know they are okay?" Barin asked, thinking of the prisoners they brought into the fortress. But Shauna and Philippe were Frituals. *Will they be treated better or worse?* Barin wasn't sure. "Right. Well, let's start with this. Get the ceremony out of the way, and we can move on to the next thing," Barin said, turning back to Alois. "What do you want me to do?"

Alois looked up into the sky, judging their position, then, using the tip of his boot, Alois drew an X in the dirt. "Kneel here, please." Barin did as he was bid, splaying his cloak around him on the ground. "Good. Now please raise both of your hands above your head." Barin felt a bit odd and unbalanced on the ground. "Are you ready?" the elf asked quietly.

Barin thought for a moment, feeling the anticipation bubbling up inside him. He didn't understand his Magick nearly as much as Lyra and Paulo did. He hadn't had the chance to explore it. But once he was marked, he knew the five of them, when they were united, would be unstoppable. He had done what his father had asked of him for too many years. It was time to create his own legacy. "I am."

Alois smiled and nodded. "Lyra, Paulo, please each grab one of Barin's wrists." The monk paused before reading from his notes, his voice echoing across the windy plain. "Each Fritual is marked in a different way, representing the different Magicks. Shauna had water drawn over her skin, Paulo you have told me the light of a stained glass window's vines chose the pattern for you. Lyra has also confided in me that she stood out in one of the many snow storms her people had and the wind itself drew the marks. I don't know how Philippe was marked, but I can imagine that it was in a similar fashion to the three of you." Alois rested a hand on the top of Barin's head. Up until then, Alois's voice had been more informative, but now the tone changed. He projected more above the wind, speaking not to just the four of them there, but nature at large. "The spirit Fritual is different. They must be marked with the support of the other Magicks. I call upon the Goddess to accept me, Alois, as the conduit for the Magicks of fire and water. Having discussed it with those you have already named, we know they would also agree that this elf is the one to control this Magick, spirit Magick. The Magick tied closest to you." From a small pouch at his side, Alois pulled a vial of oil and rubbed a small circle of it into Barin's forehead. Lyra and Paulo shifted their weight, and Barin made a mental note to thank them later for supporting his arms. He didn't know how long this ceremony was going to take, but his shoulders were already aching from the act of holding his arms above his head and his fingertips were going numb. Alois flipped open another one of the notebooks. "The spirit Fritual is one who, like his brothers and sisters, is connected to everything around him. Unlike his fellows who connect to nature, he connects to his people. With his powers, he hears and shapes the way people feel and act around him. With your guidance, he will learn to wield these powers to create a world that fits your ideals."

Alois took the oils and poured it over Paulo and Lyra's hands, then placed his hands a little lower, tipping the end of the oil over his own hands. "Please call upon your wondrous Magicks." Alois closed his eyes. After a pause, he shifted, cracking an eye open to look over at Paulo. "That was for you. Can you access your Magick?"

Paulo cleared his throat "And do what exactly?"

"That doesn't matter, we just need the current of the power," the monk muttered.

Barin glanced between the two elves, Lyra having already called upon her Magick to rearrange the wind. The yellow glow was leaching into the dark skin on Barin's wrist and running down the oil strands. Paulo pulled a few stones from the ground, his own jagged markings and green markings flowed over his own skin.

With the elves on either side of him pulling their Magick, Barin felt the Magick flowing through and around him. Barin looked to Alois. His eyes were closed, head bowed over Barin.

"Barin, pull upon your own Magick," Alois said quietly.

Barin closed his eyes and reached out to the Magick he felt singing beneath his skin. He jumped as what felt like a wave of information washed over him. A cacophony of thoughts and emotions swirling all around. Enre was apprehensive, fidgeting and ready to fight if needed. His thoughts milled around a series of strategic plans if they were attacked. Lyra was intrigued, trying to piece together bits of lore she knew herself. Paulo was also interested, but like Enre, he wanted to get this over with and get back inside the city walls. He wouldn't voice it, but he didn't understand the relationship that the men in charge of this city had with Magick, and why they feared it so much. Barin turned his thoughts to Alois. His friend was so full of pride, it oozed out of him. He was thinking of the early meetings in the fortress, when Barin would be on guard duty and would spend all of it discussing life and all he actually wanted. Barin opened his eyes and stared at his arms in amazement. A large grin spread across his face. "Whoa," he whispered. He brought his focus back, pushing away the others' thoughts and emotions.

Alois opened his eyes and started smiling as well. "Well done, everyone." He pulled a few cloths from his pouch and handed them out to the three Frituals. They wiped all the oil from their hands and arms. Barin stared at his arms. His markings were purple. Four thick bands encircled his wrists and forearms where the others had held, and thin rivers of purple spider webbed between, trailing away to nothing.

"Welcome, brother. You are officially one of us," Paulo said, clapping him on the shoulder. "All five of us have been tested. Nothing can stop us now. The Dark Ones won't know what hit them."

Barin turned back to Alois. "Thank you, friend. Thank you."

Alois nodded, the pride written all over his face.

Chapter 23 Taytra

Taytra took another bite of her soup, looking around the room. She couldn't quite place why, but everyone felt uneasy. Like there was something they didn't want to discuss. Andrew wouldn't meet her eye across the table. *What is going on?* She set her spoon down. Paulo, Lyra, and Barin sat in a row, their markings slowly fading after Barin's successful Fritual ceremony. Taytra could see the thick purple band glowing under his white linen shirt. The meeting had gone well as far as she was concerned. Serena had kept her promise and had managed to get more supplies from the council. *I still need to get her to explain how she gets anything done with them.*

She glanced over at Ward, but he was looking across at Andrew, the two of them having some sort of unspoken conversation. She had watched as Ward had folded up his notes when food came, had seen a line of text they hadn't touched on, but he had quickly stowed the page out of sight. She finished her stew, watching as the others kept glancing in her direction. Paulo and Serena were better at hiding it, but they, like the others, kept glancing away when they saw her looking. She pushed her stew away and leaned forward. "You know, I can tell when you are up to something if you look at me like that. Or should I say don't look at me," Taytra said pointedly. "This isn't just about making sure I get dinner. Though I do appreciate that. You are up to something else."

Ward looked taken aback, but in the way a five-year-old does when he has been caught with his hand in the sweet jar. He shared a look with Andrew.

"Come on," Taytra snapped. "What is going on? We already discussed everything for the day, and nobody said they had any issues with what we discussed. Serena said we are getting more stuff for our people, right? The numbers we asked for originally?" Taytra turned to the half-elf. "Right?" The elf nodded. She turned to Barin. "And you said we may be able to get help from your mother in Bulandon if we ever needed it." The elf hesitated for a moment but nodded. "Great, so," she said, turning back to Ward and Andrew, "what is going on? You can tell all of us." She turned her head just in time to see Paulo nod. "What do you all know that I don't?" She scoffed, throwing her arms in the air. "Goddess."

Ward rotated to face her. "Hang on a second, Tay. We wanted—No, we needed to make sure we had all the correct information first," Ward said slowly, his voice even, watching her like a deer who would flee at any sudden movements.

"What, did they leave Cabineral? Can we go home? Is Father okay?" She felt a surge of joy and fear at the same time. She grabbed his arm. "This is the news we have been waiting for. Once Shauna gets here, we can go home! Take Cabineral back! We will show them what happens when you take our home away from us!" She jumped to her feet, grinning, but then she saw the faces of the others in the room. They were somber, serious. Some looked a bit afraid. But she didn't know what they would be afraid of. She felt the smile drop and a stone fall deep into the pit of her stomach.

"Tay," Ward started but cleared his throat. "We insisted on the second and third reports to confirm it, which is why this took a bit to get to you. Please understand, we haven't been keeping this from you out of malice. We wanted to be sure before anything was said to you."

Andrew ran a hand through his hair, squeezing the skin at the back of his neck. "Tay, I don't know what to say, but I'm sorry. I don't know what to do."

A lump formed in the back of her throat. "About what? What is going on?" She looked around the table, trying to glean any information from them. "Did they hurt Father? I will kill them if they touched him again." She smacked the table hard and barely noted the way her hand stung.

"Tay, you need to relax. We don't want you to be upset," Lyra cooed.

Taytra roared, "Well, I already am. Great job stopping that. If you would just tell me what—"

"Shauna isn't coming!" Ward yelled.

Taytra froze, mouth agape. "Wh-what?" she croaked. All the air left her lungs, and she sat down slowly, feeling like the world was falling away from her.

"Shauna isn't coming," Ward repeated, his voice cracking on the last word.

Taytra looked into Ward's eyes, searching

desperately for the lie.

I want to tell you everything is going to be okay. That Shauna will be here tomorrow or something like that. But I can't. I can't lie to you like that. I wish I could. Ward had said that to her just a few days ago.

She gripped the edge of the table, feeling the world pivot around her. She stared hard at the table, searching for an answer. *Shauna isn't coming. Shauna isn't coming.* The words echoed over and over in her mind. "What happened?" she gasped, her voice shaking as she spoke.

"Tay, I am sorry. I wouldn't tell you if I didn't believe it was true. You know that, right?" She nodded dumbly, and he looked at her like the others did. Apprehensive, like Tayra might lash out. "She and Philippe were captured when they left Fuegaste Peak. The reports say they are headed south to Bulandon and Nurzan's fortress," he continued. Unlike up on the wall, he didn't reach out to her. He didn't try to ground her.

Nurzan. Nurzan has her. My sister. My baby sister.

The room spun again. His face, so like Barin's, loomed in front of her. Taytra retched and pressed a hand to her mouth, bolting from the room. She couldn't be in the room anymore. It was hot. She was burning up from the inside out. The food in her stomach threatened to come back up.

"Tay!" someone shouted, though she couldn't tell who. She stumbled out of the inn, stomach roiling. She heaved again and let out a whimper. She tried to swallow back the metallic taste, but it coated her mouth and tongue. She saw a barrel of water next to the building and sashed the water in her face and cupped it in her hand, rinsing her mouth of the vile taste.

"Tay? Are you alright?" Serena put a comforting

hand on her shoulder, pulling the hair out of Taytra's face.

Taytra flinched away from the contact, feeling the way the guards had ripped the dress from her shoulders. Taytra shook her head and let out another small whimper. The still-bruised lines on her back burned with shame, and pain, and fear.

Serena crouched to her level, tilting Taytra's face to look at her. "Taytra, look at me. You are in Hollens. You are safe here," Serena said slowly and grabbed Taytra's hand, squeezing her fingers hard. "You feel that? You are with me in Hollens. No one is trying to hurt you. You are safe here. They can't get you. You are stronger than them."

Ward burst from the inn a few moments later, his eyes wild as he searched for her. "Tay? Taytra?" he called.

She wanted to call to him, but the noise that spilled out from her was a whimper.

He spun on his heels, seeing her and Serena crouched in the shadow of the inn. "Tay? Oh, Tay, I... This isn't how we thought... I-I'm sorry. Paulo waited to tell us. He had to be sure. He told me today."

She nodded. "I know. Thank you for making sure." Her voice didn't sound like her own. A tear rolled down her face, but she made no move to wipe it away. She felt her stomach roil again at the thought of Nurzan and bent over, retching into the grass.

Serena gently laid a hand on Taytra's back like her mother had when she was a child. Taytra didn't flinch this time. Serena pulled the girl's long hair back. "When we got the report," Serena said, tying Tay's hair back with a leather cord, "I thought about telling you right away. But we thought you might lash out. Threaten to smack a few men upside the head?" She gave an encouraging smile. Taytra could only nod. She felt weak like she had when they had escaped. "Can you tell us what is actually going on?"

Taytra looked at Ward. His dark brown eyes were broken. So ashamed of himself. She nodded. She owed them all an explanation. Herself one. She was scared of the way her hands were shaking. "I—When everything started back in Cabineral, I—I killed Damian."

"I remember. I was angry for not acting faster," Serena said.

"The guards wouldn't let me see her at first. I wanted kill them," Taytra said, rubbing her arms. She felt cold and hot at the same time, like she was back in Cabineral, catching her sister as she fell, the guards pulling the two of them apart. "Then the next day, Shauna was completing her ceremony, getting her marks. I was so angry with her for putting herself in danger. And with the queen. With you," Taytra said, looking at Serena, "for putting Shauna in that predicament. I stabbed Damian. I killed the head of the queen's guard." Taytra paused, pressing a hand to her stomach, nearly retching again as she felt it roll. "I—I told our father that she needed me. Needed *us* to protect her. That I couldn't leave her alone. That I needed to protect my sister." Tears flowed freely down her face. She stopped to let out a few sobs, leaning against the barrel, the cool wood leaching some of the heat from her skin. She put her head between her knees, trying to catch her breath. "I am supposed to protect her. But how can I? I am here. So far away. So far away," she sobbed. She felt Ward's warm hand on her back, on the marks Nurzan had made. She flinched away and the pain on

Ward's face made her cry harder. "I'm sorry. I'm sorry. I'm sorry," she repeated again and again. She reached out to Ward, and he wrapped her in his arms. She felt like a child. "I want to go home. I just want to go home."

"I know. You are so brave," he whispered. He adjusted his position, sitting awkwardly so his hands sat low on her waist, not touching her back. She stayed there for a while, trying to catch her breath. To stop crying. "I'm sorry. I'm sorry. I'm sorry," she repeated to Ward, to Serena, to Shauna.

"You have nothing to be sorry about," he said, his voice low and rough in her ear. He paused, pressing his forehead into her shoulder. "Tay, you don't need to apologize."

"I am so afraid of him," she breathed, clutching Ward's shirt. "I didn't think I was. But I am. I want to kill him. But he was so cruel. You could feel it." Nurzan stood above her, belt raised over head. She buried herself into Ward's chest, trying desperately to push away Nurzan's face. "Nurzan has my sister. How can I save her?"

When she looked up from Ward's shoulder, the others had come outside. They sat around her in a small circle. People walked by, and when they tried to approach, Andrew waved them away.

"It is okay to be afraid. It is okay to be upset," Barin said. He kept his face down, away from Taytra, the features that favored that of his father. She had punched this elf for looking remotely like Nurzan. But the idea of her sister with him sent her spiraling. "It is okay to be afraid, but you can't let it stop you. You can't let him stop you, okay?" Barin's voice was angry., The way she wanted to be. Ready to strike, to fight. She nodded, reaching out to him, and the elf slowly took her hand. His skin was cool, and like Ward's, callused by many hours spent training. He looked up at her and searched her face. "My father is not a good person. I will stand beside you against him. I will do all I can to help you get your sister back," the elf vowed. "On the Goddess, I will. I won't stop until he is stopped. What he did to you, to your family, to all the families of Cabineral Lake and Bulandon... He didn't start this but he killed everyone who stood against him, and we can stop him."

Taytra took a deep breath. Then another. "What do we do now? This changes everything."

It was Paulo who answered, "We have spent too long training. Now, we fight."

Looking around at those who stood by her side, Taytra realized she had never felt so scared. But she was ready. "We fight."

Chapter 24 Philippe

After three days of riding, a sandstorm, and too few flasks of water, they had reached the heart of Dark One territory. Philippe's shirt was stiff with sweat and sand. The rough texture left the skin of his sides, already tender from the cracked rib, raw. He felt little stabs of pain each time the fabric brushed his skin.

Someone had decided after the sandstorm that had rushed over them, to keep him and Shauna together. They were easier to keep track of. Philippe didn't mind. They were each bound to their own horse, and the two horses' halters tied together. So, if one of their horses went off, they both would. It had already proved to be a poor idea with Shauna's skittish horse taking the lead on more than one occasion.

He glanced over at Shauna. Her mouth was pressed in a tight line, but then she looked over and shot him a small smile. "You, okay?" he asked in a hushed voice.

"As good as I can be," she replied, keeping her eyes forward.

He nodded and turned back to the line. They couldn't hope for anything else right now. He could see the outline of the fortress in the distance, the details hard to make out against the dark sky, and did his best to steel himself for what would come. They had done everything they could to break them. Now they would know if they had succeeded.

Philippe watched as Fayanna turned back on her horse and stopped to speak with a nearby guard. After a brief conversation, the guard approached, drawing a blade. "Put your hands out," he ordered, and Philippe slowly lifted his hands away from the saddle. The guard leaned over, pulled Philippe's hands away, and sawed at the taut rope. It snapped with a soft *pop*, the frayed ends smacking the horse's withers. The horse danced, and Philippe gripped the pommel tightly, wishing they would just cut him free entirely. "Oi, what are you playing at? Get off that horse before it spooks the others."

You and I both know you did this, Philippe thought bitterly as he dismounted. He gripped the pommel and only let go over the saddle when he knew he had his balance. He tugged at the ropes binding his hands. *Secure as ever.*

Philippe looked over the heads of all the Dark Ones up the line to the fortress. The walls of the fortress rose above them. Like the recruitment camp, it was partially built into the side of a mountain, the craggy hill rising high above the walls he could see. Chunks of rock and sparse vegetation lined an uneven trail up to the gates. They were open, no doubt waiting to absorb the new host into its walls.

"Let's go. The general will be waiting," Fayanna said, striding past them. "Move it."

Philippe took a half step to the left, and was pushed back.

"This way," the guard behind him said, nudging him deeper into the line of soldiers.

He stumbled for a second, trying to figure out which way he was meant to go. *Do we follow the Hunter or these guards?* His answer came half a second later when the guard growled something under his breath and took Philippe by the elbow, walking him through the ranks of soldiers. He and Shauna were walked straight through the middle of the line, forcing the soldiers to part to let them through. Philippe kept his eyes on his feet as they walked past, avoiding the eyes of those that spat in their direction and leered at Shauna, ignoring the profanities they threw at the two of them. Philippe couldn't help but marvel at the complexity of the move. While it was an inconvenience to the soldiers, forcing them to move out of the way, it also acted as a security measure, since there was no way they could escape when they were physically surrounded. But it was also a psychological move, letting them see how deep they were in the situation, see the many faces of those that hurled threats and abuse in their direction. *What do we have to do to get a chance?* Philippe wished he could be back in Damian's camp, where they had a fighting chance, even with the spells. Damian had a weak hand over his men, using tricks and bribery to get people to do what he wanted. With Fayanna, there was no questioning it—she had control. Her men didn't whisper their disapproval or question her actions. Her word as a Hunter was law and was followed to a T. Philippe watched as she quickly dismounted from her sleek black horse, pausing to give it a small sugar cube before passing it off to someone else and striding to the front of the line.

So, she has a soft spot for something in her life.

"Hands," a guard ordered, and Philippe turned, surprised at the harshness in the elf's voice. "Hands," he snapped again. Philippe put his hands up, and the guard started haphazardly slicing through the ropes binding Philippe's wrists, nicking his skin.

Why must you rush everything? Philippe pressed a hand over the cut. He clenched his jaw against the stinging pain as blood seeped between his fingers, staining them a bright red. He lifted his hand away and sure enough, the guard not only nicked his wrist but left him with a cut around an inch long. Much to his relief, the cut didn't look deep. He twisted his hand. *No veins and no muscles.*

The horses around them flicked their ears back and forth, and their nostrils flared "Can I get something to wrap this up? Is Galen around?" The guard turned to him, eyes narrowed like Philippe had threatened him. "So I don't spook the horses. They don't seem to like the smell of blood," he said, gesturing to the horse closest to them, whose eyes were wide, the whites clearly visible.

The Dark One stepped close, waving the knife with a smear of Philippe's blood on the blade near his throat. "You don't think our horses have been trained to be used to the smell of blood?"

Philippe stood a bit taller, putting another inch between him and the blade. "I am sure you have trained them well, but this horse doesn't seem happy."

"Just give him a bandage. Not everything needs to be an argument, soldier." Fayanna stepped in. "And cut the drama. It isn't helping anything."

Philippe nodded his thanks, kicking a bit of sand over where he thought the blood had dropped, hoping to mask the scent for the horses. He stepped carefully away from the closest horses, pressing his opposite hand over the cut to try to staunch the bleeding, but by the time Galen arrived, his hand was stained red and there were a few drops in the sand at his feet.

Galen made quick work of wiping clean Philippe's fingers and wrapping gauze thickly around his hand. "Try to call me earlier than you think if you need these replaced. It will be harder for me to come see you there," the elf said.

"I—Okay, I will," Philippe said, watching the elf disappear into the rows of Dark Ones. *Does he want to help us? Did he mean more than he said?*

"Are you two finally ready?" Fayanna said, pulling the two of them away from the guards, her thin fingers digging into Philippe's elbow. "You two had better be on your best behavior," she hissed. The Hunter looked like she wanted to add something, a sneer paining her lips, but something made her stop. Fayanna guided them up the rough path to the fortress. Philippe's tired legs felt like lead as he struggled to climb the hill, the sand shifting and sliding beneath his feet. Fayanna kept an iron grip on their elbows even as the sands shifted, her steps stuttering as she slipped on a loose stone that went skittering down the hill. Her nails dug into his arm, and she yanked viciously at his shoulder. "Watch it."

This whole thing would be easier if you let us walk on our own, Philippe thought as he stumbled slightly. "Sorry, I slipped," he muttered once he regained his balance.

Philippe pulled his eyes away from the looming entrance when he heard Shauna mutter, "Goddess, help me," under her breath as she lost her footing for a moment. She stumbled and twisted, trying to catch herself. Fayanna yelled as Shauna fell to her knees, pulling the Hunter down with her. Philippe grit his teeth when the Hunter's nails dug into his arm as she tried to hold on. The Hunter was back on her feet a moment later, leg raised to lash out at Shauna. "What are you doing?"

"Wait, she didn't mean to fall." Philippe clambered to stand in front of Shauna. He put a hand out in peace and slowly lowered the other, helping Shauna to her feet. He tensed a moment before her hand touched his, ready for the spark they felt back in the recruitment camp. *It's okay, just move slowly*, he said, hoping Fayanna couldn't tell.

Once on her feet, Shauna quickly broke the contact and backed away from both of them, hands up. "I'm sorry, I slipped. I didn't mean to. You were still holding my arm when I fell," she repeated. "I will be more careful, I will." Shauna said quietly, trying to calm the woman.

"You better," the woman snapped and grabbed Shauna's shirt, tugging her along. She glanced at Philippe. "Come on. And stay on your feet."

Philippe clenched his fists. He wanted nothing more than to knock this woman out and run. He watched helplessly as she dug her nails into Shauna's skin, knowing they would have matching half-moon bruises on their arms. Shauna winced but didn't move to pull away or fight the woman. *What is going to happen when we get inside?* His stomach turned again. *She did her job. She got us here in one piece, now she can be as cruel as she wants*, Philippe thought, wishing he could do more.

Fayanna stopped, scanning for something or *someone* in the distance. The Hunter gestured to one of her guards, who raced up the hill to answer the call.

Philippe shifted uncomfortably as they waited. He glanced from the doors to Shauna. *What are you thinking?* he wanted to ask but didn't dare let the question float to her. *What will they do there?* Philippe, struck by a thought, turned. "Hunter Fayanna, may I ask you a question?"

She glared at him but nodded. "You just did, but I will allow another."

He glanced at Shauna, weighing the question before asking. It was better to know than not. "As you know, we were previously captured by Damian. I am afraid he was not the best teacher of your ways."

"That wasn't a question. Out with it," she said, crossing her arm in annoyance.

"Yes, ma'am. You see, we know that this is the heart of the Dark One stronghold, but we are unaware of who Lord—or is it General? Nurzan is. You have mentioned the name a few times, but no one has told us who he exactly is. I have gathered he is of a higher rank than you. Could you enlighten us before we go in? We wouldn't want to do anything that would bring shame on you or your legion." He glanced at Shauna, but her face was locked, eyes wide like she had seen a ghost. He spun, trying to figure out what it was that would scare her like that.

Fayanna quickly moved an arm across her chest in salute.

"I am Lord Nurzan," a low, silky voice said.

Philippe turned, trying to conceal the look of surprise from his face. The elf was dressed head to toe in black, the cloak fastened at his throat with silver chains that glowed in the moonlight.

"My lord, these are the two Frituals, brought to you as ordered."

The guards shoved Philippe and Shauna forward. Philippe tugged himself free of the guards' grasp, standing tall in front of this leader of the Dark Ones. Shauna stumbled, and on instinct, Philippe moved to help her, but she waved him away even as the guards reached for him again.

"Wait," Nurzan said quietly, and the guards stepped back without a word.

Shauna kept her head bowed for a moment. Lord Nurzan watched Shauna, observing her every movement as she ducked her head and slowly got to her feet. There was a sort of fascination in the way he watched her. Like he couldn't believe she was actually in front of him. A glee in the way his eyes crinkled at the corners that made Philippe's stomach flip. *How long has he been looking for us?*

The Dark One stepped away from his own line of guards and offered Shauna a hand up. "Are you alright?"

Shauna stared at the elf, and Philippe couldn't quite place the emotions that played across her face. When she answered, her voice was restrained, like she was unsure whether to speak. She glanced at Fayanna but then something, the new, stronger version of her, took over. "I—Yes, I am alright. I will be okay."

"You are very different," Nurzan said.

"Different, lord?" Shauna asked and again glanced at Fayanna to see if this was the correct move, but the Hunter did not give any indication. Philippe watched the high elf, waiting to see if there was some other honorific Shauna should have given him.

Nurzan nodded, circling her like a predator

deciding if the prey was worth the hunt. "From your sister. I expected a lot more fight from you."

"Tay—my sister?" Her eyes go wide with fear before hardening. She stared the elf down, and the sight sent a thrill of pride and fear through Philippe. Her cheeks were flushed with anger. "What have you done to my sister? Where is she?" Her voice cracked, and she clenched her fists at her sides but didn't break eye contact. She stepped up to the elf, ignoring the flurry of movement from the guards around him and twisting away from those that pulled her back. The lord waved a hand, and the guards fell back into line, hands hovering just above their weapons.

"Ah, there it is," the elf says. "You *do* have some fight in you. I thought you might. You would have to in order to make it this far." He turned and strode back to the fortress. "Don't worry, little Fritual. You and I will have plenty of time to talk about what has happened to your sister."

Shauna blanched, her facade cracking as she glanced at Philippe.

"Hunter."

Fayanna stood even straighter. "Yes, my lord?"

"Take these two to the Monk's cell then meet me in my chambers. I want to discuss our next move." The lord of the Dark Ones stepped back through the gate, his men falling behind him in a wave of oily black cloaks.

Chapter 25 Shauna

Shauna watched General Nurzan turn his back on them without another thought and walk into the fortress. The second his cloak was out of sight, the guards swarmed around them. They yanked her away from Philippe and threw her to the ground. Shauna coughed and shook her head, trying to clear the mouthful of sand from her lungs and out of her face.

A spear butt thudded between her shoulder blades, and she spluttered, trying to get air into her lungs. She was hauled to her feet, her face inches from a guard. He yanked her head back by her short hair, forcing Shauna to look him in the eye. "Don't you ever insult the general by making a stand like that again," he spat, he pushed her toward the fortress and another guard caught her arm in a viselike grip. Shauna glanced over at Fayanna. She hadn't moved, her face an emotionless mask. She looked the two of them over, then spun on her heels, leaving the Frituals. Her job was done.

Shauna knew a bruise would bloom on her wrist shortly. The pain was welcome, though, grounding her in the moment. Pulling her thoughts away from where they could easily spiral. She took one deep breath, then another, feeling as though she had been punched in the gut a thousand times. *Breathe. Focus. Look around. What do you see? What do you hear?* She tried to stay in the present. She felt tiny scratches on her face from the sand. *Taytra. He knows Taytra.* The gates were two heavy doors several inches thick and inlaid with what looked like bits of iron. Three men on each side waited to close the doors. The moment they crossed the threshold, as if a silent command went through the air, the six soldiers heaved the heavy doors shut behind them. The lock sliding into place was a punch to her gut.

Escape will not be easy if at all possible. Here there were walls to scale, a gate to break down, and guards everywhere she looked. It was not rough ropes, or a stake in the center. It was not fabric tents Lyra could blow away in the wind. Shauna felt crazed, her eyes darting everywhere as she took in the danger all around her. She felt like an anvil was on her chest. *Breathe,* she reminded herself. *They are taking you to a cell. Who knows when you will be out again. Pay attention.* The courtyard they were led into had targets and barrels lining the walls. A few elves hung about at the lower level, lounging and talking. They turned, falling silent when they passed. She glanced away and saw a room that must be an armory, filled with weapons, armor, and piles of black uniforms. The guards pulled them down a passage lined with torches, the yellow flames flickering and popping. Her ragged breath echoed off the walls.

The head of the Dark Ones knows my sister. He knows she is a fighter. Fayanna had said that she had started a rebellion. Led a coup. But not before she had been beaten. What did that mean? Was she still alive? They would have said if she were dead. If she were dead, they would have used it as a tool to bring me down. The knot in her throat tightened. *You have to be prepared for them to tell you she is dead.*

Philippe stepped closer as they went down a hallway, the skin of his arm brushing her's. A moment of connection. *Are you okay?* he asked before stepping away. He kept his eyes on the guards' backs.

Shauna shook her head, trying to move the greasy bangs out of her face. She didn't know if she was okay, but she couldn't allow them to think she wasn't. She was a shattered piece of glass held together by the frame alone. Shauna bumped into him. *I will be.* She couldn't say that she was okay now. She didn't think she was. He stared at her out of the corner of his eye, his overgrown brown hair curling around his temples, then he nodded.

The guard led them up a staircase to a room at the end of the hall, the door creaking open on squeaky hinges. He walked around the room and touched the torch in his hand to the two on either side of the room, casting dark shadows over the windowless area. "In now," the guard said firmly once he moved back into the hall. Philippe stepped in first, then Shauna. This room was like the room in the first fortress, with a small bed, but this one also had a small crate peppered with bits of wax and the remnants of a quill and a dried-out pot of ink.

"Remember, we will still know," he said, pointing at the band of black Magick on their wrists. "Do not use any Magick." The lock slid into place with an echo of finality. She listened as they walked down the hall, leaving them alone. "Make sure someone goes and checks in on their Magick blocks later. Last thing we need is for that spell to break."

Shauna didn't move until she knew they had actually left. She moved to the door and peered down the hall. No one was outside.

She whirled around when the thin bed screeched in protest as Philippe tried to sit. The noise sent her heart skittering. "Oops," he said, lowering himself down slowly. He gave her a half smile. "Sorry, I didn't mean to scare you."

A laugh bubbled up from her stomach, the sound sharp, different from her normal laugh. It surprised her, which made her laugh harder. "Of all the things to be scared of right now," She gasped, trying to catch her breath between fits of laughter.

Philippe's eyes were wide as he pulled her down to sit on the bed next to him. "Hey, hey, it's okay." He smoothed her hair back from my forehead, trying to tuck it behind her ear. "We will be okay."

Shauna shook her head and tasted salty tears on her lips. *Am I laughing or crying?*

"We are going to be okay," he repeated, running a thumb over the back of her hand.

We are going to be okay. The words echoed in her mind. Shauna had been telling herself that for days. As the sun baked her skin, she had tried to think of a way to escape where there wasn't one. "Yeah?" She snapped, pulling her hand away to wipe at the tears streaming down her face. She looked up at the ceiling, blinking hard to clear the tears. "And how do you know? We are currently being held captive in the center of the Dark Ones stronghold, down the hall from the commander. Who *knows* my sister. How do you know we are going to be okay?"

He opened and closed his mouth several times, deflating a bit. She hated it, She hated that she did that, but while she didn't know what it was she needed right now, she didn't need fake platitudes.

"I—I don't know. It felt like the right thing to do?"

Shauna sighed and leaned forward, scrubbing at her face. "I don't know what the right thing to say is. I don't know what the right thing to do is. I just—I don't know." Her voice cracked, and she took a few deep breaths, trying to stop the floodgate of tears from bursting.

Philippe paced the room for a few minutes. Part of her wanted to yell at him to stop and save his energy, but she wanted to run laps. She felt like her emotions were lightning, zipping under my skin. "How long do you think it is going to take us to get out of here?" he asked. The question echoed in her mind, reverberating in all the corners that were filled with fear and dread.

Her eyes locked on the makeshift desk in the corner covered in small lumps of wax.

Take them to the monk's cell, Nurzan had said. *How did the monk leave? Monks don't fight.*

She dug at the dirt under her fingernail. "Probably a long time." She looked up at him, "I mean, look at that box. That buildup didn't happen all at once."

Philippe bent and pulled off a large chunk, rotating it between his fingers. He carefully pinched out the little splinters stuck in the wax.

Shauna watched him for a few minutes. Her brain felt full, buzzing with thoughts and also nothing, unable to focus on any true feeling. "What do you think they are going to do with us?"

He shook his head. "I'm not really sure. I am definitely concerned based on the questions Fayanna asked. Targeting the points where we had to defend ourselves. We *had* to defend ourselves."

"She was so upset when I talked about that. I tried to make sure my words were what she wanted." She ran a hand through her greasy hair, then shook out her fingers, trying to shake of the feeling of the residue that clung there. "It's crazy that people like the Dark Ones are going to try to hold us accountable for defending ourselves against them."

"See, that right there is going to be the issue. They don't see it that way. They have their own system of law. They are allowed to get away with things like that because it is *their* law. What they do is acceptable in their mind because they are following their system, not ours. But they aren't going to take the time to explain what it is to us. We should just know." He dropped the small ball of wax to the floor, and she watched as it bounced out of sight into one of the dark corners of the room where the torch light didn't reach. "We need to be careful what we say and do." He ran a hand over the unkempt beard he had had started to grow. "I don't know which of us is in the worst boat, because I was in their 'camp' for a while. You have always been their enemy." He sighed. "I don't know which is a bigger betrayal of their rule system."

She nodded. "And I don't know if honesty is the best course of action, or if I should hide what I say and protect myself." She stared hard at the floor. "Part of me thinks they will, I don't know, appreciate the honesty and bluntness? Or they will hurt me. Either way, I don't want to deal with the consequences." The silence stretched between them for a while. There wasn't anything they could do. They were trapped. Waiting. She glanced at Philippe. He stared into the corner, his eyes unfocused, his fingers dancing over the frayed cuff of his shirt.

Shauna looked at the door and took a deep breath. "This is going to sound crazy."

He moved, sitting on the bed beside her. "Go for it, nothing can be too crazy right now." He wraps his arm around her, and she leaned into him, savoring the warmth, the comfort in feeling his solid frame around her.

"I almost feel safer here, more than I did on the road. Like, yeah, there is probably a guard on the door, but we are locked in a room. No one can touch us, and we are together." She looked up at him, searching for the boy she used to know. The snarky boy she loved who always got into trouble.

He nodded. "No, I feel that too. Like a twisted sense of relief. We have one less thing to be on guard about, at least for the time being."

The silence that fell between them felt more comforting this time. It was just the two of them. There were a million things she could say at the moment, about what they could do to get out, about what they *were,* but it felt better to just stay quiet.

"How long do you think it will be before that Nurzan guy pulls us in for questioning?" he asked, pressing a kiss to the top of her head.

Slowly she pulled away from him and moved back to the door, peering out the small window into the hall. She pressed a finger to her lips. They couldn't let them hear what they had to say. It didn't surprise her to see not one but three guards standing outside. Two were further up the hall, talking in hushed voices. She turned back to

Philippe. "I would assume it won't take long. So we should probably take some time to get our stories straight. We can't let them use anything against us," She said, thinking of her father and Taytra and wondering yet again what this elf did to them. She took his hand *Let's see?* They both looked down at their hands, but they marks didn't appear. *Okay, what should we say?*

Chapter 26 Taytra

The dawn bell had yet to ring, and sleep still hung heavy in everyone's eyes, Taytra's own eyes felt puffy and raw from crying, but tired as she was, Taytra hadn't felt so awake in weeks. She was ready. She bounced her leg, the heel of her boot clicking incessantly on the floor.

Beside her, Ward slipped a hand to her thigh, stilling the movement. "Relax. We will get started soon," he whispered, nudging the tray of breakfast food toward her again.

"I can't eat yet. It's too early."

"You say that now, but if Serena got us in for the meeting, we might not get to eat again until the dinner bell. Eat," he said sagely. "'Cause I for one don't want to listen to your stomach howling for food later." He handed her a biscuit.

"My stomach is not that loud." She grouched, making a point to aggressively bite down on the roll in his direction.

"How are you feeling today, Tay?" Lyra asked, sitting across from her.

"Better. Ready," Taytra replied around a mouthful of food. "I was shocked and scared last night. I still am, but now I am ready. Once we figure out a plan, we will be ready to take out Nurzan." She didn't mention the nightmares that woke her all night, or how she had cried until she had no more tears, but Lyra nodded, no doubt seeing the way Taytra's skin was raw around her eyes without needing it to be said.

"I don't know if it will be that simple," the elf replied carefully.

Taytra laughed. "Don't worry. I know it won't be easy. Nothing ever is. But we can pretend that it will be, right?" She pulled out a pencil and bit of parchment, ready to take notes on their plans.

When everyone was settled round the table, Andrew called everyone to order. "Okay, we need to keep this brief and to the point. Serena was going to try to get us in on the council meetings list first thing this morning so we need something concrete to present. What do we have?"

Paulo raised a hand. "According to the reports, we have been able to confirm Shauna and Philippe have been in Dark One hands for at least a week, possibly a bit more. They should be moving in on Bulandon in the next day or so. Which means any attempt we make will have to be made directly on the fortress."

"Right. By the time we get there, they will be in the fortress, more than likely Father will put them on one of the tower cells. They are harder to access and thus easier to guard. I estimate three to four Hunters will be in the vicinity, but they won't be the primary guard. They are more mobile that way."

Taytra knew they would be guarded, but the idea of the Dark Ones having an elite force was something she hadn't considered.

Ward raised a hand to interject before Taytra could ask. "Hunters, Barin?"

Barin coughed. "Yes sorry, the Hunters are Father's elite group of soldiers. They receive the highest level of training. Father tried to get me in, but I failed too many of the standards. They run his dirty work when he needs a job done and can't trust others to do it. Think like personal mercenaries who also hold rank over the military units. I may not have passed their tests but I know what their training was. And I know how to get us in and can anticipate some of their plans. However, I am sure they know I am with you by now," Baron added. "The entire fortress will be at the ready."

"I take it Damian was not a Hunter?" Taytra asked, looking up from the list of notes. "If he was, I would say we would be in pretty good shape to take them down."

"No," Barin said, "Damian, was nothing more than a weasel. He managed to get that job over some of the Hunters because he went in with wits before force. Though I have gathered, whatever wits he thought he had diminished since he was in our force, but then it was not under my father's hand."

"So," Ward said, pushing the conversation forward. "Is it better to go at it with a small task force to get in and out, or a full force?"

The elf leaned back, pondering that for a moment, drawing figures in the air with the tip of his finger like he was tracing the surface of a map. "Either case has its ups and downs, but unless my mother is ready for all-out war, I think a smaller force would be better."

Taytra nodded quickly, finishing the note. "A small task force will be easier to supply. But that leaves the question of who should be on it. Obviously the three of you have earned your right, but I wouldn't stop you if you wanted to stay here in Hollens. You are valuable people with a bounty on your head," she said to the three elves. "I for one really want to go—I *need* to go—but I am not sure what the best course of action is. The three of us—" She turned to Ward and Andrew. "—helped all those people leave Cabineral when they never thought they would. It doesn't feel right to just leave them behind, but we can't take them to the fortress."

Ward and Andrew shared a look. "Remember you have a bounty on you too, Tay. We talked about this separately last night after you fell asleep. We wanted to make sure we made the best decision that we could," Ward said.

Paulo put up a hand "I want it to be known that I would love to travel with any of you, but you have committed yourself to these people. Unless you have someone you would trust to make sure they are safe without you. You would have Serena, but she doesn't have a lot of free time."

Andrew nodded and turned in his chair to face her. "Tay, you need to go. From day one, you built this rebellion to save people but your intention has always been to save your sister. You said it yourself, time and time again. And I am sure our people would understand," he said, putting a hand on her shoulder. "You are such a fighter. Shauna will need that." He turned to Ward. "We went through the same training, and you are the better strategist, from what Barin has told me. They will need that in the fight ahead. I will be staying. I have developed a good relationship with most of the people here. They will listen to me." He looked down. "I would also like to stay in case there is a chance that Safiya can escape. I am sure word has gotten out that we are here. I would just hope she could get here too."

"Are you sure?" Taytra asked. "We don't know how long it will take. I agree you have gotten to know more people, but is that enough?"

He gave her a small but resolute grin, "I am sure, Tay. I want to stay. I will deal with the council and make sure things go smoothly while the rest of you go kick some ass. Show you aren't to be messed with, that they didn't break you. Gotta use some of that training."

She grinned and grabbed his hand. "Yes, I do." Her eyes swam for a moment. "If Saf or Jacinta make it, please tell them I love and miss them." He nodded, and she turned to the rest of the group. "Right, then. It will be the two of us. Are all three of you coming?"

"It may not be a good idea at first," Paulo agreed, "but we need to get all five Frituals together as soon as we can."

Barin pulled out a rough sketch of the fortress and walked them through the different parts of the heart of Dark One power. "I can redraw this if you want. I just made one for today." They pelted him with questions from when the shipments would be and how many guards would be on each watch, to known weak points or areas that were often overlooked.

Taytra drained the last of her coffee, scribbling in the margins of her page as Barin said, "I don't know how many Hunters will be at the base. It changes day to day depending on what they are assigned to do. I am sure a

Hunter has Shauna and Philippe now. And like I said earlier, I am sure there are at least three to four guards on their cell. We may be able to use you, Taytra, since I have heard you look very similar to your sister?"

"Yes. We used that trick in the past, though it didn't really work very long," Taytra agreed. "It was clear pretty quickly that I wasn't Shauna and they didn't really care. They were throwing anyone they could into their cells."

A knock on the door startled everyone and they turned toward the door. "Come in," Lyra called.

A man poked a head in the door. "I am sorry to interrupt. I was sent by the Council and the Guardian. She said that you should come as soon as you could or at least before the lunch bell."

The group glanced around. "Thank you," Paulo said. "If you can, please let the Council know that we shall be there very soon. We are just about wrapped up here."

They waited until the man had left before continuing. Barin cleared his throat. "Um, so as I was saying, I don't know how visible I can be during this raid. Everyone there—unless they are a new recruit—will recognize me. And I am sure they have some sort of special reward if someone captures me."

"I agree. I think I will be in the same boat since Shauna and I look so similar, but we can solidify the plan as we go over the next few days," Taytra said. "Let's get ready to head to this meeting. I am sure it is going to be a wild time—like every one of them have been so far."

Chapter 27 Taytra

Taytra shuffled her pile of papers, ready to start this meeting with the Council. Ward sat by her side, and Andrew, having given her his seat at the table, stood at her shoulder, ready to jump in when needed.

Serena nodded to her when they were settled and mouthed, *You ready?*

Taytra nodded. She wanted to launch into these negotiations. Serena looked beautiful today in a deep olive green dress. She sat tall in her chair and shared a nod and a smile with Taytra as if to say, *This is good. You will figure out a way through this.* Taytra reread the note Serena had slipped them before they had entered. *If this goes south, I have another plan. Fear not friends, we will get what you need.* Taytra tried to repeat that notion to herself, knowing it may go south was inevitable, but the fact that Serena already had a plan to counter that should make her feel better. But she was still nervous about it all going south.

"So, what did you desperately need an appointment for this morning?" the councilman on the far end of the table asked.

Taytra nodded in his direction and waited until everyone was settled. She shuffled her notes to the right page and turned, looking each of the council members in the eyes, forcing them to acknowledge her before starting. "Well, Master Faiose," Taytra said, barely holding back a grin when the man jumped as his name was said. She had Serena to thank for the list of names and descriptions, since these men felt they were above naming themselves. "As you may already be aware, we have received news that cannot be ignored. This news has been corroborated by three separate scouts. Shauna Flynn and Philippe Mattick have been captured and are being moved to the Dark Ones' fortress outside of Bulandon as we speak. They may already be there." She scanned the faces again and focused on one who sat, stirring his coffee and ignoring her gaze. "Master Faiose, I cannot express how deeply this is an issue. I speak to you as someone who has faced the Dark Ones head on before. Their control is tyrannical. They do everything they can to eliminate the sort of peace you have created here in Hollens." She took a deep steadying breath, willing her voice to remain strong. "I also speak to you as someone who loves one of those who have been captured. I will not lie to you and say that this does not make me biased."

"What is your point child?" one man asked, his voice tinged with exasperation.

"My sister has been captured. I am asking if you are ready to accept what is staring you directly in the face, if you would finally acknowledge that there is a war at your door. And to ask, what are you going to do with this information?"

An older man in the corner stood shakily to his

feet. His skin looked waxy, like age dripped from him. "You are young and easily excitable as all young women are. You have to trust that your elders are handling things accordingly."

Taytra opened her mouth, but Ward leaned forward, jumping in first. They knew this would come up. The council had walked right into their next move. "Have you spoken to *your* elders about this, sir?" His voice, like Taytra's, was firm. It left no room for error.

"My elders?" Master Wakemen asked, clearly confused by the question. He did in fact appear to be the most senior of the room.

"Yes, sir. Have you asked your elders?" Ward proffered a hand to the four senior patrons of the room. "For I am under the impression there are some in this room who do not agree with those whom are your elder. Who have seen more than you."

The men glanced around the room as if still confused.

"Are you that closed off from the outside world?" Andrew asked with a tone tinged with pity. "Do you not realize how young you are?"

"Excuse me, we are your elders!" another man snapped.

"That may be the case for my friends who are leading the rebel sect of Cabineral," Serena said quietly, her voice soft as silk, hiding any edges. "However, for myself and the Frituals beside me, that is not the case." The men looked down in recognition. "To answer your question, I don't believe they have. They have not asked advice of me, and I don't believe they have either Paulo or Lyra, is that correct?" The two elves nodded.

"Right. So, how about you take a second and listen

to what we have to say. For we have experience and wisdom on our side," Taytra said. She did her best to keep her voice even, knowing if she did show any emotions that would appear "excitable", they wouldn't take her seriously. "Several of us will be leaving in the next few days. We want to make sure we leave our people in good hands. The enemy is at your—*our* door. But we will go willingly into that danger."

"You are leaving? Who gave you permission for that?" Councilman Kasser asked.

"I am sorry. I didn't think we needed your permission to leave," Ward said, taken aback.

"Of course, you do. You reside within our walls now."

"Okay, Father. I am sorry, I didn't know I was still living under a curfew," Barin muttered. "Oh, wait. I am old enough to be your great-great grandfather." This received several glares from the council and a grin from everyone on his side of the table.

"Everyone in our city is under a curfew. That was made very clear to you when you arrived," Councilman Faiose said. "I personally made sure the rules were taught."

"With all due respect, sir," Taytra said, "just two weeks ago, you wanted to give my people barely enough food to cover one meal a day and told them they couldn't work. That doesn't seem like a compassionate leader who wants us to stay. For most of the people who followed me through the gates, this is not a permanent home. This is a temporary period until we can return to Cabineral. Would you stop those people leaving now if they wanted to return home?"

"Well, no, but you see—"

"Then why would you stop us?"

"Do not interrupt a councilman," Councilman Wakeman roared. "You are aware of the rules." He gestured wildly at the parchment on the wall.

"Sir, your rules are trivial and are why you get nothing done," Paulo said. "I used to be a part of several groups in Gradatia to help make sure the harvest season always ran smoothly, over the course of thirty or so years. These meetings? Are the most unproductive meetings I have ever sat on." Paulo's words hung in the air like a hammer. "Now, will you please be frank with us? We are trying to have a conversation with you. The least you could do is be clear."

The Council erupted, speaking over one another in a way that highlighted Paulo's comment.

"There is no war at our door. They will leave as soon as you do."

"There is a bounty on their head. Let them leave."

"It is a suicide mission."

Taytra stood, silencing the room. "You mean to tell me you had the information and were just going to keep it secret rather than acknowledge something needed to be done about it? And to look in the face that it could be dangerous?" She sat down slowly. "I am afraid for my sister but I am just as afraid of what will happen when—not if—when we leave. There is a host of soldiers at your door just waiting for a command to attack. Does that not strike you as something you should pay attention to?"

"Your men don't seem ready to fight a war," Barin added. "I grew up around soldiers. Your men are soft."

"You shouldn't be leaking information to them!" one man says, pointing an accusatory finger at Serena.

"I am sure you won't believe us, but we have our own sources," Andrew piped up. "Serena comes in to fill in the cracks. But she has withheld a lot. She only answers the questions we directly ask. Many of which we already have some background on."

Serena nodded. "I swore your oath when you brought me in. I have not gone out of my way to break it," she said coolly. "Now I think I will point you to article 4 of your code. I believe that pertains to Hollen's stance of neutrality when war is at your door. Some of you may need to revisit that text."

To Taytra's immense pleasure, not one but two of the councilmen quickly started flipping through their copies of the code to find the text Serena mentioned.

Master Wakeman threw his hands in the air. "We can't just go fighting the Dark Ones willy-nilly. This fight is of the elves. Not humans."

Taytra couldn't help it. She dropped her head into her hands and sighed loudly. "Excuse me, but that is not an appropriate response. Let me just send a message to the battalion at your gate. I am sure they will understand and leave. Since this must just be a miscommunication." She glared up at them. "Or do you want me to leave and take the host with me? Oh, wait, didn't you just say you don't want me to leave?" She grinned wickedly at the looks of confusion as they tried to follow their own stream of logic. "Doesn't really make much sense, does it?"

Paulo took over from there, putting into words what Taytra wanted to say in a much more delicate manner. "We are currently facing an onslaught outside these walls I don't think the kingdoms have ever faced. Nearly all of the monarchies have been toppled. People are facing persecution based on their blood in a way we haven't seen in centuries. And the Frituals have returned," Paulo said, gesturing to the two other elves beside him. "Over the years it was believed that we, the Frituals, would resurface when the Magick was strong enough in the blood lines." He glanced at his fellow Frituals. "However, I think many would agree if we were to stay, the Goddess has chosen us to come now. I don't know why she chose the five of us. But I have to believe it was for a purpose. And that purpose was to stop the Dark Ones from taking over the cities. Shauna Flynn and Philippe Mattick are born of human parents. They may have some Elven blood; however, they are human. They are a clear point that this is not just a war for elves. These Dark Ones are targeting humans. They see humans as inferior and they know you are not prepared. If you do not act now, they will destroy your city." Paulo stabbed the table to emphasis his words. He scanned the face of the men. "We do not come to you to say this because we hate you, but rather because we see the weaknesses and want to help. We are asking what you will be doing if not to protect those that have come from Cabineral, then how will you protect your own people from the enemy at your door? It will be difficult for some of us to leave without knowing that we will be supported, and those of us who will remain can rely upon you for the things that may come up in the weeks to come. Winter is hard—war will make it harder."

The lunch bell peeled through the air, and the councilmen all stood. "Well, this has been a great conversation," they said, gathering their things to leave.

"What do you mean, this has been a good conversation? We have talked in circles for the last ten minutes."

"And that is all you will get. If you leave, you leave the care of your people to us. And know this—you will *not* be welcomed back," Master Wakeman said, leaving the room with a huff.

"We are not bloody children!" Taytra snapped, slamming a fist on the table. "We are trying to talk sense with you. To understand what you will do. How we can help you?"

One man, the youngest—Taytra thought his name may have been Harper—turned at the door. "For what it's worth, I think you are right. I will try to talk with them. They need some sense if we want to see spring again."

Serena stood at her place at the end of the table, staring after the men in disgust. She shook her head and sighed. "I am sorry. I feared that the conversation would go that way. You all did well on short notice." The group began to file out of the room, but Serena pulled Taytra aside. "When you go back to your rooms later, there will be a package for you, and one for Ward in his rooms. Try again tonight," she said, pressing a piece of parchment and two envelopes into Taytra's hands. "I will see you there."

Chapter 28 Taytra

The trousers and linen shirt Taytra preferred now lay in a heap on the bed, along with her belt and knives. Tonight she would need to take a leaf out of Serena's book and battle with wit. When Taytra was in Cabineral, she and Shauna would help each other tie the corsets of their dresses or do the buttons up the back when one's fingers wouldn't quite reach. Since leaving Cabineral, Taytra had taken to wearing more men's clothing. She preferred how much she could move, but also how easy it was. No buttons or ties up the back out of reach. The dress Serena had left was likewise easy. Where the dresses Taytra was used to had laces up her back, this was low cut. Not a single button in sight. Exposing her skin, every scar, and lingering bruises on her back. It made her feel both uncomfortable, but coupled with words in the note Serena had left her, powerful.

While you are here, you may as well enjoy Hollens. In the envelopes are two invitations to the Samhain festival tonight. I want you to take my extra tickets. You deserve to experience something nice, though it has been many years since I last saw it, from past experience, this is a beautiful ceremony.

I don't give this to you solely so you can have the night off, though. Use this chance to get close to the council. Show them your strength. Show them what you have been through. Sometimes a story won't take root until it is told in a different way. Tell them your story. You have earned each scar you have through your bravery and wit. Show them you are more than an "emotional young girl."

By the way, the bolero is one of my favorites. It doesn't fit me quite the same as it used to. Keep it.

Serena

Taytra read the note again as she looked herself over in the mirror on her door. The skirt of the dress was a deep navy and gathered at her waist. The bodice was peppered with bits of black metallic thread that glittered when she turned. The dress itself had a low-cut square neckline and long sleeves that would protect her from the cold. It was backless, the fabric falling from her shoulders in a deep V-shape that ended right at the small of her back, exposing every one of the lash marks and the yellow and green from bruising. The Bolero the half-elf had mentioned was gorgeous. It sat on Taytra's shoulders and flowed midway down her arms, constructed of a series of overlapping black leather scales, each of which had a smaller scale of metal within. It looked like Taytra herself had scales. Serena had even sent over an artisan to help her do her hair. After a painful hour of brushing and pinning, her hair was pulled back in a series of braids secured back with a few porcupine quills and a feather courtesy of Lyra.

She turned from the mirror and pulled up the front

of her dress, slipping her knife into her boot. *I won't go unprepared.* Though she reminded herself this was meant to be a battle of wits. There was a soft knock at the door, and she quickly readjusted the blade in her boot before standing. "Come in," Taytra called, letting her skirts fall into place.

The door swung open, and Taytra turned when Ward didn't step into the room. "Shit," Ward said upon seeing her, his eyes taking every inch of her in a way that made her cheeks flush.

Taytra grinned, stepped up to him, and tapped his chin, which he prompting him to snap it shut. "Ya' good there?"

"Uh, yeah? Yeah, I am. I'm good. Fine. Totally fine," he spluttered, stepping away from her and trying to regain a bit of his normally stoic composure. "I got you the cloak you asked for. I figured with what we will be doing the next few weeks black would be best?" he said with a question at the end, holding out the package.

Taytra eagerly ripped open the bag, letting the thick wool cloak fall free. She flung it around her shoulders, clasping it at her neck. "It's perfect. You look good too," she said of the dark brown vest and pants Serena had left for him.

"I never thought I would have someone else dress me besides my mother." He smiled, reaching out to shift the cloak so he could see beneath it. "Is that like an armored sweater?"

"You could call it that." She laughed, turning to look at her reflection in the small mirror one more time. The last time she had put this much effort into her appearance had been for Beltane in the spring, and she had never owned anything like this in her life.

"Are you sure you are ready for this? You are going to have to make nice with a lot of people."

"What, don't think I can play the act of the sweetheart?" She pouted, feigning innocence.

"No, I didn't say that. I just mean, you haven't been the nicest to some of the people you are going to have to speak with and you are probably going to have to spend a lot of time dancing with them."

She grinned wickedly. "Does that make you jealous?" she teased and lifted the last bit of her ensemble, which was a small mask, over her face. It was made of a piece of wood that would obstruct her face, giving all in attendance a bit of anonymity for a few hours.

"What, me? No, it doesn't make me jealous," he spluttered, slipping his own cherry wood mask over his face. "Why would it make me jealous?"

"Good." She pecked him on the cheek, their masks clacking together slightly. "Let's go."

Chapter 29 Ward

The library was lit up with what had to be at least a thousand candles. Each window held a single flickering flame and the doorway was filled with stacks of candles of all different heights. A thick black carpet peppered by drops of a rainbow of colored wax had been rolled out the door. A few people at the front of the line were collecting the invitations. "This sure is fancy," Ward said, leaning into Taytra so she would hear him over the babble of voices.

"I know. This isn't what I thought it would be like. It seems like it is just the upper class of the city. I wonder what our families would have done if we lived here," she said, looking down the street where people gathered in small bunches. "Are we late?" She looked over her shoulder, but no one else joined their line.

They moved up in the line, and Ward handed over the invitations. The women at the front of the line were a few librarians. Moira, the head librarian, stood at the end of the line. "I don't remember your names on the list," the woman who had their invites said.

"Oh, we were added last minute by Lady Serena

Nightcastle," Taytra said, reaching up to adjust her mask. "She said she was going to do it this morning, and gave us the invitations."

"Uh-huh," the woman said, pulling up the list again. "Ms. Senesac, do you remember any extra names being added to the list?"

Moira shuffled over. "Hmm? Extra names? I think there may have been a few." She held a large mug of tea and adjusted her glasses as she peered over the other woman's shoulder.

"I've got this," Taytra whispered to Ward, stepping forward. "Ms. Moira, how good to see you again. I didn't know you were going to be here tonight," Taytra said, slipping the mask from her face.

"Oh, Lady Taytra! You look amazing! And is this Andrew? Or is it Ward?" Moira quickly passed off her cup of tea and clasped Taytra's hands. "Is that a porcupine quill? And that feather! You must let me have it after to make a pen." The older woman spun Taytra around beaming, just as much as Ward was. "Oh, my dear, this is beautiful! You must put your mask back on! Have to keep on with the tradition," she said, helping Taytra slip the bit of ribbon back around her elaborate hairdo. "I never did anything like that when I was your age. You must teach me how!"

Ward smiled as he watched the two women bubble and gush over the dress Serena had gotten for her. *I want her to have a thousand more moments like this,* he thought as she did a little pirouette for the older woman, the skirt splaying out around her. "My name is Ward, ma'am," Ward said with a smile. He glanced over at Taytra. "I hope Tay hasn't said anything crazy about me if you already know me?"

Moira laughed. "Oh, no! She just requested that the two of you get added to the list of accepted patrons. I am sure if you work with her, you are a lovely person." She turned to the librarian who was still looking at Taytra and Ward with skepticism. "Yes, these two are definitely allowed to come in. Taytra is a wonderful girl."

Taytra beamed. "Thank you, Moira. Anything I should expect?" she asked, craning her head to see past the door.

"Oh, it is your first time! Right, of course. You're from Cabineral, you must do something different. Oh, how fun! I am glad you could be here for this. Definitely try the candied hazelnuts. They are amazing. And the cider, I heard it is a very sweet batch this year, just the way I like it. Just enjoy the night, the Goddess has blessed us with a beautiful time. As the library is the tallest building in the city, we are the closest to the stars."

Taytra nodded with every item the woman listed. "We will have to check out those candies. I hope you have a good night. Take some time to enjoy it yourself too," Taytra said, squeezing the woman's hand. "We will see you later!" she called as Ward began to guide her away.

She laced her arm through Ward's once they were through the doors. "See, I told you."

"You would have stayed there all night if I let you," he teased. "Have you talked with her often?" he asked, guiding her up the spiral staircase to the rooftop.

"Just the one time we had a really pleasant conversation before, you know, you found me passed out over a pile of books." She laughed. "Hopefully, that won't happen tonight."

"Well, keep those sweet-talking skills sharp. We

have some work to do." They followed the crowd of people through the many floors of the library to the top floor. Like the doorway below, there were candles scattered all around in glass jars or sitting atop mirrors that sent rays of light bouncing in every direction. They passed through the last door and climbed to the roof, the evening sky high above with a thousand starry pinpricks. In the center of the roof sat a large stone-lined firepit with a large stack of wood, ready to be lit for the bonfire. "Sort of ironic, isn't it?" Ward asked. "To have one of the biggest fires of the year over what could be arguably the most important building in the city." He looked out over the city, flicking torches far below tracing lines through the city.

The two made their way around the large stack of wood. There was a ring of bricks around the wood to contain it, but it almost didn't seem like it would be enough. Ward pictured the massive fire they had at Beltane that spring, the way it made the night look like and feel like a summer's day. "Well, they are prepared in case anything goes wrong," Taytra said, pointing to a series of buckets that line the rooftop. She spun and scanned the space and those around them. "So now that we are here, what do you think we should do?" The area was full of people dressed in elegant gowns and tunics, all in intricate masks.

"I think we should start with the food," he said, pointing toward the tables on the far side of the roof. Taytra shot him an exasperated look. "What? Everyone else has food. If we want to blend in, we should too! Besides, didn't your friend tell us to check out the candied chestnuts?"

"You just want to snack." She grinned, her soft gray eyes like bits of copper in the reflection of the candles.

He grinned, stopping himself before he tucked a lock of hair back behind her ear. "I can neither confirm nor deny the accusations brought forward," he hedged. *Even with the mask, she is the most beautiful woman here.*

The two are stopped by one librarian decked head to toe in brown. "Hello. I can take your cloaks, if you wish."

Ward quickly undid the clasp at his neck. "Thank you." He passed her the cloak. "Ward Hendricks." She nodded and wrote his name on a piece of parchment that she pinned to the fabric. Ward turned to Taytra, a hand out ready to help her when he saw she had frozen. Taytra stared hard at his cloak and the little bit of parchment pinned on the top. "Tay?" Ward whispered. "Do you want them to take your cloak?" He asked. "Just a moment," he said to the librarian and pulled Taytra a few steps away. When Taytra had told him about the dress he knew this may happen. But it was part of the plan. To show the council that they were strong enough to take care of the people of Cabineral, and to prove what they were willing to sacrifice to make it so. She stared at him, then looked to the librarian.

The woman holding the cloaks smiled at her, unaware of the turbulence in Taytra's mind. "Don't worry, miss. You can get your cloak at any time."

Ward reached over and gently squeezed her fingers. She shook her head, turning to look up at him, her eyes distant. "You can get the cloak back at any time," he echoed. "You have my word. You tell me you need it back, and I will get it for you that second."

Taytra nodded, and with hands that shook slightly, unclasped the cloak at her throat. "Right, you are right." Her voice cracked slightly. She passed the cloak to the woman. and cleared her throat. "Taytra Flynn." She sounded stronger, more sure of herself and her decisions. She rolled her shoulders back and took a deep breath. Ward couldn't help but smile at her resilience. "My name is Taytra Flynn."

"Thank you, ma'am. If you get cold at any time, feel free to come and find me," she said, giving a small bow and hurrying away to hang the cloaks.

Taytra stepped up to the wall and looked out over the city, a cool breeze blowing across the rooftop. Taytra shivered, rubbing her arms for a moment and readjusting the mask. Ward stepped up behind her, leaning into her ear. "I am very proud of you." He placed a soft hand on her hip, careful to only touch the fabric.

She smiled, looking over her shoulder at him, her dark lashes brushing her mask. "Thanks."

He glanced down at her back at the yellow and green bruising and the edge of the scar from her cut to her side. Every ounce of her resilience was on display, not a wound but a badge of honor. That showed just how deeply she cared for those she wanted to protect. "Now, let's get a drink and show these men why you shouldn't question what a Flynn says."

Chapter 30 Taytra

Taytra stood by the wall, shivering as the wind blew through the streets and up to the rooftop party. It was a larger gathering than she and Ward had expected, but that was good, wasn't it? It meant more people would know their story.

"Have you heard about the people by the gate?" one woman in a wine-colored dress said as she passed Taytra.

The other woman gasped. "Yes! Can you believe what has happened to them? They must have been so crazy to think that leaving their home would help. They should have just done what we have and stayed put. Leaving never has helped anyone."

She opened her mouth to say something when Ward laid a hand on her arm. "Just wait. There will be plenty more like those two tonight. Don't burn yourself out talking to people who can't help us yet."

She watched the two women join their dates. "Yes, but they seem like the perfect type of gossip we need to get this ball rolling," she said, crossing her arms, the tight skin on her back flexing as she did so. She couldn't help but be acutely aware of the way it felt and moved. The skin was still a putrid range of yellows and greens, even a month on. *This will show them*, she wanted to snap. *I am no weakling, no tiny child that needs to be cared for.*

"Taytra, Ward, the two of you look wonderful. I am so glad you got the packages and they fit well," Serena said. She was in a dark green gown with little flower details around the sleeves. Her long black hair hung free, shining in the torchlight. She wore a silver mask that hugged the delicate features of her face. "And that color! Taytra, I know you prefer reds, but you look great in blues."

"How did you get us in so soon?" Ward asked. "It didn't seem like they normally allow late entries like that."

"Oh, Moira and I go way back. You wouldn't believe the trouble we got into when she was just a page here at the library. But now she is the director and can get away with it." Serena grinned. She turned back to the rooftop party. "Now, since the two of you haven't been here before, let me explain how the night will work," she said, slipping between the couple and guiding them to the eastern side of the wall where the full moon hung low in the sky. "When the moon reaches its peak, the fires will be lit. You see those?" She pointed to a series of small firepits around the edge of the roof near the water buckets Taytra had pointed out earlier. "As the night goes on, those will be lit to mark the time." As she said this, one of the librarians carried a torch high above her head.

The young woman walked a full lap of the roof, holding the torch high. "For the Goddess, who in her goodness, blesses us tonight," she called out three times before stopping at one of the pits and placing the torch in the center of the small pyre.

"Once all the outside pyres are lit, the last and largest in the center will be lit," Serena continued. "Now that the first has been lit, the festivities can begin." She pointed to the stairs where, as if on cue, a few musicians came through with their instruments. "On the table next to the food is your dance card. It is by appearance as we are meant to be discreet. You are 'the armored one,'" Serena said, fiddling with one of the scales on Taytra's shoulder. "The council will be arriving throughout the night. We will all be wearing silver masks. They should each have a date, but I am sure a pretty little thing like you can get a dance." She leaned in. "You have my full permission to smack any of them should they make any moves you find to be too forward," she said tightly. "I did speak with a few of the wives. They are just as displeased with the progress that is being made as you are. They said they would do what they could to assist." Serena waved at a woman who walked by, copper cuffs on her wrists. "Look out for those cuffs. Those are the wives. They know what you look like and will help how they can."

Taytra nodded. "Wow, okay."

"You've got this," Serena said, stepping away.

Ward caught her arm before she could leave. "Wait, Serena, what am I supposed to do?"

"Keep the focus on Taytra. She is the representative of the Frituals, for her sister. Keep the focus on her," Serena said.

Ward crossed his arms, grumbling, "I thought we would have more of a plan than that."

"You and me both," Taytra said, reaching up to touch one of the quills stuck through her hair. "Well, how about a dance?" she asked as the musicians began the first

232

song. "This may be our only chance."

Ward gave a bow. "I think it is the man who is meant to ask for a dance."

She crossed her arms. "Are you going to deny me?"

He pulled her close, and she could feel his heart pounding through the linen of his shirt.

Not so cool under pressure after all, she thought.

"On the contrary. I am going to insist on the first two dances." He laughed.

They danced clumsily at first, struggling to find the beat to which those around them danced. But it worked almost in their favor. Taytra could feel many eyes on the pair. "You know, I still thought it was going to be you that asked me for a dance at Beltane, not Andrew," Taytra said as she spun away from him.

He caught her hand and spun her back into his chest, her hand coming to rest on his chest as she stumbled for a second, trying to catch her balance. His eyes danced, like he wanted to say something he knew he shouldn't. She felt his heartbeat get faster under her hand, but then he looked past her shoulder. "You have a new date incoming," he said quietly, his eyes darkening for a moment.

She watched him for a moment. *Are you jealous of this?* she wondered before Taytra looked up to see an individual with a black mask like Ward's approaching. "Show time," she said, turning back to Ward, and curtseys.

"Hello, madam, sir. May I cut in?" he asked, putting out a hand.

"Yes. I need a drink myself," Ward said, bowing lightly to brush a kiss across Taytra's fingertips before stepping away.

Taytra's her heart fluttered, and she was suddenly cold without the heat of Ward against her skin. Taytra turned to her new dance partner, a bit breathless. "I— Hello, sir. Yes, you may have this dance. I am afraid I haven't had a chance to check my dance card."

The music started up again at a quick tempo, and the two took off at a quick jig. Taytra practically bounced her way around the space, ignoring the delicate footwork the others around her did with ease. "You seem to have taken to our dances fairly quickly," the man said, spinning Taytra around the dance floor.

Taytra laughed breathily as she stumbled. "You give me too much credit, sir. I am barely keeping up." She regained her balance, and they danced again for a few beats. "Hang on, how did you know I am not from here?"

The man laughed, spinning her out to arms' length. "Please, Miss Flynn, you are the most notable guest we have had in Hollens in a long time," he replied.

She stared for a moment. She knew people would know her. Would have heard her story and put the pieces together, but for it to happen so fast shocked her. Her skin crawled, something about the man suddenly unnerving. "Well, I hope I meet your expectations. Can I ask who you are since you know who I am?"

The short song ended, and the man bowed. "For now, it is best that you do not. You just need to know that I am with you. What is happening to your people is wrong, and when you need the support, I will be there." He pressed a piece of paper into her hand.

"But we need your support now, sir!" But the man had melted backwards into the night. She looked down at the bit of paper in her hand as the music started up again, much slower this time.

"May I?" A hand wrapped in a delicate glove was raised to her.

"Oh, yes. I apologize. I was distracted." She slipped the piece of paper into her pocket, sending a prayer of thanks to the Goddess and to Serena for a beautiful and practical dress.

She turned to her new dance partner, a spark of recognition flashing through her. *Okay, here we go.* She took the man's hand. *A silver mask. Which of the councilmen are you?* The man's hand was soft and frail beneath the glove, the knuckles of his fingers swollen with age. *Ah, this must be the one that told me that I am just young and excitable as all women are.*

The man was much shorter than her, which was saying something. At one point, he may have looked eye to eye with her, but age dragged his shoulders down. "I don't think I have seen you at our previous events."

Taytra swayed to the beat, realizing this man was doing no more than shuffling his feet side to side. "I have not been to a celebration in some time. They seem to be ruined for me of late."

"Oh, that is disappointing. I hope this one turns out well for you."

She smiled, and over top of his head, saw Ward conversing with one of the women in the cuffs. *At least one of us is making progress.*

"You know, you remind me a lot of my daughter. The way you danced that last jig like no one was watching. You seem to be very spirited."

"You say that like it is a bad thing," Taytra said wryly.

The man nodded. "In some ways. She was a vibrant woman but she made mistakes."

Taytra paused, trying to see past the mask to the man beneath. "Was?"

The man looked behind Taytra. "You seem to have a shadow tonight. Did you come alone, ma'am?"

"I—No. I came with someone." She half turned, trying to see who the man was looking at, but he gripped her arms firmly. "Do you trust this person you came with? We can help you leave tonight if you do not."

"If it was he that I came with, I do. I trust him with my life," Taytra said solemnly. "But if you would allow me to look, I would like to determine if that is him. I unfortunately have made many enemies. I like to know who watches me." She stepped away from the man and, holding his hand, walked around him in a circle, doing a little improvisational dance. She smiled the whole time, as to not alert the person. But she saw that it was just Ward. "Yes, it is the man I came with. No need to be afraid now," she said overly sweetly. When she turned back to the councilman, he stared at her, his mouth agape as he held her at arms' length. "Sir, is everything alright?" she asked coolly. She knew what it was. He had seen her scars.

His eyes danced from her eyes to her stomach where the cut on her side disappeared too. "You are hurt."

Taytra stepped closer and stood tall, showing no weakness. "On the contrary, sir. I am healing. Yes, I was hurt in a fight, but you will find I can do a decent job holding my own." She put her hands on her hips, watching him. Willing him to fight her as the other dancers moved around them.

"Miss, please." He took her hand and led her off the dance floor. "Please tell me what happened," he said, passing her a drink.

"I believe the Guardian has already told you my story," Taytra said, taking a sip of her drink.

"The Guardian? Why would the Guardian tell me your story?"

Taytra watched as another dance began. To her left, a woman wearing cuffs nodded to her. The woman turned, and Taytra saw she stood beside Ward, who gave her a soft smile. Taytra turned back to the man. "Tell me what happened to your daughter."

The councilman looked confused for a moment, but then looked to the sky where the stars bloomed. "She was a beautiful woman. Knew exactly what she wanted. And bossy as all get out. Her mother and I tried to keep her safe at home, gave her an easy life, but she wanted more. She went off exploring with a group of traders, said she wanted to see all the kingdoms." He took a sip then stared hard at his drink, swallowing a few times. "She uh—" He stopped to clear his throat. "She was brought back to us about a month later. She had been killed by the Dark Ones."

Taytra put a hand on his arm. "I am sorry. I hope she rests easy with the Goddess." They watched as the librarians lit the next fire. The last before the grand pyre. "So you understand a portion of my pain. The fear and confusion that lies in the unknown, the danger that lies in our kingdom." He looked up at her but waited for her to speak. "My sister was taken from me. She left of her own choice to keep me safe, but she has now been taken. I have been left with the broken pieces of my people and my family. And I would do anything, as I am sure you would, to put it all back together." The man nodded. "Sir, I have fought. I have given my blood, and my sweat, and my tears for my people. And I will do it again and again, to protect them and get my family back." She took a deep breath, lowering her voice. "I may be excitable, as you say many young women are, but that doesn't mean I have any less fight in my heart then you do for your people."

He looked deep into his cup, as if the answers he sought laid deep within the amber liquid. "You truly are the one who took a whipping so your people could escape?" She nodded. "How did you do that? Was it not the man you came with who did it to you?"

She adjusted the armored bolero around her shoulders. "I knew they needed to make one of us a martyr. They thought it would break us. I had been separated from my father. I didn't want them to hurt him. So, I stepped up. We knew they would target me, but what happened… there was no way for us to plan for it." She looked to Ward. "He regrets every moment, but I don't. It proved to me that I was strong enough. You will find that we women have more to us, more drive to do and protect. The world moves on no matter what we do, and women are meant to be at the forefront." She turned back to the councilman. "I will not flatter you with my story. While portions of it are different because of my sister, the core of it, homes and families being torn apart, is happening all across the kingdoms."

"Lady Taytra." The two turned to find the woman with the cuff having approached, her eyes swimming with tears. "You will do great things for your people. We know you will." She bent, and to Taytra's surprise, laid a soft kiss on the fingers of Taytra's free hand.

At her name, the man jumped as if he didn't quite believe the story completely, but the final piece of the puzzle clicked into place. He nodded. "Yes, yes, Miss Flynn. You will do good. And we will make sure to help you with that." He looked off to the crowd. "I will find my members. Thank you, you have given me much to think about this night. Fitting that Samhain is a time of change." He looked to his wife, then back at Taytra. "Please, go enjoy your night." He pointed to Ward. "You deserve a break."

Chapter 31 Ward

Ward was waiting with a warm cup of cider for Taytra to come off the dance floor. She bowed to the councilman she had danced with and watched as he stalked stiffly away. Her cheeks were flushed pink and her eyes danced with joy. "Is that for me? Thank you! I think that was the last of them. I don't see any others to speak with," she said, taking the cup. She blew the steam from the top, the clouded bits of her breath mixing with the drink's steam.

"I figured you may need a little something," he said

She sighed in pleasure as she took a long sip. "This is exactly what I needed." She shifted the cup so it sat firmly against her palm and laced her fingers around it. "I think it is working. They are listening to me."

Ward couldn't help smiling at her. "I knew they would. They just needed a chance to get to know you." Ward said, "Like most men, they have a bit of sense when separated from the pressure of their peers. Typical." Ward turned away from Taytra as the music shifted suddenly. The light jig on a flute, blending to a lone drum beat.

"Look!" Taytra said, pointing to the stairs. Three elders came up the stairs in long, brown robes, their hands raised as they chanted a song. As they moved into the night air, they raised their hands high above their heads, raising a fresh piece of what looked like corn and a log. They moved into the open area in front of the largest pyre, their movements almost dance like as they weaved around each other, chanting something in a language Ward didn't understand. "Are they speaking in an Elvin language? Would be pretty ironic, don't you think?" he whispered in Taytra's ear.

She smacked his arm. "It is not Elvin. Do you not remember anything from lessons?" She paused, then giggled. "One of us has to remember stuff because I sure don't remember anything." She grinned up at him mischievously. "It would be pretty ironic, though, wouldn't it? But it is something for the Goddess. She branches both cultures."

He wrapped an arm around her and pulled her close. "Okay, Shauna. Pulling facts out of thin air," he whispered into her hair. He winced inwardly as she tensed at the mention of her sister. "I'm sorry. I was just making a—"

"Don't," she said firmly, watching the three elders. "It is something she would do. She would love to see this," she said almost wistfully.

"Next year, we will come back and you can show her," he murmured, and Taytra nodded, her hand coming to rest on his own.

The elders turned, each casting their piece of wood into the fire. Shouts of joy filled the air as the flames leapt and jumped, quickly consuming the logs. "Here, toss this in!" someone said, passing Ward and Taytra each their own log to launch into the greedy flames. When the last log was added, the pyre reached at least twenty feet in the air, the ring of smaller fires giving off enough light to see everyone, and enough heat to make you think it was a summer day.

The band shifted again, the drummer stepping back, and they started a slow piece. The crowd dissipated and the couple moved back to their place at the wall. In the distance, Ward heard the bells tolling twelve times. As the final note faded, he watched as everyone around them removed their masks. Samhain was no more.

Taytra swayed to the music, leaning into him.

"How do you feel?" he asked, pressing his lips to the top of her hair again.

"Good. I think we finally made some progress." She sighed, looking up at the stars. "I'm glad. I don't what is more exhausting. Trying to argue my way through a fight where the other side doesn't want to try, or running from an enemy."

Ward laughed, taking another sip of his cider. "You really think they are comparable?"

"Of course not," she grumbled. "But it is at least easier to know why they don't like you." She pulled away and looked over the people on the rooftop with them. "I learned a lot tonight. About people and how the hold their pain." She watched a few different councilmen talk, their dates hanging around, waiting for them to finish up.

Ward shifted his position, rubbing Taytra's arms where a few goosebumps started to rise on her skin. "Are you cold? We can send for your cloak."

She shook her head. "No, I am okay. Just thinking," she said, looking up into the star filled sky.

"Oh, Goddess, do I want to know what you are thinking about?" he asked dramatically.

She pinched his arm "You are feisty tonight, aren't you?"

He shrugged. "Someone has to keep you down to earth from time to time."

She nodded, her smile faltering. "I'm just worried we won't make the right decisions."

He pulled her closer, lightly rubbing her back. She jumped away when his finger trailed one of the long scars, and he stopped. She shifted and turned, pressing her back to his chest. He wrapped his arm around her, his hand resting lightly on her hip. He could feel her breath, slow and even, unafraid. "I think," he said slowly, trying to gauge her reaction, "that whatever decisions we make will be the best we can make given the current circumstances and our knowledge of the situation."

She scoffed, looking up at him. "That is a very diplomatic answer. Is the council rubbing off on you?"

"Maybe." He sighed. "But I don't regret what we have done. I only regret one decision. Every other one I look at and think that I did the right thing at that moment. I don't know if I ever will with that one. I should never have put you in that moment."

Taytra's eyes softened, and he had to look away. He couldn't let her see the pain he still held. "You know I have forgiven you for that. You don't need to feel any guilt for it. It was out of your control." She turned in his arms and cupped her face. "You have nothing to be sorry about. He—Nurzan is the one to blame."

Ward leaned into her hand, the warmth of it, and closed his eyes. He swallowed hard, the lump in his throat building. "I—I know. But there isn't a day that goes by that I don't think of it. I see how it changes the way you hold yourself and protect yourself physically. I don't need to see the damage to know it is there. I don't know if I will ever stop being sorry for it."

She stood up on tiptoes and pressed a light kiss to the corner of his cheek. "Ward Hendricks, you are a good man. One of the best." His hand caught hers, holding her against him. "The actions of others forced upon you won't change that. The fact that you are here, by my side, fighting with me and actively trying to stop them is the only apology I will ever need from you."

Ward nodded and swallowed hard. "I know, but—"

"Ward," she cut him off, her voice firm yet gentle, "Ward Hendricks, I don't want to hear a but out of you." She stepped away from him. "Now, you are going to stop this, and you and I are going to dance," she said, dropping her cup on the tray of a passing waiter and pulling Ward onto the dancefloor in time for the dance to turn into a happy little jig. "I believe you said you would get at least two dances."

"I honestly don't deserve you." He laughed as she spun him in a circle, leading the dance.

"I know. But that is what I am here for. To keep you down to earth sometimes," she mimiced.

Chapter 32 Shauna

A knock at the door to their room woke her with a jolt, her heart pounding as she rolled to her feet, the bedsprings screeching in protest. A small flap she hadn't noticed at the bottom of the door was pulled back and in slid a tray of food. She waited, watching through the small window as the shadows danced as the guard backed away from the door. She moved to the door, expecting the usual gruel she had gotten when she had been held in Damian's camp. Something like a hunk of bread or hard cheese and dried meat. Something easy to eat that didn't require a fork or a knife. She lifted the lid and froze. "Philippe, food is here," she said, staring down at the food—two large bowls of what looked like a thick beef stew, as well as fresh bread, a bottle of liquid, and two cups.

"What is that smell?" Philippe yawned.

"Our dinner," She said. "This looks really good, but we can't eat it."

He came and sat on the floor next to her. "Why?"

She smacked his hand away when he reached for one of the bits of bread. "This is too good. It has to be poisoned or something. We are prisoners. Why would they give us such good food?"

"I mean, I got good food when we were with Damian. Didn't you?"

She laughed at that. "Damian didn't feed me, remember? He tied me to a post and left me outside to rot. When he did feed me, it was stale bread and cheese, not stew, so I am sorry for questioning why the highest leader of the Dark Ones would want to give me food that smells better than anything my mother used to make me even when I was sick." She shoved the tray back toward the door.

He put his hands up defensively. "Okay, okay, I see where you are coming from."

Shauna sat back on her heels, staring at the steam coming from the stew. Her stomach growled, the sound echoing in the empty room.

Philippe stared at her stomach a moment before his own growled. He shifted, an uncomfortable smile spreading over his lips at the sound. "Maybe they want to make sure we stay healthy. We don't know how long they want to keep us here, and they won't be able to keep us long if we get sick."

She nodded, her eyes locked on the rich smelling food. She hadn't eaten food that smelled this good since they were with Amicus, maybe even the feast, though she hadn't eaten much then either. "What if they did something to the food?" She said warily, slowly pulling the tray back toward them.

A loud bang on the door sent them both jumping back, and she turned to the door. A Dark One looked down at them through the small slit in the window. "Just eat the damn food already. If you won't, I will," the guard barked.

"We didn't do anything to it."

"Okay," Shauna said, blowing air through her lips. *Because pressuring us into eating makes me want to eat more,* she looked from the food to the guard.

"You need to be taken to get cleaned up once you are done, so will you hurry up and eat?" the guard said, sounding exasperated.

Philippe reached over for the bread, ripping off a big chunk with his teeth. "What do we need to get cleaned up for?" he asked around the mouthful of food. She watched him, but his skin didn't go purple and he didn't foam at the mouth. He took the bread and dunked it into the stew. He saw her watching and nudged the food to her. "It is alright, go ahead."

She would give anything to take a bath right now, but the prospect of having a Dark One guarding her was not quite what she had in mind.

"Lord Nurzan wants to have a meeting with you in the morning, but he said you had to be cleaned up before that could happen as you are both quite rank," the guard said shortly. "Hurry up. Knock on the door when you are finished, and someone will be sent to get you."

Shauna picked up one of the bowls of stew and blew gently on the still steaming food. She and Philippe shared a look. We knew we would be questioned by Nurzan—the process had already begun with Fayanna—but the idea that they had to be presentable before being allowed to speak with him wasn't something she had expected.

"Do you want to go first or should I?" Philippe asked, using the bread to mop up some of the liquid in his stew.

She considered it for a moment. Both options made her feel sick. Shauna would rather stay by his side, but also she didn't want to be in this room alone. "I will go first," she said slowly, trying to convince herself. "Yeah, I want to go first."

"Okay, if you are sure."

She nodded, and took another bite of her stew. The rich food was almost hard to eat after having food that was easy to pack for travel for so many weeks. It sat in her stomach like a lump. She took a few more bites and poured some of the drink, which turned out to be some sort of fruit juice. Once she finished the sweet drink, she got up, putting the bit of bread under the crate for later. "I can't eat anymore," she explained. What she didn't say was that she didn't trust them to feed them this well again in the future and she didn't want to risk them taking it all away from them.

He nodded and did the same with the bit of bread that he had left. Shauna moved to the door and gave a few short knocks, pressing her hands against her sides, willing them to stop shaking. It took a moment before the elf's eye came back into view. "All set?"

"Yes, sir," Shauna said, she clenched her hands into fists, still trying to stop them from shaking, but also to show that she would be compliant and visible as he opened the door.

He looked from her to the tray, probably to see if she was going to try to stab him to death with the spoon. "Right. Come with me, Miss Flynn." He grabbed her elbow, leading her into the hall, and held her in place while turning to lock the door behind them. His hand on her arm was softer than some of the others, more of a guide than an outright threat. His grip wouldn't leave a mark.

They took a different route through the fortress, down a long spiral staircase. The walls were lined with torches, always more torches. It was dark in the halls upstairs, but she was pretty sure they were underground now. The grout lines on the walls had little bits of moss growing to them, and moisture dripped down the wall into little puddles. Surprisingly, while cold and damp, it didn't smell like mildew. Still, she shivered and steeled herself for what she was sure would be a very cold bath.

The guard stopped in front of the third door in the hall. "You have as long as you need. Inside you will find a towel, a bar of soap, and a change of clothes. There is a bell on the wall. Ring it when you are finished, and someone will come to take you back to your cell."

"Someone? Not you?" She asked, stepping into the doorway. "I will be alone?"

"I have other things to attend to." He looked her up and down. "What, did you think we were going to lord over you the whole time?"

Shauna closed her mouth after she realized it was hanging open. "You trust me?" Shauna glanced up the hall, but there wasn't another guard in sight.

The guard laughed dryly. "Look, if you are able to break out of our fortress on your own without using any of your Magick and without any of us knowing, you deserve to get out."

She nodded and headed into the room. The door thudded behind me, and she turned when she heard the deadbolt slide into the lock. *Well, that would be the first step of getting out now wouldn't it?* noting where the bell sat on the door. Unlike the cell that she and Philippe shared, the door to this room did not have a small window.

Good, she thought. *No one can watch me that way.* When she pressed her ear against it, she couldn't make out the sound of boots or anyone outside. *What, did you think we were going to lord over you the whole time?* the guard had said. That was exactly what she thought would happen. It was all she had known for the last month. *Maybe he is one of the ones that believes what they are doing right but isn't cruel about it? Maybe he would be one that would help us?* she thought wistfully.

Shauna took her time examining the room, even going as far as to remove the torch from the wall and use it to shine light into the darkest corners of the room where piles of dust gathered. Only then did she peel her clothes off. They were not salvageable. She secretly hoped someone would burn them. They were coated in mud, sweat, and blood from her foot and the Dark Ones slain on the plain. Every so often, she smelled their burning skin coating the back of her throat. She shuddered and turned to the tub. It was a wide stone basin with soft tendrils of steam rising from the water. As she climbed in, she wondered what sort of Magick was used to make it stay warm. It had to have been at least thirty minutes from the person bringing the food to the cell, the two Frituals eating, and her getting here, and yet, when she slid into the water, the heat soaked into her skin, instantly zapping away the cold chill. *Will stay warm the whole time?*

The water was a murky brown by the time she climbed out, and her skin was red from scrubbing at it with the rough washcloth, but she hadn't felt this good in a long time. The bath helped ease some aches she had blocked out a while ago. She turned to the pile of clothes that waited for her. She had assumed they would be all black to fit in with the Dark Ones' uniforms, but instead, Shauna found a linen shirt, trousers, and socks, along with a new pair of boots. The pants were a bit big but the belt that lay on the bottom of the pile was enough for her to feel comfortable to leave the room. It wasn't anything like the dresses she used to wear at home, and she felt slightly uncomfortable, exposed in a way, even though she was fully covered.

Just think like Tay, she told herself, thinking of all the things her sister would wear. Taytra didn't care what others thought of her outfits. Shauna ran her hands through her hair and felt a pang of sadness. She chopped it all off, and for what? She still ended up here. She rubbed the towel viciously across her head. *Well, at least it won't take as long to dry now*, she thought.

She turned to the door. She was stalling, and knew it. Shauna took a deep breath. She didn't need to hit the bell yet. She could stay here in this space and be alone. The door was locked. No one could get to her, and it seemed like they would let her be. *They will check on you at some point to make sure you didn't off yourself,* a sour angry part of her thought, but she pushed that thought well into the back of her mind. She couldn't stay here forever. She lifted her hand, ready to pull the short rope that would ring the bell, when there was a knock at the door.

She turned to the sound, replaying what the guard had said. *Are they checking on me already? Did I take too long?*

"Shauna?" a voice called from the other side.

Shauna. They called her by name, not little Fritual, or prisoner, or anything like that. her name. "Yes?"

"Can I come in?"

She stepped back from the door. *Can they come*

in? Who would ask permission? *Why would they ask permission of me? I was a prisoner. What would happen if I said yes? If I said no?* She knew the silence was stretching far too long. She needed to say something.

"It's Galen. I wanted to check out your foot now that you have gotten cleaned up. I can come back in a bit if it is better?"

She looked down. The bandage for her foot was in the corner with her old clothes, stained and unsanitary. She didn't think he would be coming anymore. Which meant he must have something to say. "You can come in," She said and watched as the door swung inward.

"Ah, good, you are all cleaned up," Galen said, closing the door behind him. She waited, but the lock did not slide into place behind him.

"Are you alone?" Shauna whispered, glancing over his shoulder.

The healer nodded. "We will need to be quick. They don't know I am here."

She quickly backed away from the elf. "If they find out you are here, I will be dead." She looked at the closed door, expecting it to burst open at any second. The brief moment of peace she had felt was absolutely shattered.

The elf put his hands up. "No, no, no. It isn't like that."

"Isn't like that?" She hissed, scared to speak above a whisper in case anyone came past the door and heard her speaking to someone when she was meant to be alone. "Do I need to remind you that I have been kept as a prisoner not once but twice? The fact that I have been on the run for over a month now? That I have had to learn how to fight while running for my life from people who want me dead?"

The elf bobbled his head. "Okay, okay, yes. I—I, yes, but that is not why I am here. I wanted to warn you that they are planning to do a ceremony."

She froze. "What sort of ceremony?"

The elf shook his head. "I am not exactly sure but I ran into some of the Magick users in the library. I was trying to look up where I could find certain herbs in the desert, and they were looking up different ceremonies. I heard them say they haven't done this sort of Magick in years but they were planning on doing it with three people." His eyebrows scrunched up in confusion. "I haven't figured out who the third person could be. You and Philippe are the only Frituals we have in custody."

She rubbed her face, trying to process this news. "I don't know who that could be. Galen, what am I supposed to do with this information? It isn't like I can run away from this right now," she said, gesturing to the door and the Dark Ones outside. *Look, if you are able to break out of our fortress on your own without using any of your Magick and without any of us knowing, you deserve to get out.* The guard's words echoed in her mind.

The elf deflated. "I just wanted to warn you. I thought you would want to know."

Knowledge is your weapon right now, She reminded herself. She sighed "No, thank you. I appreciate you telling me. I will—I don't know what I will do with the information, but it is better to know than not."

The elf moved back toward the door, pausing to listen before opening it, slamming the deadbolt home and sprinting away.

Shauna stood in the empty room and looked to the tub, the murky water still steaming with warmth. "What will be, will be," she whispered before reaching up to pull the bell.

Chapter 33 Philippe

Shauna stood in front of what Philippe assumed was General Nurzan's door when he and his guard approached. She looked much better now that the mud and grime had been washed away, but the bruises, cuts, and the black band that was twin to the one on his wrist stood out starkly on her skin. She did look a bit more awake, but there were deep bags around her eyes, a pain a bath couldn't wash away.

The guards stepped away for a moment, whispering about something Philippe couldn't quite make out.

"You look good," Shauna said, giving him a once over.

He noted the loose-fitting pants and the shirt that didn't quite fit, the neckline hanging askew on her shoulder. "You too. Are you ready for this?" he said lightly, trying to bring a bit of levity to what he could only assume would be a very intense conversation for them.

She shrugged, the movement fixing her shirt. "As ready as I will ever be." She glanced over her shoulder at the guards that waited down the hall. "Did your guard leave you alone, too?"

"Yeah, it was strange. It was..." He trailed off. "It wasn't nice, per se, but..." Shauna took a half step toward him before stepping back, her eyes flicking between him and the guards. "You remember what we talked about?" he asked quietly as the guards came up. She nodded, her eyes seeming to cloud with something he couldn't quite place. The guards separated them and patted them down, checking to make sure they didn't have any weapons. *When would I have gotten a weapon?* he wondered as the guard spun him around.

"They are clear," the guard said, pushing them to the door.

Shauna stepped forward to the door and turned back. "Do I knock?" she asked, her hand up and waiting to be told what to do. Philippe noticed a slight tremor to her hand that she didn't let reach her voice.

"Yes, the general is waiting for you," one of the guards said. "He should not be kept waiting any longer."

She turned back the door, and Philippe watched as her shoulders rose and fell quickly as she took a deep breath, preparing herself. He felt himself doing the same, steeling himself. Shauna brought her hand back to hit the door, and it swung open under her hand. They are met with the lord of the Dark Ones. "Hello, Frituals. Please, come in," he said, gesturing for them to sit in the chairs in front of a large desk.

Shauna slid past him and plopped herself into the first chair. She curled into herself, crossing her arms in front of her chest. *Don't let him break you.* Against his better judgment, knowing the general was probably staring the two of them down, Philippe let his hand swing out and brush her shoulder as he took his seat. He didn't know if she heard him say the word *strong* as he made the briefest contact with her skin, but she glanced up at him and uncrossed her arms, putting her hands into her lap.

Nurzan walked slowly around his desk, trailing a hand along the surface. He made eye contact with both of them before taking his seat. Philippe kept his eyes fixed on the elf's face, watching as his eyes drifted over each of the marks on his skin, then over Shauna's shorn hair. Philippe pressed his hands into his thighs, waiting for the elf to speak. *Just get on with it!* Philippe wanted to shout. Shauna shifted in her chair, and it screeched underneath her, breaking the elf out of whatever spell he was under. "Well, it sure is nice to have the two of you here."

Philippe tried not to look at Shauna, at the words, but it sent his already pounding heart skittering. *Why would it be a good thing that he has us here? What exactly does the elf want with us? They have had every opportunity to kill us if they had wanted to.*

The elf leaned back in his chair and crossed his arms. The nonchalance of it was unnerving. Philippe was sure that was exactly why it was being done, and forced himself to breathe, to keep his thoughts focused on what the elf said—and what was left unsaid. "You two in particular have caused quite a bit of trouble of late," the elf continued. "Fayanna told me what went down at Fuegaste Peak. For two untrained humans, it was quite an impressive feat." The elf turned to Shauna. "Your sister was quite—we shall say feisty—when I met her at Cabineral Lake, but those I spoke to didn't think you were going to be that much of a threat. And yet, here you are. How many of my elves would you say you have taken out?"

Shauna balked at the question. Philippe could see her trying to think of the best way that would get her in the least amount of trouble. "I am not sure, sir," she said flatly. "I did not stick around long enough to make sure that each member of your army I came across was dead. I did what I needed to do in order to escape, then left."

"But you admit that there may have been some deaths?" Lord Nurzan asked, leaning forward in his chair, fingers interlaced.

Shauna hesitated, then nodded. "Yes, there may have been some that were killed. I—" She sat up straighter, "I know at least three from Fuegaste Peak were killed. We made sure that they were dead when we left. Or tried to leave." She glanced over at Philippe.

"And what about you, Mattick?" Nurzan asked Philippe.

The young man shrugged. "I have to admit, Shauna has had more run-ins that required fighting than I have." Philippe tried to match the elf's cool demeanor. "I was taken prisoner, as I am sure you have been informed by Damian. I was—I did his bidding for a time." Philippe knew he was entering into dangerous territory, the border of whether his actions had been his own or not was a knife's edge that he didn't want to balance on for long.

Nurzan shifted a piece of parchment on his desk, a long line of notes on it, split into what looked like six columns. "I have heard," he said, holding up the page. "What I believe is the list of those that were hurt or killed by either you and your fellow Frituals." Philippe couldn't stop his eyes from dropping to the page. The ink covered both sides. "Now, we are not an unjust people," General Nurzan said as if it was obvious. "You will not be charged for injuries or deaths made by your counterparts. Their charges will come in time." He traced a finger down the list.

"What makes you so sure of that?" Shauna asked. Philippe and Nurzan turned to stare at her. The question wasn't entirely a challenge. Though Philippe could tell by the set of her shoulders, she wanted it to be. "What happens to us if you don't get the others? Will we be charged for their—" She stopped short of saying the word that would carry weight.

"Would you be charged for their crimes?" Nurzan pondered, running a hand over his short beard. "I have not really considered that. I have always said we would get them, all the Frituals, in one place. But if they are as elusive as you two were, it may be a while indeed," he mused, his lips coming together in a wicked smile. "Would you prefer that? To take the fall for your fellows? Your kin?" He fired back at Shauna. When she didn't answer, he grinned. "So, would you say Shauna has killed more of my elves than you have?" Nurzan pushed, turning back to Philippe.

"I—No, sir, not necessarily. Shauna has—" He glanced over at her. Her back was rigid, emotions wiped from her face as she stared straight ahead. He knew she was weighing every word, calculating what her next move should be. "Shauna is more merciful than I am," he said, thinking of the fireballs he had slung at the elves who had chased them across the plain. The way they had collapsed in on themselves. The horses had panicked, trampling the other underfoot. "The three kills she mentioned were just as much my fault as her own." She shot him a glance, an eyebrow furrowed. *That wasn't right. Something about that wording wasn't right.*

Nurzan nodded slowly. "Would you consider yourself merciful, Miss Flynn?" He didn't give her a chance to respond. Instead, he stood, leaning across the table at her. "If that is the case, why are there reports of you killing my elves with Magick that does not belong to you?" He hissed, the cool civility wiped from his face, replaced by an anger that sent shivers down Philippe's spine. "I am merciful. I could have had your sister killed. Instead, I had her whipped, beaten in front of everyone." He sat down. "I had hoped to make an example of her. Like that weak mayor of your town. Instead, I made her a symbol of hope."

Philippe watched Shauna's jaw work as she tried to figure out what to say. They had gotten very little information about what had happened at home, what had happened to their families. And now they had to try to figure out on the fly what was the truth. He knew the words that would come out of her mouth would be damning when she smirked. Born of this new Shauna, the one who was harder, was no longer afraid that people may judge her. She still weighed her actions like the one he had known all his life, but this Shauna made her actions count. She grinned and shook her head, clearing the hair away from her eyes. "Well, I guess that should have told you that you shouldn't have underestimated us. We can't help it if you can't see what is staring you in the face."

Chapter 34 Shauna

"Guards." Nurzan didn't look away from her, his eyes a storm of anger waiting to be unleashed. The door opened, and he flicked them the slightest glance of acknowledgment. "Separate these two. We are going to go about this differently."

Shauna did everything she could to keep her gaze locked with the Dark Ones, even as they wrenched her shoulders and pulled her out of the chair. She didn't fight them, but she didn't go willingly. He nodded to himself as the door snapped shut, as if whatever fight she displayed was what he expected. *Did he play me for a fool? Did I fall into a trap?* No, that was genuine anger in those eyes. He hadn't expected her to fight. *That doesn't mean he won't enjoy it.*

Where is Philippe? she thought, cursing herself for not paying attention. She was too busy having a stare down with the lord general of the Dark Ones to pay attention. She didn't know where they took him. She glanced over her shoulder as she was taken around a corner, but she didn't see him or the other guard. Shauna didn't hear them either. The guard pushed her into a room and quickly locked the door behind him, like he couldn't get away from her fast enough. She glanced around again, trying to see if there was anything giving away what she could expect to come next. *You challenged the lord general of the Dark Ones!* She didn't know who that girl was in that room, but she had been coming around more frequently. *You had better stick around,* Shauna told herself, *'cause you clearly made an impression on him.*

The room didn't seem to be a cell, more like an unused bedroom. It was empty save for two chairs in the corner. A part of her was drawn to the chair, wanting to sit and wait rather than stand awkwardly in the middle of the room for Goddess knew how long, but she didn't want to be seen in a weaker position from the start.

Shauna spun when she heard a key in the lock. *It's only been a minute?* She floundered, looking for something she could use to protect herself. But of course, there wasn't anything. They made sure of that before they put her in here.

An elf entered, but it wasn't Nurzan. His skin was pale like her's, nearly as pale as Lyra's. The black of his uniform made his eyes look like bits of chipped ice. "Shanna Flynn. Sit," the elf said, gesturing to the chair in the corner. She hesitated, but only for a moment when the elf made another, firmer gesture. She moved across the room slowly, hoping she didn't do anything that would make the elf perceive her as a threat. Shauna sat on the edge of the chair, gripping the seat.

The elf crossed his arms and leaned against the wall. she tried to hold his gaze, but quickly looked away. "A bit jumpy?" he asked.

"You wouldn't be jumpy?" She snapped.

He shrugged. "Why would I be? I haven't done anything to be afraid."

"Who said I was afraid?" The words escaped before she had a chance to stop them.

He grinned, as if that was some sort of cue he was waiting for. "You may say you aren't afraid right now, Little Fritual," he whispered, slowly taking the chair across from her. "You can act all tough and like nothing is phasing you. But you know what?" He leaned close, and Shauna fought every instinct that told her to move away from him. "I don't buy it for one second."

She wanted to curl up into as tight a ball as she could, to move the chair she sat on between the two of us and step into the corner. Instead, Shauna schooled her face into a blank slate. "You may have an opinion."

The elf laughed. "Alright, we can play it your way. My job is to get you to talk. So, let's talk."

"Okay," she said, opening her arms wide. "Let's talk. Where shall we start?" She leaned back as if this was nothing. She had all day to play his little mind games. *Let's see if I have half the wit Taytra does.*

The elf reached into a pocket and pulled out a bit of parchment. "Well, let's see." He ran a finger down a scribbled mess, which she presumed if he could read it, was a list of topics. "It's a pity you tried cutting off all your hair. I heard when you had it longer, you were the spitting image of your sister."

Shauna reached up and touched her shorn hair. "Some have said that, yeah."

He leaned back. "I heard you tried to trick us when we took Cabineral. Tried to swap places for a bit." He barked out a sharp laugh. "I also heard it didn't work."

She cocked an eyebrow at that. "Really? If it didn't work, where do your little notes say I was originally captured?" She grinned when his eyes dropped back to the page. "Here, let me fill in the gaps for you. Tay was captured that day, yes. But you were going to get her anyway. I think she mentioned when I saw her, you had already captured our father." Anger boiled in her chest, trying to constrict her throat, and she paused. *I am stronger than him. I know more.* Taytra had swapped dresses with her and lured the Dark Ones away on purpose. And that plan had worked. It was one of the few things that had gone well. She could still remember the sound of her crashing through the woods.

"Eh, blondie, get back to the story." The elf snapped his fingers close to her face, breaking apart the image of Taytra vanishing into the dark forest.

Shauna flashed a smile she didn't feel. "You know, for someone who is meant to be interrogating me, you sure seem to be missing a lot of the basics. Did a few too many of your messengers die on the way back here?"

"What happened outside Cabineral?" he asked curtly.

She pushed the hair away from her face. "I escaped. Made it out into the forest, for what was it? Two? Maybe three days? Before your lot caught me trying to get across the plateau. I also found another Fritual camped out in those woods you somehow missed for over a month."

The elf seethed. "My men would never miss anything like that. Those elves—" He caught himself. "Damian lost his touch."

"Okay." There were other things she could say, barbs about catching an untrained girl in the woods. Alone. But she didn't, she saved that for now, tucking away the knowledge that all that knew him thought Damian was a waste of space.

The elf looked her over. "So, your sister," he said, as if to change the subject. "She seems to have made a name for herself."

"Really? I wouldn't know," she said sarcastically. "I haven't talked to her in a month."

The elf shifted in his chair, leaning forward. "You really haven't heard anything?" he pressed.

Shauna held her fingers up as if to count. "Hmm, well, let's see. I was running in the woods alone, then I was captured, then I was running around the woods with a few others, and then I went to Fuegaste Peak, and then, oh right, you captured me a few weeks later." She dropped my hands to her lap. "Where in the 'I was running around the woods' part, would you like me to insert communication with my sister? Or a way to learn what she was doing? I only heard she escaped from you lot when I got here. And I don't know why I should believe anything you say?"

The elf scowled. "Fine. Tell me about her."

"Taytra Flynn is my sister. She is one year older than me. She didn't really have a plan for after lessons ended. We fought a lot," She said shortly.

She grinned as the elf huffed and covered his face. "No, I—Why would your sister be a good leader?"

Shauna laughed. "She wouldn't. That isn't me trying to be mean. She just isn't a leader; she doesn't like people. She gets angry and makes rash decisions. If she is some leader like you keep saying, she has her own reasons for doing it." She watched as the elf thought over those words. *Would Taytra be a good leader? Maybe if she was put on the spot. She was one that liked to get things done her way. If no one else took the job, she would.*

"So, if you think your sister would not make a good leader," the elf hedged, "you wouldn't follow her lead?"

She shook her head. "Those are your words not mine."

"Even though you don't think she would make a good leader, you would still follow her?"

She leaned forward. "What are you trying to get at? What do you want to know about my sister?"

He leaned forward too, their faces inches apart. "Wouldn't you like to know?"

"I don't know. It seems like you are the one struggling to get information," She breathed. The elf's eyes squinted in annoyance, and he sat back. *Point me.* She smirked. "So, since the information does nothing for me at this point. I am already here," she said, gesturing to the stone walls around me. "Who was Manon?"

The elf scoffed. "That brat? She is an informant. She managed to get some information we needed and got herself into a hole. Now we use her as needed for tasks. She got a pretty good promotion after your job."

Shauna blew air through her lips, puffing her hair to the side. "Congrats," she said dryly. "How many jobs has she been on?"

"Six that I know of." He said. "The Hunters just started using her, so I am sure we will send her on more." Shauna grinned, and the elf looked like he wanted to stab himself in the foot.

"You new here? You don't seem as intimidating as some of the other Hunters I have met," She drawled, wondering just how far she could push her luck with this elf. *He had to pass the tests to get here, so he must have been good at something.*

"Your father. Would you say he is a leader?"

"Again, what are you playing at? You are trying to use me to find weak points in my family, sure. But your process isn't worth my time."

The door banged open, ricocheting off the opposite wall. "Jessup, get out," a voice snarled, and the breath evaporated from Shauna's lungs. Nurzan stalked in, taking the seat Jessup had vacated. "So, you want to play games, Fritual?"

"No, sir. I just thought I would see how long it would take for him to get to the point. Which we never were going to, it seems," She said, the bravado she had been feeling wiped away.

Nurzan sneered. "My Hunters have skills that are better suited for other things."

She couldn't help but smirk. "So he said."

Nurzan pulled out the bit of parchment with her crimes on it again. "We are going to go through this now."

She tried to look as disinterested as possible. Every fiber of her being wanted to reach out and snatch up the bit of paper, to see what sort of crimes they thought she could have committed. "Okay, let's do it." She crossed her arms, hoping it hid the fact she was starting to shake.

His dark eyes looked almost black as they locked on her. "Let's start easy, shall we? I have noted here how many guards were injured during your capture on the plateau. You think you can tell me what that is?"

Memories flashed in her mind's eye. Running away from the alarms, the dog that chased her. "I—I cut one. I had a sword and I cut one. I remember." Her hand drifted to her face. The blood—his blood—had coated her face. She had tasted it. "Then I used Magick. I don't remember how many I hit. I made a sort of whip. It could have hit any number of them."

"And what about your flight from the camp?" Nurzan pushed.

Did I answer correctly? She wondered. "I was poisoned by Damian. I don't remember most of our escape. To my knowledge. I didn't attack anyone because I was unconscious."

"Ten soldiers were dispatched to Fuegaste Peak. Six were dead or injured. I want you to tell me what happened to them."

She paused, rewinding to the plain below the mountain. "Six… I knocked one from their horse? I think Philippe spooked the other horse. I don't know what happened to the riders." She looked to her hands. "We faced off with four of them. So that must have been the last of the riders." She shuddered at the memories. The blackened ribs. The elf that clawed at the water she held around his head until he fell.

"What happened?" Nurzan said, his voice low and dark.

"We didn't go with them. We had a cart, because of my foot. And we decided to face the odds three to four. Not that Manon did anything to help. She hid in the corner," she said darkly. "They approached and seemed to think that we would just go willingly." There was no real way around it. Nurzan wanted to know what they had done to those elves, why they weren't the ones that captured the Frituals. "We fought back. Rather than be on the defensive, we went on the offensive. Philippe made a ball of fire and it knocked one from his horse. He died from the burns." She stumbled over the memory, fighting to stay in the present. "You probably won't believe me, but the next wanted out. He tried to argue that if they let us go, we wouldn't hurt him. That only lasted a moment, because then one of the other soldiers stabbed him. He said if anyone tried to go against the Dark Ones, they were dead to them."

"You are right. I don't believe you," Nurzan said, sitting back.

Shauna shrugged. "You have the information, and Philippe will tell you the same thing. It is up to you to decide if you want to listen to the facts."

"Continue with what happened," the general growled, which was acknowledgement enough he knew she was speaking the truth.

She rubbed her hands over her pants. "Well, that was the first two. The fire and then the blade. Next, I think I killed him. I drowned him. I held water over his head until he stopped fighting. I didn't pause to see if he started breathing again."

Nurzan leaned forward again, eyebrows peaked with interest. "You drowned him. How did you do that? There were no rivers or bodies of water nearby."

She shrugged. "I had a canteen of water. One for me to drink and a second if I needed to use my Magick."

"You made sure you always had access to a source of Magick. Smart."

Is he really complimenting me right now? "Well, it seemed like an obvious way to protect myself." There was a long silence that stretched between them as she waited for the elf to yell at her for trying to defend herself, but he seemed lost in thought. "Um—The last soldier... I think Philippe threw a fireball, but it missed. It did spook the horse, and he fell. He was trampled. Like the others, we didn't stay long enough to see if he was alive."

Nurzan wrote down a few things and then turned back to her, eyes blazing with that same deep anger. "I want you to tell me everything you know about Barin. Now."

She racked her brain. "Barin who?"

Nurzan's eyes blazed. "The last Fritual, the spirit Fritual." He spat out the words like they were poison.

"I—We found him?" She asked. "Philippe and I didn't meet him or her. We didn't even know the spirit Fritual had been found."

"I don't believe you," the elf hissed.

She scoffed. "Do you believe anything I am saying? Get a truth blade if you don't. I don't know who this Barin is. I have never met him or even heard his name."

The pencil in his hand snapped, and the elf stood abruptly. She jumped back, putting as much space between them as she good. "Guards! Take her back to the cell. I am done with her."

"Wait!" She said, surprising herself. "What happens now?"

"You will find out soon enough," he said, sweeping from the room.

Chapter 35 Taytra

Taytra read over her notes for the fourth time that morning. She could hear the buzz of voices outside as the people of Cabineral were gathered together. It was time to update them on everything, even the bits she didn't quite want to tell them about.

Ward and Taytra's presence at the celebration the night before had worked. Enough of the council had been swayed by their story to agree to help them. Even knowing generally what to expect, the meeting this morning had shocked her. Sure, a few of the council members, namely Kasser and Fouise, had stuck to the original plan and said there was no way the city of Hollens could help them. Kasser even went as far as to claim that the wounds on Taytra's back were fabricated, created out of illegal Magick. Thankfully, Serena shot that conspiracy theory down before it got too far. Taytra had never seen Ward's face flush that red before. If Serena hadn't given them a verbal lashing, she was sure there was nothing she or Andrew could have done to hold him back from physically throttling them. But the rest had treated her with respect, and some actually went on to apologize for their previous behavior. It was like they had been replaced by an entirely different crew of men.

She turned the parchment over. This list of updates and supplies was so important, such an amazing progression, she didn't want to follow it with the news of their departure to find Shauna and Philippe. But there was no way she, Ward, or the Frituals could leave without explaining why. These people deserved to know. She had tried to find Sam and Clive before the meeting, but they were off on some adventure to explore the city. *Thank the Goddess we made some headway before we had to leave,* she told herself for probably the fourth or fifth time since the meeting had ended.

"You ready?" Andrew asked, peeking his head into the big tent.

She looked down to the list again and nodded. "As ready as I'll ever be," Taytra said, following him out. Her little cohort of three hundred people stood waiting for what they had to say. The message was for all available adults to attend, but she could see some of the children too, balanced on their parent's hip.

She smiled at the little stage Andrew had made for her to stand on. "Are these the old food crates?"

"They never came back for them, so I thought we may as well use them for something," Andrew said, helping her climb onto the stage where she could see and be seen by all.

She glanced down at her speech. Now that she was in front of everyone, it felt stiff. Impersonal. Not something these people wanted or deserved after all they had been through together. The crowd pointed in her direction, their voices growing louder for a moment before they all fell silent as she raised a hand. "In the last month, many of us have made memories I don't think we will ever forget." She folded up the bit of parchment and slipped it into her pocket. "A little over a month ago, I was fighting with my father about whether I was actually going to spend the day in the city with my friend or not," Taytra said, hoping her voice could be heard at the back of the crowd. "A little over a month ago, my sister did what many of us have done. She jumped into Cabineral Lake for the Fritual test. But when she came back up, she was different. I only saw her a few minutes that day and I haven't seen her since, but even then, I could see the change in her was great. I am sure she has continued to change. Some of you who were at the ceremony saw her Magick. And you saw how the Dark Ones had infiltrated our home. I haven't seen my sister in over a month because, as you all know, she ran to try to take them away and keep us all safe. The last time I saw my father, he watched me confront a Dark One. I haven't seen him since, because he, like many of your family members, did not escape with us. They are still under the Dark Ones' heels." Taytra paused, swallowing the lump in her throat at the thought. She glanced around, catching the eyes of some of those gathered. Their faces were pinched with sadness, some with deep purple bags under their eyes, and dull skin caused by lack of food. "Please do not think a day goes by that I do not think of them. My father, my friends, my classmates. People I don't even know. There hasn't been a day we have been free that I haven't thought of them."

"Yeah!" someone shouted, and it startled enough

people that there were a few awkward laughs.

Taytra smiled and kept going. "I don't know when we will go home. I pray to the Goddess it will be soon. But I can't lie to you." She looked for Ward. He smiled and nodded. "It may be a long time. But after another series of negotiations, I think you will find your stay here in Hollens to be more to your standards." She pulled the bit of paper out and went on to list the increase in accommodations, food, and the ability to work they should see come into effect over the course of the next moon cycle. "I really hope that this helps improve your quality of life here at Hollens. After many conversations, the council is more understanding out our cause." She shifted slightly, feeling the fabric of her shirt brush against her shoulder blade and one of the lashes that she had exposed for them to see the night before.

There was another cheer, and someone shouted, "When can we start to work?"

Andrew stepped up beside Taytra. "Soon. After this meeting, please come to me with anything work or trade you are skilled in. We will submit this list to the city, and they will work on the assignments as needed. We might not be able to put you in your respective trade, but we will get you work." He looked at Taytra before stepping down. "You've got this. They will understand," he said, clasping her arm for a moment.

Taytra stepped up and took a deep breath. "As I said and you are well aware, my sister, Shauna Flynn, was named the Fritual of Cabineral. Over the last month, we have met several other Frituals. Philippe Mattick from home was also named the Fritual who can control fire. Paulo, and Lyra here—" She turned, pointing to the two elves who stood behind her. "—helped us escape the Dark

Ones on the plain. And some of you may have had the chance to meet Barin. I come before you with both good news and bad. For the good. We have found each of the Frituals. Whether you believe in it or not, this time is blessed with Magick." Taytra paused, gauging the reaction of the people before going on to explain the predicament they were in. "The Dark Ones have a strong foothold in our cities. We believe Hollens may be one of the few safe places left."

"But for how long? They are right outside!"

Taytra didn't try to answer that. Not when one of her biggest fears around leaving was what those outside the gate would do. "We have been trying to track Shauna and Philippe's movements. They were traveling with Paulo and Lyra before splitting off so Philippe could go through his ceremony. They were meant to be back here to meet Lyra and Paulo by now. They were meant to be back a week ago." A ripple of concern went through the crowd. Taytra put up a hand, trying to calm the crowd. "We have now learned where they may have disappeared."

"Are they dead? What happens to us if they are dead?" someone shouts.

The words were a gut punch to Taytra. "We do not believe so. Our reports indicate they are alive. There is hope. The Frituals are a big part of our plan to fight the Dark Ones. They represent all our people, and hopefully under them, we can be united."

"That sounds like bullshit to me," a heckler shouted.

"Your opinion is valid, sir. Having seen the power they hold, if we can get them and an army, I believe we will have a chance," Taytra insisted.

"So, what happened? Why are they late?"

Taytra looked to Ward. "For your safety and our own, we cannot tell you specifics. But Andrew will be taking over as the primary contact between our people of Cabineral and Hollens. I will be leaving on a two-week mission to get my sister back." *A two-week mission we are hoping the council will let us return from,* Taytra thought, remembering how they said they would not be welcome back if they left.

A cry went up in the crowd, and it started to disintegrate.

"Wait, let me finish."

A disgruntled murmur held on for a few minutes but then stopped.

"I know many of you would and do feel the same having had to leave or lose family members." She unfolded the paper but didn't look at it. "Part of the reason we escaped from our home in Cabineral was to keep our families safe. This is something I must do. I have always said I don't understand why you chose me. I think it was because you saw part of me in yourselves. You want to be there for your families the way I want to save my own. Now I need to go get my family back."

"What about those that didn't get out of Cabineral?"

Taytra nodded. "That is all part of what we have been discussing. We believe once we have all five of the Frituals together, we will be able to return to Cabineral. I will admit, I selfishly would like to go home as soon as I can to get my father back. I don't know if that will be the case. It will take time, but we will go home, and having all five Fritual together will give us an advantage."

"All this Magick woo woo stuff doesn't make you a soldier!" someone shouted from the back of the crowd.

Taytra paused, tamping down the first bitter thought she wanted to throw back at the speaker, and worked to find something that would help more than harm.

"I believe you, Tay!"

She found him in an instant. Little Sam sitting up on a roof, his legs hanging down, swinging in a big arch. His hand was at his hip, on the knife Ward gave him. "Thank you. I have full faith that Andrew will be able to support you on his own just as well as he did when Ward and I were here, if not better. I don't think I am a good leader."

"Yes, you are, Lady Taytra," said a different voice, older. "You have done things others haven't wanted too and fought for us."

Taytra smiled, swallowing back a lump of emotion in her throat. "Thank you. Are there any questions I can answer?"

"When you do come back, can we join your army to fight them?" a young man who Taytra thought looked about their age asked.

"When we come home, you will have a choice. You have already given so much. And I can't ask anymore of you or your families. But if you choose to stand beside us, we would welcome your strength."

"When do you plan on leaving?" someone said from the crowd.

Taytra looked out at Ward, who nodded. "It depends on a few things, but we are looking at heading out tomorrow. There is much we have yet to discuss," Taytra said. She looked in the crowd for Sam again and saw him climbing off the roof and away from the crowd. She made another mental note to find him as soon as she could. She knew he would be thinking of the family he had already lost. "If there are no other questions, I am going to be in the big tent. If anybody needs me for the next hour, that is where you will find me," Taytra said before dismounting from the makeshift stage. She paused, squeezing Andrew on the shoulder and heading back into the tent.

When the tent doors slid shut behind her, she took a deep breath and slowly released it. The amount of preparation they needed to figure out over the course of the next few hours was a bit mind-boggling. *So, this is what it is like to go into something prepared?* she thought wryly, digging through a pile of papers to find her supply list. Tayra turned when she heard Andrew's voice just outside the tent, answering questions and deflecting people with ease. *He will be okay,* she thought, listening to him work. She stacked things into piles and compared it to her list. She or someone from their group would need to go to the market to get a few things. As much as she wanted to stand outside with Andrew and field any questions people had, she couldn't do that and get ready in time.

The tent flap at the back of the room opened, and Ward snuck in, tying off the flaps so people could only come to Andrew at the front. "That was really good, Tay. You did a really good job," Ward said, coming to the table and a pile of reports.

"Do you really think so?" she asked, pulling the bit of paper from her pocket. "I wrote down all these notes and thoughts that sounded good, but once I got in front of everyone, they just didn't feel right."

"I think that is why you did a good job. You spoke

from the heart. Anyone could see you were sincere and you were trying your best. But they could also see, or at least I could, your passion and your drive. You want to protect them but also your family." He smiled. "It's one of the reasons that you *are* a great leader. You show your heart on your sleeve in the best way possible. "

Taytra laughed wryly. "You know those people in the books that I've been reading say you would be wrong. They say you should be firm and not show too much emotion and that doing so makes you weak."

"And how long did those men last? Didn't they all die in battle?" he said with a smirk.

She shrugged. "I'm not sure I haven't gotten to the end yet."

He laughed. "Not to spoil it for you, but the military and their armies were all they had. They had to rule their men with an iron fist because they had nothing else. That is not you." He touched her shoulder. "You are brash, snappy, and angry at times. But you are kind, passionate, and caring. That is why people follow you and believe in you. That is why they will trust you when we come back."

Chapter 36 Shauna

She paced the cell, waiting, waiting, waiting. *Philippe?* She tried, and each time, pain lanced up her arms, and she felt nothing. *Philippe!*

She sat down hard and pressed her hands into her eyes. It had been hours.

Shauna had spoken to Lord Nurzan hours ago. Was it the next day? She couldn't say. She haven't seen Philippe since. *Has he been questioned? Did they hurt him? What is going to happen to us?*

She stood again and moved to the door, looking out into the hall.

"You can't use your Magick here," the elf at the door said dryly.

"You think I haven't figured that out?" she snapped. "You have been telling me that for weeks now." she smacked the door and slid back to the floor.

You are acting crazy, she told herself. *You need to hold it together.*

Her stomach grumbled, and she looked down. *I kinda wish I had eaten all of that food.* Here she was thinking they would bring her back to that cell. She was right to think they wouldn't feed her again at least.

She stood and went to the door. "Where is Philippe?" The guard glanced in her direction but didn't respond. "What is going to happen? Huh? What happens now?" They didn't even look at her this time.

She slid down the wall, not caring that her back got scratched by the rough stone. *Philippe, I am scared.* She ran a hand over her face, feeling it burning. She wanted to cry but there was nothing left. She was angry that she fell into this situation. That she couldn't defend herself.

Her marks flashed black on her arms again, but she still felt nothing.

Philippe, I am scared. But I am going to fight.

Chapter 37 Taytra

Taytra took everything out of her pack, laying it all out in front of her. *You broke out of a cell and went with just the clothes on your back for days*, she reminded herself. The few supplies she had felt both like too much and not enough to make it through this mission. *Two weeks on the road. You can manage that.*

A knock at the door gave her a moment of relief. "Come in!" she called.

She turned as the door slowly creaked open. "Hi, Tay, Andrew said I would find you in here packing," Sam said quietly. He stood in the doorway, shifting from foot to foot. One of Ward's wooden carvings twirled nervously in his fingers.

"Sam! Yes, come in. Where have you been?" Taytra said, hurrying over and giving the small boy a hug. She gently pulled him over to sit on the bed, swiping the carefully laid out supplies out of the way. "I saw you leave after the meeting but I couldn't find you anywhere. I came looking for you after I went to the market and after dinner, but Clive said he didn't know where you were."

He looked up at her with glassy eyes, fat tears already gathering in the corners, then turned away, staring hard at the carving in his hands. "I was hiding. I didn't want to see you go." Taytra's heart broke, but she could see he wanted to say more. So she waited as his fingers trailed over the mane of the little horse figurine. "But I realized I couldn't *not* see you go. I had to say goodbye to you since I didn't get to say goodbye to anybody else." He sniffled, wiping his nose on the back of his sleeve. He looked up at her just as the first tear fell. "I know you need to go but I'm scared you won't come back."

Taytra pulled the little boy into a tight hug, his head nestled in the crook of her elbow. Taytra looked up to the ceiling in her room, blinking rapidly, as his tears dropped onto her arm. *Goddess, please look over him. He has been through so much. And Clive. They need each other and they need someone who can be there consistently for them.* She took a deep breath and swallowed hard past a lump in her throat before saying, "I know. It's something that I am afraid of too."

"You are? "Sam said with a sniffle. He looked up, his little face blotchy and red.

How long was he crying before he came to see me?

Taytra nodded. "Of course I am. I'm afraid of leaving. I'm afraid I won't find my sister. I'm afraid of what may happen when I do find her. There are many things in life that we can't control. And things we don't understand. But that doesn't mean we shouldn't try." She brushed Sam's hair out of his face. "My father used to say that the worst thing that could happen if I asked someone for something or tried to do something would be if someone said no or denied me the ability to try. Right now, the worst thing I could do for myself or Shauna, would be to not try to save her."

Sam took a moment before saying, "What do you think I can try while you're gone?"

Taytra took his hand in hers and gently brushed her thumb across the back of his hand. He watched the movements and leaned into her again. "While I am gone, I want you to do one brave thing a day. The next few weeks are going to be very scary, especially with the Dark Ones right outside. A lot of adults are going to be very upset and angry at times. Ward and I will not be here to take care of you. Andrew is going to do his best, but—"

"But he's going to be busy," Sam interjected.

Taytra squeezed his hand. "Exactly. So, I think you should do one thing a day that makes you or someone else feel good or brave. That doesn't mean I want you looking for trouble, though."

Sam got up from the bed and went to look at the list on Taytra's nightstand. He carefully sounded out the letters, shaping them into words as he tried to read the page. "Do you think I could be Andrew's assistant?" he asked, putting the list down.

Taytra paused. "I think it would be best if you don't bother Andrew too much. Not because I don't think he would appreciate the help. I think some of the adults would think that you would get in the way and would yell at you." Sam nodded, agreeing with her. "I think that one brave thing that you could do every day would be to try to talk to a family every day, see what you can do to help them. Play with the other children. Show them it is safe here in Hollens. Then it wouldn't just be you helping Andrew, it will help to keep you busy too."

He nodded again. "I think I can do that." He moved

back to her side. "Can you promise me something?"

Taytra paused, then nodded. "I can try."

He wrapped his arms around her. "Will you be careful and take care of Ward and Lyra and Paulo and everyone? I don't like that I won't be able to watch you."

Taytra laughed. "You've been watching us?"

He shrugged. "Sort of like I had breakfast with Paulo a few times. And Lyra was always really nice. She helped me go to sleep a few nights when she was on rounds. I'll miss you all." He rolled the small figurine between his fingers. "I'm trying not to be too sad."

Taytra brushed a long chunk of hair out of his face. "That itself is very brave. I will do my best to protect everyone. But I think you are allowed to be sad. I am sad."

"You are?"

"Of course. I don't want to leave everyone but I need to find my sister. She is very important to me. Just like you are." Sam buried his head in her lap and sniffled for a few minutes. She rubbed his back, waiting until he chose to come up. "Do you want to help me pack up my things? Maybe you will think of something I haven't."

He got up, went over, and clipped her cloak around his shoulders. "Of course, Lady Taytra," he said, sweeping into a low bow. The two of them placed each item in the bag. He turned each piece over, examining every side before passing it over and giving that item his approval.

A knock at the door made the two turn. "Hello?" Taytra said, standing and moving to the door.

"Lady Taytra, may I speak with you?"

She narrowed her eyes. *I have heard that voice before. But where?*

Sam tugged on her sleeve and looked up at her,

waiting to be told what to do. She pointed to the bed, and he went and sat, pulling out his little figurine again. "Come in," she said, making note of everything around her in the room. *I am not being paranoid. Just prepared*, she thought, noting the knife sticking out of the top of her bag, well within her reach.

The door creaked open, and a male entered. She didn't recognize him at first but there was still something familiar about him she couldn't quite place. "Lady Taytra, I am not sure if you remember me," he said. "You and I shared a dance at the smooth celebration."

"You danced with someone who wasn't Ward?" Sam piped up. When the two adults turned to him, he fell back into the pillows. "Sorry." He looked to Taytra, and she nodded, so he went back to his figurine.

"I danced with several people that night, so I am afraid you will need to be more specific."

"I didn't realize you had a little brother," the male said, leaning against the door frame, avoiding the probe.

Taytra turned back to the man. "This is Sam. Sam this is…" She trails off. "I don't believe you ever gave us your name, sir?" She eyed him head to toe, a quiet challenge while she waited for him to answer.

He cleared his throat. "No, no, I didn't. It is best that you don't know. Wouldn't want the council members to catch wind. We are not on the best terms."

"I see," she replied, looking over the male again and calculating how long it would take her to reach the blade if she needed it. There was something about him that made him stand out. The mystery act was more annoying than anything—the masquerade was over. "What can I help you with sir? I believe the last thing you said to me was that you would know when I needed you?" she said dryly.

The man chuckled wryly. "Well, yes and no. I thought the time would've come prior to you leaving, but as you will be leaving with Ward and the other Frituals, I thought I would come and pass my token onto you to give to your people." He handed Taytra a small black coin with silver embellishments. She flipped it over, examining the images of Queen Moraine when she first started her reign and stones were still printed on black onyx. "As you may know, that coin is very old. As am I. Like your friend, Serena Nightcastle, it comes from a time of old. I have many skills that I would like to help you and your people, but I can only do so much right now," he said with the wave of his hands

Taytra watched the movements, trying to figure out where she saw something similar before. "You can use Magick?" she asked as the man put his hands back into his pockets.

"Yes, I can. Which I'm sure you can understand what limitations I work under at this time. Give that to your people when you leave, and when the time comes, I will help in whatever capacity I can. You never know when Magick will be needed, even in the city of men."

Taytra slipped the stone into her pocket, tapping it to make sure it sat safe in her clothes. "I will do that," she said. "Thank you. I don't know why you are doing this for us but I can tell you that it is very appreciated. I hope it will not be used, and when I come back, we are able to discuss this more."

"Until you need me, I would ask you to keep our discussions private." He turned to Sam. "Do you think you can keep this a secret for me, son?"

Sam nodded vigorously and made a show of zipping his lips and throwing away the key.

The man laughed. "It doesn't quite have to be like that, friend. I do ask that you keep my secrets safe, but if you see me anywhere and need something, I would be more than willing to help you with or without my mark."

"So, you're definitely a friend? You aren't a Dark One trying to be sneaky, are you?" Sam asked, getting up and coming up to stand just in front of Taytra. "Because that would be very mean, and I wouldn't want to have to stick you with the nice knife Ward gave me."

The man burst out laughing. "Little one, I promise I am not a Dark One. If I lie to you at any time, I give you full permission to use that blade of yours, as I do not take kindly to traitors."

Chapter 38 Andrew

Andrew knocked on Ward's door with a soft tap of his knuckles. He waited, nodding as someone went into the room next door. *Did he go to bed already?* Andrew wondered, turning away from the door.

He paused when he heard a sigh and the sound of bedsprings creaking.

"Come in," a muffled voice said from inside.

Andrew opened the door to find Ward stretched out on his bed, his boots hanging off the bedpost by the laces.

"Hey," Ward said. "Right, you wanted to talk tonight. I am sorry, I was going to meet you downstairs, but…" he said, sitting up and rubbing at the short beard that had grown in the past few days. "That doesn't matter. What did you want to talk about?"

"You guys really are leaving tomorrow, aren't you?" Andrew said, sitting in the only chair in the room. It creaked underneath him, and he shifted, wondering if the rickety thing would hold his weight.

"I don't know if I would trust that thing.

Sometimes it leans heavily to one side. But if you fall, I wouldn't be mad. I could use a laugh right now."

Andrew carefully slipped off the chair and onto the floor. "Well then, I don't think I should give you that satisfaction," he said with a grin. The two stared at each other for a moment, waiting for the other to speak, the silence shouting all the things they had wanted to say but hadn't since the fall of Cabineral. "This past month has been more than I ever thought it would be." Andrew sighed.

"I know. I think that's why it all went so wrong so quickly. At home, at least. No one suspected anything." Ward fiddled with the cuff of his shirt. "I mean, I know we wanted to join the queen's army and maybe someday be part of her guard, but this isn't how I pictured my career going," Ward said with a dry laugh.

"You're telling me." The two paused again, listening to the crackle of the fire in the corner. "So, you and Taytra?" Andrew said. "What is going on there?" he asked, already knowing the answer.

Ward flopped back on his bed. "Yeah, me and Taytra," he said with a smile.

Andrew couldn't help but smile, too. He knew what it was like to have a smile you couldn't contain. He had worn it all spring.

"I didn't mean for this to happen, I will have you know. I know anybody can see that, but something…" Ward trailed off.

"You know you need to be careful," Andrew said, scooting closer to his friend.

"Yeah."

Andrew pushed on. "You probably already thought of all of this."

"I've talked with her about it a few times," Ward said.

"Okay, I still want to say it. Is that alright with you?"

Ward sighed and covered his face.

Andrew paused, trying to find the words. He wanted Ward to be happy. Seeing him with Taytra made him happy, but it made him miss Safiya like crazy. Andrew wanted to make sure they weren't separated too. "You need to be careful because they could use her against you. If they transferred any of the guards that were in the palace that night to Bulandon and they recognize you, there will be instant targets on your back."

"There already is. There is one on your back too," Ward pointed out, looking under his arm at Andrew.

The young man sighed. "Yes, but I am not about to travel into the heart of enemy territory to get back my family," Andrew said, his voice coming out sharper than he meant. "You know just as well, maybe even more than I do, how scared she is going to be. I really care about both of you. I just want to make sure you can't be used against her, either. If they somehow connect your relationship and get you, she will buy into whatever tricks and won't think. The whole point of this is to get Shauna and Philippe. I don't want you to get hurt."

"Believe me, I know, but I think she will be okay."

Andrew blew out a breath. "Are you sure? What happened at the castle—"

"What happened at the castle was not her fault," Ward snapped, sitting up, his eyes fiery. "What happened was—it was…" He trailed off, trying to find words.

Andrew watched him warily. Knowing that Ward

needed to hear what he had to say from him just as much as Andrew needed to say it. "I know what you mean and I know part of you doesn't want to hear it, but I need you to listen. Love and emotions, they make coming to decisions hard sometimes. I don't know what I would do if I was in your position and it was Safiya," Andrew said. "So I can't tell you what to do. I can only warn you as a friend and as someone who wants the best for both of you, that you need to be careful."

Ward nodded. "Thank you. I know you do and I appreciate it."

"What are you gonna do?" Andrew asked, pulling his knees to his chest.

Ward sighed. "I have no idea. I know what you mean about protecting her. I tried to avoid this. But I feel like the more I try to pull away, the more I get sucked in by her."

"I don't think that is a bad thing. You just need to know going forward. Once you leave Hollens, neither of you can let your emotions get the better of you," Andrew said. "That is all I would ask of you. No matter what happens, just try to keep a level head."

Ward nodded. "When we are in the council meetings, or like up at the library, I just get swept up sometimes in her. She knows exactly what she wants and will do whatever she can to get it. That is when I really see her. Who she used to be, but also so much more."

Andrew grinned. "Are you sure it just wasn't that dress she was wearing?" Ward swung for him, and Andrew rolled away, laughing. "Alright, alright. I'm just saying, from what I've heard—since you two were in such a hurry you didn't stop by my room to see me beforehand like we planned—even if you hadn't been there to convince the council to get on our side of things, her dance card would have been packed," Andrew said pointedly.

Ward grinned and crossed his arms. "The outfit Serena got her was definitely... striking," Ward admitted and shook his head. "What are you going to do while we are gone?"

Andrew laughed. "Convince the council to let you come back?" His smile dropped. "Honestly, I don't know. Just make sure we survive long enough to go home."

Ward scoffed. "I don't know about that. I know Taytra and many of the others want to go back, but I can't help but wonder how much of that it's just an empty shell. Who even knows if her home is still there? We didn't get to go through the town, and half the people that were locked up hadn't gone to the ceremony. People said they were burning everything. Maybe we go back and we have to rebuild, but I don't know." He paused, and Andrew watched as he seemed to pull his emotions back. "I want to believe our home is still there. At least the city, if not our town, and maybe that will be good. Maybe if we can go back, we all live in the city. We would need to rebuild all the farms, but maybe in the future there won't be such a divide if everybody can live in peace."

Andrew looked into the fire as it popped and crackled. "I don't know if I ever want to go back. I just want to find Safiya and leave. I don't know why anyone would want to go back to where there was so much pain." Ward nodded, and the two of them stayed silent for a long time, watching as the flames tore into the wood and the fire slowly shrank. "I should go. You need to get some sleep before you leave," he said, pausing at the door. "We will figure it all out. We just have to take it a few steps at a time."

Ward rose and pulled Andrew into a hug, clapping him on the back. "We will be back before you know we are gone."

Chapter 39 Jamie

Jamie walked among his group, listening to the even breathing of children and the grandparents with too loud snores.

"We should be there by morning," Birsha said from Jamie's side.

"We just need to avoid the patrol again." Jamie looked toward the road. "They know we are here somewhere; they just don't know where we are." He could barely hear his own voice but didn't dare speak any louder.

Birsha nodded and adjusted his grip on the rough staff he had carved for himself. "We just need to avoid them for a few more hours. We can't take another close call."

Jamie glanced over to where Grayson slept fitfully. The boy had run for hours, leading the Dark One down a trail away from their group. He had returned to them, covered in hundreds of scratches, his knees bloodied where he had fallen, and exhausted. But he had led them away and protected the group.

"I don't know how he made it. I wouldn't have had

an ounce of his strength," Jamie whispered.

Birsha smiled. "Grayson used to win all the racing competitions around festivals. I wouldn't have trusted anyone else to outrun those devils."

A stick snapped somewhere in the distance, and the two men fell silent. Birsha pointed to himself, then in the direction of the sound before slowly standing and creeping toward the sound.

Goddess, please let it just be some creature finding it's burrow for the night, Jamie prayed, watching as Birsha's form disappeared into the dark. Jamie's heart raced, and he felt an icy bead of sweat drip down the back of his neck. *Goddess, please protect the people of Cabineral a little while longer. We are sick and tired but determined to make it.*

Jamie winced as a child cried out in the dark. It was followed by a mother's gentle coos, soothing the babe back to sleep. Jamie looked back to the road and crouched lower into the brush. *Goddess, protect us.*

It started with the sound of boots, their heavy feet tramping up the road. Then he heard the shouts of the officers. "Keep moving. They can't be far now! You there sweep the trees."

Jamie watched, wide-eyed and afraid to move a muscle as a soldier broke from the line and began to stumble his way through the woods.

"I don't see why we need to look for them like this." the elf grumbled. "They wouldn't be dumb enough to stay in one place."

A stick snapped behind Jamie, and he flinched and nearly cried out as a hand came to cover his mouth.

"It's me," Birsha hissed in Jamie's ear. "I'm sorry, I didn't mean to scare you."

Jamie nodded, and the boy lowered his hand. "We aren't getting any sleep tonight," he breathed, gesturing to the cohort. Much to his relief, the elf that was sweeping the forest had returned to the road.

Birsha shook his head. "No, we aren't. It's lucky they came through at night. We left too much of a path when we came off the road today." He pointed to several swipes of mud and broken branches.

Jamie watched as the last of the Dark Ones moved out of sight. "What should we do?" Jamie asked. "Should we send a scout to see where they go?"

Birsha chewed on his lip, the corner swollen from the repeated stress. "I don't know. Not yet. We don't want them to know we are in this area. We can't risk it. In a few hours, we can send someone out so they can be back before we move on. Just in case."

Jamie nodded. "Okay. Let's go back and tell the others." He paused. "We might not be done with this tomorrow."

Birsha sighed. "I know."

Chapter 40 Andrew

Andrew leaned against the wall nearby, watching as his friends tied the last of their supplies to their horses and climbed into the saddles. He smiled, looking at the different ways they carried themselves. Lyra had her small bag of supplies tied to her pack traveling lighter than everybody else, but that was normal. Barin had a heavy pack with a few blades sticking out of it, ready for any battles they might face.

"How is everybody feeling?" Lyra asked, surveying their small group.

Taytra looked nervous, but Andrew knew she was more than prepared for what would come ahead. Ward looked as serious ever, and Paulo looked excited, ready to do something. Andrew thought Barin looked uneasy as he ought to. Returning to the land of his father and having to face him was no simple task. *He will outshine his father's deeds,* Andrew thought, watching as the elf gathered his reins.

Andrew moved closer, his heart constricting a bit. It was time to send them off. "I almost wish I decided to go with you," he said with a wry smile. "Looks like you are off for a grand adventure."

"Oh, I'm sure you'll have your own set of challenges here with me," Alois said, his eyes a bit misty. "We will have our own issues waiting for us the moment they step out of that gate."

"What did you decide for your route?" Andrew asked, stepping up to check Paulo's stirrups.

"We are going to go south and hook around the back side of Bulandon," Paulo said once his feet were in the stirrups. "That way, we can try to avoid any patrols and use the cover of the city."

"We sent word to my mother in the city to expect us," Barin said, shifting as his horse danced beneath him. "We will see who gets there first. Either way, we will use the cover of the city to make a plan once we know exactly what happened to Shauna and Philippe. It will be safer that way."

Andrew saw Lyra glance at Taytra. *Ward didn't say how that last meeting had gone last night.* The young woman's face tensed a bit, but she said nothing. *She didn't like that plan.* Andrew turned to her. "And you will send word once you arrive?" Andrew asked. "If it is safe to, of course. I am sure the people will ask daily for an update."

"Yes, we will let you know as soon as we can that we have arrived safely," Paulo answered for her. "It may not be for a few days, but you will get an answer."

"Andrew! Come here!" Taytra turned quickly in her saddle to pull something out of a bag. "I almost forgot." She moved to her cloak, frantically digging at the pockets until she pulled out a small black stone stamped like a coin. "An elf gave this to me," she said, reaching down to hand him the coin. "I meant to find you last night."

"When did you talk to an elf besides us?" Paulo asked, peering over Andrew's shoulder at the stone. "Where did you get that? We haven't made stones like that in generations."

Taytra grabbed her reins, fiddling with the bit of leather. "Well, if I am honest, I didn't know that he was an elf at first. I met him at the library the night of Samhain." She turned to Ward. "You remember the man I danced with before I danced with the members of the council, the one with the black mask like yours?"

"Yes." Ward scowled. "The one that cut our dance short." Andrew held back a grin as he saw Taytra's cheeks flush pink. "I remember him. He seemed a bit odd. He was only there for a short time. I think he left one or two dances later," Ward said. "When did you see him again?"

"He found me at the inn last night. Someone told him where we had rooms. I was with Sam packing my things." She paused. "The night of Samhain, he told me that when we needed the support, he would be there. Last night, he said he wanted to extend that offer even if I— well, we—" She gestured to Ward and the Frituals. "—weren't here in the city. He still wanted to help our people," she said, trailing off. "I'm still not entirely sure what sort of help he really would offer us. But I believe he is a Magick user."

Andrew perked up. "It would be really nice to have someone else here that we know that can use Magick besides Enre if things go south." He turned the stone over in his hands. "But did he give you a name or anything?"

Taytra sighed. "I don't know his name. He said it was best that I didn't know it. Whoever this person is, is not liked by the council. If he is a Magick user, he probably has broken the rules quite a few times."

"Is it really wise to put all of our trust in someone we don't know? Especially if he wouldn't even give you a name?" Ward asked.

"What does the male look like?" Barin asked. He had gone still, his face stony.

"I didn't see his face the first time, with the mask," Taytra said, "but I remember his eyes. They were such a pale blue, and something about him didn't quite seem elven. He had long dark hair that he wore in a really tight braid."

Barin nodded, rubbing his chin. "The man you describe sounds very familiar to me." Barin said, "I wouldn't be able to say for sure without seeing him, but he sounds like the elf that abandoned the Dark Ones. One of the first Hunters. His name is Lochlin Callow."

"You are telling me there is a possible former Dark One Hunter in the city right now? Who has chosen to work with us?" Ward asked incredulously. "Why would he do that?"

"I think he might be right," Andrew said, looking at the stone in his hand. "I mean, this is an ancient coin. I believe it's dated right at the beginning of Moraine's reign." He turned to the elf. "What should I do?"

"Be careful," Barin said slowly. "I would not trust him right way. If he wants to help, go to him only if you must. If he comes to you, let him earn your trust. He has chosen your people for a reason. Do not reveal any information to him you wouldn't want others to know. Yes, I would keep him at arms' reach, but with the host at the gate, you can't discredit the benefit of having him possibly on our side."

Andrew nodded and slipped the stone into his pocket. He looked to the sky; the sun still sat low on the eastern front. "I don't want to keep you all waiting. You have a long couple of days ahead of you." Andrew slipped his hands into his pockets. "I wish you well, my friends. May the Goddess keep you safe and return you soon."

Chapter 41 Jamie

Jamie wanted nothing more than to sprint the distance between him and the gates to the city of Hollens. After they arrived yesterday afternoon, the group had been left stranded with the prospect of how to get inside, when no one knew that they were coming. The high wall around the city was both a blessing and a curse.

"Do you think they are waiting for us? Or did they follow Taytra, Ward, and Andrew's group?" Birsha asked.

"It's probably a combination. We need to figure out to let the city know we are here and get in without tipping them off." Jamie pointed at the dogs the Dark Ones had moving around the plain. "We can't risk getting caught by them. Not when we are so close." Jamie looked up at the wall and to the Dark Ones' encampment. The soldiers he could see in the distance huddled around their little camp fires. "Keep everyone away from the tree line. I am going to see if there is a way around them," Jamie warned. He began to creep around the edge of the tree line, keeping his eyes constantly switching from the ground in front of him to the elves in the distance.

It took him fifteen minutes to reach the edge of where the woods pulled away from the wall. He glanced again between the distance. *I have to do it,* he thought, steeling himself to step out of the tree line. He crouched low—his legs and lower back, screaming after so much time spent in the position of late—before he began to move through the thickest parts of the tall grass. He glanced toward the Dark Ones. *This should be far enough away, right?* He could see a guard on the wall overhead. The guards on the wall didn't look like they were on a continuous patrol. They kept stopping to look down at the field and then walked a few feet before going back to the same point. Maybe a twenty-foot lap. Either they were doing a lazy job and didn't care that there were a bunch of Dark Ones literally feet from their front door, or they had enough people at the gate it didn't matter.

Jamie stepped, out waving his hands all over the place, hoping the movement would catch the eye of one of the guards. He cupped his hands around his mouth and called up to the wall. "Hello, can you help me?"

The guard jumped and looked out to the plain, shading his eyes. He waved frantically when he saw Jamie, gesturing for him to come closer.

Jamie did so, watching the guard to see if he made any gestures that might mean danger was coming.

"Sir, are you okay?" he called down, leaning over the edge of the ramparts.

Jamie craned his neck, trying to see the man high above. "Yes! Much better now that I am speaking with someone. I need your help."

"What are you doing out there? You must know it isn't safe. There have been messages on the bulletins for weeks now!" the guard called down in an almost scolding tone.

Jamie wanted to laugh at the irony of it. Here he was another little rebel, being scolded by his mother. "Sir, I am not from here. I am from Cabineral Lake. I was trapped there under the castle. Me and my people recently escaped. We had heard that Hollens was a place of safety."

Jamie could have sworn he heard the man groan. "Oh no, not more of them." But when he looked up again, the man was gone. He was about to call up again when the man on the wall asked, "How many are in your party, sir? And where are they? We may be able to send out an escort to assist you."

Jamie beamed. His prayers were being answered. "An escort would be most appreciated. We have about thirty individuals. Mainly mothers, children, and elders. We do have one very sick individual whom we have been carrying."

The guard stepped away to relay the information. "Alright. We will send a group to help escort you to the city. You see that point at the edge of the forest where the trees jut out a bit? Bring your people there. We will gather a force and get you in here by sundown."

"Goddess bless you. Thank you! Thank you very much." Jamie spun and took off back across the plain, making it about fifty feet in his excitement before realizing there were still Dark Ones about and ducking.

Ten minutes later, he made it back to where he had left his group huddled in the trees.

"Jamie, what did you think you were doing? You could have been caught at any time!" Birsha said. "Are you crazy?"

Jamie laughed, too happy and excited to care about

the jabs. "We are going to get into the city. I was able to get the attention of one of the guards."

"We saw you go up to the wall!" little Noah said. "It was very brave!"

"Which means the Dark Ones could have, too." Birsha scowled. "What were you thinking?"

"We are going to get into the city," Jamie repeated, "and they are sending out an escort to assist us so if a patrol goes by we will have some protection. We need to move everyone so we can do it, though." Jamie looked out to the city. "They want to get us in by sundown. Come on, we need to get everyone moving," Jamie said, quickly moving through the crowd, passing word along.

When he got to the back where Moraine was resting, he stopped. "Moraine, you are awake! You have been out for a few days. What happened?"

She smiled softly. "I will be alright, Jamie. I heard you got us a pass into the city? We can talk more about me once we get there." Something about the way she said it let Jamie know there was no use fighting with her.

"Okay, do you think you can walk or do you need support still?" Jamie asked, looking at those who had been taking turns carrying the queen.

"I think it is best that at this time I still receive help," she said, sounding stiffer than she had in a few weeks. Like she was holding her cards close to her chest.

"You heard the queen," one of the men said, and the two lifted the makeshift sling and began following the line of people through the woods.

Jamie walked beside the group, trying to get a read on the queen's emotions. "Once we get inside, we can find you a healer to check and make sure everything is okay."

The queen nodded, her eyes locked on the city in

the distance.

Jamie hurried to the front of the group, encouraging those he passed to move quickly but quietly.

Thirty minutes later, the whole group huddled near the tree line where the guard had indicated. He glanced at the sky. The sun was beginning to set, the sky shifting to a bright orange. Jamie grinned as a line of soldiers came from the city, not from the main gate as he had expected, but from the side of the city far from the Dark Ones.

Jamie stepped out and waved to the men, who picked up the pace, moving into the woods with those from Cabineral.

"Are you the one that waved us down?" a shrewd-looking elf asked. He looked Jamie up and down, a look of barely concealed disgust on his face.

"Yes, my name is Jamie Flynn. I have about—"

"Hang on, did you just say your name is Flynn?" the elf snapped, cutting him off. "Goddess above, if you are related to that girl..."

Jamie froze. "That would depend on which girl you are referring to," he said slowly, glancing over his shoulder at those who gathered behind him. *Everyone thought Hollens was a place of peace. Maybe the guards on the wall didn't care about the Dark Ones outside because they are inside, too?* Jamie thought, his fists curling at his sides. He glanced to the blade at the elf's side. *If I can get that before he moves—*

"Oh, you know which one," the elf said. "I don't want to deal with this." He pointed to one of the others in his group. "You take care of him. I can't deal with Flynns." And then he stomped back toward the castle with no regard for his safety or that of the others.

"I—I am sorry? What just happened?" Jamie asked.

"I apologize. That is Neander. He is—shall we say, very particular about how he should be treated. I would have to assume he thought you were Taytra Flynn's father?"

Jamie nodded, grinning, beginning to put the pieces together.

"Right. Yes, your daughter, for lack of a better phrase, didn't put up with Neander's shit." The man winced, seeing little Noah behind Jamie. "She saw right through all the pomp and circumstance and stood up to him. He is not used to women being so vocal about their opinions. And he harbors a bit of a grudge." The man looked out to where the elf was walking. "I should add, your daughter was more than right on everything she argued with him about. Especially getting her people into the city. He tried to make them wait out here for a few days, and she argued that they needed to get into the walls as soon as possible. They fought. She got him to agree to get the city to move up the opening, and not even ten minutes after he went to get the gate open, they arrived," the man said, pointing in the direction of the camp. "They wiped out everything. Burned all their tents and supplies to the ground, but they got all their people inside. I hear she has been giving the council a hard time since. As you can see," he said and pointed to a section of charred earth, "that is all that is left of what her group had brought with them."

Jamie beamed. "That sounds like my Tay. Was anyone hurt?"

"Not to my knowledge, sir, no. Everyone made it in while the Dark Ones were moving in on it. They burned it after they were inside."

Jamie nodded, relieved that the group around him wouldn't need to learn what would happen to them. He glanced around. "Well, what do we need to do to get my group in?"

The man grinned. "Please follow me, Mr. Flynn."

After a few minutes of organizing, they made their move. The head of the guard put Queen Moraine, the children, and the elders in the center, with the stronger adults around them, and the guards ringing the outside. As they approached the gate, the doors swung open, and they heard a great cheer go up. The circle broke, with everyone making a mad dash inside. Jamie turned just in time to see the doors thud shut behind him.

He took a deep breath as tears welled in his eyes. He looked to the sky. *Thank you.*

Blinking back the tears, Jamie looked around. He wasn't the only one crying. Nearly everyone around him was laughing or crying. *These are them!* he realized as he recognized the faces that milled around him. They were from Cabineral. They were the trio's people. He spun, searching for Patrice. Maybe she was here and he could reunite her with Omar and Ward! He stopped when he saw Andrew with a wide grin on his face.

"Jamie! You got out! How did you do that? Is this everyone? I could have sworn there were more of you that we had to leave behind. I am really, really sorry about that. Is Safiya here? Where is she?" The young man rattled off.

"Andrew!" Jamie pulled the man into a tight hug. "It is so good to see you. There were more. I will explain later. First, Saf—" He stopped as a body came flying out of the crowd and launched herself at Andrew.

"Saf!" Andrew cried out, his voice strangled with emotion. "Oh Goddess, thank you." He squeezed her tight. "I'm here. I'm so sorry."

Jamie stepped away, letting the two have a moment of privacy. He turned, looking for another familiar face. If Andrew was here, then Ward and Taytra wouldn't be far. He looked for Omar. They could find them together.

"Jamie Flynn!"

He turned at his name, coming to face a woman he had only met one other time. "Serena! You made it here too! The queen will be so pleased. Let me bring you to her," he said, turning to lead her.

"Hang on," Serena said, putting a hand on his shoulder. "I believe Andrew was going to tell you, but he is a bit preoccupied now." She shot the young man a grin. Serena's smile faltered when she turned back to Jamie. "You should know, Taytra isn't here. She left yesterday morning."

Chapter 42 Andrew

Moraine sat up in bed, a cup of tea in her hands. "You don't need you to hover. I will be more than okay on my own," the queen said.

Andrew looked over at Jamie and Serena. Neither of them looked pleased by this answer. As the current leader in charge of the rebellion, Serena felt it was necessary he be here. Andrew would have felt differently. This was the queen. It felt like they could barely convince the council to keep up the constant patrols on the wall, let alone be a part of Queen Moraine's private affairs.

Serena crossed her arms and scowled down at the queen. "Moraine, from what Jamie has said, I beg to differ. You were unconscious for days. That is no little thing."

The queen took a sip of tea, ignoring the statement.

"Queen Moraine, what happened? Jamie said you were in the same cells the entire time?" Andrew asked, and they both knew that wasn't exactly true. Jamie had said as much.

Moraine, who saw right through the weak attempt, sighed and gave in. "That is not what he said," she said rather primly. "I know what you are doing there, young sir. But I will answer your question. Maybe you will all stop badgering me for a moment."

Serena scowled. "We would stop badgering you if you would just be honest with us."

Moraine pursed her lips but turned to Jamie. "You asked after we were taken to the cells, but I didn't tell you what happened when they split us up. I didn't really believe we could do anything about it. And I didn't feel there was a time to tell you with so many ears listening in," she explained, turning to Jamie. "I kept how I was feeling a secret. It didn't feel right to talk about how poorly I was feeling when people were suffering in the dungeons. I am sorry for the difficulties it caused the next few days."

Jamie nodded slowly. "I accept your apology. That all makes sense. Had people caught wind of what was going on, they may have panicked."

Moraine rolled her shoulders taking a moment to collect her thoughts. "When they took me to be interrogated, they had one of their spell casters there. It didn't really matter what I said. They had made their decision. When they were done asking questions that they already had answers for, they did a spell. They cut my wrist and after chanting some spell, placed this black band on it. They said I would regret ever letting them capture me." She scoffed. "As if I didn't regret every minute of being in their captivity." She rolled back her sleeve. "Over the course of the next few days, I realized I couldn't feel my Magick anymore. It was like it was just gone." She made a movement, like a dust cloud dissipating. "All I could feel was an emptiness within me, like something was missing. And then I just got so, so tired. It didn't really make sense, so I had to assume it was because of the spell.

Then I woke up, and we were out of the castle. I felt like I got run over by a horse."

"Can you sense any Magick now?" Serena asked, her eyebrows creasing in concern.

The queen shook her head. "No, I can't."

Andrew stared in shock at the black Magick on the queen's arm. *Goddess, if they can take away the Magick of a queen, how can we stop them?*

"Moraine," Serena breathed, "what are we going to do?"

The queen sat up tall. "I can tell you what we are not going to do," the queen snapped. "We are not going to make a big deal of this. We don't need a lot of people hearing about this. We will keep it quiet and figure it out," she said, shutting down the concerns.

Andrew felt like a child being scolded for stepping out of line. He tried to think of anything he could do. Serena brought him here because she seemed to think he could help. There was no way the council would be able to help, they were repulsed by Magick. He reached in his pocket for his notebook, wondering if he had a name of someone within. *Maybe Moira at the library could help? We could trust her.* His fingers brushed the onyx coin in his pocket. He slipped it from his pocket, clenching it in his fist. "Your majesty, I think I might know someone that can help." He glanced over at Serena and held up the stone.

"Are you talking about what you discussed with me after Taytra left?" Serena asked, cocking an eyebrow at Andrew.

He nodded. The conversation hadn't gone well. She wasn't happy to hear there was a former Hunter in the city, but she had agreed that it was necessary information. She said she wouldn't share it with the council unless it was necessary, there was no way they would react in any way that would be beneficial, since they still seemed to believe that the Dark Ones outside their door wouldn't be that big of an issue. "He may be a good person to reach out to. I can meet with him separately, not say who it is, and see if there is something he can do about it."

"Who are you talking about?" Jamie asked.

Andrew passed him the coin. "Before Taytra left, she met an elf at an event who said he wanted to help us. He left a token and said he would still help even if she wasn't here." Jamie passed the coin to the queen, and Andrew watched as the queen's eyes went wide. "Barin believes he is a former Hunter who left the Dark Ones because he didn't like the way things were turning out. We haven't followed up with him."

Moraine turned the coin over in her hand. "This is a stone from the very beginning of my reign. These haven't been made in over a century."

Andrew nodded. "That is why Barin believed that it was this Hunter."

"And you think this elf can help me?" the queen asked, passing the coin back to him. "Why would a former Hunter help me?"

Andrew shrugged. "I don't know if he can. I would think he could at least have an idea of the next steps to take would be. I also have access to the city library. Taytra was able to find some good information. I am sure they would be more than willing to help me look around."

The queen nodded. She didn't say anything at first, which made Andrew think he shouldn't have said anything. "Alright, you have my blessing to move forward with this. Take Serena with you when you meet him. Once you have an idea of if he is safe and if he has any ideas that sound credible, I will meet with him." She turned to Serena. "Any meetings we have will be on our terms. It doesn't matter whether or not I need to have this meeting. Our terms or no meeting," Moraine said firmly.

Serena bowed slightly. "Yes, your majesty. I will make sure your needs are protected, as always."

Moraine put her cup of tea to the side and turned back to Andrew. "That aside, tell me about yourself. How are things going? What should I know about the council?" She glanced over at Serena. "Have you told them I am here yet? That should be fun." She giggled. "I never got along with the men of Hollens."

"Believe me, I was an ambassador long enough to know that." Serena huffed. "They know 'unofficially.' I sent them a message when you arrived," Serena explains.

"Please update me on any reactions they have once they hear. From what I remember, they are not fond of elves or of any of the monarchs. The last thing I need is for them to hear I am out of Magick." She rubbed her brow. "They would never let me hear the end of it." Andrew shifted his position. "Yes, Andrew, I am sorry. Please go on."

"Well, I am not sure what Serena has filled you in on, but a lot has been happening. But it also feels like not much." He laughed a bit before going on to explain the stalled meetings, the arguments, the meetings they were left out of, Taytra's move for Samhain, and the improvements that had been made after. "Nearly everyone has already been placed in a job. There are only six people who haven't. Of those that arrived with you and Jamie, just about everyone has been treated for any wounds, and the city has given more than enough food to help everyone do better than they were. To heal."

"And yet, you didn't think you had a place here. You have done everything I would and more." Moraine smiled. "Great job. I think you and I will work well together."

Chapter 43 Taytra

"Taytra," Lyra said a gentle hand on her shoulder. "Tay, we have to get moving."

Taytra sat up, pulling the scarf to block the sand way from her face. "Okay, thanks, Lyra." Taytra blew air out from between her lips and glanced around. The rest of her party was up and moving, rolling up their bedrolls. She leaned over and poked Ward.

"I am awake," he said without opening his eyes. "You are the lazy one here."

She huffed. "I am not lazy. This just blocked the sound really well," she said, pulling it down so it settled around her shoulders. "I had to block your snores somehow." She rolled over and grabbed her boots, quickly lacing them up. She glanced around again. *Everyone is here, and no one has said anything,* she noted, and yet, something in her chest fluttered, a spark of anxiety she couldn't quite place. "Nothing happened last night, right?"

Barin looked over at her, surprised. "What makes you ask that?" He moved to the horses and began to prep them for the long day ahead.

Taytra shook her head. "I don't know. Just have this—I just feel uneasy."

Barin paused. "I know what you mean. We are close."

"Close?" Paulo asked.

"To the fortress. It's a few miles away. You wouldn't be able to sense the Magick, but maybe it feels that bad to everyone. Even those that don't use Magick," Barin explained. "It will pass when we get closer to the city." He looked to the sky. "Remember what I told you about the storms. Today looks like the perfect weather for them." He tapped the cloth that sat around his neck. "Be ready."

***

"That is the fortress?" Taytra asked of the shape in the distance. It was too far to really make out any details but the formidable building was hard to miss. Small pinpricks of light danced around the edge, and from what Barin had told them, there would be between six and ten guards on the wall at all times.

Barin glanced over his shoulder at his little parade of people behind him. "Yes, so hurry up." He glanced up at the sky. "The next watch should be changing soon. They don't usually get this far out, but if they see us, they may think it is a good idea to come and investigate." He spurred his horse to a faster pace. "The city of Bulandon isn't much farther on."

Each person in their group moved into a trot, and Taytra watched the little dust clouds puff up under her horse's feet. Barin had explained the fortress was a mammoth, able to take care of itself, but talking about it was different than seeing it. She didn't know how their little group could possibly break into it, find her sister and

318

Philippe, and get them out without being caught.

"We will find a way," Paulo said, noting her gaze. "Whatever is going on in there, your sister is holding her own, no doubt." He smiled. "You Flynns have your own way of fighting, a stubbornness about you that people don't expect."

"Sandstorm incoming. Cover up," Ward called out, interrupting the conversation.

They quickly wrapped scarves around their heads, leaving just their eyes exposed. Taytra leaned forward, making sure the wrap around her horse's face was in place before the wall of sand washed over them.

Lyra could have wiped the storm away or sent it around them easily, but they didn't want to risk sending out any Magick signals this close to the fortress. Plus, as difficult as it made it to travel across the plain, it acted as a perfect cover.

Taytra leaned into her horse's neck, pressing the cloth to her face and trusting her horse to keep her with the others.

"Tay!" Paulo called beside her. "Tay, take this. Barin said it's a larger storm," Paulo shouted over the wind, reaching the end of a rope to her.

She wrapped the end of it around the pommel of her saddle a few times. She could feel the tug of the others on the line now. It was both comforting and uncomfortable, as it made her horse jump forward a bit with each step, but she knew whoever was at the other end was moving closer, forming a huddle. *I hope Shauna is under cover.* Taytra looked in the direction of the fortress but she couldn't see through the wall of dark sand that flew in front of her. She couldn't see Paulo beside her anymore or hear him if he was trying to say anything over the roar of the wind.

She leaned forward on her horse, tucking her hands in her sleeves and away from the sand, and gently pet her horse, soothing him over the duration of the storm. It didn't last that long, maybe fifteen minutes, but once it stopped, the world felt eerily quiet. She watched the squall continue across the plain out toward the fortress. This was the largest storm they had come across.

Taytra untied the rope from her saddle, and they all quickly and quietly dismounted and took a few minutes, brushing the sand from under the horses' saddles and made sure there were no new cuts or scrapes that could become infected by the tiny particles. Taytra climbed back up on her horse after she was done with her check and started to walk circles around the group.

"Is something wrong?" Barin asked.

"Nothing, just antsy, ready to go. You were the one who said we didn't have that much time before the patrol would be coming by," Taytra replied. Barin smiled, and she felt a bit of the anxious bubble in her chest deflate for a moment. *He gets it. There is a lot at stake. For both of us.* She turned to the fortress, visible now that the storm had moved on. "Shit, is that them?" she squinted at the fortress. Even this early, heat waves distorted the ground in shimmering waves.

Barin whipped around. "It might be." He shielded his eyes against the sun. "Come on, we need to go," he ordered, climbing back onto his own horse.

Taytra turned to see if anyone needed a leg up, but they were all trotting toward her. *Good.* She turned and started an uneven trot, following the Frituals. It had been refreshing to travel so quickly with Ward and the Frituals.

Covering the distance between Hollens and Bulandon in a little over a day, much faster than they had planned. The horses were doing well too. Taytra had been afraid one of them would go lame from the hard pace, but each time they got down and checked their horse's feet and legs, there were no issues.

"If we don't run into any setbacks," he called over his shoulder, "we will be in the city well before nightfall. We just need to figure out how to lay low until Alessia lets us in."

"If you take me to any points were there are entrances, I could get us in," Paulo pointed out. "Like the one Enre opened for you."

Barin burst out laughing. "You think it would be a good idea to literally drop us into a rebel camp that is on watch for Dark Ones twenty-four seven? It would not matter that we are Frituals or that the leader is my mother. We do that and that would be a death sentence for all of us." He smiled at Paulo. "I am sorry for laughing. But I think we can both agree, I would rather not finish my day being skewered. Besides, from what Enre told me, those points in the city are shut down every so often so the Dark Ones can't try to use them. After my crashing entrance, I doubt it will be open any time soon."

They rode in silence after that, following Barin's lead across the desert.

Taytra glanced over her shoulder one last time as the fortress went out of view behind one of the many sand dunes. *Just hang on for a few more days, Shauna. I will be back. I promise.*

***

Barin took them on a path that looped around the

city of Bulandon. "When I left, there was a long train of people leaving in a caravan with supplies and trade. The city is just getting back on its feet," Barin explained. "We need to avoid those. They had Dark Ones checking each cart. I hid under a pile of hay. But I doubt we would get so lucky again. We are headed to the southern gate."

Taytra thought of the message Enre had sent before them. *Did the messenger make it here okay? Does the queen know we are coming?* The goal was to have someone meet them at the gates and, once it was safe, guide them through the city to one of the underground entrances.

Taytra reached under her cloak to touch the blade on her waist. Sam had sharpened it for her before she had left. She just prayed to the Goddess she wouldn't need to use it today. "Which plan do you think we should go with? Stay together or split up?" she asked as they pulled up a bit away from the gates to the city.

"I haven't fully figured it out. Which do you think would be most beneficial?" Barin asked, turning in his saddle and moving to a trot.

"Well, you said there probably would be Dark Ones waiting for us to arrive. Wouldn't it make sense for us to split up then? If Enre's messenger was intercepted, then they will be looking for a group of at least five people. If we split into smaller groups, we may be able to get into the city easier, right?" Taytra offered.

"But the person we are meeting with won't be expecting that. What if it is more dangerous?" Lyra asked.

Barin considered it for a moment. "It might, but I think there is something to it. Have any of you ever been here before?"

Taytra shared a look with Ward. "No, my family

never went on any long holidays around the kingdoms."

Paulo said, "This is new territory for all of us."

Barin nodded. "Right, that makes sense, of course. Perhaps I could travel between both groups? Make the rendezvous point for one, then figure out another point and take you there?"

"I don't know. It seems like traveling the city could be the riskiest for you, as you are from here and people know your face?" Ward asked.

"Let's stay in eyesight of each other for now, but head inside in groups. One group can be the lead and the other can follow at a distance. I would refrain from any use of Magick," Paulo added.

"Right. Hoods back up. Let's merge in with that group there and get into the city," Barin said, pulling his hood high on his head.

Chapter 44 Andrew

The market was livelier for this time of day than Andrew would have expected. People bustled back and forth, wool cloaks snapping at their heels.

"It feels weird to be out and about like this," Safiya said, sticking close to Andrew's side.

"If you get overwhelmed and want to leave, we can. Just let me know," Andrew said, gently rubbing Safiya's back in small, comforting circles.

Safiya paused on the corner, waiting for a cart to go rolling by. "I think I will be okay," she said. "It is almost nice. I can move and go where I want."

"Ward told me there was a shop along here that was selling cloaks at a decent rate, especially this late in the season. I am sure we will find you something. And if we don't, you can keep wearing mine." Andrew watched her as she rubbed her arms and shivered. He couldn't believe she was here, and while underfed, she wasn't hurt. Andrew had played their reunion over and over in his mind, a part of him never thinking he would actually get to see her again, let alone hold her and have her by his side. The skin around her cheeks was tight, a bright pink flush under her skin from the cold. To him, she was just as beautiful as she had been the night of Beltane when he asked her to be his wife. "I am going to say something crazy," he said, catching her hand and pulling her out of the flow of traffic.

"What? Is everything okay?" she asked, searching his face for danger.

He smiled down at his fiancée. "Nothing is wrong. I just—Part of me was scared I may never see you again. And now that I have you back, I never want to lose you again." He reached down and grabbed her hands. "I know we had plans. You were going to meet with Jacinta and get a dress and do the whole thing." He sighed. "I still want all of that but I don't know when it will happen."

"My family is still missing," she said quietly, scuffing her feet along the ground.

"I know. And that is the one thing that makes me hesitate. But we will do the whole thing when we get home. You can have the dress and the flowers, but I want to do it now. If you will have me."

"Andrew, what are you asking me?" Safiya asked, her thumb running over the callus on his palm.

"Marry me. Please. Tonight, we can talk to Alois, and he can do the ceremony. I don't want to lose you. I want you to be my wife."

Safiya grinned. "You were more confident this time," she said, stepping up on to her tiptoes to kiss his cheek. "We can do it in the camp. We may not have our close family but we can have our people around us."

Andrew's heart skipped a beat. "I know it isn't what we wanted, but I don't want to go another day without you as my wife."

She squeezed his hand, searching his face. "You have taken on so much in the last month, and I wasn't sure I would ever get out of there. That in itself is something to celebrate. Yes, let's find Alois."

Andrew grinned and bent, pressing a kiss to her lips. "I am so grateful the Goddess brought you back to me," he whispered against her lips "Come on, let's find Alois. And a cloak, we still need to find you a cloak."

* * *

"You ready for this?" Enre asked, clapping Andrew on the back.

Andrew poked his head out of the tent, looking out to the crowd. Nearly everyone from Cabineral was gathered around the front of the tent waiting for the ceremony to start. "I can't wait." He grinned and turned to Alois. "Thank you again. I can't begin to express how much this means to me."

The little elf grinned. "Oh, of course, friend! I haven't had the chance to perform a wedding in at least a century! I am honored the two of you would think to ask me."

Andrew grinned, his stomach full of butterflies. "Do you think you remember how to do it?"

The elf scratched his beard. "I will figure it out, don't you worry," he said, waving Andrew away. "Come, come. Let's get this started before the people out there start a riot. Your Safiya was right. These people need something to celebrate."

Andrew nodded and took a deep breath before striding out of the tent and stepping up onto the makeshift stage of boxes. The people cheered. Andrew's cheeks flushed with joy and a bit of embarrassment at being in such a big spotlight. *Just focus on Saf,* he told himself, scanning above the heads of all the people for his bride. The air whooshed out of his lungs when he saw her.

"Close your mouth, friend," Enre said, sliding past him to take a seat in the crowd.

Safiya walked arm in arm with Serena. Andrew watched as the elf turned to the young woman and whispered something that made her grin from ear to ear. Like with Taytra, Serena gave the young woman a beautiful gown to wear. The deep burgundy fabric complimented the girls too-pale skin, making it look as though she glowed from within. Serena lifted a hand, indicating it was time, and the crowd fell silent as Safiya passed—aside from a few little ones who asked in too-loud whispers if she was a princess. Andrew was more than impressed with the quick turnaround. From the time he and Safiya had found Alois to this moment as he helped Safiya onto the stage with him, could be no more than three hours. And yet, they had an audience, a dress, and were ready.

"You look amazing," Andrew whispered for just Safiya to hear.

Safiya twisted slightly, letting the gown twirl around her feet. "I feel really pretty. I could have tried on dresses for days. I didn't know a warrior could have so many gowns. Serena must have lived here a long time."

Alois stepped up to them. "Are you two ready?"

Andrew took Safiya's hands, then nodded. "Yes. Thank you again, Alois."

The old elf raised his hands high overhead.

"Friends, family, and strangers of Cabineral. We are gathered here tonight under the light of the Goddess's moon for a joyous celebration." Alois's voice faltered, and he cleared his throat before starting again, bringing his arms down. "Gosh, that is tiring. I am not doing that anymore," he muttered, and the couple laughed. "Andrew and Safiya came to me today, expressing that it was their will to be wed. After the terrors of the last month, who could deny them that?" The crowd around them murmured their agreement. "I would ask all those gathered here to bear witness to their union. It will be different than many ceremonies we are used to. There will be no rings, no passages read or lengthy vows exchanged. Just as the two have requested, a few simple words and a group to bear witness to their union."

"That's the way all weddings should be. They are too bloody long!" someone from the back of the crowd yelled, sending laughs out amongst them.

"He isn't wrong." Andrew laughed, squeezing Safiya's hands.

Alois placed a hand on Safiya's forearm. "Please repeat after me. I, Safiya—oh, Safiya dear, what is your surname?"

"Lunnan, sir," she said quietly.

"Ah, yes, beautiful name. I should have asked before," the elf said. "I, Safiya Lunnan, take thee, Andrew Warner, to be my lawfully wedded husband."

She grinned, her eyes dancing with happy tears. "I, Safiya Lunnan, take thee, Andrew Warner, to be my lawfully wedded husband."

Alois turned to Andrew. "It is your turn. I take thee, Safiya Lunnan, to be my lawfully wedded wife."

Andrew grinned. "I, Andrew Warner, take thee,

Safiya Lunnan, to be my lawfully wedded wife."

Alois grinned, bouncing slightly on his heels, unable to contain his excitement. "Now together. May the Goddess bless our union with peace and love as long as we both shall live."

Safiya's voice was clear and bright with joy as she repeated the words. "May the Goddess bless our union with peace and love as long as we both shall live." But Andrew wasn't looking at her anymore. He was looking past her to the wall, where a stream of soldiers raced up the stairs and along the battlements. "Andrew? We are meant to say that line together." She squeezed his hands. "Andrew, darling what is it?"

The crowd turned as they heard the shouting up on the wall. *No, no, no, no, no!* the voice in Andrew's head roared. *Not now!* Then he heard it. The twang and whistle as many arrows left bowstrings. "Get down!" he roared and shoved both Alois and Safiya off their little stage. He landed on top of the two, covering them as fire arrows rained down around them.

"Andrew!" He could hear the terror in her voice well before he saw it on her face. "Andrew, what is happening?" She spun underneath him, trying to see his face.

Andrew looked around, trying to gauge when it would be safe to move. Where it would be safe to go? "Saf, it is okay. You are safe for right now. I have you." He took her hand and helped her and the elf to their feet. "Alois, are you alright?"

The elf coughed and brushed the dirt from his beard. "Yes, I am alright. They must be at the wall!"

Andrew nodded. "I need to see what is going on."

He turned to his almost wife. "Saf, I need you to stay here. Alright, I need you to—" He looked around at the screaming families who flew from the space. They crying babies that were hauled away. Taytra had said it. She had warned them, when Hollens was attacked their people would be the first to feel the blows. "I need to see what is happening. Please." She looked at him wide-eyed. "I—I need to do this," he repeated, and she nodded, eyes wide with fear but understanding. "Do you remember where I asked you today? The little alley I pulled you into?" She nodded, tears streaming down her face unabated. "Go there. Take as many of our people as you can. I will meet you there soon, I promise." He pulled Safiya into his arms. She shuddered against his chest, and he looked to the sky. *Goddess, please don't let this be what I think it is.*

Alois grabbed his arm. "To hell with the ceremony. Andrew, Safiya. You kiss now and you are wed. Because I say so, and the Goddess will have to deal with it."

Safiya turned her tear-stained face to the elf. "But we didn't finish it."

"I don't care. You two are married. Now kiss and let's go!"

Andrew cupped Safiya's face. "In the spring, when this is all over, we will have our wedding the way we want it. Whatever you want, I will get it for you."

"You have a lot of making up to do, soldier." She laughed and pressed her lips to his. Andrew pulled her close, tucking her body into him away from the wall and the next line of arrows that rained down around them.

"I will. Anything you want. You will have," he said, breaking the kiss. "Go, go to the market. I promise, I will be there soon."

Enre dashed up to him. "Andrew, the wall."

Andrew looked from him to his bride, and she nodded. "Go," she said before she too turned and started calling out to the families and shepherding out of the courtyard.

An arrow clattered between Andrew's feet, and he turned. "What in the Goddess's name is going on?" he yelled, running for the stairs to the wall. *How could they possibly have snuck up on them? Someone should have been watching the wall this whole time. We should have seen this coming. Someone should have called a warning.* But as Andrew climbed the steps, he knew. Even if there had been a warning, there would never have been enough time.

Chapter 45 Paulo

Paulo dismounted before entering the city, using the moment to prepare himself. He adjusted the stirrups, making sure they wouldn't swing and hit his horse's stomach before leading him through the gates of Bulandon. Barin had said the city was finally getting back on its feet but that many of its inhabitants were still having a difficult time. Paulo stared at the gate house as they moved past it. Many of its beams were scorched black by flames, making the newly inserted support look like white bones. People huddled around the few braziers, but it was empty aside from the few guards that patrolled the area. At first glance, Paulo couldn't tell who they served, though he had to assume they were Dark Ones. There was no king, no outwardly established government, so who else could these guards serve?

"Keep your head down," Ward whispered as he moved past the elf.

Paulo checked again to make sure his hood was fully up, covering his face before he nudged his horse forward. The horse pulled, resisting him, and backed into someone else's path. "It's okay," he said, patting his horse's shoulder. "It's okay." The horse's ears flicked back to listen, then forward again, turning to focus on some specific sound. "This is a good thing anyway," he said quietly to the horse. "You just gotta let me know if you see anyone mean." The horse tossed his head almost like he was agreeing to the rules.

He saw Lyra turn in her saddle, trying to make sure he was okay, but he didn't look. Out of the corner of his eye, he saw Lyra also dismount and start to walk towards the exit of the courtyard.

He reached into a saddle bag and pulled out a bit of bread, munching on it as he slowly led his horse out. A few people tried to speak to him, asking for spare money and the like, but he kept his head down.

Ward had also gotten down but he was speaking with someone who looked like a blacksmith. *Maybe he threw a shoe?* Paulo wondered as he walked by. He glanced over at Ward as he passed, who nodded in his direction. Paulo hesitated for a second, wondering if he should stay behind to make sure he was okay, but figured he was doing something like he was. Trying to blend in. Paulo glances behind Ward to a bulletin board on the wall and ducked his head a bit lower. Listed among some individuals who must be real criminals, were a few familiar faces. Barin was listed at the top, his sketch the most detailed of any of the Frituals, with Paulo and Lyra's being a bit rougher. The two portraits were close enough one could match them, but some of the details were off. His nose was nowhere close to that big. Ward, Andrew, and Taytra also had earned a place on the wall, but Ward was probably safe to speak with people as in his drawing his hair was much shorter and he didn't have a beard.

Paulo passed a few Dark Ones, keeping his gaze forward. The hair on the back of his neck stood on end when he accidentally caught the eye of one of the Dark Ones. He held their gaze for the briefest moment before looking away. *Please, Goddess, let him not recognize me*, he thought, hoping the fact that he didn't jump to look away would keep him safe.

"Hey, you!" a guard in front of him shouted. Everyone in the crowd froze, and Paulo ducked his head, praying he wasn't the target. "Hold still!" the soldier said, shoving past Paulo to the person behind him. Paulo turned slightly, checking to make sure it wasn't any of his crew.

He felt a conflicting pang of relief and sympathy for the person who was led away, kicking and screaming, "I didn't do anything. Where are you taking me? Get your hands off me!"

Paulo took a moment, scanning the crowd for all five of his crew. Ahead he could see Barin talking with someone who sat on a small pony. *That must be our guy,* Paulo thought, turning to walk in that direction and continuing to nibble on the bit of bread. There were a few small children darting in and around the crowd trying to nick bits off of unsuspecting individuals.

One came near, and Paulo caught the boy's eye and shook his head. The boy froze like a deer caught by a hunter, then ran away before him or of his counterparts got caught.

"Fancy seeing you here," Taytra said casually striding up next to him with her horse on a long rein. "That was crazy, wasn't it?" she said, pointing back in the direction of the poor prisoner.

"It is sad. I thought he was coming for me at first. I don't know what I would do to be pointed out, but you never know with jumpy guards, right?" he commented, trying to act casual and like his heart wasn't pounding from the close encounter. He glanced over his shoulder and saw that Ward was back on the way, about a hundred yards back. "Looks like our friend is up ahead. Shouldn't be long until we find our inn," he said, nudging his chin in the direction of Barin and their escort.

Out of the corner of his eye, he saw Lyra apologize to someone nearby who her horse nearly kicked. She moved her horse to the corner and spun him in a circle to test if he had gone lame.

Barin and the person started to move, and Taytra noticed, shifting her horse first to follow them. The first duo led them down the street and took a quick turn, pulling them onto a quieter street. There wasn't a single Dark One in sight. Paulo took what felt like his first deep breath since getting into the city.

"Is this all of you?" their escort asked.

"Yes, we are all here," Ward said, coming around the corner. He flicked a new knife around in his hand before slipping it in his belt. "What?" he asked, seeing Taytra's scowl. "I was making sure I gave them a sale today. Just helping out the local vendors. I am sure a stall there costs a small fortune."

"Right," the person said. "My name is Saxe. It won't take us long to get to the tunnels. Before we do, we will be stopping by a stable. We obviously do not keep the horses with us," he said, and Paulo had to agree, the idea of keeping horses underground did not sound pleasant. For the horses—or those that had to clean up after them. "We will show you where to go to get them should you need them at any time." He scanned the group. "Any questions?

We won't be able to talk much once we get going. In fact, I would refrain from mentioning anything you wouldn't want others to catch wind of," Saxe said, gesturing back the way they came.

Right. While the rebels hold the city, the Dark Ones have a grip over it as well.

"How long will it take us to reach the inn?" Lyra asked. "Me and my fellow travelers could do with a bath and a hot meal."

The elf grinned. "Yes, I did notice that. We should have you settled into your rooms within the hour, miss. If you will just follow me, we will get your horses set up in the finest stalls." The elf turned and began walking back up the busy street.

Paulo kept alert, trying not to tense or duck his head in any obvious way when a patrol went by. *Just a little bit longer and we will be undercover*, Paulo told himself. His horse tossed his head as if he could sense Paulo's unease. "I am okay, just a long day," he murmured to the beast, petting his neck as they turned another corner. "We will get you set up with a big old thing of hay. How's that sound?" Paulo grinned when the horse turned his head to him, the animal's big brown snout sniffing his shirt for snacks. "Not quite yet. In a few minutes."

"Well, you certainly made a friend." Barin laughed from behind Paulo. He held a tight lead on his horse. "This one tried to bite me again this morning. Luckily, we haven't bucked at all today though. Gonna have to work on that, aren't we, sir?" Barin said. He reached up to pet his horse's neck, and in response, the beast flattened his ears and tried to back away from Barin, pulling the elf along with him.

"You will just have to give him a bunch of treats.

He has worked hard the last few days. But he will warm up to you eventually. Or he won't. Horses have a mind of their own." Paulo grinned. "I have always had special luck with horses."

Barin scowled, and Paulo couldn't help but laugh. He knew what the younger elf was thinking without having to ask. *How much of Paulo's luck with horses was of his own doing, and how much was his Magick?*

"Okay, right this way," the elf leading them said, turning into the courtyard of a large inn with dilapidated sides. Paulo could see a few people inside, but it looked like they were the sort of patrons that couldn't tell their ale had been watered down to nothing.

Paulo saw a pair of Dark Ones walk past the gate, their pace slow, clearly listening in as Taytra turned to Ward. "Really, here? You booked our rooms here?"

Ward shrugged, playing right into the ruse. "What, you said you wanted somewhere cheap. And look at the barn. The horses will be happy."

She threw her hands in the air, spooking her horse slightly. "I'm sorry I didn't mean to scare you," she said, patting the horse, then turning back to Ward with a fire in her eyes that made Paulo almost burst out laughing. "At least someone will be happy with this situation. I said somewhere cheap, as in, won't break our bank. Not someplace we have to worry about someone stealing our money!" She turned to the rest of the party. "I am sorry. He can be a bit daft sometimes."

"Miss, would you like to still rest your horse until you find quarters that suit your fancy?" the elf asked as the Dark Ones rounded the corner out of sight.

"Fine, I guess so. They need to rest just as much as

we do. This place will work for now." She huffed, following the elf to the door.

Lyra grinned. "Better watch out, Ward. She's got some pretty high-class tastes. It's gonna be a real issue one of these days."

He barked out a laugh. "Don't I know it!"

Their guide called over his shoulder, "Food for your horses can be found in the tack room. If you want to hang up any saddles, use the door on the left. Any other *valuables* you may want to store should go to the room to the right. I can help you with that."

We are going through the right hand door to get into the tunnels, Paulo thought, and the others nodded. Barin led them in, and they headed to the stalls at the far end of the barn.

"Hello, sir. I can care for your horse, if you'd like?" a little boy said from the top of a pile of hay in the corner.

Paulo looked to Saxe, who gave him a small nod. "Sure. Let me grab my bag and then he is all yours." Paulo untied his bag and pulled out a stone, tossing it to the boy. "As a matter of fact, can you take care of all of our horses?"

"Yes, sir!" the child replied, catching the coin. "I will get right on it. I'll give them a bath and everything!"

Paulo smiled and passed the reins off. "I trust you will take good care of him. I will let you know when I need him again and make sure to request you get him ready."

After the horse was led away, Paulo headed back up the aisle to the tack room. Like Saxe had said, the room lined with bags of grain and hay for the horses also featured two doors on either side. Paulo opened the door on the right, where he would 'store his valuables.' This led to a small room with a series of drawers.

"How do we get in?" Taytra asked, peering over his shoulder.

Paulo ran a hand over his chin. "I am not sure."

Taytra slipped passed him,. "Well, if I wanted to be secretive, I would make it difficult or inconvenient." She scanned the many rows of drawers. "There." She crouched low in the corner and opened a drawer that was nearly on the floor. "Gotcha."

Much to Paulo's surprise, the drawer had a lever, that when Taytra gave it a good tug, opened the wall of drawers on a set of secret hinges. "So you can still store stuff," Paulo said, opening one of the drawers at eye level.

"But if you know where to look, it isn't hard to get in," Saxe said. "Come. I am sure Queen Alessia is expecting you."

Chapter 46 Andrew

The thing they had been telling the council for weeks had finally begun. The siege of Hollens. As Andrew looked out over the plain, he saw not just a group of Dark Ones that had followed those from Cabineral and had been waiting outside the gates for well over a week. Now there were at least three other battalions, and they had brought siege weapons. He watched in awe and horror as the ranks to the far left began the slow trudge to the gates, pushing a heavy battering ram between them. The large fire harden log swung on heavy chains, its spiked wheels slowly tearing the ground apart as it crept forward. The Dark Ones who pushed the machine surrounded by a ring of additional guard, who held shields ready to ford off any attacks.

The soldiers on the wall stumbled and clattered around him. Their shouts full of fear as they fumbled and dropped weapons and struggled to follow orders and create formations.

We knew this was coming, Andrew thought,

watching in dismay as one man chased his spear as it rolled down the parapet. *Have these men no real training?*

"By the Goddess," Enre said, staring out at the carnage that would unfold. "What are we going to do, friend?" he said, turning to Andrew.

Andrew turned, watching as the last of the people from Cabineral left the square, heading to the market district with Safiya and Alois. "We need to find the commanding officer," Andrew said. "Someone around here has to put things in order." He spun, trying to find said officer, but every single person around him appeared as unhinged as the next. *Where are they?* he wondered. *There should have been some officer at least in the area? They should be here by now.* Someone ran by, and Andrew reached out and grabbed them by the shoulders. "Sir, tell me what is going on. Where is your commanding officer?" The boy, who couldn't be older than fifteen, stared at Andrew and Enre, mouth agape, as another volley of arrows flew overhead. "Boy, what is going on?" Andrew asked again, shaking him.

The moment cracked the spell of fear, and the boy spluttered, looking at a body in the corner. "He dead. The officer is dead," he gasped out. "We don't have anyone. I can't find any of the officers."

"Goddess," Andrew swore, letting go of the boy. "Okay, you and I are going to work together." He pulled the two of them to the side as a man went barreling past, the smell of urine rife between them. Andrew glanced around. *How the hell did I get here?* he wondered. A month ago, he did a test to come of age and now he was in a war zone. *I can't know enough to control this,* he thought but tamped down that fear. He didn't know what he was doing but he knew enough to know that they needed to get this wall under control. "I am going to give you a task," he said, keeping his voice firm but comforting. "First, I need you to take a few deep breaths. Rushing around will get you hurt." The boy nodded and took a few shaky breaths. He turned to look out on the plain, and Andrew pulled him away. "Here, focus here in the city." The boy looked down at his feet. *How did he get here? He never should have been on this wall.* Andrew glanced around. He and Enre needed to gain some traction and control before the Dark Ones and their battering ram reached the gates. "I want you to go to the bell tower. Do you know if there is a way to signal that there is danger? We need to send the message out to everyone in the city so they know to get to safety."

He stopped. "There is, but—" The boy shook his head. "We honestly haven't used that sequence in years. I don't know if people will recognize it. I don't think we have used it since I was alive. Not even practice drills."

Inwardly, Andrew cursed the council but said nothing to the boy. "Even so, there will be those that remember the last time they rang it and will pass on its meaning. I want you to find two or three others and ring that message through the city. Is that clear?"

"Yes, sir!" The boy nodded and took off running, grateful to have a purpose that took him away from the walls.

Andrew turned to back to Enre. "We need to get these men in some sort of order. We need to delay them," he said, pointing out to the battering ram just as the Dark Ones released another volley of arrows at them. Everyone on the wall pressed themselves against it, hoping the arrows passed them by. They struck the floor around them, the points sparking against the stone.

"We need to get ourselves some weapons," Enre shouted over the clatter. "I, for one, don't want to be a sitting duck!"

Andrew gripped the elf's shoulder. "Run to the armory. See what you can find for the two of us. And if you can find anyone in charge, get them up here! Or to the other flanks. We need to be strong on all sides."

"I'll be back soon!" the elf said before darting in between the men who gathered on the parapet.

Andrew looked out over the wall, trying to devise a plan. Out on the plain, he could still see the scorched black earth where they had set up camp before they had made their retreat into Hollens. This was meant to be a haven for their people. He, Taytra, and Ward knew it wouldn't be long before the Dark Ones came for them, but he had thought they would be better prepared for something like this. *How did nobody sound an alarm when more soldiers came? How did we miss this?* he wondered. *Did the council know something like this was coming? Did they purposely hide this?* He turned away from the wall. *What would Ward and Taytra think if they knew that just days after they left, the city would fall?* He took a deep breath. "Men of Hollens!" he called, hoping his voice carried out over the din of battle. "Now is your chance to take a stand. I need archers to the wall!" Andrew shouted, watching the men on the wall slowly turn to face him. "Now is the time to show them this is your home and they cannot take it. I need archers to the walls," he shouted again and watched as the men moved as if thawing their movements slow and jerky, as they tried to get their brains to fight against the fear that clouded their judgement.

"Sir, how can you possibly think we can fight

them? Look at all of them!" one man asked, his voice cracking with fear.

Blood pounded in Andrew's ears and his chest tightened. He watched as the men turned, looking to him for an answer. With so many untrained men who had never really believed they had to raise a weapon, it would be hard to hold the Dark Ones off for long. Impossible even. But they had to try. "We are better off than them. There is a wall to protect us. We can keep making weapons and have beds and places to rest. They need to wait for things to come back and retreat to a camp set up in a few days. We have the upper hand," Andrew said, trying to imbue his words with power and confidence. Andrew didn't mention the fact that supplies could run out, or that there were women, children, and elders who lived in the city, or that the wall could fall. "Are you ready, men?" A weak cheer rose along the wall, and Andrew smiled. "Archers to your arrows." He moved along the wall, surveying those that drew arrows to bows, nocking the arrows to their strings. "I want you to target that battering ram. We need to take that out first," Andrew said. He leaned out over the wall, looking at the ground far below. The sun shifted behind a cloud, and he could see with that the weak autumn light reflecting off a dull cap at the end of the wood. He couldn't be positive at this distance, but Andrew would bet a few copper stones that it was cast iron. "We need to take that out before it reaches us. Take aim!" He raised a hand and heard the drawing back of many bow strings. He watched as they sighted their shot down the arrow's shaft. "Fire!" The twang and snap of arrows leaving strings made him grin. Many of the arrows were short, but one or two struck home. *Goddess, help us. Give us better odds,* Andrew prayed. If each volley was like that, they would waste more arrows than have successful shots. *It's a start,* he told himself. "Ready arrows!" he commanded. "Take aim… Fire!" Andrew watched as more arrows made it to the slow-moving group this time. The arrows pinging off the shields of those protecting the battering ram. Some of the surrounding men flinched at the sound of the Dark Ones crying out in pain below, while others smiled, knowing they were protecting their people. "Again!" he shouted. Andrew glanced over his shoulder as more men came up the stairs, weapons in hand.

A boy came up, who looked no older than him, but like the others around, he wore a guardsman's uniform. "Sir, I don't have a bow or arrows but I have a slingshot," the young man offered.

Andrew glanced out onto the plain. "What sort of range can you get with it?"

The young man put a stone in the pocket and drew back until his arms were shaking, then brought it back down. "I mean, I don't think I can make it reach that far, but if they get closer?"

Andrew squeezed the other's shoulder. "If they get close enough for you to use that fire at will, do not wait for my order," Andrew said and prayed to the Goddess he would not need to use that slingshot.

"Andrew!" The young man spun when he heard his name called and turned to see the guardian in all her power. Serena Nightcastle stood on the stairs, a sword at her hip and a bow and arrow slung across her back. "What do you need?" she asked, surveying the men around Andrew.

"I need another officer," he said. "I need to know what's happening on the other walls. We need to get a message to the council. I am not a member of their guard. I should not be running things."

The half-elf opened her mouth to say something but waved him down the stairs toward her.

"Fire at will!" Andrew told the men on the wall. "Take down as many as you can. I will be but a moment." The men turned to their task, fingers fumbling over the arrows.

Andrew took the stairs two at a time to reach the half-elf, and she grabbed his shoulder, pulling him close. He could barely hear her over the din and clank of battle, but the words sent a chill through his bones. "The council will not listen. They've closed their doors and are unwilling to help with what happens at their gates. They are unwilling to take action. We are all that stands in the way of the Dark Ones taking this city."

He stepped back, mouth going dry. He had feared it may be the case when the alarm hadn't been raised but had prayed he was wrong. That it wouldn't come to this. "Are you serious?"

"Yes, I am." The half-elf nodded solemnly, anger dancing in her eyes. "I would not lie to you, friend."

Anger crackled between them. Andrew turned to the council's tower. *I thought we made progress.* He wanted to scream across the distance between them. He thought they had done it, gotten them to understand the severity of what was happening outside their gates. That Taytra's work the night of Samhain had helped. But clearly, they were too dense to see. An angry, cynical part of Andrew thought they should just let the city fall, let the council see what happened because of their inaction, but he couldn't. His people were there, the people that had taken them in and shown them true kindness were there, and they didn't deserve that.

"So, we fight," Andrew said.

"We fight," Serena agreed.

"Andrew! I have supplies." Enre panted, coming up the stairs behind Serena. "Hello, Guardian. Here to join the fun?"

Serena grinned savagely. "I am always ready for a good battle."

Andrew took the sword Enre offered him and began buckling it around his waist. He paused, looking up at the elf. "You need to go."

The elf spluttered, his eyes dancing between the half-elf and the human. "What do you mean, I need to go? You need all the help you can get!"

Serena nodded. "Andrew is right," she said, looking at the young man. "See, this is why the council should listen to you. You lot think of things experienced individuals don't think of right away."

Enre threw his hands up in exasperation. "You want to fill me in on what is so smart?"

"You need to go to Bulandon. Get a message to Barin's mother. Tell them what is happening here. They need to know that—" Andrew dropped his voice. "They need to know what is happening to the city. Maybe they can send help. If not, they need to know Hollens may fall soon."

Enre's jaw set in a firm line. He wanted to fight. Andrew could see his mind working, mulling over all the ways to argue about why he needed to stay, but he nodded. Enre was one of the few people who knew how to get to the rebels and the queen there.

"I will be back. I will not abandon you," he said,

pulling Andrew into a tight hug. "Stay strong. It will be a long fight. I will bring help as soon as I can."

"I know you will try," Andrew said, "Now go. I am sure they will be watching for riders."

Enre looked like he wanted to say something more, but shook his head and turned, running back down the stairs.

Chapter 47 Barin

Barin shifted from foot to foot as anxiety gnawed at his stomach.

"You alright, Barin?" Ward asked. "You seem sort of… antsy."

Barin looked up, stilling his movements. "Let's just say the last time my mother and I spoke, we didn't end it on great terms." He scoffed. "That was after I thought she was dead for five years, but turns out she was alive and creating a secret underground city of rebels to stand up to my father." Paulo's eyes went wide, and Barin laughed. "Yes, I have some family issues that really need to be taken care of."

Acton, Queen Alessia's commander, stepped out of the room. He was just as Barin remembered. Tall, with sun-tanned skin and the strength most men dreamed of. "Ah, yes. Frituals and friends," he said.

Taytra and Ward shared a look. "Yeah, that's about right," Ward said.

Acton nodded, the movement short and direct. "Yes, good. If you will just follow me. Please take a seat wherever you would feel comfortable."

Barin was pleased to see his mother had decided to set up an actual table for this meeting rather than the low tables and many pillows he had seen the last time in the space.

"Ah, Barin!" said Queen Alessia, who was queen in name, but Barin knew was more akin to Ward and Taytra than she would care to admit. "How are you? I heard you have some friends you need to break out of the fortress." She swept him into a hug.

Barin looked awkwardly over at his friends. "Ah, yes. Mother, may I introduce you to Paulo, Lyra, Ward, and Taytra. Paulo is the earth Fritual and Lyra the air."

Alessia went right to Lyra. "Oh dear, wonderful. I used to be able to control air Magick. But after—well, we don't need to go into that. It is just good to meet someone who can touch the same Magick. I haven't talked to anyone like me in a long time."

Lyra grinned. "You and I will need to take some time to discuss our different training. Perhaps there is something we can learn from each other."

Alessia turned to Paulo. "And you! You can control earth Magick like my Enre. I am sure the two of you met in Hollens?"

"Yes, ma'am, we did," Paulo said.

"Good, good. Please, find a seat," Alessia said, moving to the head of the table.

Paulo caught Barin's eye and mouthed, *my Enre?*

Barin shrugged. *I have no idea.* The elf nodded and sat down.

"Acton has given me an overview of the situation, but how about you tell me your perspective?" Alessia said, sipping from a large goblet of wine.

Paulo and Taytra shared a look, and she started. "Ma'am, my sister, Shauna Flynn is able to control water Magick—she is the water Fritual. She is kinda the reason everyone came together. Her testing is what brought out Philippe's powers and how we found out the Dark Ones had infiltrated the castle at Cabineral Lake. She found Paulo and Lyra, and they eventually found Ward and I and our group of rebels from Cabineral."

Paulo took over. "We, meaning Lyra, myself, Shauna, and Philippe split up a few weeks ago. Lyra and I started to head here, actually, to see if we could find the spirit Fritual." He glanced at Barin. "We did find you eventually, just not in the right place. Anyway, we split up. Shauna and Philippe went to Fuegaste Peak so Philippe could be tested and receive his markings. They were captured. We received word a few days ago that both Shauna and Philippe were either on their way too or were already held here within the fortress at Bulandon. I don't think I need to go into much detail on why that is something that cannot be much longer, and the danger it poses."

Alessia nodded somberly. "No, unfortunately I am well aware of the danger Nurzan poses to others. How do you intend to rescue them?"

The group was silent for a moment. They had a plan, but it hung in the balance. Without her approval, the group would need to find another solution. "Mother, we would like to ask for your assistance. Any move we make will reflect on you and the people you serve here in Bulandon. We would be remiss to make any decisions without your input."

Alessia cocked an eyebrow. "Is that a bit of

diplomacy I detect? Alright, let's see what your plan is," she said, leaning forward. "I am game to play."

Ward leaned forward, and Barin nearly lost the impassive look he was trying to express. *She is falling for every single motion,* he thought.

"With all due respect, ma'am, this isn't a game to us," Ward said, his voice an even line. "People's lives will be on the line. Some of which are our close friends or family members. We don't have time for games." Alessia nodded, and Ward pushed on. "We would like to propose a small task force to get in. But we may need support from you and your men to get that entrance."

Alessia waved a hand and shared a look with Acton. "We don't have the time to launch a large-scale assault. The only way to defeat them would be to start small. Peck away at the foundation they had built until it comes crumbling down."

"Fair," Ward countered. "But I would argue a small task force doesn't need to have the support of, as you put it, a 'large-scale assault.' We would just need someone to make a distraction."

"We would like to send a few people into the fortress while splitting some of the others to lead them away," Barin noted. "We feel this would work in our favor in a few ways. One, as we said, a distraction. But we also don't feel entirely comfortable with having all of the Frituals together at one time. It makes the group more recognizable, but in the assumed state of Shauna and Philippe, they can't really defend themselves."

Acton leaned forward, placing his hands on the table. "I can get behind that. What is your proposed split?"

"Barin is highly skilled and knows his way in and out of the fortress. He has to lead the group going into the fortress. The benefits out way the risks. Paulo and Taytra would go with him as well," Ward explained, "while Lyra and I lead the distraction and pull the focus away long enough to get in and out undetected."

"Acton and I will consider this and let you know our answer shortly. I don't believe it will be an issue, but there are other matters to consider," Queen Alessia said. "As you noted, any action that is taken will reflect on our people here in the city."

"There is one other matter we have been trying to understand that we would hope you could assist us with," Lyra said.

"We know that Shauna and Philippe were captured. But I was previously captured with Shauna. She is a fighter. She wouldn't let others hold her back for long," Paulo said. "She is strong. Stronger than others may think she is. She knows how to read a room and how to play her cards."

Alessia pursed her lips. "You want to know what could have stopped any attempts at escape?"

"Yes, if you know of anything. It would be good to know so we could help them, and to protect ourselves if we go with the plan where one or more Frituals would be entering the fortress," Paulo said a bit too eagerly.

"And what do I get in return for this information?" Alessia scowled.

Barin leaned forward. "I am sure I can provide you something of use, Mother. Just give me a minute. While I consider my knowledge of the Dark Ones, how about you share what you know?"

Acton scowled, but after a wave from Alessia, said, "We believe—There have been rumors that the Dark

Ones are perfecting a form of Magick that limits the abilities of others or disrupts their powers entirely. We don't know how they perform the Magick or if it is permanent."

"So hypothetically, they could have done something to take their Magick away? Entirely?" Taytra asked.

"Yes," the commander said, "and you will have no way of knowing if these individuals are still Frituals until you find them."

"It's a good thing Shauna will always be my sister then, isn't it? Wouldn't want her worth to be tied to anything she couldn't control," Taytra spat. "Magick or not, I am going after Shauna."

"Tay," Ward warned

Barin marveled at the way he was able to calm her with a word and a hand on her arm. *Okay, calm wasn't the right word,* Barin thought as he watched Taytra's eyes narrow in anger. *More like corralled.* "Do you know if this Magick is reversible?"

"No, we haven't been able to study it. We just have heard snippets," Alessia said, watching the young woman down the table. "We will, of course, assist you in any way if that should be the case, but we don't know much more than that. I can show you the reports we have. Perhaps you will take something away from it we have not."

"We would greatly appreciate that." Barin looked at a map, surveying the distance between the base in the city and the fortress on the outskirts and found a point, grinning. "Mother, have you and your people found the craggy trail and the secret back entrance?"

Alessia's eyes narrowed, and she leaned forward, trying to see what Barin could be looking at. "No, we don't know of any secret entrance into the fortress."

Barin grinned. "Well, now you do, and I have a plan." He pointed to the back edge of the fortress. "This is how we will get them out."

Chapter 48 The Sisters

Shauna pulled at the ties on her wrists, but they held firm. Her heart raced, and she bit hard on the cloth that was bound in her mouth, muffling her cries. She flinched as the door banged open and Philippe was shoved in beside her. She leaned toward him, not caring if they knew anymore. *They are going to kill us. I am going to die tonight.*

"Hey. No moving," the guard said, holding a blade between them. She glared at him but stopped. Philippe was only kneeling a few feet away but he had never felt further away. The guard moved behind them, and she was acutely aware of the fact that she didn't hear him sheath the blade.

She shifted slightly. The Dark One who bound her wrists made sure the ropes were savagely tight. In minutes, she wouldn't be able to feel her hands anymore. Rocks bit into her knees, and her calves ached. *I won't be able to stand up quickly*, she thought, preparing herself for the blow that would come when she didn't answer the order fast enough.

Shauna glanced down at the black band of Magick that had been encircling her wrists for well over a week.

The scratches where she tried to claw it off in her sleep had nearly healed. All she wanted was to remove it from her skin, to get rid of the feeling of it touching her and making her stomach roll.

But she feared it might be traded for something much worse.

Outside, the Dark Ones gathered, and she got a glimpse of the platform before they closed the door on them. "Have them ready. You will know when I want them," was all Nurzan had said. The cool calculating look was replaced by the evil of a Dark One lord. The look she always felt was lurking under the surface. She had seen a glimpse of that anger when he questioned her, and now she would see why he was the one whom even the Hunters obeyed.

A soldier opened the door. "Wouldn't want you to miss your cue." He grinned. "Thought you might want to watch the show before it was your turn." He looked over her head at the guard with the blade at their backs. "Nurzan will be making his entrance in a minute. You better get out here."

"Right." He moved to stand between the two Frituals. "Before I do, you two can have these removed. Not sure if the lord wants you to speak or not." Shauna flinched as he reached for her and he grabbed a chunk of her hair, holding her head still so he could cut the cloth that bound her mouth. "I should just leave you," he said, pushing her out of the way. She watched, hoping he could feel her hatred burning into him as he removed Philippe's gag and stepped just out the door.

She watched as Lord Nurzan took the stage, and she took a deep breath, trying to steel herself for what would come.

***

Taytra peered over the edge of a rock at the fortress, the moon overhead casting long shadows over the boulders "How long until we make our move?" she asked

"It shouldn't be long now. Ward will give the signal shortly," Paulo said

Taytra looked out towards the plain, waiting to see the glimpse of a mirror's reflection in the distance. The plan was fairly simple. Ward and his small band of fighters would distract the Dark Ones similarly to how they had on the plain when they needed to escape with the caravan. He had half a dozen archers at his disposal and four men for close quarters should it come to it. Barin had snuck her and Paulo through the private trail and discovered there was a large gathering of Dark Ones within the fortress near the gate. The plan was to pull those soldiers to the wall and sneak in through the back. It surprised Taytra that there would be such an easy opening, but from what Barin had said, it was used often for the Hunters to leave on missions without a fuss, and his father used it previously to escape quickly. That was exactly what they would use it for.

"It was always part of my patrol on the wall to check and see if there was anyone trying to use the trail. It was usually something that we would check at the beginning of the night and sometimes at the end, but the only people that really ever used it were the Hunters because they didn't want to go through the whole rigmarole of going through the front gate." They had no way of knowing if there were Hunters using it tonight, so they just had to wait for the signal from Ward that they could make their move.

Taytra pulled out her knife and turned it over and

over in her hands before slipping it back into the scabbard. What she wanted to do was to pace back and forth but didn't want any dust to give away her position. She fiddled at the end of her braid, lightly tugging on the hair.

"You've never done anything like this have you?" Paulo asked, watching her fidget.

"What gave it away?" she asked, tossing the hair over her shoulder and gripping the pommel of her sword.

He grinned. "It's okay to be nervous," he said. "Getting ready for something like this can lead to a whole bunch of pent-up energy. You just need to know how to use it most effectively so you don't burn yourself out. It's the same idea with the Magick we have but it can be used for normal combat as well."

"Who said I was nervous?" she asked, mentally storing the advice. She took a deep breath and looked out to the plain where their soldier should be waiting.

"There it is," Barin said, pointing out a small reflective circle. "That's our sign." The trio started to move, quiet footsteps and creaking leather armor the only sound as they moved up the path. Taytra kept her eyes on the ground in front of her, doing her best not to kick any loose stones.

Taytra had assumed by Barin's description of the well-used back entrance and the fact there was a path, that there would be a small door or gate they would need to break into. "Well, this makes things a bit simpler," she whispered. "So, we just slip in through there?"

Barin nodded and waved a hand, motioning for the others to hold back for a moment. Their entrance was nothing more than a crack in the wall. By the look of it, someone used Magick and blasted out a hole, the large stones and cracked pieces of rock littering the area in front of it. He crawled up the embankment and paused in the gap, listening for any guards. Slowly, he drew a knife from his hip and swung through the hole. After a moment, he came back "The guard isn't here. We're good to move," he said, motioning for the two of them to follow him.

"What do you think is going on?" Taytra asked, straining to hear exactly what the Dark Ones were saying in the distance.

"I don't know. It is very rare for my father to gather everyone in one place. They don't even do that when the Hunters are named. It must be something to do with Shauna and Philippe. We will have to hold back for a moment to see what's going on."

Taytra nodded and swallowed the acid bubbling up from her stomach. "Okay, we follow you," she said, hoping her companions didn't notice how her hands shook.

***

She couldn't see Nurzan, but his voice sent a chill down her spine.

"My brethren. We are gathered here tonight to try several prisoners. These children of man claim they did nothing wrong. That they are innocent."

Shauna looked at Philippe, but his eyes were locked forward, as she watched him, the color drained from his face.

"But in the same breath, they claim they are Frituals. That the Goddess above blessed them with Magick." A chorus of laughter and boos followed.

She turned back to the door and slowly tried to slide closer to him so she could see what he was seeing.

So they could face it together.

"We know this is not the case. How could they speak the truth? Charlatans! The children of man cannot touch Magick. So, what does this mean? These claims?" She saw him. Nurzan pointed at them, to the room they were in, his eyes blazing with anger. "They stole the Magick. These Frituals they claim to be are nothing more than criminals."

We didn't steal it! She wanted to scream back. *I don't want to hurt anyone!*

"After careful examination of the evidence, we have decided these two children are deceptive. They use elven Magick for their own reasons and they should not and will not have it any longer." A loud cheer rippled through the Dark Ones, and Nurzan stopped his speech to bask in the sound.

"Will not have it any longer?" Philippe echoed. "What does that mean?"

"They have already caused too much damage to our cause and what we fight for. They must be punished and held accountable for their actions."

"We have to escape! We have to try!" Shauna hissed, she pulled at the ropes binding her wrists in vain, hoping that she could break them, loosen them, *something*! The ropes creaked, and she bit down on the inside of her cheek, trying not to cry out at the pain. Even if she couldn't access her Magick, she had to do something. She reached for it, searching for it. But again, she felt so empty and cold.

"Stay strong," he said.

Shauna thought she heard him wrong at first, that he didn't speak. It was just a whisper in the wind, but when she glanced over at Philippe, he was smiling. It was a smile Shauna used to think about all the time, that made my stomach turn with butterflies.

"I am right here beside you."

She reached for him, turning so she could hold him even with her hands bound. She didn't care if they saw. *I love you.*

He smiled. *I love you too.*

"Bring the prisoners forward!"

Chapter 49 The Sisters

Paulo and Taytra nodded and waited for Barin as he moved down the hall before signaling for them to follow. He guided them down a hallway, pausing every so often to listen to the sounds in the distance.

Goddess, please give us more time! Taytra peeked through an open doorway as they walked past and froze.

"Hey, you! Who are—"

He can't sound the alarm!

Before her companions had time to react, she moved into the room and lifted her blade. The guard tried to step past her, and she leapt, bringing the blade down into his neck with a spray of blood. She stabbed a second time, hoping to cut off the sound of the elf's gurgling death cry.

She looked down, and her hands were covered with blood. She quickly wiped them on the leather of her pants. Her hands shook harder now, and she took a deep breath and curled her hands into fists until she felt tiny half-moon indents of her nails sticking into her palms. She held the position for ten seconds, then unclenched, willing herself to release the fear and nervousness she was holding. *I'm doing this for Shauna. That person would've kept me from her. He was a Dark One.*

Paulo put a hand on her shoulder. "Are you okay?"

Taytra bite the inside of her lip nervously. She nodded and wiped the end of her blade on her pants. Something about that strike was different than when the two Dark Ones caught her in the clearing. Then she had a group of people to protect. Now it was preemptive, that Dark One didn't have a chance to defend himself.

She watched as Barin pulled the dead elf further into the room and tucked him in the corner. "This will have to do," Barin said. "He's at least out of sight. It should be a little while before anyone finds him. Hopefully by that time, we will be long gone." He looked to Taytra. "You did well. I see what Serena meant about you having quick reflexes." Barin moved to the doorway, looking for other foes. "If we keep going down this hall, it will take us to the courtyard. As much as I want to know what is going on, I think we should go around." He pulled out a small map smudged with charcoal lines. "If we take this staircase, we can try an upper balcony. We will be able to see the crowd and maybe get an idea of what is going on and what to do."

"We follow your lead, brother," Paulo whispered, but Taytra noticed he was looking past Barin to the noise in the distance. It was getting louder by the second.

Barin nodded, stepping out of the room, and the trio backtracked up the hall. Barin stopped at a door, pressing his ear to it. "It's hard to hear anyone over them," he whispered. "Hopefully, the same can be said of us." He opened the door, and the three hurried up the stairs. Barin motioned, and Taytra crouched low, keeping her body below the wall of the balcony. She and Paulo stayed near the door, moving a brazier to block it, while Barin worked his way around the wall to the next door, ensuring they were the only ones on that level.

"Can you see them?" Taytra asked and slowly raised herself so her eyes hovered just above the edge of the balcony's wall.

Paulo's face darkened. "I see Nurzan." He glanced over to Taytra. "I see why you punched Barin."

She shifted her position and froze.

"Bring the prisoners forward!" Nurzan roared.

Taytra nearly stood, but Paulo's hand clamped down on her shoulder. "Wait! We need to see what is happening."

"If you had your bow, we could end it all right now. We could take him out."

"No," Paulo cut her off, "Remember what Queen Aliessa said. We can't take him out yet." He gripped her shoulder. "Besides, if we did, the rest would murder them. Look."

From the back of the crowd, she watched two Dark Ones dragged out her sister and Philippe. Taytra felt a bubble of rage in her throat at the sight of her sister.

Thick black bands of Magick circled her forearms and her wrists were bound with rope. Her clothes were clean but ill-fitting and hung off her body.

She was so much thinner than the last time Taytra saw her, and bruises mottled her skin. Most surprisingly, her sister's hair was short, hacked off in uneven chucks that hung around her face. Taytra only got the briefest of glimpses of her sister's face, but deep bags were under her eyes. She looked so tired.

"Goddess," Paulo whispered. "It's only been a few weeks since I saw them? What did they do to them?"

"Dark Ones are cruel," Barin said, his voice monotonous, deadpan. His face was full of utter disgust.

Taytra looked back down at the two.

"Untie them," Nurzan shouted. "Let them stand before us."

Taytra watched as a guard moved forward and sliced the ropes free. She felt a pang of sadness in her chest as the two immediately reached for each other, hands clasped between them. Something came over Shauna, and she stood tall, as if the contact gave her all the strength she needed to stand up to all the Dark Ones.

"What do the two of you have to say for yourselves? Any final words before you are stripped of what should never have been yours?"

"Barin, what are they doing?" Paulo asked, his voice dangerously low.

"I don't know."

"We aren't afraid of you!" Philippe shouted, and Taytra couldn't help but wince at the words. "You can't crush us. We will keep fighting."

Nurzan laughed. "Like how you have fought us this whole time? You have lost. You have no weapons. No Magick. You are powerless, and soon, we will make sure that is permanent."

"That's what you think!" Shauna shouted, and together she and Philippe raised their free hands. Taytra gripped the wood of the balcony as flames rippled down Philippe's arm and water shot from all directions, coming to her. As if from some silent signal, the two lashed out, Philippe's flames flying over the crowd while Shauna sent her water lashing out. Their markings were a dazzling dance of blues and reds.

"Stop them!" Nurzan roared as the two of them launched their Magick at the lord general. It took a moment, but several guards tackled the two, separating them, and the Magick died.

One of the guards slammed a spear butt between Philippe's shoulder blades, and he bent over in a coughing fit.

Taytra winced but watched as he came up, glaring. He looked just as tired as Shauna, but he kept fighting. "We have to do something!" she whispered as someone smacked Shauna, sending her sister careening sideways.

"Guards!" Nurzan shouted, standing and dusting himself off. "Take them. Now," he growled.

As they fell on Shauna and Philippe, Taytra tore her eyes away when she saw movement out of the corner of her eye. Despite what was unfolding below, she grinned. "Now, we play. That's Ward, he has started his attack," she said, pointing to the arrows that streaked over the wall, the sounds mixing with the fight below. Taytra wasn't the only one that noticed it either. A group of Dark Ones broke away, sprinting in that direction.

"Pretty good timing," Paulo said. "They did say they wouldn't stop fighting. They just didn't know they had backup coming."

The alarm sounded as the Dark Ones realized they are under attack from outside as well.

Taytra turned back to the fight below, her eyes locking on three Dark Ones who approached the crowd, their faces shrouded by hoods.

Barin scrabbled backward. "Shit, I think I know

what is happening. Come on." He moved the brazier out of the way and started back down the stairs. "I know where they will be going."

"What? What is going on?" Taytra asked, trying to take three steps at a time quietly and keep up with him.

"Those are the Dark One elders. The ones that teach Magick. Capable of very powerful Magick. This is bad and good. If they are here, it means things are going very bad for those two, but good for us. They never do Magick in front of others. They will be taken to the chambers," Barin called over his shoulder.

"So, what do we do?" Paulo asked.

Barin paused before a door, motioning for them to stay silent before moving into the room. A few moments later, he was back with a bundle of black clothing. "We blend in," he said, tossing the clothes at them.

***

Pain lanced through her forehead. She tried to look around and get her bearings, but the moment after she hit the ground, someone yanked her to her feet.

"Let's go, little Fritual. Time to face the consequences for your actions," he snarled.

She twisted away, ready to fight. If she could touch Philippe, they could do it again. When they were touching, their Magick couldn't stop them. Shauna reached for him, but he was down. Thrashing and fighting with three guards on top of him. "Philippe!" She cried out, launching herself into the midst. But she was in no state to fight. She was on the ground a second later, a Dark One pressing a boot into her back. He lifted her by her hair, a knife pressed at her throat. "I see you have chosen to do this the hard way. No matter, it's all the same to me." He walked Shauna through the crowd, but she spun, trying to keep her face on Nurzan while she was led away.

"You won't get away with this!" She screeched. "All of this will be the start of your downfall!" There would be others. There always had been other Frituals. But if she was going to die today, she wanted him to remember her. Shauna heard Philippe still struggling behind her as she was shoved into a room off the courtyard.

The elf pushed her into a chair, pressing the point of the blade into her shoulder as another tied her to the wooden chair. She looked around the space, the dark stone adorned with harsh runes that made her blood run cold. On a dais before the two chairs was a long, silver knife etched with more runes and a book that looked like it hadn't been touched in a century.

They are preparing some sort of ceremony. Galen had warned her. He had tried to prepare them, but it hadn't changed anything. They were still here.

Three hooded figures stood before them. In the dark of the room, she couldn't see anything beneath the hoods.

"Get out," the first said, his voice like brittle bones snapping. The guards obeyed, half running out of the room.

What was about to happen if they couldn't stand to be here a moment longer? They didn't even ask if they needed assistance.

"Where is Nurzan?" Philippe panted.

"Lord Nurzan will come after to ensure our work is done," the hooded figure said, lifting the blade.

She scoffed. "What, he can't even come to see—"

With a flick of his fingertips, the third robed figure

sent a black band that covered her mouth, muffling the end of her words. A second cut off the protests from Philippe.

"Now, let us begin."

Shauna thrashed and fought, pulling at the bonds until a noise she couldn't fight spilled from her lips, silenced by the black Magick. But nothing she did stopped the Dark One from lowering the knife and sliding it across her skin. It was so sharp she didn't feel a thing as the blade sliced through the skin, letting the blood run down her arm, sliding between her fingers. They did the same to Philippe. Between the sounds of him fighting against his bonds, Shauna could hear the quiet patter of their blood hitting the stone floor.

The figure nodded and the two behind the dais opened the book and started chanting in a language she didn't understand. It didn't sound like elven, it was too harsh. As the words filled the room, her vision went blurry, and she gritted her teeth against the searing pain flaring up her arm, centered on that cut. It felt like someone was sucking her dry, pulling her Magick out of her skin. Shauna's markings flashed again, a sea of blues, before sinking to black.

She looked to Philippe, and he was tense, pulling at his restraints, the ropes biting into his skin even as his markings winked out and he slumped forward. She wanted to cry out, say something, to try and get him to respond, but it felt like her tongue was swelling in her mouth, thick and heavy. She felt heavy, like she couldn't possibly hold her head up another moment. Her eyes fluttered closed so all she could do was listen to the voices chanting the dark Magick around her and fight the swell of darkness that threatened to make her pass out.

Shauna heard a clattering outside and tried to open

her eyes. If this was the moment she died, she wanted to look them in the face. The door slammed open, the noise pounding in her skull. Everything hurt. She couldn't quite hear anymore, the sounds were delayed, happening a world away. She strained, trying to get her eyelids to respond, to open a crack.

The chanting stopped with a loud crack, and she felt like an anvil had been lifted from her shoulders. She tried to look up again, but the room spun. A hand touched her face then fell to her wrists.

"Stop... Don't touch me," Shauna tried to shout, but what came out was breathy and garbled.

"Goddess, we need to get them both out of here now."

"Get away from him," she mumbled again and felt a hand on her arms undoing the ropes.

"I need something to bandage these."

There was another sharp sound and someone said, "Here, use this."

She tried to open her eyes, but they felt so heavy.

Someone grabbed her face and lifted it, and her neck ached with the weight of it. "Shauna, we are going to get you out of here. I promise."

She flinched. "Who are you?" Shauna mumbled.

"We're going to have to carry both of them," another voice said, and she felt myself being lifted onto someone's shoulder. "That will have to do. Once we get to the infirmary, they can get stitches"

Finally she pried open her eyes, wriggling. *I have to fight. I have to fight.*

"Shauna, relax. It's Paulo."

She blinked, trying to get her eyes to focus on the

face of the elf. "Paulo?" she asked, not believing him.

"Yes, it's me. We are going to get you out of here, okay?" Paulo asked, shifting her again.

"Go ahead and warn the others we are ready."

"I need to stay with her," a girl's voice snapped.

"We need to warn the others. Go. We will be right behind you," the second voice said. "Ward needs to know we are out."

Ward? Paulo is with Ward? She thought as her head lolled against Paulo's chest. "The guards? Nurzan? They were everywhere." Shauna's head felt like it was being squeezed, everything was too bright, but a bit of her strength was coming back.

He nodded. "Don't worry, they are dealing with other things." He squeezed her arm and carried her from the room.

The courtyard that just a few minutes ago had been filled to the brim with Dark Ones, was now empty, but she could hear them screaming in anger in the distance "Paulo, what is going on?" She asked. "What happened to all of the Dark Ones? Where did they go?"

"Lyra and Ward are distracting them, but we don't have much time. We don't know exactly where Lord Nurzan went," Paulo said.

She tried to wiggle her toes then her ankles as Paulo carried around the edge of the courtyard. "I think I can walk."

"If you are sure. You lost a lot of blood." He slowly placed her on her feet. At first, her ankles gave out, and she started to stumble, but he caught her, and she slowed down a pace, lifting one leg and then the other. "I think I will be okay. Just don't go far, okay?"

He nodded and guided her around a corner, a hand

hovering at her back ready to catch her at the slightest change.

"Is my sister okay? And Ward, you said he is here?" she turned to see who was carrying Philippe.

"That is Barin. You will have a chance to get to know him soon," Paulo said, and she noticed his hand tighten press a bit more firmly on her back nudging me along.

It's Barin who answered that time. "We can answer all your questions but we need to get out of here. The last thing we need is my father catching us here."

She stopped dead in her tracks, and Barin nearly ran into her and dropped Philippe. "Father?" She hissed, glancing from Barin to Paulo who sighed covering his face like he knew this would happen.

"God, you and your sister are so alike. At least you aren't punching me," Barin muttered, pushing past her. "Yes, Lord Nurzan is my father, and you are Shauna Flynn. My given name is Barin Nurzan. For obvious reasons, I have denounced my father, but that doesn't stop him from popping up from time to time, ruining everything. I will explain everything once we get out of here."

"I am not going anywhere with you!" She snapped, pulling herself away from Paulo.

"Shauna, come on. We need to hurry. Your sister is waiting for you," Paulo said, reaching for her.

"But where are we going?" Shauna insisted. She was angry now, and it was the only grounding she needed.

Barin shifted his hold on Philippe. "It will be easier and safer to explain all this to you when we are in Bulandon. We are going to the city." He didn't stop moving. "Now, come on. We can't risk being caught."

Shauna glared at Paulo in a way she hoped conveyed she wanted answers soon, but followed after Barin. "Where is my sister?" she asked. "You sent her out here alone?"

Barin laughed. "Do you not remember where I said your sister punched me? It is the Dark Ones who should be scared of her right now. She is on a rampage. She wanted to burn down this entire building to get to you."

Chapter 50 Taytra

Taytra paced back and forth, looking at the sky. The moon was starting to make its descent. *Shauna was going to be okay,* she told herself, looking to the fortress where Barin, Paulo, Shauna, and Philippe would be any minute.

She crouched low to the ground, glancing over her shoulder every so often toward the fortress, then out to the plain where Ward and half a dozen fighters were keeping the Dark Ones distracted on the wall. She saw the dancing light of the fires they had created behind a few boulders. They were using these tiny flames to light arrows and shoot them over the wall. A few well-placed shots had caused fires within the fortress, but most just left the Dark Ones confused. She watched as one by one the men lit the arrows, waiting until one arrow was about to hit before sending off the next. It was a perfect way to keep the Dark Ones pinned. She grabbed the mirror from her belt and tried to do her best to angle the thin rays of moon light toward the rock she thought Ward was hiding behind. She did it for about thirty seconds before ducking out of sight. She waited to see if there was a response before doing it again. This time, she got an almost immediate answering reflection back. Knowing the message that Shauna and Philippe had been freed had been communicated, she made her way back down the trail, ready to strike out at any Dark Ones that might have been lurking in the shadows.

She stumbled a bit coming up the hill and winced as half a dozen stones went skittering down the embankment, the noise seeming to echo across the desert sands. She slowly turned back to the fortress and froze. She could hear a few voices. She crept as close to the wall as she dared, straining to hear the voices more clearly.

"It's ridiculous, you know. There are at least two hundred of us in the middle. And we were picked for the watch."

"Right? We were on patrol last night. We were meant to have the day off."

Taytra crouched low and slowly drew her sword, raising it in front of her. *I have done it before I can do this again,* she thought, then she jumped through the gap in the wall, taking the two Dark Ones by surprise. Neither of them had a weapon drawn. *Some guards if you can't hear the ruckus? Though maybe they thought it was part of the gathering Nurzan had in the courtyard.* She sliced the first's arm, praying to the Goddess it was the elf's dominant hand, and kicked him back hard, sending him thudding into the wall. His head slammed against the stone with a loud crack, and he didn't get back up.

The second got his sword out during the process and swung wildly at her head with a two-handed swing. Taytra ducked and stabbed at the Dark Ones exposed midriff. They jumped back just in time, slicing downward. Taytra cried out and jumped back, falling to a crouch, feigning an injury. She clutched her arm and watched the Dark One circle her and reached to grab a handful of sand from the earth. When the Dark one stepped closer, she flung it into his face. He scratched at his eyes with one hand while flailing the other at her with the other hand still wrapped around the blade, a loud string of curses spewing from his lips.

She quickly disarmed the elf and knocked him back with a sharp kick to the chest. He tumbled back, and Taytra planted a foot on his chest.

"Do it. You wouldn't dare," the elf spat at her.

She contemplated what to do for a moment. This Dark One had seen her here. Knew they were using this entrance. The last thing she needed was for them to track her and the others some way or to sound the alarm. *Well that decides it,* she thought grimly before stabbing her blade into the Dark One's chest.

She spun when she heard a loud gasp. Taytra ripped her sword from the Dark One's chest, splattering her shoes with gore, and turned to face the new opponent. But she dropped the blade a moment later and was running the distance between them. "Shauna!" she cried, wrapping her little sister in her arms. "Oh, Shauna, you are awake."

Shauna was stiff in her arms, looking from Taytra to the body on the ground. "You've gotten a bit better at stabbing people, I see."

Taytra let out an empty laugh. "Well, I had to practice. Can't promise to be your personal bodyguard if I can't uphold my end of the bargain." Barin motioned to Taytra, and she nodded, turning back to Shauna. "Are you okay? We are going to have to move pretty fast for the next few minutes. It might get a little messy."

Shauna nodded. "If I need help, I will let you know."

"Okay, what do we need to do?" Taytra asked, turning to Barin, who pressed a hand to the first guard's throat, making sure they were down.

"The original plan was to wait for Ward and his crew to get back here and go from there to the ridges. I think we should split up. Shauna, Taytra, and I will get going so I can get a head start with Philippe. Paulo, can you wait here for Ward?"

"You got it," the elf said, drawing his blade. "I will make sure no one follows you. Ward and I will be right behind you."

"Come on," Barin said, leading their little group down the trail.

"Is he going to be okay? Why hasn't he woken up yet?" Shauna asked, following a few steps behind Barin, peering at Philippe's face.

"He should be," Taytra said, bending to scoop up her blade and act as a rear guard. "He woke up for a second when we came in. He kept fighting, like you did. He thought we were more Dark Ones, which like was the point. We wanted to trick them. I think he got hit during the scuffle." Barin glanced over his shoulder, an eyebrow raised.

"Wait." His hand hovered between them, and he rotated, listening. "We need to move faster."

"What if it's Ward? Shouldn't we wait up?" Shauna asked, turning.

Taytra grabbed her sister's hand and pulled her along. "Come on, we can't wait."

Shauna stopped short. "Can you please fill me in on some things? All I know is you are here somehow and Ward is here too. What is going on? How did you get Nurzan's son on your side?" she asked, pointing to Barin.

Taytra waved Barin to keep moving and grabbed her sister's hands, turning her to look at her. "Shauna, we don't have a lot of time. This attack is meant to be quick, in and out. Get you and get *out*. Ward is here leading a distraction team, but once they stop shooting at the fortress, the Dark Ones will follow us. I am sure they have put two and two together. If not yet, they will very soon." She glanced back up the trail. "Barin is the last Fritual you were all looking for, and he has been marked. We didn't want to use any Magick in case they could track it. Barin is Lord Nurzan's son, but he has fully denounced him. His mother is leading another secret rebel sect in the city of Bulandon. That is where we will be staying and were you can get help for Philippe."

Shauna's eyes were wide, but she nodded., "I— Okay. Yeah, we can talk about this more when we get to the city."

Chapter 51 Ward

"Ward, how are we going to break?" one of his men asked, hiding behind a rock as the sky rained stones and arrows around them.

Ward glanced at the quiver at his side—he only had three more shots—then to Lyra. She had her bow at her side, ready to strike anyone who came too close. "We have been given the all clear We are good to move once we get a chance." The soldier passed the information down the line, and Ward looked to the cracks. "You take off first. We need you to be safe as well."

Lyra pouted, "Oh, come on. We both know you need someone here to have your back," she said with a grin. "I could knock them all off the wall in one go."

Ward shook his head with a grin. "While I would love to watch that happen, you need to go. We will be right behind you." He pointed behind to the series of cracks and crags through the desert. She nodded and slinked off. Though the desert had rough terrain that would be difficult to navigate at night, it was their best and straightest shot to the city. If they got pinned down there, at least they wouldn't be as exposed. "One more volley," Ward ordered. "Once you make your shot, head that way into the shadows until you are out of range. Try to move when the moon is behind a cloud, then head for the cracks."

The first of the volley went off, and the soldier next to Ward took off running in a zigzag between rocks until he was at least one hundred yards away. Ward watched as one by one the men left. He looked to the wall in time to see a soldier pop up over the wall and duck away as a well-timed arrow fell a few feet away from him. "We need to move faster," Ward called out. Once the last man left, Ward shot off his three remaining arrows and took off running after his men.

Roughly ten seconds after the last arrow would have hit, Ward heard the twang of many arrows leaving bows and thuds as they started to rain around him. They were far enough away that only the strongest of shots landed near him, but the thuds of the impact were more than enough to get his heart rate up. He slid to a stop next to Lyra. He peeked around the edge of a rock, watching the deluge continue, but not for long. "We need to keep moving," Ward said, fighting to catch his breath. "They are going to come out to get us soon."

She nodded. "I will lead. You take the rear." She shifted to a low crouch, stepping between the soldiers and collecting a line of them behind her.

How much time do we have? He turned back to the gate. *Shit.*

The Dark Ones moved like a sea of ants along the wall, standing and looking out into the desert without any arrows to pin them down. There was nothing stopping them from coming to hunt them down. He turned and ran, following the last man out of the rocks and down into the craigs.

He squinted into the darkness, looking for the front of the line. Ward caught a glimpse of Paulo near the front with Lyra before they disappeared behind a large set of rocks. *Did they just get out of the fortress?* He felt a pang in his stomach and turned to look back at the gates that were starting to crack open, red-hot torchlight burning across the sand. "Gates are open! Let's move!" Ward shouted, turning back to the soldiers under his guard. Some looked back at him in surprise, their eyes wide like they didn't think the Dark Ones would really follow them, while others jumped to action, pushing past them. Ward sprinted to the front where Paulo and Lyra led the group. "Where is Shauna and Philippe?" he said, looking around. "Barin? Tay?" He panted, his hands on his knees

"They are ahead. Barin had me stay back to let you know. He took them as soon as we got out of the fortress. Barin is carrying Philippe as he is unconscious. We couldn't wait. They had a five or ten-minute lead on you. Shauna is up and walking, disoriented but okay."

Ward nodded. "Good." He glanced over his shoulder. "Do we have reason to assume they know we took Shauna and Philippe yet?"

"I am sure they have figured it out. Unfortunately, they aren't dumb. I would think it would be one of the first things they checked on," Paulo said. "I would assume they know and are coming with a vengeance," Paulo warned. "Nurzan is going to come to Bulandon and rain hellfire, especially if he thinks all five of us are in one place." Paulo shook his head, and they jogged in silence for a minute. "Queen Alessia was right, by the way," Paulo said under his breath. "I am fairly positive we were able to stop it in time, but they were attempting to cast a spell that would take away Shauna's and Philippe's Magick."

Ward tried to keep his face even. "But you haven't had the chance to test it because we don't want to give away our position."

Paulo nodded. "Yes, we will need to do something about that."

Ward turned and headed to the back of the line. "Come on, men. We need to keep a move on. Your only job is to catch up with the other Frituals and protect them. Get to the city safely. Dark Ones are coming. We have to presume they know we have the Frituals. Let's go!" Ward shouted, hoping the Dark Ones weren't close enough to hear them yet.

"I am sorry, Ward," the person at the back of the line panted. "I am awful at running. Especially in armor." She squinted against the sweat that drips in her eyes.

"What is your name, soldier?" Ward asked, slowing to her pace.

She looked to the ground, watching her footing on the slopping path. "Blackery, sir. Faith Blackery."

"Okay, Blackery. You were recommended by Acton, who is the head of your military, is he not?"

She nodded. "Yes, sir, he is."

Ward smiled. "So, whether or not you can run well, you had a purpose here, did you not? You don't need to apologize if you give me your best. Why don't you tell me why Acton picked you? What is the thing that cancels out your running? Which, if I am honest, I am not very good at either."

"But, sir, you have been running all over the place," Faith said.

"I have, but it still hurts. I've had a stitch here

under my ribs for the last ten minutes. Just gotta breathe through it. It'll go away eventually."

Faith nodded, and Ward heard her take three slow breathes, moving through her own stitch. "I am an archer," she said. "Acton had me start training people last year. About a month ago, he put in in charge of all the archers."

Ward nearly tripped. "Why didn't you say anything earlier?"

She grinned and shrugged. "You are the officer here. And you weren't doing anything I wouldn't do. The flaming arrows were a good touch."

Ward shook his head. "What else would you have done?"

She took a few more breaths so it was easier for her to speak. "I might have used the last few shots to shoot a few flaming arrows at the turrets at the corners. They looked like they were made of wood. It wouldn't take that long for them to put out, but it would still be some time that we would have to escape."

"Or it could have just taken a different way down," Ward countered.

She mulled it over for a second. "They could have, but I think they would want to keep their fortress intact. Plus, armories tend to be at the base of turrets. Makes it easy to restock quivers."

Ward nodded. "I see why Acton sent you. Keep up as best as you can. I think Taytra and I will need to talk to you some more at a later time," Ward said. "You have more skill than you think you do, Blackery." He looked over his shoulder. "Got any ideas on how to keep them from following us?"

She grinned wickedly, slowing to a fast walk. "I thought you would never ask."

Chapter 52 Taytra

Taytra could hear people coming up the trail. Her sister had slowed to a walk, her feet scuffing over the uneven ground. "Come on, Shauna. We've got to go a bit faster," Taytra said for the fifth time in as many minutes.

Shauna mumbled a reply, her gaze unfocused and at her feet.

Taytra had considered pulling her sister onto her back, but if anyone came up on them, she wouldn't be able to fight and protect her sister that way.

Barin was farther up the trail. His pace had slowed too, but he continued to fight on. They were moving up and out of the craigs when Taytra heard the sound of stones falling, smashing together with loud cracks. She turned to see a plume of dust go up in the moonlit sky. The noise woke something in Shauna, who scurried up the embankment, following Barin.

He paused at the top and turned to Taytra. "I really hope that was Ward and he did that on purpose," he said before turning and moved up the steep embankment with renewed vigor.

Taytra stopped and drew her sword. Part of her wanted to turn back and go up the trail to see what had happened. If it wasn't on purpose, they would need help.

"Tay, hurry up here, we should be able to see what is going on from up here," Barin said.

At that, Taytra hurried up the trail, running past her sister and Barin to the top. She looked around the area, checking in the undergrowth to make sure there was no ambush waiting for them before turning to look down. The dust in the distance made it hard to see what exactly happened and who did what. She saw movement she had to assume was Ward and his soldiers. They were moving at a fast pace, covered in a layer of dust. A few were climbing down from the cliff walls, dropping down to the trail below. She squinted into the distance beyond and saw some Dark Ones attempting to climb over the pile of stones.

She jumped back when she saw a light reflected on her chest. *The mirror.* The light bounced for a moment then went away. "It's Ward," she called to Barin and Shauna, who climbed up the embankment and out of the craigs. "He just sent me a message." She held up her bit of mirror. "I think they did it. Or at least they are okay."

"Good. Can you help me put him down?" Barin asked. "I need to rest for a moment. It won't be long, then we can keep going. I just feel a cramp coming on." Taytra hurried over and grabbed Philippe under the armpits so Barin could shift out from underneath him. She grunted from the effort and nearly dropped him, but Barin came back a moment later to help support him to the ground. Barin bent and checked his pulse. "He is okay for now." He pulled back the sleeve and unwraps the make shift bandage on his wrist. Black stained his wrist in a thick band, but it looked more like soot than Magick that lingered on his skin.

"Is it gone?" Shauna said behind them and ripped her own bandage from her wrist.

"Shauna, what are you doing?" Taytra asked, grabbing Shauna's hands.

"They tried to take our Magick away. They gave us these cuffs that would let a Hunter know if we ever tried to cast, but I couldn't reach my Magick. The only time we were able to feel any of our Magick was if we touched. They—the room. They were trying to take the Magick away." Her voice cracked and raised in pitch, and Taytra had to fight to hold her sister back.

"Shauna, please. It's okay."

"Shauna. Take a deep breath." Barin turned and moved Taytra gently out of the way. He took Shauna's hand and gently wrapped her arm back up. Taytra saw the lightest shimmers of purple marks on his wrists. "Shauna, I know you don't know me, but I want to know everything that happened. Whatever my father said and did. But you need to do that in a space where you feel safe and can speak freely without being rushed and can process what happened. Please wait until we get to the city." His words relaxed something in her sister. Shauna's shoulders fell from her ears and some of the tightness around her mouth faded.

Shauna nodded. "Yeah, yeah, okay. I can't do Magick right now, right?"

Barin shook his head. "Not unless we think it is absolutely necessary. We will make sure you can still cast when we are safe. I promise."

Shauna turned and looked down to where the soldiers should be following. "Do you think they used Magick?"

Taytra looked as well, searching for Paulo and his green markings. "I don't think so. Paulo works a bit more cleanly."

Barin motioned, and Taytra helped him to move Philippe onto his back. "Come on. Our tunnel entrance isn't far."

"I wish we had some torches," Shauna muttered, stumbling over a stone. "But that would give us away, wouldn't it?"

Taytra nodded. "You have always been pretty good at sneaking around. Is this too difficult for you?" She joked, trying to keep the mood light.

Shauna laughed dryly. "I only ever snuck out in the daytime. At home when I knew exactly where I was. This is a bit different."

Taytra turned. "I think the first people are coming out of the embankment. You keep going. I am going to make sure they are friendly."

"Tay," Shauna said, grabbing her arm. "Please be careful."

Taytra nodded. "I always am. Others just make that difficult sometimes. Go. I will be right behind you."

Shauna nodded and hurried to follow Barin between the cacti in the distance. Their shadows were quickly distorted by the silhouettes of the tall plants.

Taytra spun and ran in a crouch to wait at the top of the trail. The first soldier came over the hill, and she grabbed them, pressing her knife to their chest.

"Lady Taytra, I am with you. Paulo and Lyra are just behind me," they said quickly, eyeing the blade.

She turned and looked down the trail, holding onto the person until she found the two Frituals on the trail. "Okay." She let them go and pointed up the trail. "Keep going that way, and you will find Shauna and Barin. He needs assistance to carry Philippe."

The soldier nodded and ran up the trail, eager to follow her orders and get away from her blade.

"You can't threaten every soldier you see," Paulo said, climbing up the trail.

Taytra laughed and gave him a hand. "Watch me." She pointed at the cloud of dust still rising into the sky. "What happened?"

Lyra was next up, hurrying past and following the line of soldiers away. "One of the soldiers had an idea to delay the Dark Ones. They noticed a weak point in the cliff walls on the way in and helped Ward set up an avalanche as the Dark Ones came through."

Paulo turned and gave a hand to the next few soldiers coming up. "Exactly, and no Magick was used. Ward had Lyra and I lead. He should be coming up in a few minutes. How are the other three?"

Taytra and Paulo started to move back toward the cactus field. "Doing okay. I told some of the soldiers to go help Barin carry Philippe. He is tiring, as to be expected. He did have to use a smidge of Magick to calm Shauna. She is overwhelmed and confused. Again, to be expected. I hardly saw his markings."

Paulo nodded. "I thought we might have had to. I feel bad, but we don't exactly have time right now to explain it all to her, and who knows what the two of them went through?" He sighed, glancing over his shoulder. "I hope the head start is enough. We need to get to the tunnel."

Taytra turned, jogging backwards. She can't see into the crack in the earth anymore but she can't see the end of their line of soldiers either. "It will have to be. How many men did they send after us?"

"I didn't get a good look. Ward stayed near the back the most. I don't think the avalanche will take out all the soldiers, but it probably took out quite a few. So maybe we got a slight advantage."

They were nearly to the cactus field and the tunnel that led them to the underground city. "We are going to have to collapse the tunnel," Taytra said.

"The queen knew it was a risk. She told us it was fine."

Taytra picked up the pace. "I know. I just hate feeling like we leave a trail of destruction wherever we go."

"No," Paulo said sternly. "We do not. Any damages caused are as a result of actions we needed to make to keep us safe. No more than that. Each sacrifice is necessary. Do not feel bad for taking actions that are required to keep yourself safe." He held her gaze until she nodded. "Let's go catch up with Lyra," he said, picking up the pace again, forcing her to work harder to keep up with his longer stride. She knew he was doing it on purpose. Pushing her to make her stop overthinking things. A move she appreciated.

She glanced over her shoulder one more time. *Come on, Ward!* Taytra skidded to a stop when she saw another person climb out of the trail. They were carrying someone across their shoulders. "Paulo, Wait!" she shouted.

He turned and squinted. "Is that Ward? Who is he

carrying?" But Taytra had already taken off back the way
they had come.

Chapter 53 Shauna

"Okay, we will go right through here," Barin said over his shoulder, hurrying into the entrance of the tunnel.

Shauna paused at the top. *The last time I went into a cave or a tunnel I was captured.* She shook her head, pushing away those thoughts. *No. This is not the same*, she thought before stepping into the entrance.

She only made it a few feet before an elf was at her side. "Hi, you must be Lady Shauna? Please come with me."

"I—Hello. Yes, I am Shauna," she stammered, blinking against the shadows in the tunnel.

"Forgive me, Shauna. I know you have been through quite a bit the last few nights, but I need you to follow me quickly. We need to get everyone out of the tunnel. The moment the last soldier is through, we are collapsing this sector," the person said, grabbing her elbow gently and guiding her through. "We need to make sure you are out of danger when that happens," He added.

Shauna followed as quickly as she could, trying not to trip on her tired legs. "I'm sorry, did you say collapse this sector? How many tunnels do you have? Is your base entirely underground?" she asked, looking around for Barin and Philippe. She saw them up ahead. Barin had his head down and was quickly rattling something in elven off to a soldier who took off running back up the tunnel past her and out into the night.

"Yes," her guide said. "Nearly everything we do is underground. Keeps us safer. The city is crawling with Dark Ones. They think the city is still just as dilapidated as it was a few years ago when they burned it down, but really, we are doing quite well." They came to a crossroad of tunnels. "Just this way, dear. Let's get you to the infirmary. Get you checked out. I will have someone send for food as well."

Shauna stepped back. "Please, I want to stay with Philippe. Barin had him"

He nodded. "Yes, Lord Barin was taking Philippe right there. We are going to take the next left."

"What is your name?" Shauna asked. "Can I know that?"

"Yes, I am sorry, I should have told you sooner. My name is Scota." He smiled.

"Scota. Okay, thank you." They walked quickly, people around them jogging past, going both away and toward the direction from which they had come. Some carrying weapons, others with shovels and pickaxes.

"How long will they wait before they collapse the tunnel? I know my sister, Taytra, she went back to check on the progress of the soldiers."

Scota nodded in understanding. "Yes, yes. They have orders to wait until the last person is back but they will have to make that judgment call. If they need to, they will collapse the tunnel earlier, as discussed before they left."

"They can't! If they get left out there, the Dark Ones will kill them. Paulo is still out there too. He is one of the Frituals. We can't let them have any more of us!" Shauna said, her voice growing loud and pitchy. "We have to go back."

She tried to turn and start making her way back up the tunnel, but Scota grabbed her elbow more firmly. "Lady Shauna. Your sister and every single person on that mission knew the risks going into it. They have a plan should they get locked out. They didn't go into this blind." He looked into Shauna's eyes. "Your sister knows how to get back to you. She is a very strong woman. She will be here soon."

Shauna stood in the hall, looking between where her sister and Philippe should be in the infirmary. "Scota, I don't know what to do."

He pressed a comforting hand to the small of her back and guided her down the hall again. "I know. That is why I am here. You need to go to the infirmary. We will get you checked out and make sure you are safe and out of the way. I will make sure someone will send you an update the moment we know where your sister and the others are."

Shauna nodded and allowed herself to be pulled along to the infirmary. *What about Ward? He was out in the desert. Does he know what to do about the tunnels?*

When they got there, Philippe was laid out on a bed, and a few people are huddled around him with clothes and bandages, taking care to make sure he is okay.

"Shauna. Good, you can come right over here," a nurse said, "Thank you, Scota. You are free to go." She waved him away.

"I will get you an update as soon as I can," he said before exiting the wing.

She followed the nurse over and sat on the bed, glancing over to Philippe. He looked like he was just asleep. "Is he okay?" she asked, trying to get a look at him between the bodies around him.

"He should be. We are just waiting for him to wake up. The healers don't see anything wrong. Barin said they tried to do some sort of Magick, but we don't think it was completed." She took her arm and started to unwrapped it. "Let's get this cleaned and stitched up. Is there anything else you want to get checked out?"

"They did the same Magick on me, but I stayed awake. Well, barely. I don't think I passed out, at least." she pulled off the boots given to me by the Dark Ones. "I think it should be okay now, but I previously had stitches in my foot. They gave me a healer, but I wanted to make sure it was okay." She thought of the elf and the warnings he had tried to give them. *What will happen to him? Will they find out what he was doing?*

The nurse grabbed a tray of supplies and put it on the bed beside her. "Alright, we will get that checked out for you in just a moment." She pulled off the wrap on her arm, got it cleaned up, and began to stitch it up. She flinched a few times at the tiny needle pricks but the nurse's work was so quick Shauna hardly noticed. She wrapped a bandage and tied it off quickly. "That is all set. You should be okay in a week or so. Now, let's check on that foot," she said, shifting to the end of her bed. The cleaned her foot, looking at the thin scar. "This looks great. I don't think this needs any more treatment."

Thank you, Galen, wherever you are. He probably

saved Shauna from a lot of pain.

"Is there anything else you need? We are going to send down some food. Just a bit of soup and bread, not too much. We don't want you to get sick."

Shauna nodded. "Okay. I don't think so? I think I will be okay."

"Good, then I need you to rest. No walking around, stay put. The tunnels can be very confusing if you don't know your way around," she said on her way out of the room.

"Okay." Shauna turned to Philippe. They hadn't had a chance to really talk since before they got to Fuegaste Peak. She had avoided the conversation. And now all she wanted to do was talk to him. To try to put the pieces together and understand exactly what had happened. She moved off her bed and grabbing a nurse's stool and sat beside his bed, taking his hand. She leaned forward on the bed and pressed her forehead to his hand. "Philippe, I don't know what to do." She whispered into the heavy silence.

Chapter 54 Paulo

Paulo pulled Taytra behind a clump of cacti, trying to shield their position.

"Who is that?" Taytra asked, squinting into the distance and the dust on the trail.

"It must be one of the soldiers in his group. Maybe something happened with the trail."

She turned to him. "You said it was on purpose?"

"It was, but that doesn't mean there weren't issues. He peeked around the edge of the plants. Ward and the injured soldier were making progress but it was clear they were struggling. Paulo glanced up the trail ahead. "We don't have much time. We have to help them! We can't just leave them out here to try to make the cut off." Taytra stood and started to move toward the duo.

"Wait." Paulo grabbed her arm. "We need to make sure it is clear."

"Paulo, we know for a fact it isn't! We need to move now before the Dark Ones get closer. If we don't move now, we won't have a choice but to go for the secondary route. We can't lead them straight to the base."

Taytra pulled her arm away. "I am going. If you want to go for the tunnel, I won't blame you."

Before Paulo could form a reply, she was up and jogging to Ward. *Goddess help me*, he thought. Of course, getting captured right now would be in no way ideal. The whole point of this mission was to get them all together. "Tay, slow down," Paulo said, trying to catch up with her while running in a low crouch. "You know you are just as important as any of us, right?"

She scoffed but kept moving, her blade drawn, ready to strike anyone who came too close.

The tramping of feet could be heard not too far off, along with stones skittering down the embankment and the echoing clank of weapons. Ward looked up the trail and it looked like he could barely contain the fact that he was *not* happy to see Taytra. "What are you doing here?" he hissed when Paulo and Taytra were within earshot.

The man's eyes stayed locked on Taytra even as Paulo answered for her. "We saw you helping this soldier here. We couldn't leave you behind," Paulo said, moving to help take the other side of the soldier. "Everyone else made the tunnel," he added.

"Good," Ward grunted. "We need to move fast. We took out or stalled most of this force but some still got through." He shifts the elf's weight. "Blackery here deserves all the credit. She was the one who saw the weakness in the Canyon wall. She got the men organized very quickly and probably saved us all."

Paulo noticed the dark red, wet stain on the elf's shirt and caught Ward's eye.

"It was nothing," Blackery panted, her head rolling to the side.

"We thought the force of the collapse would be

focused towards the Dark Ones, but there was some blow back of shrapnel. Blackery was standing in front of me giving orders." Paulo could feel the guilt radiating off Ward in waves.

"Right. How much further is it to the entrance?" Ward asked, turning to Taytra.

The woman was facing behind them. "Incoming. Looks like three of them."

Ward picked up the pace, dragging Blackery's feet through the dust. "Tay, how far is it to the entrance?" Ward asked again, his voice a bit tighter. Paulo glanced over at him. Ward's jaw was set in a hard line of determination.

Taytra stepped toward the incoming soldiers. "Keep going. I've got this."

Blackery groaned in pain and shifted her weight between Ward and Paulo's shoulders. "Tay, focus come on," Paulo snapped. "We don't have time to play hero. We need to go. If you stop you will be killed."

Taytra whirled. "I am not trying to play hero. I am trying to assess our situation," she snapped, spinning the blade around in a small circle and walking back towards the trail.

"It's about eight hundred meters," Paulo said, finally answering Ward. "It isn't too far. We might not make it before they catch up, though." He looked at the young man. "We can make it…" Paulo trailed off. *We can make it if we leave this girl behind who may not make the night.*

Ward grunted in response, turning slightly to look toward Taytra.

"You two keep trying to stay out of sight. I will

take these three out. Try to pull them off the trail. If I don't follow right behind, close the tunnel," she said before dashing out of sight behind some of the scrub.

"Tay!" Ward shouted, but the girl was out of sight. "I can't—Tay! Goddess, that woman is going to be the death of me," he said, trying to move a bit faster.

"The best women are," Paulo pointed out. "As much as I hate to admit it, she has a point. I think that is the best thing to do right now." When Ward didn't answer, Paulo pushed on. "No doubt they saw you, but they didn't see Tay or I cut back. They will assume you are flagging behind. She will have the advantage of a surprise attack. Three to one aren't the best odds but, she is smart. You and Andrew have done a good job training her."

Ward nodded. "I know. She is right. Pulling them from the entrance is the best thing. But I am not happy about it."

Blackery coughed again, and Paulo noticed a thin layer of blood on the elf's lip, pooling in the corners. "You shouldn't worry about me."

"No, you will be alright. It isn't that much farther to the infirmary," Ward insisted.

The girl barked out a pained laugh. "Don't try to be gallant with me. You just told Tay not to be a hero."

"Let's see what we can do."

"No!" the man snapped. He shifted his weight, pulling Blackery away from Paulo. He quickly bent and caught the small elf behind the knees. He grunted as he lifted her, cradling her weight to his chest.

"Ward," she croaked, trying to say something, but blood trickled down her chin.

Ward stumbled but caught himself before the two went tumbling. "You deserve to live," Ward panted. "You saved all of us. There was no way we could have outrun them if not for you."

In the distance, Paulo saw the dark indent that is the tunnel's entrance. "We are nearly there."

He dropped back, trying to hear Taytra or others approaching. He turned back to see a few soldiers sprinting in their direction, a stretcher spread out between them. "See," Ward said. "Help is on the way. Just hold on a bit longer!"

"I—I—" Whatever the elf tried to say died on her lips.

"Excuse us," the two with the stretcher said quickly, lifting the elf between them. "We have to move."

Ward stared at the elf in shock as they took her away. "I—she—It should have been me."

Paulo took the young man and pushed him along. "Come on. We need to get inside," he said even as he looked over his shoulder for Taytra. He grinned. "Looks like you trained her well."

Ward turned, and Taytra was sprinting past them a moment later. "Come on, slow pokes. The time has passed for hunting Dark Ones. It is time to go."

Chapter 55 Shauna

Shauna woke and jumped at the sound of a distant rumble and a jarring crash she felt in her chest. *That's the tunnel!* Her heart rate spiked. She sat back down and took a few deep breaths, trying to focus on the room around her and not the fact her sister might be locked out. She might be locked out with a bunch of Dark Ones on her tail. *I just got her back. I can't lose her again.* Tears pricked her eyes, and she turned back to Philippe. Shauna rubbed the palm of his hand, feeling the rough calluses on his skin. "What are we going to do?" she thought aloud, wondering what could possibly be their next steps. If they had all of the Frituals, what would they do? She was as overwhelmed as she had been on the lake when she found out she was a Fritual. Her brain was buzzing with unanswered questions.

"Shauna, are you okay?"

She jumped up and turned.

"Tay?"

Shauna rushed over to her, throwing her arms around her sister's neck. "They said they were going to collapse the tunnel and if you weren't back in time you

402

might've had to find another way back," Shauna said into her neck.

"I am okay. We made it. Ward was carrying one of our people. It slowed him down a bit. Paulo and I went back and helped him, that's all. We are okay," she said, rubbing her back in small circles, just like thier mother used to do when they were upset or sick. "Come on. Come sit down," she said, guiding Shauna back to a bed. "You need to rest. You have gone through a lot."

She buried her head in Taytra's shoulder, holding her close. "How long has it been? A month? It felt like a year."

"I know. But we are together again. That is all that matters right now. You don't have to worry about any of it," she said, and Shauna felt like a child. Like when she got picked on by her classmates and Taytra cheered her up.

"You saved me." Shauna whispered. "Again. You saved me again." she laughed through the tears.

Taytra laughed too. "You know, I told Father when you were doing that ceremony with the queen when you got your markings that you needed me. You needed us there to make sure you didn't get into trouble."

Shauna laughed, but it faded, and she sat up. "Where is Father? Did he get out when you did? How did you do that? What happened? How did you even get here?"

"I think this would be best explained over dinner."

Both girls turned to see Ward leaning against the door frame with a tray of food in his hands. "Ward!" Shauna jumped up but sat down quickly as a wave of dizziness washed over her. "Whoa," she murmured while holding her head.

"They said that might happen, thus why we need to get some food in you. With the blood loss and the running, you are pretty depleted right now," he said, placing the tray on the table beside her bed.

The moment the tray was down, she flung herself at him. Shauna just wanted to hold all her friends and family close. "I missed you. I am sorry I lied to you."

He pulled away a bit. "Lie to me? When did you lie to me?"

She laughed. "At the feast. I told you I was nervous just because I didn't like ceremonies, and that was why I wasn't eating. It really was because I knew what was going to happen. I mean, I was still nervous. But the reasoning was different." She sat back down and took the tray of food, her stomach rumbling as she bit into the thick bread.

Ward just stared at her for a moment before he burst out laughing. He covered his face and tried to stop but only laughed harder. "We just broke you out of a Dark One fortress, and the first thing you want to do is apologize for lying to me about not eating at the ceremony where you were named a Fritual a month ago?" He kept laughing, "Goddess, Shauna, I missed you. I miss when little lies like that were so important."

Shauna laughed too, because really, it was ridiculous. "I was so scared. I thought I was going to throw up." All three laughed harder. "You all still had to jump into the lake after I took my test even though I had already figured it out." Tears streamed down her face but this time it was from laughing. "You were soaked!"

"Shauna?" At first, she missed it. "Shauna? Where are we?"

She jumped to her feet, ignoring how dizzy it mader her and grabbed his hand, "Philippe." She sat on the edge of the bed and leaned over so he could see her. "Hey, hey, love." He sat up slowly, and Shauna held his hand to her chest. "We are safe. We are free."

Chapter 56 Taytra

"So, here you are. All five Frituals in one room," Alessia said, sweeping into the room.

Taytra smiled at her friends. It really was a miracle that they were all together. She squeezed her sister's hand, and Shauna smiled.

It was so good to have her back, but Taytra would do anything to take the dark purple bags under her eyes away.

"Shauna, Philippe, how are you doing? Is there anything I can offer you during this time? Barin has told me all that transpired. I can't imagine. I am so glad we were able to assist in your escape."

"I've definitely been better," Philippe said.

Shauna punched Philippe's thigh. "What Philippe means to say, is we are managing. Thank you for helping us and giving us a place to stay while we come to terms with what has happened."

Philippe turned to Alessia. "With all due respect, ma'am, I want to apologize. I am sure helping us is going to cause an obscene amount of hardship for you."

The queen looked to her commander.

"You are not wrong, Master Mattick," Acton said. "That is something we are already working on."

Barin leaned forward. "What are you planning? I may be able to offer some insight."

Acton nodded. "Yes, I was hoping I could meet with you this evening to go over the plans we had drawn up to see what you thought of them, and what our enemy may think of to counter it." The commander looked to the queen again, who nodded. "While we of course want to make sure you are all okay," Acton said, scanning the faces of each member, "the main question we have for you now is what are you next steps? How will you defeat the Dark Ones?" He focused on Barin. "You know, of course, we cannot spare your father."

Barin's eyes narrowed. "Have I once said I wanted to spare him? I—" Paulo put a hand on Barin's shoulder, and the young elf stopped. "I am well aware of this, Acton. I was ready to take him out if we had the chance when we went to the fortress, but per my mother's orders, I did not seek him out."

Alessia held her chin high, moving past the comment. "This is something we have been wrestling with for the last few years. If I am honest, we have *just* been surviving by the skin of our teeth. So, if you have any ideas, this would be greatly appreciated."

"Well, what have you been trying?" Taytra asked. "We may be able to offer insight if we know."

"What haven't we tried, is a better question. Your mission into the fortress was the first direct attack like that we have made. We haven't been able to break their defenses. We mainly would do attacks on patrols and their supply lines."

"Have you connected with any of the other kingdoms?" Paulo asked.

"Not beyond the light cooperation we have gotten with Hollens. Nobody else has responded to us. Not in a long time."

"Hollens," Taytra whispered, thinking about what they said at the last council meeting.

"What was that?" Alessia said, leaning forward.

Taytra glanced over to Ward. "We finally made progress with Hollens right before we left. It was like banging our heads against a wall for a bit. But after some work, we were able to show them why we should work together. Hope."

Acton's face fell. "Hope? That's it? You don't think we have been surviving on hope this entire time?"

"But that is just it. You have been surviving, you haven't been living. Now you have something to fight for, something to live for. That gives people hope. We saw that firsthand. When we connected the pain to something tangible, we were able to make progress. The people of Hollens didn't care that those from Cabineral were hurting. Not until they realized we were fighting the same evil. That *together* we stood a chance. Through hope and unity, we were able to bring something forward for our people that should help them!"

"What exactly are you suggesting?" Alessia asked.

Taytra took a deep breath. "We need to show everyone scattered around the five kingdoms that we have something to fight for. The Frituals have united. Together they can do extraordinary things. They can defeat the Dark Ones, I just know it. I mean, look around. We had to knock down a whole portion of your tunnel system. That is bad.

However, the difference in morale between now and when we first got here. Your people are ready to fight in a way they weren't two weeks ago. If we show the other kingdoms that? The Dark Ones don't stand a chance. You haven't heard from people, but there has to be pockets of rebels."

Paulo nodded, picking up the thought. "The Dark Ones started hundreds of years ago as a small movement that gained power over many years. We can't deny that their roots have grown deep, latching themselves to our society. But the rebellion that Andrew, Ward, and Taytra created proves you can make momentum. There must be pockets like yours, Queen Alessia, all across the kingdoms. If we show them we are here and ready, I am sure they will come to fight with us. We need to show them there is something to stand for."

The door crashed open and everyone turned.

Queen Alessia rose to her feet. "Enre? What is going on?"

The elf was haggard, covered in dust and sweat. He looked like he hadn't slept in days. "Queen Alessia, Frituals, Commander Acton. Please know I mean no disrespect by interrupting, but you needed to know."

"What is it, Enre?" Ward asked, his face pale.

Taytra felt a pit of dread opening up in her stomach.

Enre glanced between the two rebel leaders. "I have both good news and bad news, I am afraid."

Alessia sat again, her face stony. "Speak, sir—out with it."

Enre twisted the edge of his cuff, an anxious tick Taytra had never seen him do. "The good news is that those that were still trapped in Cabineral have escaped. They made it to Hollens. Lady Taytra, Lady Shauna, well, and Master Ward, your fathers were there. Master Ward, I am afraid there is still no sign of your mother."

Taytra glanced across the table as Ward sat back, his face a wash of relief and pain. "Father is free?" Taytra whispered. "How did they escape?"

Enre winced. "I am afraid I didn't see him long enough to get the full story. Andrew sent me to warn you." He turned to look at the queen. "The city of Hollens is under siege. I was only in the battle a short time. But the men I saw, they were not trained. The force will not stand for long."

"Andrew," Ward murmured. "Is Andrew okay?"

Enre smiled but there was not warmth. "He was leading the fight on the wall. I am afraid the battle interrupted his wedding. His bride came with those from Hollens."

"Safiya?" Shauna said. "They were getting married?" Her face fell. "I wish we were there. Is she okay? What happened?"

He nodded. "When I left, she was. She was taking people further into the city away from the gate."

"You said the men on the wall..." Paulo said. "They didn't know what they were doing?"

Enre swallowed hard. Even through the fear, Taytra could tell Enre would do anything to be back there. "When I left, Andrew was doing his best to collect the men. There was no officer. No organization. Half the men on the wall were too young to have any decent training." He looked to Acton. "We will need to make a plan. I don't expect that the city will last the week."

Taytra stood and she felt all the eyes land on her.

"This is it. This is what we need to do. If—When the city falls, we reclaim it. We reclaim Hollens. It has always been the city to stay away from the battles. It has been steadfast against all war. We go back, we claim it. Make our stand and tell everyone. Send messengers to what is left of all of the kingdoms. That is where we will make our stand."

Lyra smiled and reached across the table take both Barin and Paulo's hands, and they take Philippe and Shauna's. "This is the first time all five Frituals have stood together as one. Even if we fall, our story will carry on. Others will learn our names, and our story will live on beyond us. A testament to peace. That the kingdoms can unite and come together for one cause."

"For the Frituals," Ward said.

"For the Frituals," Taytra echoed.

Chapter 57 Shauna

The desert sky was a deep purple, the sand reflecting the light of the moon in pale gold strands of shifting dunes. The cool breeze that she tried to avoid when she was in the control of the Dark Ones feels calming now. It lifted the short strands of hair from her face, the uneven edges tickling her cheeks.

"That's definitely a look, Flynn," Ward said, glancing her way. "It isn't bad, but next time, maybe see someone that knows their way around a pair of scissors."

She laughed, and it felt strange. Good—it felt good to laugh with her friend, "You're one to talk. What happened to Mister clean-shaven? I'm going into the queen's military. I have to be perfect."

He pulled at the thick beard he had going on. "You know, I've found the military isn't all it's cracked up to be. I don't think I am up for this kinda pressure for the long haul. Might not make it. Then there's your sister." Shauna watched him as he looked up at the stars. "You wanna see someone work Magick? Watch your sister." He laughed and pointed over his shoulder. "I have never seen someone with a bigger attitude win over so many people.

They think she has this charismatic air. Like they know they can trust her word. We don't know what the hell we are doing half the time." He laughed harder. "We literally had to hold her back from yelling at the high council in Hollen's. And then she could turn around and be calm and collected and talk to our people, reassuring them it would all be okay. We didn't have shit, but she made them believe it was good shit."

She smiled. "I never would have guessed it. Think she could make it in politics?"

"Goddess no! She would murder everyone." He scoffed. "We trained her how to do it too. She picked it up a lot faster than we thought she would. She had too." He turned to her. "Your Magick? Is it… okay?"

Shauna smiled. "Yeah, it's back." She waved her hand over the sand, and after a moment, small droplets pushed the sand aside. "There is water just about everywhere. If you know where to look," She explained. "It's definitely back. But it still feels far away sometimes. It's like I have to learn it all over again. Philippe's Magick is back too. I don't know how, but you all came at the perfect time."

They sat in silence for a few moments. Neither of them really wanted to touch the subject of the past month, just brush past it.

"So," Ward said, standing and brushing the sand from his pants. "Now that you are safe and secure, are you and Philippe going to get hitched? Or are you going to wait until you can see your father again? Since you know you had the surprise engagement then didn't—" He paused. "Are you engaged anymore? You gave him back the ring, right?"

Shauna looked down at her hands, picking at a bit of dirt. "I don't know anymore," she said quietly. It felt like a betrayal to say it out loud.

Ward was startled at the words. "Really?"

It hurt to hear him ask the question. But she couldn't lie and say it didn't feel good to say it out loud. "We—" Shauna paused, trying to find the words that matched what she felt. "We have been through so much. And I wouldn't want anyone else to go through what we have. And—I know I wouldn't want to have anyone else with me. But when all this is said and done..." she looked down at the dark bruise and raw skin of her wrists from the Dark Ones chains. "I don't think I want to be with someone who went through this with me."

He looked puzzled. "You wouldn't want someone who understands?" He sat back down, and she could feel his face turned to her but she knew she couldn't meet his eyes.

Shauna shrugged. "That would be nice, but even without this, I don't know if we would have worked. You know about Damian's camp?" Ward nodded. "We— When we escaped, he was him again. I know he has been trying really hard." She tucked her feet beneath her and leaned into her knees. "He has been trying, when we had time, before all this." Shauna said, gesturing toward the fortress and the desert. "To get me to trust him and get back where we were, before *everything*." Her throat choked up, and she had to swallow the emotions when she thought of how happy she was when he gave her that ring. "But I don't know if *I* can go back to that." She waved her hands vaguely. "But then in the fortress, I thought we were going to die, so I told him. I told him I loved him. I think a part of me still does. But it isn't the same."

Ward didn't say anything at first, just rubbed her back in small circular motions. The warmth of his hand seeped through the linen of her shirt, easily relaxing her. He used to do this when she got overwhelmed with lessons. It felt like a lifetime ago. She leaned into his touch, a familial comfort she hadn't had in a long time. "It sounds like you two need to have a conversation soon," he said. "You let me know if you need any support with that, okay? But first I think you should try to take some time for yourself. Try to collect your thoughts. Your honest thoughts."

Shauna nodded, her eyes burning at the idea of the conversation. It wasn't one she wanted to have by any means. But one she needed to have. Ward was right, she needed to be honest.

The wind blew, kicking up chunks of sand, and she shivered against the cold.

"You know, you are just like your sister," Ward said, pulling his cloak from his shoulders and wrapping her up in it. "Never prepared for the winter weather."

"Kidnapped and nearly killed, remember?" She joked. "Didn't get to pack for the weather."

He scoffed. "Don't act like you didn't always forget your cloak. Come on, you should rest some more. We have a lot…" He trailed off.

"Yeah. We have a lot," Shauna said. "Just a lot."

Chapter 58 Andrew

Andrew leaped down the stairs, clambering over the bodies of those that had fallen around him. For two days, they had fought. He had hardly slept. His body was slick with sweat and blood of his men.

"Andrew, we need to fall back," Serena shouted.

He cursed. "There is nothing left. If we fall back now, they will take the city."

"Neander's line holds the eastern front. We can join up with him," she insisted, trying to get the man to leave. "If we stay here, we will die."

He held up his sword, ready for the next wave of soldiers to come through. "We must hold this sector. If we don't, there is nothing standing between us and the market district. I have to do this." Goddess, he was tired. He had little left in him but he had to stand firm. They had moved boxes and carts and closed off large portions of the city as best as they could, forcing the Dark Ones into a gauntlet. The passage had narrowed, making it easier to fight the next wave, but now, down to just fifteen men, he knew they wouldn't stand a chance.

"Andrew, we can't do this," Serena said firmly. "I

know where you are coming from. I have been there. I have seen how this plays out. We and the people behind those doors," she said, pointing to the gates to the market district, his people. "Those people deserve to live. This battle right here will not give us that chance."

He charged, taking on the few that made it to them. He hacked and slashed, all the form and finesse he spent hours teaching Taytra gone in his exhaustion. *You can't keep doing this*, he scolded himself as a soldier slipped past him. *I have to!* he battled back, hacking at the next.

Serena spun past him gracefully, quickly taking out the oncoming opponents. She turned to him, fire blazing in her eyes. "Andrew Warner. We are not doing this." She grabbed his shirt and dragged him to the door. "You are going to live through this. And if I have to force you, I bloody will." She shoved him against the gate. "Open those doors and get people moving now." Andrew opened his mouth, ready to fire back some reply when she cut him off, her voice level and firm. "That is an order. Now. Move. Take these men with you. Drop back now."

Andrew growled out a few curses but turned as ordered and pressed his full weight against the doors. They opened a few inches before he was met with the tip of a knife. "Who is it?" a voice barked on the other side. "Oh, it's Andrew. Get these doors open now!" the voice ordered, and seconds later, the doors were opened wide enough for the men to slip in single file before they were slammed shut.

Andrew looked around in shock. The men and women of Cabineral were armed with an assortment of weapon blades, staffs, and what looked like quickly made clubs and other such objects. "What are you doing?"

"Get these doors barricaded!" someone shouted, and Andrew was quickly pushed to the side as people began to move, shoving boxes, carts, and hay in front of the heavy doors.

"Andrew!" Safiya came flying out to the crowd and wrapped herself around him. Sam was just a few steps behind. "We have been getting ready. We knew you would try but you wouldn't be able to hold the gate forever."

Andrew stumbled a bit in his exhaustion. "I tried. Serena made me fall back. They will keep coming," Andrew said.

"Sir, name is Chapman. While you were gone, we tried to get ourselves organized the best we could. We have some ranged weapons and some close quarters. We will be ready if they break down those doors." Chapman passed a quarterstaff from hand to hand.

"Where did you find weapons?" Andrew asked. "The armory is near the gate," Andrew said as a man jogged passed him with a spear with an iron spade tip.

"We—uh, we stole them from the stalls here in the market," Chapman said. "We don't expect the vendors would be too mad at us. But if we need to, we will work off any debts after we chase the Dark Ones out." Sam shifted, and Ward saw he had added a dirk to his hip but he still carried the knife Ward had given him too, ready to fight off any opponents. Chapman went on, "We have most of the women and children at the back of the market. We have a path out of here at a moment's notice." He glanced at Sam and Safiya and scowled. "You two should be with them."

"Buzz off, Chapman," Safiya said, turning to Andrew. "The flaw in our plan right now is that escape route leads to a portion of the residential district. We—I believe it is just a few streets over from where Neander and his men are fighting. They haven't cleared the quadrant yet."

"What miss—Safiya is saying is we may get pinned down from both sides," Chapman said.

Andrew turned to his new bride. "Go make sure everyone is back there that isn't fighting. Do you have something?"

She nodded, eyes burning with tears again. "I do. Most of the mothers have some sort of knife."

Andrew smiled wryly, thinking back to the camp on the plain

"You'd be surprised." He had laughed. "You tell a worried mother her child is in danger, and she will come up with some pretty interesting ways to attack you. I'm sure some of these mothers would be more than willing to learn how to pick up a blade, even if it was just a dagger."

"Besides, who said women can't fight?" Taytra had said.

"We will hold this position for as long as we can," Andrew said to both of them. "You lot seem a hell of a lot more organized than those I had on the wall. Serena went to get information from Neander. Hopefully, we will know their status soon—" Andrew was interrupted by a loud bang against the gate. "Safiya, go!" he ordered, turning back to the door. "They have a battering ram," he explained. "Get ready!" He glanced over his shoulder, watching Sam and Safiya sprint away hand in hand. "Do we have any way to get some height here? To see over that gate?"

"Yes, sir. If we use this building here, we can get on the roof," Chapman said, leading Andrew to a building a little down the way. "We just need to be careful. Some beams are rotting away."

Andrew jumped as another loud boom echoed through the space. He turned to see some of the barricade shift from the force of the blow. "Right. I want archers or anyone with a ranged weapon up on buildings now. We need to have range to get to them before they get through. We will try to stop them at the gate. If not, we need the space to stop them from getting far."

"Yes, sir. I will have people follow you up momentarily," Chapman shouted, taking off the way they had come.

Andrew sprinted through the building and climbed out the open window. Below, on the other side of the wall, Andrew saw a dozen or more archers preparing to fire over the wall. He turned when he saw movement to his right. *Did they find a way through?* Andrew thought, but no. Andrew looked over to see Sam peering over the edge of the building next to him. "Sam, what are you doing here?" Andrew roared as arrows flew up the wall. They rained down around them as Andrew leaped from beam to beam, closing the distance between him and the boy. "You aren't meant to be here! Where is Safiya?" Andrew grabbed the boy and ran away from the building as arrows hissed around them.

"I deserve to fight too! I want to protect my family. I ran away from her," the boy cried, wiggling in Andrew's arms.

Andrew stopped, putting the boy down. "We need to get you down from here. It is too dangerous!"

The boy sobbed. "Taytra told me to do one brave thing a day. She told me not to get into trouble, but I want to do this. Let me be brave."

Andrew shook his head. "Sam, I am so proud of you for wanting to fight, but this is not *your fight*. I don't even know what I am doing. I can't worry that you are in danger too. I need—" His voice cut off, and he stared at Sam. The boy's expression was frozen in fear, red droplets of blood spattered across his face.

"Andrew!" the boy screamed. "Andrew! No! I'm sorry. No, I didn't want this! No! I need you!"

Andrew knew Sam was screaming, but his voice was growing more and more distant. The world grew fuzzy around the edges. Andrew looked down. There it was. An arrow, the barbed edges protruding from his chest. Andrew tipped forward, and Sam tried to hold him, but both went sliding. Slipping down the thatched roof, he scrabbled weakly at the edge then they were airborne. Distantly, Andrew heard someone scream, but he didn't feel when they hit the ground.

Costello

Legacy

About the Author

Katelyn Costello started writing when she was twelve out of spite. Her best friend got to go to a writing workshop, and she didn't. So, Costello begged her way in and brought at twenty-eight page short story to what turned out to be a poetry workshop.

Bitten by the storytelling bug, Costello is a graduate of Wells College, where she received a B.A in English: Creative Writing and a minor in Theatre.

For regular updates on her writing process follow Costello on her social media or sign up for her monthly newsletter.

Instagram and Facebook @authorkatelyncostello

Legacy